I0772345

TALES FROM STOLKI'S HALL

A THRONES & BONES ANTHOLOGY

EDITED BY
LOU ANDERS

TALES FROM STOLKI'S HALL

Lazy Wolf Studios | www.lazywolfstudios.com

Editor: Lou Anders

Copyeditor: Gabrielle Harbowy

Cover Illustration: William O'Brien

Cartography: Rob Lazzaretti

Cover Design & Interior Layout: Lou Anders

ISBN: 979-8-9851531-2-5 (Hardcover)

ISBN: 979-8-9851531-3-2 (eBook)

 Created with Vellum

For Joe Monti
Who set the snowball rolling down the hill

Dwarven Rui
NORRØNGARD
Umsborg
Raven's Perch
8
Sindholm
Wendholm
2
Aarvik
Verborg
Ravenkeep
6
Dragon's Bay
Korjeng
The Cold
Grimsgard
Sea
9
Mórheim
Herkeby
Oslendholm
1
1
5
N
Dragon's Wood
Svartálfaheim
Ri
Mountains
W
E
S
3
Nilmgard
0
100
200
Miles

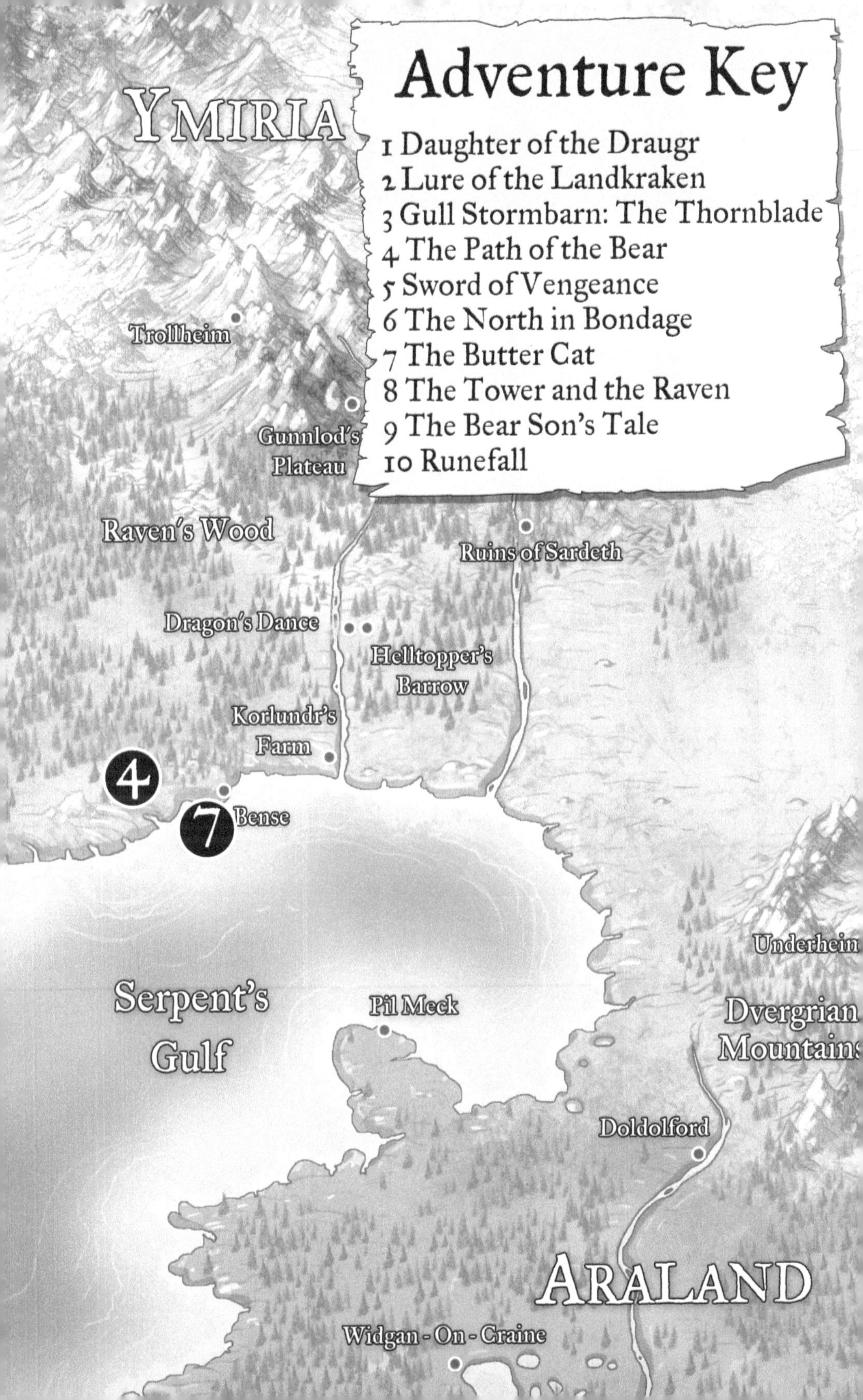

Ymiria

Adventure Key

1 Daughter of the Draugr
2 Lure of the Landkraken
3 Gull Stormbarn: The Thornblade
4 The Path of the Bear
5 Sword of Vengeance
6 The North in Bondage
7 The Butter Cat
8 The Tower and the Raven
9 The Bear Son's Tale
10 Runefall

Trollheim

Gunnlod's Plateau

Raven's Wood

Ruins of Sardeth

Dragon's Dance

Helltopper's Barrow

Korlundr's Farm

Bense

Serpent's Gulf

Pil Meck

Underhein

Dvergrian Mountains

Doldolford

Araland

Widgan - On - Craine

CONTENTS

INTRODUCTION: RETURNING TO THE LAND OF THE ICE AND SNOW

Like a dragon devouring its own tail, this book is a journey come full circle. *Tales from Stolki's Hall* is a book based on a game based on a book!

The land of Norrøngard where the stories herein are set first appeared in my novel *Frostborn* in 2014. Norrøngard is a snowbound country that draws heavily upon Norse mythology and Scandinavian culture. It tells the story of a girl named Thianna who is half-human and half-frost giant. She meets a human boy named Karn who is very, very good at a popular game called Thrones & Bones (which is also the series title), and the two of them go on the run together through the snowy wilderness, facing off against trolls and linnorms (northern dragons) and draugar (undead northerners). Three subsequent novels deepen the lore and extend the stories beyond the borders of Norrøngard.

However, a lot more goes into world-building than what appears on the printed page. Before I can create heroes to populate my stories, I must know everything about the places they inhabit. Before constructing a word of plot, I work out detailed histories, naming conventions, pantheons of gods, cultural traditions, and more. My intention from the start was to craft a playground bigger than any one book or series, with an eye toward reaching beyond children's books, across categories and media. With the wealth of world lore, roleplaying games were always on the table (pun intended). But the idea of doing a game manual was backburnered until the pandemic began. That's when *Thrones & Bones: Norrøngard* was born. This was a complete campaign setting, with pages of never-before-seen world lore. It was followed by two adventure books, *Sagas of Norrøngard* and *Vengeance of the Valravn*. As of today, there is also a musical soundtrack from a Grammy-nominated artist, numerous digital map packs, 3D printable terrain, and other accessories. Several more projects are in the works as I write this.

Now, roughly a decade after *Frostborn*'s debut, my fantasy creation enters on a new phase. *Tales from Stolki's Hall* marks the first time that other prose writers have been invited into Norrøngard. Before I became an author and game designer, I worked as an editor in adult science fiction and fantasy publishing. For this anthology, I've dusted off my editor hat and asked some old writer friends (and a few new ones) to pen tales of the frozen north. The results are spectacular—a range of stories set across the land that both showcase the world-building and extend and deepen it in exciting new directions.

It should be pointed out that while *Frostborn* is a children's book, the roleplaying game is all-ages, and the stories here are very squarely adult. After all, some of those children who began reading me in 2014 *are* adults now! Norrøngard is a big land. It can hold a lot of tales targeting different audiences. Here are some truly great ones —epics to make any snowbound warrior proud. Whether you're a returning reader or are taking your first steps into my frozen north, enjoy this latest foray into Norrøngard!

As the Norrønir say:

Be healthy. And never leave home ahead of your axe and sword!

—Lou Anders

WELCOME TO STOLKI'S HALL

Come on in. All are welcome. We have meat and drink to satisfy any hearty adventurer.

Herring is always on the menu here. As is blood and offal sausage. Horsemeats are reserved for holidays only. We recommend the barley porridge with either apples or mixed berries. That's a local favorite. We also offer a variety of cheeses, both domestic and imported, served with either rye or sourdough. Weak, watered-down beer is on hand for the children. Strong beer and mead are adults only. If you want some imported Dvergrian ale, or perhaps a bottle of fine wine from Escoraine, we can usually accommodate, but they do cost a fair handful of hacksilver. So most folks just stick with the mead.

Don't be shy. Grab a seat on a bench. A server will be right with you. Well, maybe not right away. Stolki's is after all the most popular mead hall in the city of Bense, which makes us one of the most famous mead halls in all of Norrøngard. But we'll be with you in a moment. In the meantime, why don't you strike up a conversation with one of the locals? You never know what sort of stories you'll hear. Epic sagas of adventure, or frightening accounts of encounters with spirits and malevolent monsters. Tales of bravery or stupidity—they often go hand in hand! From the humorous to the horrific, heroic to heart wrenching, you'll hear it all. Some of the tales might even be true! Regardless, the patrons of Stolki's can spin yarns to rival the best of the skalds. So eat up, drink up, and, most of all, listen up.

Just remember to duck when the food fight starts.

DAUGHTER OF THE DRAUGR

JOEL SHEPHERD

Sten rides, across green fern and thick moss. The last of spring snow lies in crystal patches upon the ground, and the sun is still low at mid-morning. On the saddle's rear clutches his sister, cheek to his back as they raise to a gallop along a straight stretch of path.

"Frida?" Sten shouts above the hooves and wind. "Frida, you have to hold on tighter! You'll fall!"

He clasps her wrist, trying to pull her arms more tightly about him. Ahead, the forest resumes, as scrub, fern and rock end at a wall of trees. Beyond, Dragon's Bay glitters gold in the low sun, beneath a scatter of pink-edged cloud. The air is chill, and Sten pulls the scarf that Aunt Olga gave him more firmly about his neck, tucking the longer end into his tunic.

He feels Frida slipping, and realizes he won't make the trees. He reins the horse to a stop, and catches her just as she falls, near falling himself in his hurry to get his weight beneath her, an awkward dismount and collapse.

"Frida!" He's come down in some snow, the icy wetness through his pants is unpleasant. "Frida, wake up!" He holds her upright, and slaps her cheek lightly.

Frida's eyes open. Light blue, within deathly pale skin. Her eyes were bluer than that, when she'd been alive. Now she stares past him, at the broken cloud, pink and yellow in the low light. "So cold," she murmurs. "So dark."

"It's not that cold!" says Sten, attempting cheerfulness. It blackens his heart to look at her. His sister, older by two years. She's always been the one to cheer him. Now this. He props her, holding the reins of the horse so that it does not wander. Sitting in ferns beside the trail, she can see Dragon's Bay, and the Seal Islands, dark rock upon the glittering blue sea. "You see, Frida? You see the bay? We're nearly home!"

"It's so dark," Frida murmurs, gazing at the scene in bleak distress. "How can you stand it?"

Sten gazes at her in dismay. "Stand it? Frida, it's Skagilund! It's home! You love it here!"

You stole her, whispers a voice on the wind. Sten stares about, upslope, where the ragged cliff of the Harðrtönnbjarg glows bright against the sun. *Bring her back to me.*

A boiling river of swords, axes and other weapons. Jangling and clanging as they swirl and tumble, a sound terrible like a thousand blacksmith's anvils. Sten blinks hard, and shakes his head to clear the vision. Had he been there? Had he truly? He must have, because Frida is here now. But it seems like a blur.

His eyes drop to the silver pendant on Frida's tunic. It's shaped as a silver stag, hanging upon a necklace of twine. Another of Aunt Olga's gifts. She must wear it at all times, Olga insisted. If she doesn't, she'll turn.

"Come on," says Sten, and tries to drag her up. Frida's eyes fix on something beneath his sheepskin jacket. A pale hand reaches, and withdraws the carving. How could she have seen it, hidden in the jacket's sole pocket?

Sten stops trying to lift her, and lets her sit, as she considers the piece of wood in her hand. Oak wood, best for carving, Aunt Olga said. The form is of a stag, its head, antlers, shoulders and back emerging from the wooden block. The legs are not yet done, spindly and difficult, as the antlers are not complete either. Sten has been scared he'll mess them up, without Olga's guidance.

Frida runs a finger over the curve of wooden neck. "It's beautiful. Like the ones in the cave."

Another flash of memory. Black rock, and bare walls. Pale people, sitting or standing in rows, staring blankly into nothing. Pale shapes, barely moving, for all eternity. "What are you talking about?" Sten mutters. "That place is horrible. There's nothing there."

Frida's pale eyes look away to the trees. "The cave is beautiful. It's filled with forests, and the land is fertile. I wandered among trees and butterflies and rainbows." Her eyes return to the carved stag. "It's my home. Take me back. I don't like it here."

"No," Sten retorts. "We have to go on, before our father destroys all of Skagilund. It's the only way."

She lies, whispers the wind. *She lies to you. She wants Frida for her own plans.*

For the first time, Sten feels paralyzing doubt. Aunt Olga is a völva. Among the Grímsgard folk, whispers abound of the nature of her magic. Sten's Uncle Hagen wedded her five years ago — bewitched, some say. They'd made a new home in Grímsgard, up-coast from Sten's home of Fylgjavik. Hagen fished, while Olga made potions and charms, and arts that she claimed were enchanted.

Sten had been with her when his family had died. Strong, tall and good with an axe, he should have been at home with his father, assisting on the boat, and helping Garth chop trees to make new boats. Instead, he'd been with Olga and Hagen, learning the old lore, wandering the woods as she taught him the true names of birds and animals, and practicing his carving. Darr would be disgusted with him.

On an impulse, Sten grabs the carved stag from Frida's hands, and hurls it down the slope. Frida stares after it in dismay. "I'm a follower of Darr, God of War!" Sten shouts. "I should never have fallen for this women's crap!"

He hauls at Frida, and finds her energy returned, though barely. He pulls her onto the horse, then mounts before her, wrapping her arms about him so that this time, hopefully, she will not fall.

He rides into the forest, dark and cool. The low sun does not penetrate here, and the air smells of things green and thick. Sten knows this trail well, linking Morheim to Grímsgard, then winding up the rugged coast to Verborg, out on the Northern Peninsula.

Ahead is Fylgjavik, his home. He passes a well-remembered bend, the path weaving about a gnarled birch tree, where once, as a boy, he'd killed his first boar with his father's spear. Where is his father now? What horrors has he inflicted, further up the coast?

The path becomes more and more familiar, downslope toward the sea. The trees thin, to clear fields about Fylgjavik, a cluster of longhouses by the shore. Sten steels himself for what he knows he'll find. Longhouses can be rebuilt, he reminds himself. New boats can be made. Even people are never entirely gone.

Dark shapes lie in the fields. Cattle, Sigmund's milk cows, all slaughtered. Raiders will take cows, not kill them. Cows are worth gold. Raiders did not do this.

Sten rides closer, and sees longships pulled to the shore, sails furled. Typically in late morning, the catch would be in, and villagers unloading fish and squid in baskets. Sten recalls mending the nets with his father, cold, wet yarn and frayed knots. His father's gruff approval to see his work, a prize as grand as gold.

Fylgjavik lies empty now. The rear of Sigmund's longhouse sees no clothes on the drying racks, no bustle of women with the laundry. No dogs bark, and no children laugh. Upon the road between houses, the cairn stones lie scattered across the ground. Pushed over, Sten thinks, in a deliberate act of vandalism. A ward against evil spirits. Perhaps some evil spirit objected.

Sten grasps the head of his axe, and pulls it from the saddle binding by his leg. A heavy, comforting weight. It calms the pounding of his heart, as he passes houses, and enters the town square. He's heard that Fylgjavik was attacked. He expected more destruction than this. Certainly he'd expected bodies, but the square's dirt lies bare. No sails lie in mid-repair near the slope, no salted fish drying on racks. Just cold silence, and a chill wind off the sea.

No, he thinks as he sees something new — a pile of charred wood where Jarl Skarde Olafsen's house once stood. Jarl Skarde was the richest man in Fylgjavik. Frida's former husband.

Sten turns in the saddle to look at her. She's staring at the ruins, with those chill blue eyes. One hand clutching the stag necklace, close to the blue scarf that wraps tight about her neck.

"Do you remember now?" Sten asks her. He's been asking endlessly on the road. Something to explain this calamity, of lives upended.

Frida's lips move. "I think I..." she begins. But cannot complete the sentence. "I don't belong here. I cannot remember. Take me back."

You take her to your doom, whispers the wind. *The völva wishes to end the world. Return her to me.*

"Father should never have married you to him," Sten says fiercely. He suspects what happened. Jarl Skarde is rich, but among his least worthy possessions is a temper. Handsome, headstrong, and a great warrior. Tempers on such men are to be expected, and welcomed. To be desired, if one is a twenty-year-old girl, and in search of an adventurous marriage. "Where is he, Frida? Is he with you in the cave?"

Footsteps crunch in charcoal ruins. Sten looks, and sees a man. No, two men. Long hair, beards, tattered tunics. One wields an axe, the other a spear and shield. Both are clearly dead, pale faces tinging to green and black, corruption and decay. This, too, Sten has been warned of.

"Brandtsen?" says the big one with the axe. His voice is like a blunt knife against a sharpening steel. "Is it Brandtsen?"

"The boy returns," says the one with the spear, solemnly. "Join us, boy. Join your father."

"Where is he?" Sten demands, steadying the horse as it shies. "What happened here?"

The axeman points at Frida with a discolored hand. "She knows," he says, grinning unpleasantly. "She started it."

"You take that back!" Sten growls.

"Didn't do what your master wanted, did you lass?" The axeman advances, boots kicking through broken house beams. "What was it this time? Something like the animals do in the forest? And you said no, didn't you? Thought you were marrying a *good* man, did you?"

Sten is staring at the solemn man with the spear and shield. It looks like... "Rangvald?" he asks. "Is that you?" The solemn man gazes back. Lean and gaunt, familiar cheekbones and nose beneath his helm. The same helm he was buried with, just weeks before.

The axeman laughs, an unpleasant rasp. "Like you've never seen a dead person before! You're sitting with one on your horse! Why don't you tell him, girl?"

He's getting too close. Sten swings from the horse, handing the reins optimistically to Frida. "She can't remember," Sten replies, hefting the axe. It requires two hands, like the one wielded by the draugr before him. "You tell me."

The axeman scowls. "What do you mean, can't remember? We all remember, boy. Unless..." his eyes widen, and he stares at Frida on the horse. "You went all the way to Nethahellir to fetch her?"

Something cuts the air with a buzz, then a thud, and an arrow protrudes from the axeman's side. He looks in that direction, with annoyance. Sten does too. There's a man there, before Vali's house fronting the square, hastily loading another arrow.

"Ambush," says the axeman, with contempt, and advances on Sten. "Living scum." He pulls out the arrow as he comes, to free the full motion of his arms. Sten rushes as he does, and is on him before the surprised draugr has replaced both hands on his axe.

Sten's swing smashes the axeman's arm, a horrid cleft through corrupted muscle, breaking bone, leaving the arm dangling. The draugr tries to swing back, but one-armed gains no leverage. Sten steps aside the weak swing, and his second swing sends the draugr's head bouncing into collision with a longhouse wall. The body falls like a stringless puppet, and is still.

Sten stares at the man that was once Rangvald, standing amidst the charcoal ruins of Jarl Skarde's longhouse. "Idiot," says Rangvald. "That's how he died the first time."

"You want some too?" Sten asks. Suddenly full of a young man's rage and confidence, shoulders heaving, yearning to hack another head. "You see that, Darr, God of War?" he wants to shout to the sky. "I haven't been corrupted by all that women's magic! I'm a warrior, like you!"

Rangvald smiles drily, the unpleasant wrinkling of decaying skin. "So you heard what happened, and Aunt Olga sent you to Netha-hellir to find your sister, and bring her back to Brandt. I imagine Olga gave you some enchanted trinket for her to wear, so she doesn't turn completely into one of us. Probably she's going to beg Brandt to stop."

Sten stares at him. He'd never known draugar were this talkative. He shrugs, unwilling to answer. Chopping heads is easier. From Vali's house, the man with the bow is approaching, from the corner of Sten's vision. Another arrow nocked, seeking a better line of sight.

"You don't have to answer," says Rangvald. "I've seen enough." He turns to go. "It won't stop Brandt, though. He brought me back from the grave. He's brought a hundred others. No one's seen anything like it. It's terrible."

"Then why don't *you* stop him?" Sten shouts. "He's going to kill everyone in Skagilund if someone doesn't!"

Rangvald turns back, with a final, thin smile. "You don't understand, boy. I *like* terrible."

The man with the bow arrives at Sten's side, arrow nocked and pointed at the draugr's back as he leaves. The man who was once Rangvald slings the shield onto his back, just as the bowman fires, and takes the arrow through the shield. He keeps walking, heading for the field beyond, where Sten thinks he spies horses.

The bowman curses, and goes to pursue. "Wait!" says Sten. The man stops, and looks. It's Halvar, from a longhouse to the edge of town. A part-owner of Vali's boat, a fisherman, like most in Fylgjavik. His eyes are wild.

"Sten!" says Halvar. "I thought you were in Grímsgard?"

"I was," Sten agrees. "I heard what happened. I went to get help." From the direction Rangvald has gone, a horse's whinny, and hooves, galloping away.

"He'll have gone to tell Brandt," says Halvar in disgust. He's a slim man, often mocked for his lack of strength, hair long and blond to the back of a bald head. His beard is thick to make a weak chin seem fiercer. He wears a long knife in his belt, but prefers the bow, unable to match the likes of Brandt hand-to-hand.

"Where is Brandt?" Sten demands.

"Don't know. Up the coast somewhere." Halvar kicks at the headless body on the ground. "Fair swing of the axe there boy. Much like your father."

"Where is everyone else?"

"They ran. The ones that lived." Halvar jerks his head back the way Sten has come, toward Morheim. "Hiding in the forest, some. Leif has a shack down there, and a boat. We can fish."

Sten shakes his head, not understanding. "Why not just go to Morheim? It's only draugar, we've had draugar problems before."

Halvar's wild eyes get wider. "Oh, not like this, boy! Not like this!" He turns, and considers the charred ruin of Skarde Olafsen's longhouse. "They'll lay siege to Morheim and kill everyone! They said they would!"

"Who said?"

"Your father did! Brandt Gustavsen! He's leading them, boy! He died at the hands of Skarde Olafsen, after Skarde killed your..." He stops, blinking as he looks at Frida on the horse for the first time. "Where..." He looks confused, as though seeing a ghost. Which is about the truth, or close to it. "Where did you come from, girl? I didn't see you there!"

Didn't see her? She was sitting astride the horse right in front of him.

A boiling river of swords, clashing and tumbling toward the sea. Sten blinks hard, and grasps for the horse's bridle, to balance himself. In the saddle, Frida is holding something in her pale hands, ignoring the two men entirely as she gazes at it.

Halvar looks more closely. "Is that Frida? Frida, girl? But... but the town saw you dead! Your father saw you dead, and he..." Halvar turns again, and stares at the charcoal ruin, then back again. "Boy," he tells Sten, an earnest, fearful rasp. "Everyone's rising. They don't stay dead around here, boy. This whole stretch of coast is cursed; I didn't want to believe it, but now it's coming true. You can't keep your draugr sister on the horse, boy. She's only still here because she's mad, she'll put a knife in you, in all of us. Best to put her out of her misery, send her to Neth if she'll have her."

"She's already been with Neth," Sten says darkly. "I took her back."

Halvar stares at him, as though he's gone completely mad. "How did you even get there?"

"I went to..." Sten begins, and stops. Where did he go? Places and faces and events are all blurred together in his mind. "I mean I just..." And how long did it take him? Brandt can only have been on the rampage up this stretch of coast for a few days, but going to Neth's cave must have taken... how long? Sten grasps a memory of a face and tries again. "I just talked to... a lady at a bar, and she showed me..." But then that line of memory is gone as well.

Halvar watches his confusion in growing dread. "Why?" he asks finally.

"Aunt Olga told me to." That much, Sten remembers clearly. "She said it's the only way to reach my father."

"Sten, your father's a draugr jarl! I've seen it with my own eyes! Skarde killed him, buried him in the field yonder, but Brandt came back! He had such rage, Sten! He killed Vali, Sigmund and Torvald, all Skarde's friends! He turned them, they all fell on Skarde, here at this house! Burned it down, killed him, dragged him off! They killed others too, Einar and Balder, and Folke, plus some more! They should hate Brandt, but they don't, they hate us! The living!

"The rest of us ran off, grabbed the women and kids and ran, but Haugtoft up the coast got hit next, and they're all draugar now too! He's raising them from the graveyards, even those who should be all dust by now, but when they rise, their flesh comes back! He's raising an army! And I'm sorry, your dead sister's not going to stop him!"

An ill wind whips the charcoal, raising it to the air in swirling clouds. Halvar and Sten shield their eyes. On a tree branch beyond the ruins, as the wind dies, Sten spies the dark form of an owl. Watching them, with golden eyes, in daytime.

Halvar looks as well. "Oh no no no," he mutters, backing away. "You've gone and messed with the gods, boy. That Olga was always crazy, you don't go stealing from gods."

"Neth's not evil," Sten retorts.

"She's Goddess of the Underworld and you stole from her!" Halvar makes a superstitious sign with one hand, retreating back as he came. "If you come to your senses, boy, you come down the coast with me and the others! We could use a firm axe! Stay away from the big towns, your father's going to raze those to the ground!"

He turns and scurries away. Sten looks back to the owl. It's vanished. Was it truly there? Is anything, lately? Messing with the gods indeed.

Sten looks at Frida, her attention buried still in the object she clasps. It's a half-carved stag, looking very much like the one he threw away. Too much. Sten grasps her slim, cold wrist, to stare at it. It *is* the same one, he recognizes the stray cuts of his knife.

Stupid to ask how she got it. Stupid to ask why he can't hold thoughts of Neth's cave straight in his head. Stupid to ask why Halvar has gotten scared and run away.

"Frida!" he implores her, gazing up at her vacant blue eyes, clasping her wrist more tightly. "Try to remember! What happened here?"

Frida slides from the saddle. Sten catches her, but she hasn't fallen, just dismounted, her gaze somewhere up the rocky coast where the wind drives small waves upon the shore.

She walks to the ruin of Skarde Olafsen's house, stroking the carved stag as though it were a new kitten. "I looked pretty on my wedding day," she recalls.

"You did," Sten agrees as he follows. There's pain in the memory. Too much pain.

"All dressed up," she muses, and performs a soft pirouette, boots dancing upon the charcoal. She's almost smiling as she remembers, eyes dancing from one happy wedding guest to another. As though here, standing in the remains of her husband's house, she's moving once more through the world of the past. Time does not matter to the dead, Sten thinks. What is this one moment, against all eternity?

"Such a handsome man," Frida says wistfully, clasping the carved stag to her chest. She steps over charred roof beams. "Such a strong and handsome husband."

"I warned you," says Sten. Swallowing hard against the pain in his throat. "I warned you about him. But you didn't listen."

"Silly brother," Frida murmurs, with an almost-smile. "I'm so in love. Love is all that matters." She turns again, gazing up at the walls of her grand new home. Walls only she can see.

It's too much for Sten. He crouches on the edge of the ruins, balanced with both hands upon his axe, hilt to the ground. Recalling happy faces, drinking and feasts. Skarde, powerful, hair in warrior's braids. Drinking horn in one hand, handsome eyes upon his new bride, with hunger.

"Don't make trouble," his father had warned him. "She'll calm him, you'll see. He'll behave better with her."

"How do you know?" Sten had retorted.

His father had smiled, the smile of a man who loved his daughter more than anything in the world. "Because that's what she did to me. I used to have a temper, ask anyone. Now look at me."

Sten takes a hand from his axe to wipe tears from his eyes. Within the ruins, his sister slowly twirls, lost in her world of beautiful weddings and endless joy. Now she stops.

"No," she says firmly, talking to some invisible person. "No, that's not right. I'm married to you, not to them."

"Frida?" Sten asks.

"No!" she yells, and slaps at invisible hands. "I won't, do you hear? I'm your wife! You must honor and respect me!"

Her head snaps around, as though struck by some invisible blow, and she falls to a crouch. Sten watches in horror, hands gripping white upon his axe. Frida stares up at her invisible attacker. She's crying now, shoulders shaking.

"My brother warned me about you!" she cries. "I didn't want to believe him, but it's true, isn't it? I can divorce you if you strike me! And I will, I swear it!"

She stands, to confront her attacker directly, blue eyes defiant. Brave and reckless, Sten recalls, at times. But then, if she weren't, she'd never have chosen this match in the first place.

"You put that away!" she snarls to the empty air. "You wouldn't dare use it! My father and brother will kill you!"

Then a scream, in pain and horror. Sten looks away, eyes shut and tears leaking. He hadn't been here. He'd gone to stay with Olga for a while, unable to bear the sight of his sister married to a monster. And in his selfish pain, he'd left her undefended. And unavenged.

His father had gone to take revenge alone, and lost. Brandt would have blamed himself, for being talked into it by all the cowardly, toe sucking townsfolk who loved Skarde for his warrior skills, and his arrogant boasting. All the fools who were only disappointed that *their* daughters weren't the ones being offered. But Skade Olafsen only had eyes for Frida.

Of course his father hadn't stayed dead. Skade's fault for not having foreseen it, for not having taken precautions. But a man of Skarde's arrogance and power would feel more than equal to any draugr.

Sten rises, and walks to his sister. She's sitting amidst charcoal ruin, gazing at nothing, a hand to the blue scarf about her neck. It's slipped, revealing a dry, open wound. That hadn't been there, when he'd found her in the cave. It had only appeared once he brought her out, to the world of the living.

Sten crouches, and pulls the scarf more tightly about her neck. "I'm sorry I left you, Frida," he murmurs. "I'm sorry I wasn't here."

He wants her to smile, to acknowledge, to forgive him. Dead Frida just stares, lost in her world of the past, having just died, in her mind, for a second time.

She doesn't belong here, whispers the wind. *Bring her back to me, before it's too late.*

Sten looks up, and finds the black owl settled on a charred beam right alongside. Its golden stare is alarming, at this range.

"She can convince our father to stop," Sten insists to the owl. "You know she can. Stop being so selfish."

Olga Estridsdottir trades in the dark ways, the wind replies. *The Draugr Jarl will gain a draugr daughter, and his power will grow. Many more will die.*

"What do you care?" Sten growls. "You'll just gain more souls for your cave!"

The owl takes flight on soundless wings.

Sten takes Frida's hand, and helps her to rise. They walk back to the horse, which is eating Vali's cabbages from alongside his house. Sten supposes Vali won't mind. Being dead, killed by Brandt, and doubtless with matters of greater vengeance on his rotting mind than cabbages.

He helps Frida aboard, then climbs on himself, and rides in the direction that Rangvald took. On the way from town, he passes a field of burial mounds, fenced with a low stone wall, with yellow myrtle growing every few strides. Local belief holds that they stop the dead from rising. In other towns, Sten has seen corpsedoors, and other tricks to stop the dead from rising. Given the number of draugar reputed to roam those places, he doubts they work either.

Here on the edge of the burial mounds, furthest from the town, is a new pile of stones. Hung upon the mound's doorway, untouched by man or draugr, Sten recognizes his father's old coat. A favorite thing, made of skins, many-times patched and re-sewn. Hung there, Sten knows, to honor Brandt's favorite daughter.

Alongside the new grave, a shallow depression that might have recently been a new grave, but now appears to have been filled in. No time spent, no effort made, to build a proper mound. A marker stone, broken upon the ground. Brandt's grave, Sten thinks, though he feels no urge to check for sure. Dug alongside his daughter, and not occupied for long. Filled in, perhaps, from rage. A message for the living.

Sten looks back at Frida as they pass. She gazes at the graves, though it's unclear from her blank eyes if she comprehends what she's seeing. Another thought hits him. If she's buried in there... then what is this physical thing upon the back of Olga's borrowed horse? The chill in his bones grows worse.

"Too many questions, boy," Brandt would tell him with gruff affection, on days when they were tending the catch, and Sten would rather wonder at the state of the world. "More scaling, less talking."

"I don't want to be like them," Frida murmurs. "Take me back."

"The pendant will protect you," Sten replies with determination. "Don't lose it."

At mid-afternoon, Sten and Frida pass through the small fishing village of Haugtoft. All is deserted, boats idle on the rocky shore. There are no bodies, but upon the ground before one longhouse, a scarlet spray of blood, and a helm abandoned. Stray arrows stick in house walls. From one wall protrudes a long spear, upon which hangs the shirt of the man who'd been wearing it. Of the dead man inside it, there is no sign.

Just out of town, Sten takes the hunter's trail, winding uphill through the forest away from the more obvious ambush spots of the main road. This is the Dragon Wood. Rising beyond the trees to the south, the Svartalfaheim Mountains, dark in shadow against the lowering sun.

Sten hears a cry. Perhaps a gull, he thinks. More alarming would be a bear cub, having lost its mother. But no... he hears it again. Bear cubs don't sob, nor speak what sound like words, fading on the salt breeze from the north-west.

He dismounts, takes the horse's bridle and leads it off the trail. Fallen leaves, needles and twigs crunch underfoot. Ahead, a slight clearing in the trees, where the stone of nearby mountains rises to displace the earth. The sound of a woman, sobbing.

Sten wants to move on. His father is laying siege to Grímsgard ahead, no doubt warned by Rangvald of what's coming up the road from Morheim. But no follower of Darr can pass by these cries of distress.

He loops the bridle about a tree fork, having no faith that Frida can hold a spooked horse, nor that she'd even try. Hefting his axe and crouched low, he advances to a better vantage through low-branching leaves.

Two men stand above a third, who lies dead on the rocks, a large spear rising from his ribs. Nearby, a woman clutches a child, and cries. All seem dark in silhouette, the sun low against the mountains behind. Though Sten cannot make out the features of the two standing men, their movements seem to him disjointed. Light shows between the exposed twin bones of one's forearm, yet still he moves.

The other clicks his fingers above the fallen man's face, as though trying to rouse him. They seem impatient, as men might be, waiting for a third who is taking too long to relieve himself in the woods. They're waiting for him to rise, Sten realizes. He doesn't know what draugar will do to a living woman and child then. He can't wait to find out. Any longer, and he'll be facing three instead of two.

No more women's magic and other nonsense, Sten thinks as he strides from the trees, hefting his axe. It settles to the familiar calluses of his hands, wood matching skin, as both draugar look up. The woman's sobbing stops with a gasp of astonishment.

The near draugr snarls, and charges like a wild animal. It wields a two-handed axe like Sten, but the shaft is rotten, like the draugr's clothes and body. Bones show in the arms as it raises the weapon, teeth grinning in a lipless mouth.

Sten anticipates the side-cut, grasps his axe handle with both hands and blocks far away from his body as his father taught him. A hard two-handed yank then catches the other's axe head at the base of the blade, and pulls it clean from bony hands. Sten reverses his swing and brings his weapon down on the draugr's shoulder with all his power, and a crunch of collapsing bones.

The draugr falls, and Sten puts his boot on its chest to pull his axe clear of shattered ribs. The second draugr is tall, dark and impassive, corrupted face half-hidden within a dark hood. It raises a shield, a smaller axe in opposite hand. Sten has no such defense. The greatest defense of the two-hander is the simple fear it instills in an opponent that if he misses, a great battle axe can smash even a hard shield in reply, or at least the arm of the one wielding it. If this fear translates to draugar, Sten doesn't know. Darr is watching. Time to find out.

He lunges, trying to provoke an attack. The tall, dark draugr merely circles, not taking the bait. Sten sees that if he circles the way the draugr intends, he'll find slippery moss on a sloping rock underfoot. Death does not make draugar stupid, it seems. The stupid ones were that way while alive.

Sten stops circling, moving sideways instead, as both opponents crab away from the woman and child, toward the forest edge. Sten lunges once more with a yell, but again the draugr merely steps back.

If Sten strikes first and misses, he'll be defenseless for a moment in the follow-through.

The draugr lunges low, aiming for Sten's legs. Sten swings, but the blow is not vertical enough, and bounces off the draugr's raised shield. He scrambles back, as the draugr's axehead nearly takes his leg, recovering for a second swing. But the draugr is on him fast, hitting Sten hard with the shield.

Sten lands hard on his back, momentarily stunned. The draugr's dark shape blocks the low sun as he looms above, easily adjusting the grip of his hand axe, like a man who recalls from a long life's experience how it was once used.

A figure moves behind the dead man as Sten prepares to roll and scramble. Female, pale, a slim hand raised as she passes like the breeze. The draugr stops. The hand falls. The axe head hits a rock with a clank. The knees fold next, as the draugr slowly topples, collapsing to the ground as though from a great weariness.

Sten stares, pulling himself up, heart pounding and back aching from the impact. Somehow he hasn't cut himself on his own axe as he fell. Frida passes on, to the fallen man skewered by the spear.

Sten comes after her, as the woman with the child stares in astonishment. The child is perhaps five, a girl with white hair. Her cheeks are red, and her eyes, from crying. She looks confused, past the fear.

"He's yours?" Sten asks, about the dead man.

The woman nods, tearfully, clutching her little girl. "He saved us from Grímsgard. He was seeing us to safety, and to get help from Morheim. But the woods are not safe."

"No," Sten agrees, getting his breath back. Frida touches the man's chest. He looks young, perhaps early twenties, like his wife. His beard is thin, and his vest hard, armored leather. But the spear has gone through it like paper.

Should have stayed where you were, Sten thinks angrily. Defend your town, and your family, in the place where you are.

But you left, whispers the wind. *You left Fylgjavik for Grímsgard.*

Then you left Grímsgard to get help when Olga asked. What will Darr think now? Sten looks up at the neighbouring trees, angrily. The black owl sits on a low branch, gazing with golden, unblinking eyes.

On the rock, beneath the impaling spear, the young man's eyes open. A dark, expressionless stare. The eyes flick, and fix on Sten. There is no life in them, only malice.

"Hush now," Frida murmurs, and places a slim palm upon his forehead. "Hush, my brother." The dead man's eyes flick to her. They widen, as though with recognition. Then emotion. Astonishment. "Sleep now. Go with Neth."

The dead eyes dissolve to grief. Gratitude. Relief. Frida's hand slips across his face, leaving closed lids, and peace. His young wife sobs anew into their daughter's hair.

"Help us," Sten growls at the owl. "Be useful."

Child, whispers the wind. *I have only ever served you.*

Sten walks to his sister. One hand clasps the silver stag pendant, the other resting upon the young man's chest. Her eyes remain blank, little more animated than the draugr. Sten recalls the tall fallen one, the one he didn't kill. Couldn't kill, perhaps. A great warrior, no doubt, while he was alive.

He looks, and sees no life in the fallen corpse. Such power in Olga's pendant. Or was it the pendant at all? Was it Frida? Or both, together in the real world, performing some great and terrible magic?

"Have you food?" he asks the young mother as she struggles to her feet.

"You're leaving us?" she asks fearfully.

"We go to Grímsgard. We can stop the siege." Sten takes his sister's hand, and to his surprise, she rises without complaint. "But we'll be there tonight, I have more food than we need. If you head to Fylgjavik, I met Halvar there. He says there are more folk sheltering down the coast, near the black rock by Seal Island, I think. It's not far, you'll be safer there than elsewhere."

"Don't go!" the young mother begs him. "The one leading them is terrible! Our best warriors fought him directly, but he slew them each in turn! They say he can't be killed! He must have been a great warrior in his previous life!"

"A good warrior," Sten says quietly. "Not a great one. Just an angry one."

The woman stares at him, horrified. "You know him?"

"He was my father." He looks at Frida. "Our father."

Frida pulls the half-carved stag from her coat, and holds it as tight as the little girl clutches her mother's hand. Her pale eyes scan the trees, in search of owls.

Sten crouches in the treeline overlooking Grímsgard. The slope is only small, but high enough to see the walls encircling the great central longhouse, all bright with torch flame. The Grímsgard townsfolk have divided into groups, to defend the wide perimeter. Every twenty strides, a fresh pile of stones has been laid to make a cairn.

But now as Sten watches, and the last glow of sun fades purple in the sky toward Oslendholm, there come cries and clashing steel, the sounds of battle. Before the walls, dark shapes prowl and cluster, scuttling up the sides of log walls, or trying to. There is too much perimeter wall to be successfully defended by shield, flame, spear and axe alone, Sten thinks. Olga must have made charms to keep them out all this time. But now the last light is fading, and the charms with it.

"There's no time!" he tells Frida, swinging astride the tired horse. He'd thought to sneak in, but Rangvald came this way and alerted them all. If they've not yet breached Olga's defenses, then Grímsgard has lasted longer than he'd have guessed.

Sten kicks the horse's sides, and it raises a weary gallop along the outer fence of clear farmland, toward the road into town. He's seen one hometown emptied of people today. He cannot bear to see it happen to a second.

Sten turns onto the road, Frida clutching him from behind. Ahead, fires atop the main gate in Grímsgard's walls light passing fenceposts to dancing shadow. The wind off the water is chill, now colder still at speed, and carries the smell of smoke. The horse shies its head, smelling something more — draugar, corruption and death.

Sten steadies it with difficulty, and kicks again. He can ride, but the horse is Olga's and Hagen's, and he has no particular skill. As he rounds the last post of cleared fields, and sees Grímsgard's gates broken open, and knows he has no choice but ride hard through the thick of it. Grímsgard has warriors, but the draugar are too many, and fight too well. If he can't find Brandt, they'll all die.

There are no draugar at the entrance, and as the high gate flashes by he sees why. Here about the great longhouse and surrounding buildings, amidst a scattered panic of running, flapping farm animals, draugar fight against men and some women in the confusion of dancing flame.

Sten pulls the axe from its place alongside his saddle, knowing too well that he's had no practise at swinging it from horseback, and that two-handed, he's more likely to lose an arm than anything else. He pulls up, as the horse shies aside, warriors yelling as blows exchange about him, axes and a few swords finding shields with a sound like a hundred blacksmith's shops.

A river of swords, tumbling over and over toward the sea, with a deafening clangor.

Sten blinks his eyes clear, and sees a woman amidst the warriors, down by the side of the great longhouse. A headdress of antlers, armed with shield and sword. Sten kicks the frightened horse once more and gallops. He passes the longhouse side, reining past combatants, intent only on reaching Olga.

From the darkness burst a pair of draugar, who hit the horse in unison. It shrieks and loses footing, and suddenly the ground is rushing up to hit him. Sten throws the axe clear so it does not decapitate him on impact, rolling clear to grab it up once more.

A draugr rushes him, only to be felled from behind by an axe. The man wielding it is large, with thick arms and a bushy blonde beard beneath his helm. "Sten Brandtsen!" exclaims Gorm the farmer. "Good timing lad!"

"We must get her to Olga!" Sten yells, running to the fallen horse. It's dying, with feeble kicks as blood gushes from a severed throat. Pinned by one leg beneath the saddle, Frida lies as though unconscious. But how can that be, with the dead?

Sten tries to drag her clear, but the leg is properly trapped. Gorm heaves to lift the horse's body, just enough for Sten to pull the leg clear. Gorm abandons the horse to swing at an attacking draugr, as Sten looks about desperately. Further down the longhouse Olga fights with several men. Her skills are not great, and she's slender against the men's bulk, but sure enough, her sword is gleaming bright with blue fire.

She blocks a draugr's attack with the shield, then barely slaps its side with the blade, and it bursts into flame. Some have doubted Olga's powers, a few to her face. Never angered, Olga only smiled and ignored them. After tonight, none will doubt, if any live.

As the burning draugr shrieks and flails, Sten hears Gorm smash his opponent's skull with his axe. "Frida!" Sten shouts, and slaps her cheek. "You can't be asleep, you're dead! Wake up!"

Perhaps she doesn't want to, he thinks. Perhaps, in her desire to be elsewhere, she's refused all consciousness. Slight girl she might be, but she's heavy to carry.

"Hey!" Gorm takes off running, and Sten looks. Ten strides away, an embattled warrior is cut down by a new draugr joining his evenly-matched fight. "Play fair, deadman!"

Gorm swings, and the new draugr blocks easily. The return blow smashes Gorm's defense, and half his face. The next sends a sword through his gut.

Sten rises as Gorm falls, revealing a dark, broad-shouldered figure in a black cloak. A thick brown beard, long hair about a haggard face. Eyes that burn, like dark jewels in the firelight.

Sten stares in horror, as Brandt Gustavsen approaches. The sword and shield are familiar. Sten recalls trying on the shield, as a child, and marveling at the terrible weight. Leather straps to bind the forearm, the stuff of boyhood fantasies. Now it approaches, bearing some of the marks Sten himself delivered upon it, in training. The sword is newer, a recent gift from a man in payment of a debt. It has new notches, and is streaked red.

Upon the belt hangs a human head. In the firelight, Sten recognises the face of Skarde Olafsen. Many days dead, if Sten's grasp of time is right, but not so corrupted as it should be. The eyes are open. *Moving*, Sten notes, in horror. The gaping mouth works, silently, as Skarde seeks to speak. To protest this endless torment.

Sten raises the axe with both hands. About him, others are fighting, but none now approach. Can draugar be scared? Several of those behind Brandt seem to hang back, as though distanced by fear. At least, Sten thinks, he need not worry about his back. None would dare sneak in and deprive their lord of another kill.

"Father," he says.

Brandt's lips twist, with bitter humour. "Boy," he spits. "You ran away."

Sten knows he dare not let Brandt near Frida in this state. Whatever Frida is supposed to do to stop him, she can't do it now. The other draugar won't kill Frida, but Brandt might. The stories say that Draugar Jarl can do anything.

"I came back," Sten retorts.

"You ran away from Fylgjavik," Brandt growls. "You ran away from your sister. You ran away from me."

"You married her to a monster!" Sten yells, losing control of the fury that's been building for many days. "I warned you he was a monster! I warned her! No one listens to me!"

"A lesser monster now," says Brandt, darkly amused. He pulls a knife from his belt, something once used to scale fish, and stabs the living head at his belt through one cheek. Skarde's mouth screams in soundless pain. "At the wedding, he suggested we should get to know each other better. And now we are."

"You've had your revenge!" Sten shouts above the crashes and yells of battle. "These people did nothing to you! Leave them be!"

"You ran away," Brandt repeats, with menace. "They let you. Some of them came to the wedding. Some are friends of Skarde. There's no one innocent, boy. Not you, not me. Not them." He points around with his sword. "They'll get theirs. I've had mine." His sword finishes its sweep, to point at Sten. "And you'll get yours."

Sten swallows hard, blinking back tears. "You'd kill your own son?"

"One more torment for the man who's lost everything." Beyond the pain, Sten feels a rising disgust at the depth of this self-pity. "Life is pain, boy. All those I kill rise again. Join me, and we'll end this pain together, across all these lands."

Brandt advances, sword ready. Sten backs up, axe braced in a tight, two-fisted grip. And pauses, as Brandt pauses, hard eyes fixed on something past Sten's side. Sten does not look, suspecting tricks. Until someone steps to his side, and stands there, facing Brandt.

Sten risks a look. It's Frida, gazing with calm detachment.

Brandt's lips twist again, and he spits. A harsh cough that is almost a laugh. "*This* is why you left? To play this trick? And she's supposed to do what? Talk to me? Convince me that I'm wrong?" Brand resumes his advance. "I *know* I'm wrong, boy. I don't care. I like it. I am beyond your judgement, forever."

The air seems to grow bright. It is a silver light, not the yellow of torchlight, and burning firepits. It grows and glares, so bright that Sten has to shield his eyes. Brandt ducks his head behind the scarred shield, growling as though the light causes him pain.

Sten stares narrow-eyed at the stag upon Frida's chest. It glows like silver fire. Beyond Frida, upon the edge of the longhouse roof, a black owl lands. And transforms, with a leap and fall to the ground, rising to become a woman, unarmed, in dark robes.

"How did you do it?" wonders the woman. The light grows brighter, the pendant glaring, but the woman peers close, without so much as a squint. "How did you know?"

"The only ones who can move between the realms are gods, and the souls of the dead," says a new voice. A woman's voice. Sten looks left, and sees Olga, sword gleaming blue in one hand, one of her paired antlers on the headdress missing where a draugr blade has lopped it. "A Draugr Jarl is the most powerful. The pendant is my own magic."

The light forms a bridge, between Frida and Brandt. Colors mix, as reality itself swirls within. Sten glimpses something more. Green fields. Trees and mountains. A new world, somewhere in the growing maelstrom. A wind begins to blow, toward the rift, whipping hair into his face.

"Women's magic!" Brandt snarls. "Leave, both of you! Neither have any power here!" But he remains hunkered behind his shield, as though fearing the light will do him damage. About the longhouse, all fighting has stopped, draugar retreating from the light, arms and shields raised to their eyes.

"And this is the true reason you sent the boy after his sister?" asks the lady in black. She sounds sad. "To do this cheap, petty magic?"

"There's nothing cheap or petty here!" Olga shouts, braced as the wind grows to a howl. Only the woman in black appears unmoved. Neth, Sten realises. She's not supposed to come here, in the world of the living. Olga swore she had no power here. But then, the living intruded into her domain first. "The rift will grow! Souls move between realms! The realms aren't as stable as the gods pretend, are they? They're not made as the gods pretend! I have two of their greatest travellers here, a draugr from this world and a girl from yours, his daughter, bound to him by blood! Between them they burrow between realms like an arrow through flesh! Together the power multiplies!"

"While the pendant binds," Neth says thoughtfully as she sees it.

She has the look of a woman who may have been beautiful once, and is now satisfied with seeming dignified. Her dark eyes, as they settle upon Olga, are cool with scorn. "And you hope to see what? The secrets of the universe?"

"Everything!" Olga yells. "It's not fair that gods alone wield the power to move between realms when you've made such a mess of everything else!"

"And you think that if this power were granted to mortals, things would be so much better?"

To his side, Sten sees Frida's hands pulling the pendant over her head. "Frida, no!" But his hands on the axe will not move.

"Child no," Neth chides with matronly concern. "Put it back on. You'll turn. I cannot stop it, my powers in this world are limited."

Frida ignores them both, and walks forward to the light. The rift moves away from her, forming an equal distance between herself and the cowering Brandt. She reaches him, and it seems to spread, forming a ring about them both. Wind kicks dirt and debris into the air, in small whirlpools against the side of the longhouse.

"Father," says Frida, and grasps the edge of his shield. Pulls it gently downward. Despite the slenderness of her arm, Brandt does not resist. Cannot resist. Dark eyes stare at hers, above the rim of his shield. "I don't need their magic, Father. I will go with you. I will fight at your side."

Brandt stares. Blinks hard. Hollow eyes, alive with silver light. "I... you can't." Sten has never heard a draugr uncertain before. "You can't join me. Not you."

"I wish to," says Frida. "Your love for me brought you here. Let us be together once more."

Brandt blinks once more. The uncertainty grows, like gathering clouds. "Not like this. No." The eyes abruptly darken once more. "Don't trick me!"

Frida turns, and tosses the pendant in her hand to Sten. Her eyes, once so dazed and absent, are bright with determination. "Break it!" she commands.

"No!" Olga yells. Sten loves them both, but there's only one he's ever truly trusted. With all matters, at least, save those of her heart.

He drops the pendant to the ground, raises his axe high, and brings it down hard. A flash clefts the air like a lightning bolt, tearing the axe from his grasp. Then he's on the ground, blinking his eyes clear, ears ringing from the blast of sound.

Olga lies motionless upon the ground nearby. About the long-house, most others are also laid flat. Some now stir, like Sten. Propped on his arms, he sees Brandt, kneeling before Frida, the only two still standing. Of Neth there is no sign.

"Girl," says Brandt, in a tight, strangled voice. "Girl. You give yourself for me. You shouldn't."

"I love you, Father," she says solemnly. "Where we go, we will go together. You will choose."

Brandt bows his head to the rim of his shield. His shoulders shake. He's crying, Sten sees in astonishment. The tales tell of love as the strongest magic, but Olga says there is one kind stronger. Sacrifice.

Brandt lifts one corrupted hand, and strokes at his daughter's cheek. His dark, sunken eyes fill with tears. "Then let us go. Together."

About the yard, remaining draugar fall. Their bodies ease to the ground, as though with a great, collective sigh. Frida stands to her father's side, and bends to embrace him. Her face upon his shoulder, her eyes meet Sten's.

She smiles, the brightest of bright smiles from Sten's childhood. It lit his life then, and does so now. From Brandt, a small, approving nod. Then he falls, a collapse to motionless bones. Of Frida, there is no sign.

In the sky above, a black owl flaps on soundless wings, headed for Nethahellir, and the cave that is home. Carried upon its wings, a hundred new souls.

Sten emerges from the longhouse the following morning, limping and sore all over. He's had little sleep, as the surviving townsfolk of Grímsgard have spent the night arranging burials, and Sten with them.

The many graves make a trench in the earth beyond the main walls, where all night the bodies of draugar and newly-felled Grímsgardians were hauled. New stone and earth is piled to one side, for new mounds. Sten walks past them now, on his way to the fields with a spade for morning toilet, then a wash in the bay. Still the axe is in hand, because despite the events of last night, one never knows. Morning sun glows yellow and red behind a plane of broken cloud. Dark rocks make a line along the horizon, headed north, out to Verborg. Good fishing here, and only the occasional dragon.

Townsfolk who insisted last night that he at least should get some sleep, now nod at Sten as he passes, hard at work filling in the graves. There's hope that these ones will stay in the ground. Olga insists that it's most likely the case.

Olga herself attends to the construction of cairns along the row. She looks at him grumpily as he approaches, still clad in armor with sword at her hip, though her shield rests against paddock wall nearby.

"Did you really give me the pendant so I could save everyone?" Sten asks her. "Or so that you could glimpse what lies between realms?"

"I'm cold, boy. But not that cold." Olga stretches the kinks from her back, as others work on, stacking stones. "Call it a happy coincidence." Hagen is back at their house, attending to animals and children. He and Olga have two, both girls. "It took me so long to get that pendant. No idea how I'll get another."

"What is it? What does it do?"

"Another day," Olga sighs, "and I'll tell you." She looks at him shrewdly, beneath falling curls of hair. "You did well, Sten. Better than most men could have dreamed."

Sten nods slowly, looking along the row of graves. Only a few new ones for villagers, thankfully. Most of the bodies in here died long ago. Sten turns, and resumes his walk, out to the fields.

"What are you going to do?" Olga calls after him. "You're free to stay with us, if you want?"

"I don't know!" Sten calls back, with hard exasperation. As he walks, he contemplates his life. He's all alone now, save for Olga and Hagen and the girls. Grímsgard likes him, he's a hero now. But somehow, he doubts it will be enough to make him stay.

He pulls the carved stag from his jacket as he walks. It was lying on the ground where Frida had last stood, embracing their father. Incomplete, like Frida's life. Like his life. Like everything. He'll finish it soon, Sten thinks. He'll get Olga to show him how to do the antlers properly, and the legs. Women's magic, perhaps, but worth the knowing. And if he just abandons paths half-walked, how will he ever learn who he is? Even the All-Father uses women's magic.

After some distance, he finds a fence for privacy, and digs with his spade. When the hole is done, he feels someone watching him, and looks up. A man stands beside the fence, ten strides away. The hood of his cloak is down, revealing dark red hair and beard, loose fringe blowing in the morning breeze off the sea.

"Greetings stranger!" says Sten, warily. Not especially worried, as most folk around here are good, save the walking dead ones. And the bad living kind tend to travel in packs. "I don't recognize you from around here?"

"No," the man admits, walking over. His voice is rough, powerful. "I heard there was a big fight here last night. Pity I missed it." He carries a big two-handed axe of his own, Sten sees. "Trade you. A look at mine for a look at yours."

Sten hands him the axe, taking the stranger's at the same time. It's a real beauty, of lovely oak grain, smooth-polished with a leather-bound grip and simple steel stud in the end, to keep the axehead in place. A warrior's decoration, not a show-off's. The blade looks sharp enough to split hairs, and Sten can see his reflection in the steel.

"Wow," he admits. "So much nicer than mine. I polished it this morning, but it'll never come up like this."

"An honest weapon," says the red-haired stranger, hefting Sten's axe with a powerful, expert fist. He's not much taller than Sten, but something in his stance, and his grip on the axe, Sten finds impressive. "It looks well used." He smiles, a glint in his blue eyes. "I like that."

"What brings you out here?" Sten asks.

"You do."

Sten frowns. "Me? Why?"

"Introductions," says the stranger, "and I'll tell you."

They swap axes back, and Sten extends his hand. "I'm Sten Brandtsen." It is a relief, he thinks, to be able once more to say that name with pride.

"Well met, Sten Brandtsen," says the stranger. "I'm Darr. God of War."

JOEL SHEPHERD is the Australian author of eighteen SF and Fantasy novels in three series. They are "The Cassandra Kresnov Series," "A Trial of Blood and Steel," and "The Spiral Wars." Visit him online at www.joelshepherd.com, on Facebook, and on Twitter @ShepJoel.

LURE OF THE LANDKRAKEN

ED GREENWOOD

The fog was heavy, a ghostly cloak that glowed in the night.

A cloak they were getting all too used to. In the days when spring warmed into summer, sea-fogs beset the lower streets of Sindholm after dark, on nights when the winds howled not.

This was just one more such night, the fog a wet and clinging cloak with tentacles that came creeping in under the warmest wool and furs. Shivering weather, when folk who had no need to stir from hearth bided indoors, leaving the dark streets and alleys to scuttling rats and those driven by their needs.

Which at this moment very much included the huldra shield maiden Halla Skogsdóttir and her steadfast companion Luta Ragnarsdóttir, for their needs included eating.

Often and well, if possible.

Yet good food—and drink, the drink was not to be forgotten!—and for that matter warm, snug accommodations required hacksilver, and it had a habit of running low. It was running low right now. So Halla and Luta were getting bone-cold and wet, out here in the night. Luta had found work, which was why they hadn't yet resorted to prying the more decorative gable horns off roof-ends and selling them elsewhere on behalf of a fictitious sick aunt demolishing her smokehouse. Yet.

Luta was the arch-tongued beauty, so Luta found most of the work. And it was retriever work suited to Luta's most often used skill: she was an expert climber very much at home on walls and rooftops not her own.

Which was why Halla was sitting on the slick-damp wooden planks of the street in this thickening fog pretending to fix her boot heel. A pretext to loiter.

Somewhere in the eddying coils of fog above her, her beloved—her exasperating beloved—was on the roof of the house she was keeping her back firmly to. The abode of one Brandr Fire-Eyes, reputed to be a wizard and definitely the man who'd swindled Luta's current client, Jora Ulfsdóttir, out of an amber pendant, a keepsake of her dead grandmother she very much wanted back.

Halla snorted. Humans. We could both die for an amber pendant.

Oh, well, it was a living.

Oh, well, it was a living. Of sorts.

Luta closed her eyes. They were doing her no good in this fog anyway, and the blindness might help her listen more intently at the smoke hole she was pressed against.

That voice had to be Brandr. Aye.

"Arnorr's magic was powerful. His corpse door is not unguarded."

Luta was up on this cold, slippery roof trying to learn the routine of the house, how many dwelt within, and when a retriever desiring to search for an amber pendant and bear it away back to a grateful Jora Ulfsdóttir could best enter the place without being seen.

"A wizard's rune," said a deeper, rougher voice, like a boot stirring gravel. It was not a question.

"A rune," Brandr agreed. "Likely the most powerful in the whole Barrow. It sucks the life out of whoever disturbs its chalk in the slightest. Or so the old men say."

Luta had never heard of Arnorr before, but it was clear enough: he was a long-dead—must be, or it wouldn't be "old men"—wizard. And now in the Bjarg Barrow, the labyrinth of tunnels under most of Sindholm where the dead were housed, and folk just a little more desperate for hacksilver than Luta and Halla sometimes went hunting tomb treasures.

"And your way past it? A spell?" A new voice, a weasel voice, higher and younger.

"A hand not ours to wipe right across the mark, and break its power—and pay the price."

"Whose?"

"Who's been most persistent in demanding his hacksilver back from me?"

"The older Snari. Snari Grimsson."

"Indeed. A hint that he'll get his loan back should bring him within reach like an eager valravn. Then we beat him senseless—I thought you'd like the sound of that—drag him down the Barrow and use his hand to wipe the chalk. That crutch you kept from the beggar we fed to the eels should serve to move his arm and keep the curse on him and not us."

"And then what? We get inside, and then?"

"Then you leave matters to me."

"What I mean is: why did they call him Arnorr Eyehands? Is 'eyehands' some sort of spell? That might be on his body, waiting for us?"

"You listen to too many skalds when you go drinking," Brandr replied severely, and then added something else that Luta couldn't hear, for all the men she was listening to were on the move now, striding away, wooden furniture groaning across a floor as it was shoved aside. She listened a little longer, but only to silence. They were gone.

And might well be going out, where it wouldn't do for them to stumble over a woman on their very doorstep with a bootheel that wasn't broken after all—let alone a second woman up on their roof, uninvited. Wherefore Luta moved. Spiderlike, patient. Stealth over swiftness, on the damp slickness.

Well, now. Why disturb a long-dead wizard, but for treasure? Powerful magic, according to this Brandr-thief who was also a wizard. Treasure. Moreover, men down the Barrow were men not at home when Luta came calling, at this smoke hole or another one...

Men who could be disturbing something that might make it healthier to be far away from Sindholm, no matter how unpopular the duo of Luta and Halla might be in some other places. A duo who'd not bided in Sindholm long enough to know what it now seemed they very much needed to know, to not put a boot wrong in the next little while.

She dropped down quietly enough, but of course not quietly enough to not startle a huldra.

"Well?" Halla might not be the sharpest blade in any town, but she was long-suffering when it came to her friends, even amiable, and that counted for much.

"The Raven, and Eldgrimr."

Halla merely nodded, and they retrieved their barrel and trudged off down the street together, bent forward as if it was full. Never skulk when you can seem to be carrying out a needful task, wearily or sullenly. The curious lose interest when they see something they know all too well.

The Sipping Raven might be the most rundown and little-known mead hall in Sindholm, and on a mean street indeed, but inside, it would be slightly less damp than out here in this fog. And it was where Eldgrimr Ivarsson, a talkative old local they'd befriended as a useful expert on Sindholm, liked to drink. Or more likely, could afford to drink.

Luta and Halla had found an empty barrel tossed aside as being too rotten to bother recaulking a few days back. They now each carried an end of it when they walked the streets of Sindholm, to appear to have a purpose for going hither and yon—and if ever someone discovered it was empty, they could play at being two touched-wits women, if it came to that. Luta had already discovered the old cask made a rolling seat she could readily balance on—and kick at drunkards if a brawl erupted.

"To ask him about what?" Halla murmured, when they were well away from the house of Brandr Fire-Eyes, and had turned a corner or three.

"Wizards," Luta muttered back.

"Wizards," Halla growled, missing a step. "Don't like the sounds of getting mixed up with wizards."

Luta shrugged. "If we avoided everything dubious in life, what would be left?"

"Ale."

"More ale!" a familiar cracked voice called, from the darkest back corner.

The woman with a heap of empty drinking-horns on her tray balanced that load on her beefy bosom long enough to turn, put hand to hip, and bawl back, "Oh? You suddenly have silver enough, Eldgrimr?"

The response was a sigh, a scowl, and a morose peer into...mere dregs.

"You do now," Luta murmured into Eldgrimr's ear with a grin, sliding him a coin as she grounded her barrel beside him—and Halla sat down across from him.

Eldgrimr looked at her, then picked up the coin, flashed the few teeth he had left in a smile, and cheerfully bellowed, "Droplaug!"

And when Droplaug lurched around to glare at him, he brandished the coin at her.

Then without sparing her another glance, he cupped both gnarled old hands around it and bent forward over the table to mutter, "You two'll be wanting to know something."

"Indeed," Luta said smoothly, into his ear. "What can you tell us about Snari Grimsson? And where he lives?"

Eldgrimr made a face. "Him."

He put one bent old forefinger down on the table and told them more than they needed to know about what a nasty man Snari was. Well, now, it seemed they'd not feel any sadness watching him getting beaten.

Then Eldgrimr slapped down his middle finger and told them what Snari looked like, the long hair with one lock darker than the rest, just here, and the nose like a boar's snout.

Then his next finger descended. The house where Snari lived, and what its roof and door looked like. One of the better thresholds in Sindholm.

Then the littlest finger, the one forever curled like a bird's claw. The latest dark rumors about the recent swindles and misdeeds of Snari Grimsson.

These were many, and Halla's lip was curled in real disgust by the time Droplaug came stumping up to loom over Eldgrimr with her pitcher—and her hand outstretched for the coin.

Coin first, a hard and suspicious peer at it, then the pour. Brim full, ere she waddled off again.

Eldgrimr drank deep, and came up gasping in delight. When he was finished grinning at them, above a bare swallow more than dregs again, Luta slid another coin along the table to under his nearest hand with the words, "And what can you tell us about Arnorr Eyehands?"

Eldgrimr recoiled as if she'd thrust a knife up his nose.

"That's not a name remembered fondly here," he growled.

"Oh? Why?"

Old eyes shot her a dark look. "Disturbing the dead is never wise."

"Which is why neither of us was considering such a thing," Luta replied without hesitation—but not too quickly. "Do we look crazed to you?"

That earned her another wide smile. "You want the truth? Or polite words?"

Luta shrugged, but the old man cut through whatever cleverness she was starting to say by asking sharply, "Who was speaking of him?"

"Never saw, but heard. House with a green door flanked by two lanterns, the left one cracked, five doors up from Gunnarr Ívarsson's. I believe I was hearing one called Brandr, who seems to know things about wizards."

"Brandr Fire-Eyes," Eldgrimr growled. "That's his house, right enough. A wizard himself, or wants to be. I down ale, but he likes to drink power. Cross him, and you're his foe—and must die. Wants every last jarl and the High King himself swept away so Brandr can king it over the rest of us, he does. And there are others here who feel as he does, and they mutter together behind closed doors betimes. Itching to burn all Sindholm down and start anew. Better, this time. With them on top, of course. He's their leader, and he's been hunting something called the Lure of the Landkraken for years."

"And what might that be?" Halla asked softly. "A spell?"

The old man winced, leaned closer across the table, and lowered his voice to a rough whisper. "Well, a landkra—"

"I know what a landkraken is, and I know what a lure is," Halla growled. "I'm guessing a wizard might be the sort of crazed dolt who'd seek to bring a landkraken anywhere near. Being as it will tear apart and devour any number of jarls, kings, and anyone else within its reach."

"Yes, but are they real?" Luta asked. "Or did skalds turn a dew-worm into a linnorm? Is this Brandr chasing an empty tale?"

Halla shook her head. "I've seen one. Seen tentacles tear two men apart in a trice."

"After how much drink?"

"Lute," the lady across the table snapped.

"Sorry," Luta said swiftly, reaching across the table to touch Halla's hand. "So what's this lure he's been hunting? A spell?"

Eldgrimr nodded. "Spell, or some sort of magic you can hold in your fist." He tried to drink deep, found he had nothing much left, and half-rose to wave his horn at Droplaug and tap it meaningfully with the coin Luta had just given him.

As he slumped back down again, he growled, "Take care. I don't want to lose my suppliers."

Halla arched an eyebrow. "You're not going to warn us off?"

"And send you striding off in a hurry to confront Brandr and Snari, in Arnorr's tomb?" the old man snorted.

His two guests exchanged glances. "Are we that obvious?"

"I know you."

There was no fog this night, just a cool ghost of a breeze. So the grunts and thuds of the three burly men beating Snari Grimsson to reeling, bleeding unsteadiness in the street below carried clearly up to the rooftop where Luta and Halla were lying watching.

The shortest of the trio had an old, heavy seax hilt with no blade left that made a vicious club, and wasn't shy about using it. The tallest one ensnared Snari's arms from behind, and held them in a grip like iron despite Snari's desperate kickings.

Overmatched and outnumbered, Snari was soon enough sagging down the nearest wall, and the tall man could whip his cloak off his shoulders, toss it over Snari's head, and bundle him away.

Luta and Halla watched them go. And take a turn at the next corner that they'd fully expected.

"Headed for the Barrow," Luta observed. "So skulk after them, but don't get seen."

Halla gave her a gentle slap. "I'm careful with my words, Lute, not a simpleton. So while I'm risking my hide with all of these large, hairy sword-brutes, you'll be...where, and doing what?"

"Looking in Brandr's upper chambers for an amber pendant," Luta replied sweetly.

"You're just going to walk in on him? And smile?"

"Oh, he's waiting at the Barrow right now. His sort have to gloat—have to be there. He won't be letting anyone get to loot Arnorr's baubles before he does."

Soon. Brandr could almost taste the magic flowing through him, like sweet mint and hot iron entwined at the back of his throat. For about the score-and-tenth time, he strolled oh-so-casually across the dark threshold that was the lower entrance to the Barrows to the far stone pillar, then back again.

Patience, he told himself, not for the first time. *Magic takes time. Patience.*

He strolled across to the pillar again. *I must learn it sometime.*

A scrape of a boot brought him around in a spinning instant—in time to see Hrólfr and the others coming out of the night-gloom, half-carrying, half-dragging Snari Grimsson.

Brandr went and got the lanterns from where he'd put them, out of sight of anyone who might take to watching him while he waited at the Barrow door. Áskell shielded him from any such eyes as he lit them both and then reshuttered them to keep things dark until they were well in.

They all knew the way by now. He'd walked it scores of times, and made all of his men do it a dozen times this month. No one wanted to get lost in the Barrows.

Just the cold, the bone-chilling cold, could kill you. Not to mention someone desperate for food or coin or better boots, who knew you were alone and couldn't outrun his knife. Or hers.

Anyone who went alone into the Barrows knew fear. If they didn't, they were mad. Into the mountain they went, carved into the rock, corpse door after corpse door. Brief, distant screams echoing, the scuttlings of things unseen retreating before lanternlight. Even four strong—five, if you counted still-blinded, captive Snari—they were all uneasy, wary. Weapons came out, men walked slowly.

There. A scream, brief and cut off horribly; wet choking. A throat slit.

And now a scuttling, much nearer but getting less near as fast as whatever it was could move, on its claws they could hear on the stone.

Smooth and even underfoot, here, this close to the entrance. It would get rougher later, as they walked older stretches.

Still rougher, once they got past the wizard's door. For Arnorr Eyehands did not sleep unguarded.

The base of her tail was starting to itch. It always itched when fear stirred in Halla.

She stood as still as a tree in the night, watching the men disappear into the Barrow. She wasn't going in, there was no need. It was a place of death, of cold stone, where the whispering wind of no forest would ever reach.

They were men of ruthless hearts, going to plunder magic, to do murder to get it. There was no need to go in.

So why was she sidling closer, softly silent in the night?

Why was excitement rising in her, until it tasted almost like glee?

Halla shrugged, and advanced.

Smiling.

Hrólfr had gone first, sword ready. The man-mountain, the open slit of his lantern tilted at the floor to show him footing and not light him as a target. He knew the right door, stopping before it ere Brandr had to say a word.

Nor did Brandr have to tell Áskell or Eiríkr what to do. Gloves on, they took Snari's elbows from behind, forcing his blind-blundering arms up and forward. Brandr shone his own lantern back behind them to make sure no one was skulking close—the passage behind was empty—but really to make it seem like his wary step back was but a step sideways, to turn.

None of his men looked his way, though. They were all watching Snari's right hand strike the stone of the door, then slide hard across the old chalk rune as Áskell shoved him, abruptly and timing it perfectly. Then everyone let go and sprang back as the rune blazed into eerie life, a cold radiance like blue-green-edged moonlight, utterly silent.

As Snari Grimsson gasped in its ghostlight, staggered sideways, and seemed to slump and dwindle.

It took the time of a fearful indrawn breath—for Brandr, at least —before Snari fell. His body hit the floor and bounced, mere bones in a skin sack. He'd withered away to a husk. Just like that.

They stared down at him for a long and silent time ere Hrólfr silently handed Áskell his lantern and dared to stoop and touch what was left of Snari Grimsson.

And lift it, like an empty sack, head lolling, to turn and thrust it forward to try to use its hand to open the door.

And then freeze, all of them, Eiríkr drawing breath so sharply it was almost a gasp, as they saw the door swing open by itself, inwards, into darkness.

It was a long time before Hrólfr trudged through the doorway, and when he did, he was holding Snari's remains before him like a shield. Hrólfr's sword, still in hand, jutted untidily up and out.

Brandr turned slowly on one heel, shining the lantern all around. The passage around them was still empty. They were alone.

Alone with the dead.

A cheery thought. Feeling that Hrólfr's broad shoulders, before him, were his own shield, Brandr warily entered the dead wizard's tomb. Stepping to the side the moment he was sure of safe footing, to see all he could and to make sure Áskell and Eiríkr weren't moving to get behind him.

They weren't, and it seemed even wizards weren't worthy of large tombs. A small, bare room hollowed out of bedrock. No doors, or anything at all except on the slab that filled its center.

Where there was quite a display. Bones were all that was left of Arnorr Eyehands, a shorter man than Brandr had thought he'd be, whatever clothes or shroud he'd been laid out in now mere wisps and shadows on the stone. His bones not disarranged. Around him, an oval of small, interlaced runes, spidery faded marks that by the black hue of their smears had been written in blood, runes Brandr couldn't read but could feel were magic. And within them, close around the body, the things they'd come for: a bare-bladed tiny needle of a knife with a clear yellow gemstone in its pommel—and no sign of a sheath anywhere— a book of two crisscrossing belts of some sort of scaled hide buckled around what looked like sheets of silver-hued, untarnished and unrusted metal, and bone tubes, long hollow bones—from the legs of oxen? No, something larger—that would have scrolls in them. Spells.

And the spider and the snake which the writings had warned Brandr about, frozen by magic, awaiting the unwary. The beady eyes of the spider seemed to be glaring at Brandr as he gazed at it, though he was well away of its fabled jumping range, the most distant of the four living visitors to the tomb. The snake lay like dusty dark purple rope, not coiled to strike. Not yet.

As big as his fist, that spider, covered with sparkling gray-white fur like new-fallen snow. A rime frost spider. The snake—a viper of a sort he'd never seen before; the writings called it merely a "serpent" —looked lifeless, eyes closed.

Brandr shot Eiríkr a look, but again didn't have to say a word; the man had remembered his orders. The long cudgel he'd carried slung on his back was now wedging the corpse door open behind them.

Brandr nodded approvingly, and unhooded his lantern.

Hrólfr did the same, then set it down a good two strides away in the back corner, and approached the slab, hefting his sword in one hand and Snari's lolling emptiness in the other. Catching Brandr's eyes, he pointed with his blade at the snake.

Brandr nodded, mouth suddenly as dry as sunbaked stone. No change in the plan.

Which meant Áskell and Eiríkr were supposed to use the magical daggers Brandr had lent them, and stab the spider hard, pinning it down ere starting to slash outwards in opposite directions and slice it apart. He hoped they all remembered how fast these guardians were likely to be, the moment they were freed from the magic that bound them motionless.

Hrólfr was wise enough to use Snari's corpse to break the ring of runes. He shook the dead man first, to warn Brandr and fetch another nod of approval.

And then brought Snari down, his sword right behind as the runes boiled up into moonlit, racing wisps of smoke that faded almost as fast as they'd appeared—to behead the rearing snake in a shower of eerie sparks out of nowhere, its long curved fangs biting the air in hissing agony as the head spun away trailing gore. Brandr never saw where it went, as the busy arms and shoulders of franti-cally-stabbing Áskell and Eiríkr blocked his view, cursing and almost sobbing in fear as they struggled with the squalling, dying spider. It was spurting its innards all over the—

"Off the slab!" Brandr roared, fearful the spider's blood would ruin the scrolls they'd come for. "Get it off!"

His shout echoed weirdly around them, magnified thunderously, and through its din the spider, or various wet pieces of it, hurtled across the room to hit the wall. And slide down it, leaving glistening marks, and a smell that set them all to gagging.

"The bone tubes," Brandr ordered Hrólfr, "All of them."

The big man nodded, already grabbing at his hip-pouch for the sack. Brandr himself took the dagger and the book, into his own sack with only the slightest of hesitations that some magical doom might smite him—none did—and then they were all stepping back from the table.

"Make very sure of the spider and the snake. Hack them if need be," he ordered Áskell and Eiríkr briskly.

Ere looking at Hrólfr and adding, "Now we leave the body as if it was bold brave Snari the Fool who tried to loot a wizard's tomb."

Both things were done, and the lamps reclaimed and shuttered down to their former slit-gleam, and then they were all making for the door, hearts leaping with sudden glee.

They never saw the huldra watching from outside, who faded back into the darkness as they approached the tomb door.

And so, never knew how tempted Halla had been to try to entomb them all alive.

The same smoke hole she'd listened at, earlier, had been her door. Its shutters had been pulled to and fastened within, of course, but a clumsy child could lift those hooks from their eyes if they climbed to where Luta had, with a sword or hairpin or anything else long and thin enough—and Luta had both.

So now she was creeping around inside the home of this Brandr the ambitious wizard like a cautious cat, listening to the distant bangings and chatter of women below, cooking. The din of servants who knew their master was out and they could make noise.

Luta just hoped none of them were in the habit of darting

upstairs without warning but with a little stealth, on some errand or other, but so far they'd shown no signs of doing so.

And she could hear nothing in the way of movements nearer.

Brandr Fire-Eyes was a wizard who felt the cold, she judged. Dark rugs were everywhere underfoot, and hangings that were more like heavy blankets than fashion adornments befitting a rising, ambitious wizard cloaked all the walls. The room she'd entered by was an office of sorts, and she'd been all over it with probing dagger and gloved hands and her eyes, disturbing as little as possible because with a wizard, you never knew, but of amber—or pendants, for that matter—she could catch no glimpse. There were intriguing little things galore, some likely magical. The carved statuettes of naked ladies likely not, but the little polished-slices-of-gems eyes had a prickling feel about them, though she'd touched them not; she hoped they weren't really watching her. Human skulls as weights to hold down stacks of parchments, of course, but…no pendants! Anywhere!

She dared not go downstairs, where the open space seemed larger and brighter; she somehow doubted the wizard left those sorts of valuables lying out on display. Yet up here, in the smaller and more private chambers, room after room held other sorts of treasures, but…

She'd run out of places to look, and likely most of the time she'd have for searching, too, when she glided to a stop for the sixth time in front of a closed door with an intricate rune chalked on it that fairly shouted "MAGIC WITHIN. DOOM NIGH."

It led into a hexagonal central chamber she'd circled several times; the passage with the rest of the rooms opening off it ran around it. That rune was a peril, or the door held other traps, almost certainly, but…a client was a client, and it was high time to begin filling her purse and not emptying it daily.

Luta drew in a deep, soundless breath, flexed her fingers, listened intently to what sounded like the beginnings of a friendly argument coming up the stairs, punctuated by a metallic crash that meant someone had dropped a metal pan or some such…and approached the door.

By flattening herself against the wall on its hinges side. Why open a door and trigger it, if you can just remove it?

Well, the builder not being a dolt who left you anything you could reach from the outside that had to do with the hinges, that was why.

Luta swallowed a soundless sigh and looked again at the ceiling. She'd studied it before, seeking lurking traps, guardian creatures, and trapdoors, and had seen only tiles. Now she peered more closely; could any of these tiles be readily pulled down, or pushed up, to open a way?

Not that she could see. Of course not, this not being some skald's tavern tale…

She set off around the passage again, opening each door in turn and looking at the walls of the room beyond. Was there space unaccounted for, between one room and the next?

Between the fourth and the fifth, there was.

Fast now, Lute, this is all taking too much TIME.

Here. It must be here, where this fanciful hanging of the World Tree hides…yes. A panel with darker edges than the others, a seam, the edges of a narrow door. Push, slide…no…lift with splayed fingertips, slide, and—it moved. Not used often, but greased. Darkness. Into which she thrust her little Fang, slicing empty air. A closet, or… up first, and nothing, but down and the push-dagger grounds on a wooden step. She reversed it, to slide the T-handle along and not make marks with the point, and so trace that step, the riser, another step: stairs up. Found. Now to see how solid the attic floor was, above the rune-guarded sanctum.

Be a soundless shadow, among the shadows.

Up, cautiously probing in the darkness, to stirring air, colder and damp, carrying the small sounds of Sindholm at night, and the ever-restless waters of the Vestrifjord to her. An attic, then, with an old roof that had its gaps and needed attention, like so many nigh any damp seaside. So, this way would bring her over that rune-guarded room…

Not just the roof needed attention. The attic floor was of stout old boards, and if they hadn't been so stout, would already be near collapse. The boards were the cheap salvage builders so often used when no visitor would ever see them. Six rough bark edges just at first glance, with at least five gaps between them she could see already. There'd be more.

Luta crawled softly to a large gap, and peered down.

There were glows down there, dimly illuminating what would otherwise have been utter darkness, glows coming from…books, on two of the shelves that ran around the inside of the hexagonal room. Old, eerie-looking books, that had runes on them Luta couldn't see properly, as each was partly obscured by the next book. But they were what was glowing, right enough. The books were thick, and worn, each leaning its own direction, like an old man who'd seen long years and now limps with a stick. Magic books, of course.

The shelves ran around the walls everywhere except where the door was, and framed a hexagonal table at the center of the room, a table of black-painted wood that had chalk smudges on it where things had been written or drawn and then wiped away. Two identical unlit lanterns stood on opposite points of the table, an expanse of bare tabletop between them.

She couldn't see the floor; it was lost in darkness…dark fur rugs? Or woolen rugs? Too dark to tell, but nothing moving, no creature that she could see, and nothing looking back at her. Which meant she could take a proper look at what was on those shelves.

One wall had the door and no shelf, and on the walls to one side of it were two runs of shelving holding all manner of interesting things, then two adjacent runs of books, then another two runs of interesting things, and finally a bare shelf awaiting interesting things, ere someone circling the room came back to the door again.

Make the circuit again, eyeballing those interesting things. A cup filled with a splay of tapers, ready for lighting, what looked to be a little metal pouch-box for flint and steel ready beside them, flanked by a larger box...kindling? Wood shavings, torchlight fungus, or some such? Closed, so she couldn't see.

Then what looked like a set of traders' weights, cubes of metal bearing owner's marks too small to see and likely unfamiliar to her. Then a square frame enclosing a bulge of blown glass that likely magnified whatever it was held over. Beyond it, a wooden stand with what looked like the skeleton of a snake wrapped around it in a spiral, its shed skin intertwined with the bones and spiraling the other way. Some sort of magic?

Luta shrugged, looked past the two runs of books, and found herself gazing at a mummified man's hand set up on a spike and wooden base so it jutted up into the air. It had runes written on back and palm, and with them, script, too. She probably wouldn't have been able to read any of it with her nose almost touching it, and certainly couldn't from up here. The hand had what looked like slivers of gemstone affixed to the fingertips, she couldn't see how. Definitely magic, and fell magic at that. Then a stone smoothed by the sea, like so many on beaches, but with natural markings that made it look startlingly like a staring eye. Then two hooked, polished-bladed knives, with grips made of antler. Wizard knives, not the slaying fangs of a warrior, and these looked to have never been used.

Then a corner, and on the next shelf, a cloth bag that might hold coins, and next to it—the amber pendant!

What she'd come for. None of the rest of what was down there mattered.

Except, of course, that it did. Those books. Priceless, or to the right buyer, if they could somehow stay alive through the negotiations and sale, enough to make her and Halla very rich. Stealing them would be wrong, but leaving this mad wizard to use them...worse.

Yet it might be death to touch them. Who knew what sort of evil magic might guard them against the wrong hands?

Not that she had to touch them. She could use her daggers, or doff what she wore to make a carry-apron, and…do what with them? Take them where? Could this Brandr feel their whereabouts, and track them like a good stag-hunter? Following her wherever in all Qualth she went?

Um.

Ah, but what if she didn't take them from this house? But hid them from him. Down inside the walls, perhaps, or where the roof drew down to meet the attic boards, all around her. Not stealing, but "mislaying" them.

Yes. Yes.

Confound all wizards, whenever possible.

Now, to lift one of these boards…

Easier thought of than done, of course, but the boards were pegged down to crossbeams, and some of the shorter boards not that securely; the wooden pegs were old and dried out and loose. So…

The cord Luta wore wound and wound around her midriff was poor armor, yet made her look fat rather than wearing rope around herself, and she always brought it along on bold forays such as this. In a trice, two boards were up and aside, the cord was tied to an attic roof-brace that was making up for short ends of treetrunk that were too flawed to take the full weight of the roof, and she was…

Dropping down into the still-locked hexagonal room like a large and ungainly spider, dagger ready, peering everywhere for a pet snake or some other guardian.

And finding nothing. Her man's kyrtill came off to be a book apron; she'd fill it and tie the cord to it and draw the bundle of tomes up into the attic in her wake. Business first: amber pendant into the soft doeskin pouch she wore around her neck, normally hidden under her kyrtill. Then books, thumb thud thump no matter what care she took, but touch nothing else, and…done, and back up into the attic, with the books—curses the dead hiss, but they were heavy! —following her, hard haul by hard haul, and…they were up. Boards creaked under their weight, so she hastily tugged on her kyrtill and spilled them from their heap. She was just pulling her kyrtill back on when—

Rat-tat-tat-TAT-TAT, startlingly loud up here in the attic, where she could hear the sounds of Sindholm around the house.

Hurled stones, on shutters close below: Halla's signal that the wizard was returning home, so bold retrievers had best begone. Now.

Which was when, of course, a board groaned under the weight of books and a half-naked Luta, and—split with a crack that momentarily had her hanging head-downwards into the wizard's sanctum.

Luta spat out all of the most colorful curses she knew, but she spat them out in a whisper.

They looked smug and sneering, the four men, striding up the slope of the street like conquerors. So the living wizard had got what he'd wanted from the dead one.

Halla quelled her desire to look back over her shoulder—and so betray Luta. Who wasn't out yet and signalling she was clear, so it was already too late.

Which meant it was this foolish huldra against four. Such a pity.

Halla hid her gleeful grin by ducking her head as she playacted at losing her grip on her faithful barrel, rocking it as if struggling to hold onto it—and then toppling it and her with it so the fast-approaching men wouldn't see she was in truth carefully aiming it, so that when she let it go...

She knew the planks were uneven, on this steep stretch of street, but not that uneven. The barrel had barely begun to roll when it bounded into the air, only to bounce with a loud and solid CRASH and then land, rolling hard, and sweeping one man—the one who looked most tired, and had his head down—right off his feet.

Halla was running after it by then, calling, "My cask! My CASK!"

The man on his back on the planks reacted just as she'd expected. Amid snarling curses, he struggled to one knee, glared at Halla racing right at him—and took a swing at her.

So she leaned in and punched him very hard in the throat.

"Hoy, now!" the next nearest man barked, reaching for her. She grabbed his hand and sat down abruptly, bringing him crashing down over her head, crotch right in front of her swift kick. His barking roar became a rising eeEEEEP of pain, and Halla was rolling away as fast as she could, fearing a sword-edge would be viciously seeking her already.

And it might well have been, had not Brandr the wizard bolted in front of the big man in his haste to get to his home with his tomb-stealings, and leave the fray to his men. And snatched a sack from the man's shoulder as he did so, its fall checking the man's reach for war-metal.

So it was that the wizard's front door banged in his wake when the man-mountain was still drawing his sword and showing teeth to Halla.

Halla showed hers in return, just to be polite.

Smarting from fresh scrapes, and breathing hard from the frantic effort that had righted her, Luta had just finished setting all boards back into their rightful places and started winding the rope around herself again when a door below her swung open, and a man chuckling gleefully strode through it.

She froze, but there was a hubbub of women's voices and then a nearer, louder male one commanding, "No, no, my stomach can wait! I've important work to do first, but mind you keep it warm. Now go, and disturb me not! I'll be down when I'm ready!"

Luta snugged down the ends of the rope and reached for her

kyrtill by feel, peering intently through a gap. At the bobbing head of Brandr Fire-Eyes, home from the Barrow and full of triumph.

She watched him bolt the door of his sanctum from within and put a prop against it that had been hidden from her in the darkness, behind the doorframe. Then he lit the two lanterns—flint and steel in that box, right enough—and began doing something to...bones longer than her arms, that certainly hadn't been in the room when she'd been peering around it, but were now on the table, so he must have brought them back from the tomb. He was...he was teasing something out of one, that had been rolled up within it. Eagerly, breathing fast, intent.

Which was why he hadn't noticed his books were missing, yet. That and his cook or maid asking about the meal. Well, the gods be with her that far, at least.

Luta settled her kyrtill back into place and felt for her belt. Her gaze never leaving the wizard below her, as scrolls emerged from their bone homes.

She saw Brandr frown in bewilderment at one, and frown in interest at another. Only to lay them aside in favor of a third that made him smirk and begin his gloating.

"The Lure of the Landkraken," he read aloud in tones of triumph, holding the scroll up. Then he set it down on the table, did back his sleeves, and reached under table-edge for...four flat stones that must have been on some ledge or open shelf. He slid two of them to pin down the top corners of the scroll, then unrolled it almost reverently to reveal it all, placed the stones to hold the bottom corners, stepped back to regard the entire scroll—he still hadn't noticed the absence of books, gods be thanked—then stepped close again to adjust the lanterns, shifting them just so.

Then the broadest smile yet, a deep breath, a wipe of sleeve across forehead, and Brandr leaned in and began to intone the words. A rune flashed momentarily as he read it, hand passing over it but not touching...

"Au kalaumadoth hyee maharokhau dardren..."

And Luta knew she must interrupt this casting. No matter the danger. There'd be longer, harder peril if the High King and all jarls were dead, and everyone was fighting for thrones across all the lands, like so many hungry leaping wolves...

"Suu maeretra thalthul daroo. Hrist marrek treia..."

Thankfully, she'd not had time to try to replace any pegs; the boards under her were lying unsecured. So if she could get that board aside without him hearing, she could then snatch and toss that one and be down on his head, and kicking, before he could get a knife out, or—

Planning never got anything done. She lifted the first board with infinite care, and again the gods were with her: in his rising excitement, Brandr Fire-Eyes raised his voice and exulted, gesturing grandly, and so heard not the faint thud as the far end of the board grounded in the attic darkness.

"Andurae lothont kreev autaunnadroth tarVAE!"

As two runes near the bottom of the scroll flared into cold brilliance, Luta plucked up the second board, flung it, and plunged boots-first through the gap she'd just made, shoving on the edge of the floor still in place to swing herself so she'd arrive not on the tabletop, but on the wizard's head and shoulders—could she break his neck?

He heard her scrambling, and the clatter of the board bouncing, and flung his head back to stare up at her.

Just in time for her boot to slam into his nose.

He went over backward like a rag doll as the lanterns toppled, one of them bursting to shed flaming oil everywhere. Too far for Luta to wrap herself around his head and shoulders and dagger his throat, as she plunged down, just missing the edge of the table, to land jarringly on the floor—dark soft carpet furs, tacked down so they didn't slip—and spring right back up in a frog-hop so she'd be ready for anything an annoyed wizard could—

She almost wasn't. Fire was spreading, that coiled snake-skin flaming up like a torch, and Brandr was coming at her with eyes blazing almost as bright in his rage, shouting something incoherent but likely unkind, nose streaming blood. A wicked-long curved knife he'd snatched from somewhere gleamed with the light of its own fell runes as he swept it up to stab down at her—

Like any grand hero-playing fool.

As fresh flames blossomed somewhere on the shelves behind her, Luta plucked the nearest of Brandr's stone scroll-weights off the table and flung it in his face, then clawed the next stone up without looking and hurled it at his knife hand.

They both thudded home, and the wizard shrieked and fumbled the knife away. He lashed out wildly and blindly with his other fist, bruising Luta's shoulder as she tried to duck past. Feeling the contact, he whirled on her as swiftly as any hunting cat, but Luta raked his forehead with the fingernails she kept long—the middle and the third of her left hand—for slicing purposes, and drew more blood.

Some sort of magic had awakened on the shelves behind her, causing small spittings and flares of gouting flame, but Luta hadn't time for see what and where, as she tried to get around behind the wizard, sprinting as he turned and clawed at her, still shouting, still incoherent—or perhaps he was trying to spout another spell amid his shrieks of pain, as Luta sprang high and kicked away his fingers, he looked wildly around for his fallen knife, saw it and rushed to bend and snatch it up, and Luta vaulted up onto the table so when he whirled with knife in hand and a shout of triumph, she greeted him with the other two scroll-weight stones.

The second one struck his nose again, and he dropped the knife to clutch at his face in pain. Giving Luta time at last to draw her own favorite dagger with one hand, and with the other whip the scroll up off the table and thrust it into the merrily-leaping flames of the toppled lantern that hadn't made it off the table.

"NNOOOooooooo!" Brandr desperately lunged to snatch the scroll to safety, just as it caught fire and flared, and its lowest-down rune blazed with sudden, eerie light, like an angry emerald eye glaring at

Luta—and the wizard's lunge brought his throat right onto her ready, jutting dagger.

Luta drove it home with a lunge of her own, making sure his throat was pinioned on it, and Brandr gargled horribly, clutched at her and at the scroll—

And then sank down, sliding down over the table-edge like something dripping, and out of sight with a thud.

As the scroll blazed, burning in earnest now, almost seeming to push out smoke, greasy green-black smoke with winking sparks in it, smoke that curled strangely. Luta watched it coalesce into…

Thick, dark tentacles, reaching for her!

Luta flung what was left of the scroll away from her and herself back off the table, so frantically that her shoulders struck the wall beneath the shelves. It boomed thunderously.

Was the wizard moving? No. Were the tentacles still lengthening and thickening and reaching for her?

Reaching, yes, but already fading and drifting, dissipating…

Which meant that she didn't have to claw open the door, but had time instead to fight the fires—or, no. Something else to do first.

Back onto the tabletop, and then a leap. Clutch, scramble, and up into the attic, to sweep the books crashing down through the gap.

She was almost weeping, but it had to be done. Tentacles…

They were gone, she saw thankfully, even before she returned to the tabletop, plunging down balanced and ready this time, to begin feeding the dead wizard's books to the flames.

And he was dead, lying on his face unmoving, blood from his throat spreading enthusiastically across the furs.

Luta plucked everything that was so much as smoldering onto the tabletop, built it up into a merry little fire, and fed it its first spellbook. Which spat at her like a cat ere it caught, then blazed up and unleashed shrieking, wailing magics as little flying shadows, shadow-serpents of the air that soared free but twisted in seeming agony as they rose.

One almost carried its flames up into the attic ere it faded, and gave off a murmuring that changed things unseen beyond the walls around her.

Suddenly chilled at the thought of what she might unleash, Luta thought better of burning the rest. Besides, if the attic went up, there went her safer way out.

She unpropped and unbolted the door, and risked a peer, but no servants—or anyone else—was waiting outside.

So she strode to the room she'd marked earlier as the wizard's bedchamber, took his cleanest robe from where it was draped ready over the back of a chair, wrapped it around the rest of the books in a secure bundle, belted it to the wizard's body, and went looking for Halla.

She didn't have far to search. Outside the front door, Brandr's men lay sprawled and dead, with a barrel upright in their midst, and Halla was sitting on it.

"Done yet?" Halla inquired with a smile.

By way of reply, Luta beckoned her and murmured, "How are you at stuffing wizards into barrels?"

The Barrow was colder than Halla remembered. It didn't look as if anyone had dared to disturb the wizard's tomb since Brandr's visit. Good.

Luta and Halla lifted the dead wizard's body up out of the barrel and dumped him atop Arnorr's bones. Forever staring at nothing, and looking horrified.

It was a good look for wizards, Halla decided.

Luta removed the bundle of spellbooks. Halla unwrapped them, and held up the robe, surveying it critically. Brandr's blood on it there and there, and...

She shook her head. "No. Not me in the slightest."

Luta gave her a look, tugged the robe out of her grip, and

rewrapped the books. Wordlessly Halla held out the barrel, for her to drop that bundle in.

The bundle of books settled into the back corner as if it belonged there, as Luta and Halla sipped their mead ale and waited. Eldgrimr hadn't been sitting in his usual spot when they'd reached the Raven, so they were waiting for him. And wondering how much useful he'd know about wizard-books.

"We're lucky to have the Barrow, I say," someone growled, at a nearby table. They started listening, without seeming to.

"How so?"

"Last village we came through, they have family graves. Dig open the same plot when younger kin go to the gods, put them in atop their ancestors—so over time, family mounds rise up, see?"

"Aye, so?"

"So they uncovered an old warrior too well, and put his son in on top of him—and the old warrior's body came back as a draugr, stalking the living. Fed on his son's blood, he did, and rose."

Halla looked at Luta.

Luta looked back.

With one accord they raised their drinking-horns to their lips, and regarded each other over them.

Then Luta lowered hers enough to say, "I'm not going back to look. I'm thinking business might be better in Wendholm, anyway."

Halla shrugged. "Better or not, the forest beckons ever more strongly."

"Eldgrimr will have to drink without us," Luta agreed.

They drained the last of their mead, took up the bundle of books, and banged open the door of the Raven.

At the same moment, deep in Bjarg Barrow, a tomb door boomed open.

A man trudging along the passage on burial detail, heard it behind him but decided to hasten away.

Leaving the dead be is always wisest. Everybody knew that.

ED GREENWOOD is a Canadian writer, game designer, voice actor, and librarian best known for creating The Forgotten Realms® fantasy world, starting at age six; he still works on the Realms every day, more than fifty years later, but over those years has created or co-created dozens of other settings, such as Stormtalons and Mornmist, and contributed to the fantasy settings of others, including Oz and Middle Earth.

Ed's 400-plus books have sold over 40 million copies worldwide and been translated into over 40 languages. Ed was elected to the Academy of Adventure Gaming Art & Design Hall of Fame in 2003, and has won multiple ENNIE, Origins, and other awards. He has judged the World Fantasy Awards and the Sunburst Awards, hosted radio shows, acted onstage, explored caves, jousted, and been Santa Claus—but not all on the same day. He is likely the only Canadian to have scripted comic books for multiple companies and appeared as himself in the pages of comic books published by several imprints.

He shares a house in the Ontario countryside with over 300,000 books. Not counting the secret bookroom. Join Ed's Patreon for his Realmslore, watch his YouTube channel for the fun stories, and follow Ed on Twitter @TheEdVerse for daily doggerel and ongoing Lord Wolf snark fiction.

GULL STORMBARN: THE THORNBLADE

K. V. JOHANSEN

When I saw the stranger, I was halfway down the cliff, toes dug into a crack in the rock, angry gulls mewling and sliding through the air about me. I was leaning just a little too far to take an egg from a last nest, and she was climbing up the path from the bit of gravel we called the beach. Climbing was the right word, because that path was narrow and crumbling and nearly steep as a ladder. Even the goats thought twice.

Not only a stranger, but a ship, slid silently in to rest in the shallows. A crew of five; the sail furled now, only two pairs of oars. I didn't recognize it; not a Norrønian vessel at all. It hadn't been there when I'd started my climb down, barefoot, the better to cling to every crack in the cliff-face, and with a grass-lined basket on my back for the precious eggs. It hadn't even been nosing in from the open water; I would have seen. I had taken a good look down below at the stony beach and the waves churning white over the hidden rocks of a fallen sea stack called Jötunnsoppr, the Giant's Toadstool. There had been a seal hanging about the day before. Ari and Tora had seen it when they took our boat out, hoping for capelin, but the great spawning schools of silver fish that usually filled the cove had not yet come this stormy spring, and the seal had taken too great an interest in them, which I didn't like to hear. They'd had the sense to get themselves back ashore and up the cliff, rather than venturing out to open water.

We had become wary of taking the boat out beyond the cove; for years now there had been rumors of a ghost ship haunting the coast, but sightings had become more common this spring, especially in these waters west of Nilmgard. Watching from the cliff-top at dusk, the day's work done, dreaming of—it doesn't matter what, I couldn't run and leave Ari to cope with his father alone—I had seen it myself, more than once, ragged dark sail limned in eerie corpse-light, ragged figures leaning to the oars.

Bright sunlight, nearly noon, and the ship below was fine and trim; the men who crewed her no draugar returned from the dead. That did not mean they were friendly.

I had a loop of walrus-hide rope about my shoulder, made fast to the lonely boulder sitting on the clifftop above, and the stranger was well below, so I abandoned my reach for just one more egg and went scrambling up. I was waiting by the top of the cliff-path when the stranger reached it, where one good blow could have sent her right back down again by the shortest route, if it seemed necessary. I had seen she wore a sword and glimpsed the vest of good scale armor beneath her dark cloak.

"Gods be with you," she said. She spoke Norrønian like a native, but the scarf about her neck was worked with what looked like Aralish embroidery to me, all thorny sprays of roses, and a sheen to it like nothing I'd ever seen. I thought it must be silk. "This is Yngi's Cove?"

"It is, mistress," I said. "The farm of Eirik Olavson. I'm called Gull Stormbarn."

I waited for the questions. The answers are: Gull, because I was found at the bottom of that very cliff one morning after a storm nineteen springs before, a child of maybe two years lashed to a raft of broken oars and planks with the gulls shrieking and diving about me, probably working up to pecking out my eyes; Storm, for the obvious reason; and -barn, well, I made it clear I was having none of this -son or -dóttir nonsense when I was still quite small, and Vanna, the bride of young Eirik Olavsson, said I might be a foundling and a thrall, but I had a right to the shape of my own life in that much at least.

I waited for the questions, but there weren't any.

"The farm of Eirik Olavson," she said. "Olav the Shield is gone to plough the fields of Neth, then?"

"Four winters back," I said. I was surprised she knew of Olav. He had been a hero, yes, but his was a small tale in the end, and I doubted the songs had ever been carried far from Nilmgard. But then, she'd come seeking Yngi's Cove by name.

"So," she said, as if that settled something, or confirmed it. The stranger looked me over again. "Call me Finola," she said. "Finola the Traveler." She was tall, almost as tall as me, and dark-eyed, with a weathered complexion and hair of a muddy red-brown color, all loose and wind-tangled, hiding half her face, but she pushed it back when she smiled. Good teeth, she had, and good cheekbones, too. Very fine and foreign she looked, with her silk scarf and her armor and a bit of gilding on her sword's hilt, a noblewoman herself, or someone high in the service of one.

"I would have words with the master of the farm, Gull Stormbarn," she said. "Will you take me to him?"

We walked together along the grassy track up the valley. Finola the Traveler stopped where the path bent around the mound of boulders we called the Huldra's Tumble, though I'd never heard why, and she got a good look. I was a bit embarrassed, though it was no fault of mine the place was so run-down. It had been prosperous once, before Olav Yngason was blinded, fighting at his jarl's side against a Svartálfar raid. Some vial of burning poison flung down from a bat on high; he saw it coming, the last thing he ever did see, and raised his shield over his jarl's head to spare him. Took the full splash of it across his own face, they said. That wasn't our Jarl Ranundr the Red, but another jarl, who went adventuring in foreign lands in his youth and was, they say, the lover of a Queen of Araland, but things like that are always told of those who go traveling, aren't they? Anyway, it wasn't Olav the Shield's blinding that brought the farm to ruin, but the grief and shame that came later, which broke his heart and his health and made him an old man before his time.

"What ill-luck's come to the place?" Finola asked, not of me but speaking to herself, forgetting even that I was there. I wondered if perhaps she might be older, and have been wandering longer, than her looks said. Maybe she'd known Olav the Shield. She'd never come our way before in my lifetime. I'd have remembered.

I looked at the farm, and saw it as if for the first time, all ramshackle and ill-kept. Rotting thatch sprouted weeds, even sapling birches; the palisade enclosing the yard was leaning, pushed over from the windward side by winter's drifts; the fields that should have been green with the first growth of peas and rye were patchy and thin, struck by late frosts and washed out by heavy downpours where ditches hadn't been kept clear for years. The húsvættr who had lived in the goatshed even when I was a child had fled and taken the blessing of the farm with it. Most strangers expected the stony, wind-ravaged lands about Nilmgard, clinging between the mountains and the sea, to be poor, but this woman was shocked, as if she knew that our green hanging valley over the sea, half a day's walk westerly from the town, had once been one of the most prosperous farms on all this coast. True, it had been a bad winter and a worse spring, with storm after storm falling upon us out of the west like hammer-blows, but I felt I had to make excuses.

"The family's not had bountiful Gaesa's favour these past years," I said.

"How so?" Finola asked.

"It's a long story." I was fairly certain I shouldn't be telling it to strangers. I wasn't meant to know as much of it as I did myself. But after Vanna left Eirik (she went off with a skald, a woman of Oslend-holm, and I don't blame Vanna, except for leaving her child behind), I'd been set to look after Ari, though he was only a few years younger than me. I found things out.

Well, the fact is, Olav and Eirik often quarreled, and weren't careful in what they said, and I was quiet, and nobody sees you when you're always underfoot and belong to the farm as much as the plough and the looms and the muskoxen in the high pasture. Also, I have a knack for lurking unseen in shadows. I wouldn't say I'm proud of it, but it saved me a thrashing, a time or two.

Finola the Traveler gave me a long, careful look. She smiled again, as if liking what she saw.

I wasn't used to being seen at all. Not like that.

"I think perhaps Eirik Olavson can wait," she said. "Tell me this long story, Gull Stormbarn." She sat herself down on a sun-warmed boulder at the foot of the heap, with her legs drawn up and her shoulders set comfortably against another warm stone.

I hesitated. Duty said any stranger, especially one arriving armed and mysterious, with who knew how many more ships waiting out of sight beyond the jutting headlands embracing the cove, needed to be brought before the master of the house, who was Eirik Olavson, sober or otherwise.

Probably otherwise. Eirik had begun the morning yelling at Tora's mother, who tended our hearth, made our cheese, baked our bread, and brewed our ale, because there was less remaining in the granary than there should be in this season, though it was hardly her fault the harvest had been poor. From there, he'd moved on to yelling at the field-hand thralls for being fat and greedy and not worth their keep, as if we weren't all winter-lean alike, and at me, for teaching Ari to defy him and letting the boy roam where he would with a thrall's daughter. All that anger, but we folk of the farm had learned to shut our ears to him and keep out of his reach, and carry on caring for the farm and for each other as best we could. Eirik's yelling would by now have turned to self-pity and the consolation of a jug of strong ale, and there'd be little welcome, whatever courtesy to guests might demand.

"Tell," Finola said, and patted the rock beside her.

So I shrugged off my basket of eggs and sat myself down. And this is the story I told. Somehow—maybe it was the shape of her cheekbones, but I think more likely it was the dark gravity of her eyes, like wells of deep water hidden from the sun, and the way she watched me—what I told was the true story, or so I thought, and not the one of sea-raiders by night that they still share over the mead-horns in Nilmgard.

It goes like this:

Olav Yngason was a stern and upright man, who held his people to no more rigid code of honorable behavior than he did himself. He only wavered once, when he betrayed his marriage vows with a black-haired weaving-woman named Riva, a thrall of his household. He maintained he had been enchanted and seduced; rumor said her father had been Svartálfar and that Riva knew some of their secret arts of potions and poisons. Just a man looking for someone else to blame, Vanna had once said to me, but she had no great opinion of men. Be that as it may, Riva had a child, a daughter born not a month after Olav's own wife bore him a son, and when the weaving-woman died giving birth, Olav acknowledged the child as his and gave it to his wife to raise with their son, Eirik. So Eirik and Gunnhildr were suckled at the same breast and grew up close as twins, and if one was in the trouble, both took the blame. What Olav's wife thought of it I never heard, for she died when brother and sister were just turned fifteen, the same year the Svartálfar came raiding and Olav Yngason won the name of Olav the Shield and lost his sight.

He'd been a stern, strict father before, though neither unjust nor unloving, and remained so after, a widower alone and having lost, he felt, what most made him worthy of respect, his ability to defend his farm and folk. What he could not do, young Eirik must do for him, but Eirik had a love for songs and tales of the great deeds of the heroes who served the High King at Ravenkeep, and yearned for such glory himself. The land of Nilmgard's coast was too small to content him, the grim necessity of the yearlong fight against storm and cold and winter's ever-threatening hunger not the battle he dreamed of. I think he felt that the everyday courage of those who stood against Svartálfar raids out of the mountains lacked chances for glory and the generosity of jarls who had more in their treasury to reward their followers with than words of praise and respect alone.

Maybe I'm not being fair. I have this view of him from Vanna, who was bitter and angry at where she had found herself, when the bold, eager boy she had married become a sullen, grasping, hard-fisted man. Maybe Eirik had yearned to see a wider world for its own sake. I could understand that. But either way, his father's injury clipped his wings. The weight of caring for the farm fell heavily on brother and sister, on brother most of all, because he must be the man of the farm. Olav had always had a softer heart when it came to Gunnhildr's venturesome ways as a child, though now that she was older he expected her to put aside her dreams of serving the High King as a shieldmaiden and take charge of the hearth till Eirik should take a wife. Despite that, neither of them kept always so close to home as they should, roaming into Nilmgard, running with a band of young people who thought themselves certain to be the next genera-tion of heroes in the jarl's hall. No harm in most of them, and respectable farmers and fishers they became, and carried axe and spear for their jarl when need arose, but there were a few with no good in them who mostly came to bad ends.

So, there came a time that the man who was Jarl of Nilmgard in those days, the one who'd been a sword for hire in Araland and loved a queen, heard that he'd left a daughter behind him. Such things happen. But he had a sword, a gift from his lover. It was a Thorn-blade forged and blessed by their druids for use against the Fey who are such a trouble in that land, and holding, maybe, secret magics. It was time, the jarl decided, that this gift went back to Araland, to be his daughter's. So he chose two of the most trusted folk of his hall, and a loyal ship's crew, and he gave the sword into their keeping. But he did all this in secret, because there was a lawless ship hunting the coastal waters about Nilmgard at that time, and he did not want the raiders getting wind of this treasure.

Secrets have a way of getting out, and word of the druid-blessed sword escaped. And in the dark of the night down along the water-side there was a short savage battle, and two men died and the Thornblade never came to the ship that should have carried it back over the Serpent's Gulf to Araland.

Now, Olav the Shield might have been blind, but he still liked to feel the rising sun on his face as he always had, good farmer that he was, and it was his habit to go out to greet the dawn on the cliff above the cove. Which you'd think was a risky thing, for a blind man, but he knew every rise and dip and hummock of his land, and he felt his way before him with his staff at need. But that dawn, as he came near his usual place, where there was a lone boulder on which he was accustomed to sit, Olav the Shield heard an uproar of angry voices raised, which fell suddenly silent. But he had heard words of theft, and murder, and flight.

Neither Eirik nor Gunnhildr would say what their quarrel had been and all three went back to the farmhouse in silence, and grim silence ruled them all that day. In the evening, a man who had gone in to Nilmgard on some errand came back to tell the tale of an attack on the jarl's chosen messengers, and the theft of the gift, the Thornblade sword he had meant for his Aralish daughter. Dreadful, that the sea-raiders ventured even into the very lanes of Nilmgard, and already the jarl was summoning ships to sail in pursuit of them. Whether they ever found and slew those raiders I don't know, though I have my own reasons for thinking it was a storm that did for them a few years later, but Olav Yngason knew what he had heard, and thought what he thought, and his thoughts were terrible. Early the next morning, before any in his house were awake, he summoned his son and his daughter to walk with him out along the track to the cliffs.

But at the pile of boulders called the Huldra's Tumble he stops.

"Tell me truth, Eirik and Gunnhildr," he says. "What do you know of this treachery in Nilmgard, this killing of good men and the theft of the Thornblade sword, that should have gone to the younger princess of Araland?"

"Nothing," says Eirik, and Gunnhildr says nothing at all.

"I heard what I heard," Olav says.

Imagine how he gazes at them, with his burned and sightless eyes, and how Eirik pinches his mouth shut and ducks his chin, not meeting that gaze, with a hectic red flush on his cheeks, because that was always his look when he went sullen, before the anger began to gather and seethe. But what expression might have been on Gunnhildr's face I can't imagine at all.

Then, "I stole the sword," she says. "I wanted it, to go to serve as a shieldmaiden at the High King's hall. But I killed no one—I went into Nilmgard that night, yes, though you'd forbidden it. I heard the fighting, down by the ships, and after the raiders fled I found the sword dropped in the dark."

It was an obvious lie, trying to shift murder, at least, off her shoulders.

"Where is the sword?" Olav asks, and I can hear how his voice would go, low, quiet, grim, in the asking.

"I threw it into the sea," Gunnhildr says. "I realized no one would believe that I was not involved."

And then Eirik says, "I would have stopped her going to town that night, Father, if I had known what she meant to do."

Even he did not believe she had only picked it up after the fighting was over. Her own brother, her almost-twin.

"Give me your sword," Olav says to Eirik, throwing down his staff.

Think how they must have stared at him.

"Run!" Eirik says to his sister.

Maybe he gives her a shove, to start her on her way.

"I don't *know*," I told Finola the Traveler. "I'm only making this story out of what they said to one another in after years, Eirik and Olav, their hearts and their mouths bitter with festering old anger."

"It sounds true enough to me," Finola said to me. "I think you have the bones of it."

Well, Gunnhildr didn't run, and Eirik drew his sword and put the hilt in his father's hand. And still Gunnhildr didn't run.

"Let her go, Father," Eirik says.

He pleaded for her life then, and Gunnhildr said no word in her own defense, begged no mercy at all, only waited.

And Olav groped out, and caught his daughter's hand, and slapped the sword's hilt into it.

"Go," he says. "Go to your raiders, go to your Svartálfar kin, go where you will and live what life you can. You are no daughter of mine."

And he took Eirik's arm to find his way and walked back to the farm, bent and stumbling like an old, old man. And though he lived long years after, he never went out again in the morning to feel the rising sun on his face.

And Gunnhildr took her brother's naked sword, and without a crust of bread nor a rind of cheese she went, and where she went, they never heard tell, from that day to this.

I looked at Finola, not the fine black eyes under those dark brows, but the height and the bones of her, and the thin mouth and the set of her jaw, so like, not Eirik, but young Ari his son, and old Olav the Shield. And the way, maybe, the loose tangle of her hair hid the maybe-pointed tips of her ears.

"You've dyed your hair," I said.

She shrugged. "Henna. It will wash out soon enough."

"Black would suit you better," I said.

She gave brief bow, hand on her chest. "Gunnhildr Rivudóttir, captain of the guard of Lady Mora Nic Fray."

I wasn't surprised that she named herself her mother's daughter, but I frowned, puzzling over the Aralish lady, whose name sounded familiar.

She saw my expression. "Mora," she said, "is half-sister to Queen Ulla Nic Fray."

"Oh," I said. And what I hadn't learned from my eavesdropping seemed so obvious now. "Eirik took the sword."

"He and the worst of us," she said. "Wild young fools that we were. He had a pair of cronies he never brought home, and never let Vanna nor I come near. No raiders came to Nilmgard that night. It was an ambush in the dark, and murder, and the jarl's men betrayed."

"But," I said, "your father heard you and Eirik arguing. Why accuse you and not him?"

She shrugged. "At the time, I could hardly think. I was so sick, so afraid of what doom awaited my brother. Afraid of what that would do to my father. But then he accused me—and Eirik let him. It was as if I had been dealt a mortal wound. So I was not thinking and wondering at it, only learning that my father could turn on me, that all the love I had thought mine was fragile as frost in the sunlight, with no trust in it. But, later, looking back, I think this is what he heard. 'What were you thinking?' I shouted at Eirik. 'I'll have that sword and be away to the High King's hall? Leave this gray hard coast behind and be a hero, with a hero's blade?' Olav only heard the last of it, and Eirik crying out, 'No, not murder. Not murder, Gunnhildr.' He swore he'd meant only robbery, as if somehow such men with such a charge should have stood back without fighting and let him and those fools with him do as they would. He said the two companions with him were killed in the ambush and he hid their bodies, and I still don't know whether to believe it, or whether there was murder that followed. But Eirik my brother, my almost-twin, looked at me, with my father railing, how could I so dishonor him, and myself, how could I so shame us all—base thrall's brat, he called me, and Svartálfar bastard, born to bring ruin to all who came near me—Eirik looked at me, and he said, 'I would have stopped her, if I'd known.'"

Old anger cracked Gunnhildr's voice. "And that," she said, "was the blow that finished me. I could find no word in my own defense, though I had not even been there that night, only gone looking for Eirik and met him coming home. I knew it would be useless. Olav would not hear. A lying Svartálfar, lacking honor, treacherous. And—if he had believed me over Eirik, it would have broken his heart."

"I think his heart did break," I said. "But better truth had broken it than Eirik's lie."

"Despite everything," Gunnhildr said, "I wish I had not come too late to see him again. Though I don't know what I could have said. What I would have said. Things better left unsaid, I suppose." She rose to her feet, looking down at me. "Now, Gull Stormbarn, take me to my brother."

But when I stood to join her, he was already there, striding up the track from the farm with a scowl like a thundercloud on his brow, Ari and Tora running to catch up behind.

A big man, Eirik, with a red-mottled face and a drinker's belly, but the axe over his shoulder was sharp.

"What's this of a strange ship putting in to my cove, Gull?" he said. "What are you doing, dallying out here with strangers when you should be about your work? Plotting with raiders?" Ari's look of guilty apology told that he'd been the one to catch a glimpse of the ship out along the cliffs somewhere and to take word back to the farm.

"What do we have that sea-raiders would want?" I asked. "This is—" I'd forgotten the Aralish name she'd taken. Not that it mattered, because Eirik's eyes had gone wide, his mouth working, silent, words choking him.

"Brother," Gunnhildr said. "I won't say, well-met. I've come home. The Fey are pushing at the doors between the worlds that keep them from Araland, and Princess Mora Nic Fray has need of her Thornblade sword."

The blood drained from Eirik's face; I've laid out corpses that looked more lifelike. Then he flushed dark as beetroot and roared, "Traitor! Be gone, before I—"

"*Traitor?* You *dare*—"

"You could have said we were away together drinking with Vanna's brothers. If you'd stuck by me, Gunnhildr, Father would never have—"

"A murderer—a thief—and you were happy for me to take the blame—"

I feared they'd come to blows, but Gunnhildr shook her head and took a step back.

"Where's the sword?" she asked. "That's all I want. I've come to take it to the one the old jarl meant it for. It's done you no good at all."

"How could it, when you left me trapped here?"

"*I—?*"

"I couldn't *leave*. If you'd stayed, *you* could have looked after the old man. I'd have been free to go to Ravenkeep."

We were all a little stunned, I think, at this.

"With a stolen sword," Gunnhildr said. "With the blood of loyal men on your hands. Of course, you'd have had a place among the heroes then."

The look on Ari's face—his father had never done much to earn his respect, but he'd tried to be a dutiful son by him. Not betrayal— just a weary grief. The finishing blow, for what had been a long time dying. Then he set his jaw, caught my eye, and took Tora's hand. She stepped a little closer to him. And he couldn't have said any clearer if he shouted, he was done with giving Eirik what he'd never earned: obedience, respect, love.

Gunnhildr shook her head. "Where have you hidden the Thornblade?"

I expected Eirik to shout again, brandish his axe. But abruptly, he gave a snort of laughter, lowered his axe, and turned away. "It's gone where neither you nor I nor your Aralish princess will ever have the good of it," he said. "Gone into the sea."

"You threw it into the sea!" Horror in Gunnhildr's voice.

"Am I a fool?" Eirik snarled. I resisted an urge to answer that. "I didn't throw it. It was safe enough for years."

"You didn't have it, when I found you coming up from the beach that morning," Gunnhildr said. And she grinned. "I remember it was low tide, then. The Giant's Toadstool." Her grin faded. "Oh Eirik, you fool."

Because the Giant's Toadstool, that top-heavy sea stack that had been a landmark all my life, had finally crumbled and fallen outwards, its stem whittled away to nothing by the waves, in the last of the winter's storms, which might be why my stranger had needed to ask if she had found Yngi's Cove. It was nothing now but a shoal, hidden save at the lowest tides.

It had been a fine nesting-place for gulls and puffins, all crumbling ledges and deep fissures. I'd used to climb it. Apparently, so had Eirik and Gunnhildr. I could have laughed. When I was a child sent up foraging for eggs, I'd used to imagine how I would hide my bits of treasure there, deep in some puffin's tunnel, saving up to buy my freedom, if only I could ever come by any bits of treasure at all.

As if there were nothing more to be said, Gunnhildr turned away.

"I've searched, and it's gone, and if you'd backed me up I'd never have had to leave it there in the first place!" Eirik howled, and I yelled a warning as he raised his axe again. Gunnhildr sprang around, drawing her sword, but it was Tora who leapt and caught his arm and Ari who wrested the axe from his grip.

"Go home, Father," he said coldly. "You're drunk."

Eirik staggered back and tripped. Gunnhildr just shook her head and walked away.

We followed, all of us, leaving Eirik sitting on the ground like a disgruntled frog.

The morning had turned cold and cloudy, another storm moving in, I thought.

Gunnhildr stood by the boulder where her father had been used to greet the dawn, staring down at the choppy gray water.

"It's not quite two months since the stack fell," I said. "Two months in salt water, but it might not be rusted past saving."

"It's a Thornblade," she said. "Druid-blessed and pattern-welded with orichalcum. It might not be rusted at all."

"I've searched," Eirik said, coming up behind. "It's buried, lost forever."

I remembered Eirik going down with a fork and a sudden interest in digging clams. I didn't remember he'd ever come back with much in his bucket. I didn't remember he'd gone more than a morning or two.

Damned seals, he'd muttered. They'd driven him off, with their snarling and snapping and their fishy stink.

"We know Eirik's a great one for finishing what he sets his hand to," I said.

Gunnhildr took my meaning. So did Ari. If Eirik had been the type to put some work into the task at hand, instead of expecting an easier, more exciting road to open before his feet, we'd not have been where we were.

"You don't want a pitchfork, for moving rocks," Ari said.

"You want a pickaxe," said Tora.

"And low tide," said Gunnhildr. The tide was almost at its highest, now. "How about a tour of the farm, nephew?" But first she went to call down to her crew that they might as well row along the coast to Nilmgard; she would spend the night with us.

It was nearing sunset when we all trudged back to the cove, armed with pickaxes and a five-foot long iron crow, trailed by Eirik, a jug in his hand and nothing but mutterings of how ill-done-by he was on his lips. The tide was nearly out and what had been the Giant's Toadstool was a long spill of broken rock.

Gunnhildr sent Eirik down first. No, I didn't want him on that steep climb behind her, nor behind Ari, who was acting like he had discovered a long-lost and adored sister himself.

The gray evening drew darker, the cloud-blurred sun dropping below the western curve of the cove as we worked, shifting and heaving the stones small enough for two or three to manage, prying between or under the rest. A chill breathed off the water, tendrils of fog rising. Tora kindled a small driftwood fire on the shore, and then more on flat stones atop the fallen Toadstool. We thrust burning brands into gaps and crevices, looking for anything that wasn't stone. Eirik perched sullen on a rock, not lifting a hand to help. Hopeless, he told us. If the sword could have been found, he would have found it.

I should have been watching the water.

Gunnhildr and I had the heavy crow wedged between two great slabs of stone and were heaving together to shift one aside when the faint splash of water and creak of timbers made me look around. A fog-shrouded ship was rounding the headland. I took it for the Aralanders returning, and, "There!" Gunnhildr cried. "Ari, Tora, quick."

Ari jabbed his pickaxe in next to the crow and we three heaved together, while Tora risked her arms to snatch something out from the hollow we'd revealed. A waterlogged bundle of heavy cloth, certainly long enough to be a sword. The stone thumped down; we crowded around her as she stripped the wrappings away.

"Hah!" Gunnhildr said, drawing the sword from the dark scabbard. Water and mucky silt came with it, but it was not the ruined mass of rust I had expected. "The lost Thornblade. Druid-blessed indeed."

It was a beautiful thing, a fit weapon for a warrior-princess. Golden vines twined about the hilt, with a silver rose where the quillons met the grip. The blade itself was patterned like water or leaf-dapple light. It had a coppery, nacreous sheen and glimmer to it in the dusk.

The seal came surging up over the shingle. Stink of rotten fish, clatter of stones—already turning, yelling a warning, I lifted the heavy crow like a club. Crooked yellow fangs, gray hide mangy and peeling, a pale glow in its eyes, it heaved forward again and stood up on two legs, a man, or something that had been a man once. Gaunt, his leathery flesh clinging to bones, beard and hair lank and dripping, clad in rags and the rotten ruin of a leather vest. Unarmed—his fingers, with long yellow nails like claws, reached to seize the Thornblade. Tora scrambled back, dropping the scabbard. She slipped on the slick wet stones but Ari hauled her to safety as Gunnhildr sprang forward to meet the draugr. The blade swept head clean from neck and the blow I was already swinging struck the thing across the chest and sent it flying. It crashed not far from its empty-eyed skull, a wreck of bones and shrunken skin.

"The ghost-ship!" Ari shouted.

Riding low in the water, half-foundered, the ship swept toward us like something from a nightmare, fog roiling thick about it. The tattered sail bellied in a ghostly wind that stank of rot.

"Get to the cliff!" Gunnhildr ordered. "Tora, Ari, go!"

I didn't know how far from the water the sea draugar would venture, but it was wise. From above, we could hold the cliff-path against however many might try it.

Ari and Tora ran.

"Eirik, come!" Gunnhildr shouted to her brother, and she grabbed at his arm to haul him down from the pile of rocks where he still sat gawping.

The ship came thrusting up the beach, keel grating, and the crew leapt over the sides like a raiding party, six fell sea draugar.

"It's mine!" Eirik roared. "Foul things, you won't have it!"

He leapt on Gunnhildr and they both went crashing down to the stones of the beach, with him on top. She lost her grip on the sword. He seized it and went running not for the cliff but down to meet the draugar. They closed in on him, or on the Thornblade that had drawn them all this spring, a treasure flung into the sea. The Thornblade they had come for now.

"Father!" Ari shouted. He bounded back down the path, and "Ari!" Tora shouted, and she followed.

"No!" Gunnhildr roared. "Children, get out of here! Gull, get them away!" She drew her own sword and ran to her brother.

They were surrounded, swarmed like when wolves run down a kid. Back to back, they fought, but I could see that despite Gunnhildr's skill, her blade did not bite as it should. Mighty blows. The draugar reeled back, one falling, another lacking swordarm and sword, but the one picked itself up, head lolling, stretched and rolled its neck, and rushed in again, axe swinging, while the other groped for its sword with its remaining hand, found it, and attacked once more. Gunnhildr had no shield. And though Eirik wielded the Thornblade, and every blow that connected bit, he was no longer any warrior to rival his sister, if ever he had been. Clumsy, slow, flailing at his enemies as if he threshed grain. He took a few hands off, sliced some bone, but only dropped one for good. Even as I ran to put myself ahead of Ari, Eirik fell to his knees.

Gunnhildr screamed his name, whirling, striking a blow that should have taken a draugr's head but it only staggered back and came on again, and a descending axe laid Eirik out on the stones unmoving.

I swung my iron crow like a bludgeon. A bearded draugr went flying, but in the tail of my eye I saw it crawling up again, though I'd stove in the side of its skull. Gunnhildr was down. I smashed the draugr raising its axe over her, smashed it again when it did not fall and Ari leapt in swinging the pickaxe. Tora swung a burning brand but it sizzled and went out on sodden rags, and the fog curled around us. I heard her scream, saw Ari, with a sob, turn away from Gunnhildr to run to Tora, slammed my crow through the chest of another draugr and felt cold slimy fingers close on my throat from behind, bone digging in like claws as I struggled and choked, losing my grip on the iron bar. And Gunnhildr rolled aside from the sword that would have skewered her over her brother's body and came up with the Thornblade. It sang in the air, took heads, one and two, and she leapt and thrust past me even as breath failed and a red tide rose to drown me. I fell gasping, clasped in bony dead arms, and she jerked the sword free of a ribcage and disappeared into the fog toward where Tora had cried out. She was limping.

I scrambled up. So did the draugr with my crow through its chest. I put a foot on it and wrenched my iron bar free, swung, and swung again, and again, and when it fell I kept on smashing. My face was wet. It could have been the fog. The tears weren't for Eirik, anyway.

And a seal came swarming up the beach and rose into a tall, yellow-haired figure in a long scale shirt. No beard. Might have been a woman, but who can tell, once the crabs have had their way? She ignored me and passed like a storm in a stench of rot and a wave of cold, snatching up a fallen axe and the fog and night wrapping her like a cloak that drank the light of our still-burning fires.

I ran, fell on treacherous stones, scrambled up and ran again. Found them. Ari was down, crouching over a heap that might have been Tora. The draugr had his pickaxe and Gunnhildr was having trouble closing in with him. She moved awkwardly, lacking her former grace. A swing of the axe—she dodged, her leg failed her and she stumbled down, landing turned on her hip, but she slashed through the draugr's leg even so and as it tumbled over her, she split its skull.

But the tall captain was running up behind her, axe swinging.

"*Mother!*" I screamed. "Don't!" I hurled the crow like a spear. Too heavy; it didn't cover the distance and struck stones clattering as the force of my throw and the uneven footing sent me sprawling. "*Mama...*" But that was only a whisper.

She heard me. She checked in her rush, and she turned and for a moment, for just a moment, I saw a living woman, tall, golden-haired, bright-eyed and laughing and the ship leaping the waves, spray flying. Her arms open to catch me and swing me up as I run to her...

And in one motion Gunnhildr rose and slashed and the Thorn-blade sword took her head.

Bones and rot and rags, falling.

I was on my knees. Maybe I was weeping, I don't know.

Gunnhildr came limping to me and knelt down, laid aside the sword and put her arms about me. Maybe I cried on her shoulder.

Maybe she'd heard what I shouted. Maybe she understood what it had meant. She didn't say anything, only let me have those brief moments of sobbing like a heartbroken child, till as Ari and Tora came stumbling to us she gave me her silken scarf to dry my face so I could pretend that hadn't happened. Then we all picked one another up, and Gunnhildr took the Thornblade again and we went back to find her own sword, and Eirik.

He was dead. The axe had sliced deep, half-severing his shoulder. The tide was coming in, lapping about the wreck of a longship, all blackened timbers that looked as if they'd lain twenty years at the bottom of the sea.

"We need to burn these bodies," Gunnhildr said. She looked at Ari. "All of them," she said gently.

He understood. Eirik, draugr-slain, had long ago flung aside his honor, and he'd lived so petty and grasping a life... no matter that he'd died well in the end. I wouldn't want to trust he'd put this world aside and move on as he should. We couldn't risk him coming back, to haunt the blighted farm.

That curse would be lifting now, I thought, whether it was Eirik's hidden treachery and murder that had brought it, or only his drinking and bad husbandry. Ari would be a far better master of the land. It had been Tora's mother and I who shaped the man he would be, more than his kin. And his own just and kindly nature.

Tora bound up Gunnhildr's leg, which was the worst of our wounds, and we carried Eirik up above the high tide mark, fetched pitch from the farm stores, and made him a great pyre of driftwood. We burnt the remains of the draugar separately, but we laid them decently together, not in a heap like rubbish. They'd not been good people, pirates and raiders caring for none but themselves, and clinging too hard to love of treasures laid up in this life against some grand future they'd never achieved, but...

But I remembered the surge and the leap of the ship on the sea, and the waves laughing under the prow, and a lullaby sung in the night when the ship rocked gentle and the stars were bright, and sleeping tucked in warm against a mother's side, her arm over me and her voice gentle and filled with love.

The flames roared up, hot and hungry, and lit the cliffs bright. The tide rose and fell again and the sun rose, and there were only ashes left.

Ari and Tora were wed three days later. Why wait longer, for what we all knew would be? Already the farm felt a lighter and happier place, and all its folk, free and freed—because Ari said he would have no thralls, since it was those bound in servitude here who had been the ones to love him and raise him and show him what a good man should be—ate together at the great table, one family.

And when Gunnhildr's leg was healed, and she sailed again for Araland with the blessing and the friendship of her nephew and his bride, bearing the Thornblade sword back to her liege-lady Mora Nic Fray, I went with her. There was a great wide world out there, and it was time I saw it.

K.V. JOHANSEN is the author of the five-book Silk Road epic fantasy series *Gods of the Caravan Road: Blackdog* (shortlisted for the Sunburst Award), *The Leopard*, *The Lady*, *Gods of Nabban*, and *The Last Road*. She holds an M.A. in Medieval Studies and another in English. While spending most of her time writing, she retains her interest in medieval history and languages and is a member of the SFWA and the Writers' Union of Canada. In 2014, she was an instructor at the Science Fiction Foundation's Masterclass in Literary Criticism held in London. She is also the author of two works on the history of children's fantasy literature, two short story collections, a number of books for children and teens, and writing as Kris Jamison, a contemporary novel, *Love/Rock/Compost*. Various of her books have been translated into French, Macedonian, and Danish. Although not a player of RPGs, she does play classical guitar, electric guitar, and bass with dogged persistence. Visit her online at http://www.kvj.ca and on Twitter @KVJohansen.

THE PATH OF THE BEAR

SARAH L. MILES

The mist settled back on the grass, the merest ripple indicating that it had been disturbed. Urszula let her shoulders drop with it and slowed her breath. She could see the deer several feet ahead of her, its head raised as it watched for danger, ears twitching. Barely perceptible under the mist, Urszula raised her left arm, hefting her spear. It was hand whittled and amateurishly made, shorter than average, but the point was sharp and her aim true. The whistle of the spear caused the doe to raise her head, seconds too late to successfully bolt. She moved enough for Urszula to curse under her breath, springing up from her hiding place and throwing herself in the direction of the fleeing deer, pulling her knife from her belt as she did. The doe dropped with the spear protruding from one flank as Urszula hit it in the side and swiftly slit its throat, ending the deer's life and bringing a smile to Urszula's face.

The family gathered around the firepit, the remains of the deer roasting on a spit. The skin was hanging from a beam to one side of the longhouse, scraped clean, and Urszula's mother Perla was washing the innards in water brought from the stream by one of her many younger siblings. A feeling of satisfaction washed over Urszula as she had provided enough food to last the next few days. Her father clearly disagreed though, seated on a bench, his back against the wall, scowling. His ruined arm was held in a sling, fashioned by Perla to try to ease the burden on him. His injury had affected his mind as well as his body, not being able to provide for his family had taken a toll and he had retreated from village life more and more.

Urszula picked up the slack where she could, trying to set an example for the younger children, while ensuring her mother was taken care of as best she could. The villagers could talk all they wanted, but as the oldest her priority was to the family that raised her, not the expectations of others. Einar would simply have to weather the perceived embarrassment of going from the head of the village's hunting party, to an injured veteran who could no longer fight. Both Perla and Urszula knew that he was sinking into a deep depression, his extended family–gathered from waifs and strays on his adventures to make up for his own childlessness–now a burden that he could not countenance to let down. Urszula was well known for her cheery outlook and positive nature, always having a kind word when meeting others from the village, despite how she was often treated by them in return, and she now made a stark contrast to her father.

All of the children were well known in Smárvik. Their father was a veritable hero and no one would treat them as anything less than he deserved, even if they came from all over Norrøngard and Araland, or even in Urszula's case from deep within the Dvergian Mountains. The villagers were a tight knit group, their distance from the nearest town making neighborly behavior a necessity. Einar's drop in stature had not reduced him in the eyes of anyone but himself, the villagers seeing his injury as proof of his bravery and the reason for a well-deserved early retirement. With a loving wife and a whole household of adopted children, outwardly there was no reason for him to be bitter. But he could see no future for himself, shoulder shattered on his final trip to the northern forests and not even a carcass to show for it.

It was almost time for the annual trip east to Bense for the Winternights festival, when the young people of the village would go to offer their support to the Jarl. Roald was preparing his finest clothes, poor furs by the standards of Bense, but fine enough for the village. This was the highlight of the year when they could travel to show fealty to the Jarl, prove their worth as hunters, fighters, and merchants, and win their place in the village hierarchy. Roald was planning on winning more than just accolades. With the demotion of Einar from head hunter, and de facto leader of the village, Roald was looking to secure the hand of one of the many adopted daughters in Einar's household, and take his place. He knew that his family farm was not of high enough stature—unjustly, in his opinion—to earn one of the better-looking daughters, so he set his sights lower, on Urszula. Roald chuckled at his own joke and looked around to see if there was anyone with which to share his wit. Given how little the other men of Smárvik thought of Roald, despite his high opinion of himself, it was unsurprising he was alone.

He considered it unlikely that there would be many suitors for Urszula, her dwarven ancestry and copper hair making her stand out in the village, even before people learnt of her disregard for tradition, passion for hunting, and rumored fast temper. He knew that she was fiercely loyal to her family, and that hunting the animal that had maimed her father would stand him in good stead persuading the old man to give her up to be his bride. What Roald lacked in ability, he made up for his misplaced confidence, and despite a legendary hunter not having been able to take down a brown bear he was convinced of his own ability. Once he had finished packing for the trip to Bense, he planned on taking the north road out of the village to the forests, finding and killing the bear, and triumphantly leading the party to meet the Jarl with his new bride in tow.

Urszula knew of the planned trip to the town; the eldest of her siblings planned on making the trip this year to see if he could apprentice to a master craftsman. With so many mouths to feed, even with one departing soon, she knew that there would be even more need for food than the regular amount of deer she could catch would cover. With the upcoming trip to Bense there were fewer hunters abroad, so she planned on making the most of the quieter season by heading further north to see what she could procure from the forest. She knew that Einar would not let her go willingly, so planned on tracking south first, before cutting back on herself.

Armed with an old short sword that had belonged to his grandfather, and the sense of entitlement that a spoiled childhood can bring, Roald swaggered along the path out of the village. He was alone, partly as he wanted any glory of the kill for himself, and partly because it was unlikely anyone else would join such a foolhardy escapade. As the son of a farmer, he was used to thralls doing work for him, and thanks to his overbearing mother was unused to being told he could not do something. The further he got from Smárvik, the more he lost his surety. He was in uncertain territory, noisily scuffing his boots on the well-worn path and wondering how exactly one went about finding a bear. He was snacking on bread and dried meats, leaving a trail behind him of crumbs and scraps that the smaller woodland creatures would make a feast of later, showing little concern for his surroundings. Biting the last chunk of meat off a bone, he casually threw the bone off to one side, into the trees.

Roaring its disgust at having a projectile thrown at it, a giant brown bear reared up on its hind legs between the trees. Claws flared from paws bigger than Roald's face. It was a terrifying sight, awesome in size. Dropping to all fours, the bear began to run toward Roald, who was petrified in fear, dropping his sword and snacks. A dark patch appeared on the crotch of his trousers, the acrid smell piercing the air and causing the bear's nostrils to flare wider. Self-preservation kicked in and Roald turned to run, slipping on the dropped sword and falling to the ground. Scrabbling backward on the path, Roald tried to find a grip on the pebbles beneath him, his fear making him desperate. The bear was almost upon him. Roald could see the whites of its eyes. Its breath was rancid. There was rotting meat stuck between its teeth. The gravel of the path was flying from beneath its feet. As it reached the cowering Roald it roared again, twisting to one side seconds before impact, one paw crushing his ribs as it changed path.

Stumbling backward under the weight of the spear sticking from the side of the bear, Urszula bared her teeth in a grimace. She had been following its tracks from deep within the forest and was surprised when it deviated from its course and ran into an attack. The change shook her out of her hunting trance, and triggered a response buried deep within her.

Screaming back at the bear, she pushed on the spear with all her might, a strength she had never possessed before surging through her small body. The move shocked the bear, which stumbled prone to the ground, giving Urszula the time to flick her knife from her belt, slicing the throat of the raging bear and ending its life. Panting with the exertion, she ignored the cowering figure of Roald and began to remove the hide of the bear, her rage making the task simpler than it should be. Splashed with blood, she worked fast and dirty, slashing the skin from muscle and fat with ragged cuts. Roald dragged himself off the path, away from Urszula and the carcass, holding his broken ribs, tears streaking his terrified face. He watched in horror as she worked, removing the entire pelt but leaving the top of the head attached. Her eyes wide in her frenzy, she raised the dripping skin over her short body, placing the bear's head over her own, and spreading the gore spattered fur behind her, a stinking bloody pastiche of a wedding veil. Urszula screamed her triumph to the sky, as Roald turned tail and fled back to the village.

SARAH L. MILES is a comics fan, tabletop gamer and competitive strongwoman. She lives on the south coast of England with her partner, one excitable Springer spaniel, and an uncounted number of house plants. You can find Sarah on social media, where she is @iamgiantwoman.

SWORD OF VENGEANCE

JON SPRUNK

Geth yawned as he opened his eyes. Errant rays of sunlight pierced the roof above the loft where he slept. Judging by the angle of the light, it was well past dawn.

He stretched as he rolled over, luxuriating in the soft furs that made up his bed. He should get up. His mother would be calling any minute to demand that he rise, but Geth wanted just a few more minutes of blissful sleep.

The ladder leading up to the loft creaked. Geth lifted his head, and groaned aloud as Calder appeared. The oldest thrall working on the farm, Calder claimed to be eighty years old, and Geth believed him. Despite the old thrall's age, he was a tireless worker, up before the sun and always the last in the household to retire for the night.

"It's past time to be up and about, young master," Calder said as he climbed up the ladder.

After a moment to catch his breath, Calder reached into a satchel slung over his shoulder and pulled out folded clothes, and not just any clothes. They were Geth's linen shirt and pants, the ones he only wore on holidays. Suddenly, he remembered what day it was. Gustav

Hidasson was coming! He threw back the covers and rolled out of bed.

Calder had also brought a pitcher of water. It was warm – thank the Gods! – as Geth splashed it on his face. He ran a comb through his hair as Calder laid out his clothes on the bed. Along with the pants and shirt, there were woolen socks and his good boots, cleaned and polished.

Calder went to a chest in the corner and sighed as he knelt down to root through the contents. He pulled out a pair of tooled leather bracers and the silver torc that Geth's father had given him last year.

Getting up with another small sigh, Calder took up the comb while Geth dressed and fussed with his hair, which hung down to his shoulders. "Hold still, young master. You need to look presentable today."

Geth glanced back over his shoulder. "So why is this man coming all the way out here?"

It was several days' travel to the farm from the town of Morheim. With winter's bite still hanging in the air, it was considered an ill time for a journey.

"I'm sure I don't know," Calder answered as he lifted a fur-lined buckskin vest for Geth to put on.

"They say Gustav Hidasson is the richest man in Norrøngard. Even richer than the jarl."

Calder brushed Geth's shoulders for imaginary lint. "Idle talk is worth less than the air that carries it. Hidasson may be rich, but he's not half the man your father is." With a grunt, he added, "He's coming here to pay his respects. It's an honor."

Calder held up a bronze mirror, which Geth ignored. "Speaking of my father, where is he?"

"Out in the barn, I believe. Overseeing the preparation of the gift."

Geth left the old thrall to tidy up the loft. Their home had three sections. The family slept in the north wing, while the servants and housecarls bedded in the south. Between those two wings was the great hall. The interior was paneled in dark wood, with a high, sod-covered roof. The house had originally been built by Geth's great grandfather and expanded over the generations.

Servants and thralls passed him in the hallway, all of them moving with purpose. A moment later, he heard his mother's voice coming from the great hall.

There, Geth was greet by a host of delicious smells. A pair of servant girls rolled dough and minded the ovens at the rear of the hall. Over the large fire put in the center of the room hung half a steer, with several iron pots nestled in the coals.

Geth's mother stood in the center of the maelstrom, overseeing the work. She was a beautiful woman, almost as tall as Geth, with wheat-blonde hair that hung down her back in a long braid. She was wearing a kirtle of sea-blue wool, and silver earrings shaped like tiny crescent moons, which he only saw her wear once or twice a year.

Geth gave her a kiss on the cheek. "It smells good in here, and I'm starving."

His mother held him at arm's length so she could inspect his outfit. "You missed breakfast, so you'll have to wait until the feast."

"That will be hours! Do you want me to waste away until I'm as skinny as Helga." He winked at the heavyset cook, who was cutting up turnips.

His mother pursed her lips. "You *are* too thin. Take a biscuit."

"How about some meat to go with it?"

Helga swatted him with a hand towel as she went back to her work.

Geth stood beside his mother and admired the cool efficiency of the work. She ran the house like a warlord on the battlefield. And, he knew, she could wield a sword as well as shoot a bow. Fierce and proud on the outside, warm and kind on the inside, she was the best mother in the world. Yet, today, she looked anxious. She kept rubbing her hands together.

"Mother, is something wrong?"

She spared him a small smile. "Today is a big honor. I just want everything to be perfect. Now go on, Geth. Go bother your father. We're busy here, and the guests will be arriving soon."

Swiping a hot bun on his way out, with a wink to the girls, Geth left the hall and headed out back.

Gustav Hidasson shaded his eyes as he gazed up at the mountains rising in the distance. Sunlight glinted on their snowy peaks. Dark forest blanketed their sides and spread across the flatlands. A lone road cut through this land, south of Dragon's Bay.

He rode on a painted gelding of high breeding, the best horse-flesh available in the markets at Morheim. Behind him followed six bodyguards, loyal only to him and his gold, and two servants leading a pair of pack mules. He usually traveled with far more retainers, but this was a special journey.

Gustav shivered under his thick fur cloak. "This damned winter is lasting forever."

The man riding beside him replied with a voice that rumbled like boulders rolling down a mountainside. "You Skagilund folk are soft."

Several inches taller than Gustav, who was not a small man by any standard, Azulf stood out as the oddity of the group. Almost every inch of his flesh was inked with woad-blue tattoos. He came from Araland, far to the southeast, where his people lived in caves amid primeval forests, or so Gustav had heard. He had never been there and had no intention of visiting. He had purchased this man from a foreign flesh-peddler, which was not strictly legal by the laws of Norrøngard. But he with the most money made the rules, or so Gustav's father had told him, and this tattooed savage was as invest-ment in his future.

"Soft, eh?" Gustav reached up to touch the antique bronze amulet hanging around his neck, and had the satisfaction of watching the pale thrall shiver. The talisman had cost more than

Azulf, but its value was priceless, for it allowed Gustav to keep him on a tight leash. For Azulf was no ordinary man.

"You may hold my soul in that bauble. But one day I will be free and I will make you—"

Gustav grabbed the amulet in a tight hold and squeezed. Large beads of sweat ran down Azulf's face, until he finally bowed his head in acquiescence.

Gustav allowed himself a smug chortle. "Good. You may have been a powerful shaman back in your barbaric land, but here you are my property. You will speak to me with a respectful tongue, or I will have it torn out. Now attend to my words."

He pointed ahead. Far in the distance appeared the peaked roof of a longhouse amid several broad fields. The farm sat at the foot of a mountain, with a lake and dark woods beyond. "That is the place I told you about."

Azulf looked for a moment. "Another farm. You own many like it."

"Not like this one. This is some of the best land for miles. It is owned by Ivek Erikson, a stubborn fool of a man. Three times I have sent offers to buy this land. Three times he has denied me, but he will not deny me today."

Azulf made no comment, but Gustav ignored that. Nothing could spoil this day for him. By night's end, he would have this land and be one step closer to his penultimate goal, becoming jarl of Morheim. And beyond that, who knew?

He stroked the amulet again, and smiled as he watched Azulf shudder.

Geth found his father in the main barn. He and several of men from the farm were standing around a tall, sable-coated stallion. The men worked for his father. Many tended the land, while others were skilled tradesmen. In return for their service, they were paid a wage and provided for by his father. Geth had grown up with some of them, and they were like family.

"He's a fine animal, my lord," said Einar, the farm's foreman. "Too fine for the likes of some ship merchant, if you asked me."

Geth's father saw him enter and beckoned him over. "Here's my son. Let's hear his opinion. What do you think of our guest gift?"

The throng of men made room for Geth. He had never felt comfortable around adults. When he was younger, these men had seemed like the Jötnar out of stories, huge giants with cold eyes who could crush you with ease. Even now, though he was as tall as some of them, he felt small in their presence. Part of him wondered if his father cared more for these men than for him.

Geth looked over the horse. It was seventeen or eighteen hands high, with a glossy black coat and muscular flanks. Physically, it was impressive. "He's not bad."

"Not bad?" Einar repeated, as the other men laughed. "Your boy is harder to impress than a Unglander merchant."

Geth looked down at his feet, embarrassed by the mocking. He felt his hands balling into fists, and he wanted to leave.

His father wasn't laughing, however. "What's wrong with the animal, Geth?"

Geth shook his head. "It's fine. Forget I said anything."

"No." His father had taken on a stern tone that Geth knew only too well. It meant he expected to be obeyed. "Tell us what's wrong with this gift?"

Geth sighed, wishing he could disappear into the ground under his feet. Yet, he answered. "Its withers are too high, so it will never be comfortable to sit. And, well, it looks rather dumb."

"Dumb?" Einar spat out. "It's a horse, Geth. Of course it's dumb."

"I've known horses that were smarter than some men," Geth's father said, which elicited a few sage nods from the group. "Geth has a good eye. This animal looks like a champion, but it has flaws. Which means it's the perfect gift for our visitor."

Geth didn't understand. Why was a flawed gift perfect? Before he could ask, a horn called from the house.

They headed out to the front of the farm, where a long, hard-packed walkway ran half a bowshot to the road. To the north, less than a quarter mile away, a band on horseback approached. They were fewer than Geth expected. He'd thought an important person like Gustav Hidasson would bringing scores of warriors, and perhaps even a wagon train to carry his household. Instead, it appeared to be less than ten people altogether. It was disappointing.

Yet, as the party got nearer, Geth made out a few interesting details. First, he had no trouble picking out the merchant, even though he had never seen the man before. He wore fine leathers with fur trim covering his bulk, which was sizable. He also wore a few pieces of jewelry, including a golden torc hanging from his neck and a wide band of gold across his brow. He looked very much like how Geth imagined a hero out of a story might look, sitting straight up on his magnificent steed, with his chest out and an imperious expression.

Yet, as bold and vibrant as Gustav appeared, the man beside him dwarfed him in almost every way. This unknown man sat at least a full hand taller, with bare shoulders that looked strong enough to wrestle a bull. And he was covered in blue tattoos. Geth had seen tattoos before. A couple men on the farm had them on their arms or chests, but this man had them on every exposed inch of skin. The inkings were oddly-shaped, too. Some were straight and others curved into what almost looked like writing, but Geth knew his letters and these symbols were nothing he had ever seen before. They made the tall man appear even more menacing. Perhaps that was their purpose.

The visitors stopped with Gustav in front. The merchant addressed Geth's father. "Ivek Erikson, we have traveled long and we seek shelter." He held his open hands out to his sides, showing they were empty.

Geth's father gave the traditional response. "Come and be welcome at my hearth, Gustav Hidasson."

Gustav climbed down from his horse. As he and Geth's father embraced, Geth noticed the merchant's sword. The guard and hilt were bright silver, with a large green jewel sparkling on the pommel. Geth had never seen anything so beautiful before.

His father introduced the family, starting with his mother. She bowed her head in greeting. Gustav took her hand and pressed it softly. She stood very still as he whispered something, and then dropped her hand to her side as soon as he let go. Geth noticed all this out of the corner of his eye. He was watching the tattooed giant still seated on his horse. The man did not move. He just stared over their heads as if he was bored.

"And that is Geth, my son."

Gustav greeted him with a firm grip. "Ah, the young hauld. He has his mother's eyes, but I see your influence on him, Ivek."

Up close, the merchant looked older. His jowls were puffy, and his nose red from the sun and wind. Still, his clothes and ornaments were of excellent quality. Geth found himself standing up straight under his scrutiny.

"If you are tired after your journey," Geth's father said, "there is shade and drink inside."

Gustav waved away the suggestion. "Nonsense. I have traveled days to see your fine estate, and I would love nothing more than a tour."

As his father led them around to the yard, a pair of the merchant's warriors followed behind, and Geth trailed after them. He was startled to see the tattooed man come along as well, walking just a few steps behind him. He dropped his head and quickened his pace, darting past the warriors to walk beside the lead men.

His father was pointing out the various outbuildings: the hog pen, the chicken coop, and the workshop shed with an anvil sitting outside the door. Newly-tilled fields surrounded the yard on three sides. As they approached the barn, Einar brought out the stallion on a lead.

"What an animal!" Gustav exclaimed.

"A gift for you," Geth's father replied. "In honor of your visit."

Gustav ran his hand through the stallion's mane and down its back. "For me? Ivek, you do me too much honor."

"Not at all."

The merchant walked around the animal with a broad smile, until he came around the other side. "I have a gift for you as well, which I will present tonight as we dine together. In the meantime, I wish to speak of another matter."

Geth could tell by his father's stance that he knew what was coming and wanted nothing to do with it. Yet, this man was their guest, and so he had to remain polite.

"As you will, Gustav. You have my attention."

The merchant nodded, still looking at the stallion. He held the lead rein tight, forcing the animal to bend down its neck so he could peer into its eyes. "Good. I came here for a single reason. To buy your farm."

"I've told you before. It's not for sale."

Gustav held up an open hand. "Please, hear me out." When Geth's father didn't object, he continued. "I own several farms around here. In fact, many of your neighbors work for me. I'm sure you know this. They still live on the land of their forefathers, working it just as they always have. They receive a fair share of the bounty every harvest. Yet, they don't have any of the risk of owning a farm in these uncertain times. If there is a bad harvest, I am the one who takes the loss. If their herds are stricken by sickness, I am the one who loses money.

"That's what I can offer you, Ivek. Peace of mind. This is a large farm. One bad year could wipe you out. Why not sell to me and be rid of the burden?"

Geth was confused by this talk. Why would anyone want to own so many farms? There wasn't much wealth to be gotten, not compared to the riches that Gustav Hidasson had made with his shipping trade. Perhaps he wanted to settle down to a quieter life.

Geth's father wasn't looking at the merchant now, but past him, to the fields beyond the yard fence. "I will keep this farm, and it will pass to Geth when I am gone."

Gustav dropped the lead rein and stepped closer to Geth's father. "Ivek, be sensible. I'll give you double the price I offered before."

His voice sounded friendly, but there was a look in Gustav's eyes that made Geth uneasy. Like the eyes of a wolf running down a hare. But his father was no hare.

"I've given you my answer. It's final. Now, over here we're building a second barn to store the summer hay."

His father started walking toward the east end of the yard. Gustav followed, but it was clear he was not paying attention. The warriors trailed after them, but Geth stayed back. He had seen enough for now. He didn't like the tension between the men.

The sound of the merchant's thrall's voice startled Geth. "This place is thick with spirits."

Geth turned sideways, not wanting to fully face the painted giant. There was no one else nearby. He had to be talking to him. "What do you mean?"

The thrall looked up at the sky and breathed deeply, letting the air out in a long sigh. "Spirits of the earth and mountains. Spirits of the air. They abound here."

Geth wasn't sure how to reply, or if he even wanted to. He did not like this man. Not the look or sound of him. "What would a foreigner know of such things?"

"You think I was born in bondage, boy? I was free, too. Once. And shall be again."

Geth didn't like being called 'boy,' but there was a menacing tone in the man's voice that made him forget the slight. "Well, you don't talk like a thrall." A question came to mind, and Geth asked it without thinking. "What would you do if you were set free?"

The thrall stood still for a moment, staring south at the mountains. Then, he answered, "I will make myself free. Someday. And when I do, this land will tremble at the sound of my name. Mothers will strangle their babes. Men will slay their brothers. And all shall grovel at my feet."

Geth shivered at the passion in those words. He had taken the man for an impassive clod, but there was a volcano seething inside him. He wondered if the merchant knew this.

"No, you won't," Geth replied. "We would stop you."

"Who will stop me, boy?"

"Men like my father, that's who."

The thrall turned to Geth, with a look in his pale eyes that was truly terrifying. "Run along, little pup. Hide in your blankets at night when the wild winds blow, and pray I do not come for you."

Geth was trembling now. Not only from fear – though he *did* fear this man – but also from anger. His hands had balled into fists. He could strike the man, and there would be few repercussions. Gustav Hidasson might demand a small payment from his father for the deed, but nothing more. However, Geth had been raised to respect all people, even thralls. And that upbringing warred with the anger rising up inside him.

Geth forced himself to meet the thrall's gaze without flinching. He wanted to say something to shut up this man, but the words wouldn't come. He was saved by a call of his name. Calder stood by the house, beckoning to him.

With one last glance at the tattooed thrall, Geth turned and left. He thought he could feel the man's gaze upon him, but he didn't look back, determined not to give him that satisfaction.

A bell later found Geth carrying a keg of ale out from the cold shed. The feast was set up. The entire house smelled delicious, making his stomach growl. He lugged the wooden cask into the great hall and set it down on a side table.

"You need anything else?" he asked Helga, who was minding the ovens.

"No, that's all for now." She shot him a wink and nodded to a plate of fresh honey cakes.

Grabbing one, Geth went over to his mother, who was making final preparations. The great hall had been hung with garlands and sheafs of wheat. She was fixing an arrangement of the flowers at the head table as he came over. She looked up, saw the half-eaten dessert in his hand, and gave him a rueful smile. "I see you've started early."

"Yes, ma'am." He hesitated, unsure whether he should mention what had transpired out in the yard. Instead, he asked, "Will the merchant's thrall be coming to dinner?"

"I don't know, Geth. I imagine so. Why do you ask?"

"I don't like the look of him."

"Don't be cruel. Sometimes people look different."

"It's not just how he looks. He feels wrong."

His mother sighed and bent back down to fool with a sagging blossom. "Geth, I don't have time for games."

When she glanced at him with an arched eyebrow, he blurted out, "Gustav Hidasson made father an offer for the farm."

She didn't reply at first, as her delicate fingers sculpted the flowers into a more pleasing shape. Then, "I guessed as much. No one comes all this way just to admire the view. But don't worry. Your father would never sell this land. It's been in his family for generations."

Geth nodded, but he was worried. The merchant didn't look like a man who liked to be denied.

The front door of the hall opened, and the men entered, with his father leading the way. Geth was relieved to see that the tattooed thrall was not with them.

As the men came nearer, Geth could tell that his father wasn't happy. He wasn't frowning or raising his voice, but he had a look that could carve stone. All the while, their guest chattered in his father's ear as they walked to the head table, making Geth guess that Gustav was still trying to convince his father.

He spotted Calder entering the hall and waved him over. As the old thrall came near, Geth asked in a low voice, "The painted one isn't with them. Do you know where he is?"

"Perhaps to your mother and father's chamber. It's been set aside for our guests during their visit."

Good, Geth thought. He didn't want to have to eat with the strange man.

"Shall I fetch him for you?" Calder asked.

"No!" Geth replied, a little too loudly. Then, quieter, "Leave him be. If we're fortunate, we won't see him again until they leave."

And good riddance to them both.

"None too soon," Calder muttered. "The entire south wing stinks. Damned foreign savage, burning incense and who knows what in there."

But Geth wasn't listening. He chose a seat along a side table abutting the head table and stood behind the bench as everyone began to gather. He watched as his mother went to stand beside his father. Gustav stood on the opposite side, at the place of honor.

As everyone sat down, servants carried baskets and platters to the tables. Geth was hungry, but anxiety gnawed at his insides. He just wanted this night to be over so these guests could leave and things could go back to normal.

Azulf knelt on the floor of Gustav Hidasson's borrowed room. The door was shut and secured to prevent any disturbances. Dozens of candles in black and red surrounded him on the floor in pools of melted wax, their dancing flames casting deep shadows across the walls. In the corner, a bronze brazier burnt a mixture of rare herbs, gums, and spices.

He was bare to the waist, eyes closed tight, swaying forward and back as he chanted softly. Sweat rolled in large drops down his chest and back. The words he uttered had been ancient before men first learned to cultivate crops and husband animals. They harkened back to an epoch when elder gods ruled.

"Come, Spirit of Destruction. Answer my call.

"Come, Spirit of Enmity. Answer my call.

"Come, Spirit of Desolation. Answer my call."

He focused on the chanting with all his being. If he wasn't careful, he could lose himself in the rite, and his spirit would fly off into the invisible ethers of the cosmos, to wander forever, formless and alone at the mercy of the many malevolent forces beyond the ken of the mortal world.

He felt a presence on the edge of his awareness. A thing of the netherworld. He could feel its hunger, rapacious and never-ending, as it pushed against the boundary that separated their worlds. With the skill of a chirurgeon, Azulf reached out and parted the ethereal fabric, inviting the spirit in with his chant.

"Come, Spirit of Anger. Follow my call."

He promised it the sweet taste of blood and flesh, incensing its appetite. He wished he could send the spirit to tear Gustav to pieces, but as long as Hidasson possessed the amulet, he was untouchable.

Other spectral entities gathered around the temporary bridge between worlds, answering his call. A handful quickly became a multitude before Azulf closed the breach.

Breathing heavily, he concluded the chant and allowed his chin to droop to his chest. The shadows on the walls writhed in ways that had nothing to do with the candles' flames.

A small smile creased his lips. They were coming.

Geth reached for a horn of ale with his left hand while he used the right to shovel stew into his mouth with a hunk of bread. Helga had outdone herself, with trenchers of beef, fowl, turnips, beans, corn, tiny onions, and four kinds of bread. Not to mention skewers of tender goat and bowls of piping hot gravy.

On either side of Geth sat his father's tenants, laughing and taunting each other good-naturedly as they ate. Tanya was pouring mead down her husband Allan's throat while the others cheered her on.

Geth noticed that Einar and a couple of the freemen were wearing swords, something they rarely did. When he mentioned it, the foreman shrugged.

"These are dangerous times. Better to be wary than caught off-guard, eh?"

Geth looked to the other side of the hall, where the merchant's guards sat alone, eating little but drinking quite a bit in silence. Dogs lolled in a broad space between the tables, chewing on bones and scraps.

Geth was finishing his stew and looking for his next victual conquest when sharp words echoed from the head table. Everyone froze. Geth turned to see his father standing up. His face was a mask of barely-restrained rage as he towered over their guest. "I will not sit in own home and be forced to listen to this!"

Gustav leaned back in his seat, thumbs tucked into his wide leather belt. "You are an obstinate pig, Ivek. But I will have this farm and everything in it. I came here in good faith to make a fair offer, but you won't even consider it."

"I considered it, and the answer is no. Do you hear me? No! Not today. Not in a hundred years. Never."

Benches scraped against the floor as several of his father's freemen stood up. Hands were placed on the hilts of swords and axe heads, though no blade was drawn. But Geth's father did not look to need any aid.

"Get out of my home, Gustav," his father said through gritted teeth. "Get out and never come back here again."

The merchant held his gaze for a moment, and then threw back his head and laughed. Geth was shocked. His heart beat hard in his chest. No one had ever dared to disrespect his father this way. He had never seen his father fight, but he had heard the stories of his father's younger days, the many times when he had been forced to fight, and even kill, to protect their land from marauders. Those stories had always seemed fantastical to Geth. Yet, seeing his father's face now, he believed them, and he was shocked to think that he would witness such violence in his own home.

Geth gripped his eating knife tightly, determined to rush to his father's side if a fight broke out.

Just as his father lifted his hands, perhaps to lay them on the merchant, a keening howl pierced the night. It was a wolf's howl, and it sounded as if the beast was just outside the house, but wolves never came that close to the farm.

Some inkling made Geth turn toward the front of the great hall. He didn't notice anything awry at first, but then a chill ran down his spine. The heavy doors were open. He started to say something to Einar, but before he could get the words out, several large shapes stepped through the doorway and stood on the threshold. They were wolves, but larger than he had ever seen.

Someone cried out. As if waiting for a signal, the wolves burst into the hall, spreading out as they plunged into the crowd of feasters.

Geth hunkered behind the table as a wolf, huge and black with eyes the color of pitch, raced in his direction, scattering the dogs before it like a tom cat through a nest of field mice. Einar started to draw his sword, but too late as the wolf leapt over the table and bowled him over. Geth flinched. Before anyone could aid him, the wolf was at the foreman's throat, rending the flesh with foam-flecked fangs.

Screams broke out. And suddenly, as if that cry was a harbinger of mayhem, everyone was moving. A couple freemen tried to aid Einar. The black wolf, as if sensing their intent, turned and leapt at them in a growling fury.

Geth edged away from the violence, heading toward the head table and his family. Yet, before he could take more than a few steps, Geth turned to see his father wrestling with a giant white wolf. His mother ran to help her husband, knife in hand, but Gustav Hidasson wrested the blade away and pulled her down on his lap. She hit him and tried to bite him, while he held her down and laughed uproariously at her attempts to get free.

What was happening? Wolves never attacked a homestead like this. And why was Gustav so unconcerned. Geth would have thought the rich man would have been the first to run away, but the merchant seemed merely amused by the carnage.

Geth almost tripped, and saw the body of a warrior at his feet. He thought it might be Allan, but the man's face had been torn off, leaving only a bloody ruin behind. The man's sword was still in its scabbard.

Geth dropped his knife and drew the sword. Yet, before he could go to his parents, a deep growl rumbled behind him. Geth's stomach dropped to see a shaggy wolf behind him. Blood flecked the beast's gray muzzle, and its eyes were a feral shade of yellow that turned Geth's legs to jelly.

The creature lunged, and Geth leapt over the feasting table beside him, barely clearing its wooden planks as the jaws snapped in his wake. Most of the hounds were dead or fled, but a couple fought their wild cousins on the floor. Geth dashed between them, anticipating the sharp pain of fangs any moment.

He angled back toward the head table, but stopped cold when he saw that his mother was no longer fighting. She lay limp on Gustav's lap. Blood stained the front of her fine gown from the knife jutting from her chest. Meanwhile, the merchant drank from his cup, laughing and spilling red wine down his chin.

Red-hot rage exploded in Geth's chest. He ran toward them,

sword raised, intending to avenge his mother and save his father, until a heavy body from behind knocked him to the floor.

Geth squirmed and tried to swing at the wolf bearing him down, but he only managed to banged his knuckles against the top of its head. As he fought to free himself, its jaws clamped down on the upper part of his right arm. He yelled as the wolf shook him from side to side. Pain tore through his shoulder. He kicked and pushed, dropping the sword in his panic, but all he could do was grab onto the beast's fur with his left hand and hold on tight.

His head struck a wooden support post, and bright stars burst in front of his vision. Geth tried to call for help, even though he knew it was useless. The wolves were everywhere. Through the forest of table legs and bench feet, he saw a figure lying on the floor, facing him. It was his father. Blood covered the older man's face, dripping down into a widening pool beneath him. His eyes were open, but blank like glass orbs.

The wolf's thrashing threw Geth against the wooden post again, and darkness swallowed him.

The dark seemed to last forever. Wrapped in its thick, cloying embrace, Geth felt nothing. No pain or sorrow, no longing for the life that he had lost. Just a cold numbness of body and soul that he thought would carry him down to the gloom of Nethahellir.

Then, a sensation penetrated that murky cocoon. It began as an itch in his shoulder, which grew into an irritation. Geth tried to move, to wriggle, to relieve himself of this growing annoyance, but without hands or form in this nebulous realm, he was powerless to do anything but endure it. The sensation swelled into a burning pain that began to radiate through his entire being.

Suddenly, he awoke with a low cry on his lips.

The pain was even worse awake than in the dusky dream. It seared in his shoulder like a red-hot iron.

He was outside, but it was dark. Tiny bites of sleeting rain fell upon him, and a harsh wind moaned in his ears. He was moving, being dragged actually, over the cold ground.

Geth stiffened as he remembered the massacre in the great hall. The wolves. His father's corpse, staring at him under the table. He looked up, expecting to see a wolf pulling him, but his gaze fell upon a pair of old, withered hands and followed them up to see Calder. The old thrall was wheezing hard, his thin hair drenched in the freezing rain. Geth almost cried with joy to see him.

Then, he hit a bump in the ground, and a sharp stab of pain shot through him. Geth looked down, and a shout died on his lips as shock took hold of him. Where his right arm had been, there was only a stump, sheared off just below the shoulder joint and wrapped in a thick cloth that was soaked through with blood. Geth's heart beat hard and fast, threatening to burst from his chest. This was impossible. He must be dreaming still. But no, he could feel the realness of the cold rain, the sting of the wind. He was awake. This was happening.

Suddenly, his gorge rose, and spewed up the remains of the feast down his drenched tunic, and tears came to his eyes because the warmth of his vomit felt so good against his icy flesh.

Calder pulled him up against the bole of a tall tree and stopped, collapsing beside Geth in a gasping, shivering mass. They had reached the forest south of the farm.

Geth looked up, wanting to see the stars, but the sky was pitch-black above the evergreen boughs.

"I'm sorry," Calder said between gasps. "I can't . . . I can't go any farther."

Geth reached out with his remaining hand and touched the old thrall's leg. "Thank you, Calder."

The old man sat up and leaned against the tree beside him. "I'm sorry."

"Stop saying that. You saved me."

Calder nodded toward the bloody stump of Geth's right shoulder. "I had to take the arm, young master. It was hanging off when I found you on the floor, too far gone to save." He drew a long, ragged breath. "I did the best I could."

Geth squeezed the thrall's arm. He couldn't imagine the courage it must have taken to go into that hall, with the wolves killing everyone, and pull him out. He didn't feel worthy.

"Everyone else is dead," Calder continued, "including your blessed parents."

Geth thought of his mother and father, lying in their own blood, food for beasts, and was sickened by the image. "What about Hidasson."

"The last I saw, he was strutting around the hall like the cock of the walk."

"But the wolves . . . they didn't attack him?"

Calder shook his head. "No. The blasted beasts left him alone like he was one of their own. Damned uncanny."

Geth didn't know what to make of that. It sounded like Gustav Hidasson had made an alliance with the animals, but how was that possible? Had he trained them to kill for him?

Geth laid back and watched the sleet come down. He felt hollow inside, like a gutted fish, just waiting to die. The only emotion he could summon was a wish that he could make Hidasson pay for his crimes, but that was impossible.

A howl made them both sit up. Geth couldn't see in the dark, but the sound had come from the direction of the farm. Another howl erupted closer, and he knew what it meant. The wolves were tracking them.

He tried to get up, but pain tore through the right side of his body, and he crumpled back against the tree trunk. Calder struggled to his feet. "Stay down, young master. I'll lead them off."

Geth grabbed the old man's leg, which felt like a rod of ice under his thin pants. "Calder, wait! Maybe they'll pass us by."

The thrall looked down with a kindly smile. "No, young master. They won't. But don't you worry. Calder will take care of it."

Geth tried to hold on, but he was too weak. Calder pulled free of his grasp and strode off through the trees, into the night.

A great, terrible sigh rose within Geth. The hollowness inside was spreading up his chest and down into his legs. He was dying.

It wasn't so bad, he reflected. His vision was fading, closing out the world around him until only a narrow tunnel remained. Geth closed his eyes and imagined how the morning would look, when the sun came up over the mountains and bathed everything in a golden glow, how the sunlight reflected off the waters of the lake as he fished, with the tall stalks of summer wheat waving across the farm. He would miss his life.

Finally, too weak to hold up his head any longer, he let it fall and drifted into his last slumber.

A chill colder than ice encased him. It froze the breath in his lungs, and yet, there was no pain. No other sensation at all except the cold.

Geth awoke with a start, to find himself lying in a shadowed cave. The ceiling overhead and walls around him were dark, craggy stone.

Confusion swaddled his mind. Was this death? Oddly, it occurred to him that he didn't hear the rain anymore.

He sat up, and there was no pain. However, his arm was still gone. Clean, dry bandages bound the stump at the end of his shoulder. An image flashed through his mind, of the great wolf biting down on him. He remembered the sharp pain as his flesh and sinews were torn, but the memory was a distant thing. Almost as if it had happened to someone else.

To his left, the cave opened in a wide mouth. No light shined through from the outside, making him assume it was still night time.

Yet, the darkness beyond the mouth was so deep that it was almost palpable. For some reason, he feared it.

In the other direction, the cave extended in a long tunnel. More or less straight, it was swathed in shadow, but he saw a dim, ruddy glow down that way.

Geth turned away from the dark night outside and headed deeper into the cave.

He walked for some time. A few minutes? A couple hours? He found time difficult to gauge. His body felt lighter than normal, but his movements were slow, so that each footfall seemed momentous.

The glow slowly became brighter, until he came to the end of the cave. Against the back wall stood a low stone table. Upon its flat surface sat several objects. A cuirass of black armor, worked to resemble a shirt of broad scales, with matching leggings. A black helm with a closed face, and a broadsword resting upon a black metal scabbard.

The objects all looked antique to his eyes, although they held no trace of rust or corrosion. The illumination was coming from strange runes engraved into each item, glowing deep crimson like molten steel.

As he gazed upon these things, a voice spoke in the empty air, seeming to come from all around him. "Geth, son of Ivek, son of Erik, you stand upon the doorstep of death."

Geth looked around, but there was no one here except him. *I am dreaming. Or I'm dead already. This isn't real.*

Yet, the voice was deep and unyielding, the kind of voice to be obeyed, or at least heeded. "You must choose. To take up these arms and return to the mortal world as Our instrument. Or pass into oblivion. You must choose."

Geth placed his hand on the sword's cross guard. It was icy cold to the touch, yet he felt an energy vibrating within the metal. And he realized that he wasn't afraid.

Having made his choice, he closed his fingers around the hilt, and darkness slammed down over him, sending him into uncon-sciousness.

Geth opened his eyes to see the trees around him once more, and the dark sky overhead. The stinging rain beat down on his face. He was back in the forest. However, he felt different.

Looking down, Geth saw he was wearing the black scaled armor. It fit him perfectly, like a second skin. He sat up, and the scales rustled softly, but otherwise the armor did not impede him at all.

The sword rested on the ground beside him in its scabbard. He started to reach for it, and froze as he saw his right arm reaching down, encased in armor. Geth raised that arm, marveling at its return. It was impossible. He had seen the bloody stump where this arm had been, and felt the pain of its loss. Now, here it was, back and whole again, although it felt odd, almost as if the flesh were slightly numb. Geth pulled off the scaled gauntlet, and dread seized his insides.

Instead of the flesh he expected to see, the hand and wrist were merely bone. He clenched the fist, and watched the skeletal fingers curl together. He opened them, and the bony digits extended to their full length. He could feel the rain striking the hand and running down the bones, but unlike living flesh, there was no sensation of cold. No discomfort at all.

Geth used the skeletal hand to grasp the hilt of the sword and draw it from its scabbard. The blade came free with the ring of steel sliding over steel. It was lighter than he expected, but the razor-sharp edges gleamed in the darkness. As he held it up, the runes along the length of blade flared brightly, and a jolt of energy surged into his hand and up his arm. Geth gasped as the power flowed through him. He felt invigorated, and strong. Very strong. But there was something else, too.

Anger.

Deep inside, Geth felt a wellspring of rage. Images of his dead parents became fixed in his mind. He tried to blink them away, but the images remained, reminding him of what they had suffered at the hands of their guest.

Geth stood up, sword in hand. He picked up the black helmet with his left hand and placed it on his head. As the metal visor came down over his face, the rage found a purpose. He knew, then, what he needed to do, and he was glad for it.

Encased in the eldritch armor and righteous fury, Geth began walking in the direction of his father's farm.

Gustav drank deep from the cup. Finishing the sweet ale, he threw it across the hall and wiped his mouth with the back of his hand. Sitting in the former owner's tall chair, he was drunk and loving it. Drunk on ale and besotted on the satisfaction of his conquest. Without an army, he had come here to this great estate and wrested it from the hands of that bastard Ivek, and now it was all his.

The wolves had been thorough in their slaughtering before they ran back out into the night. The only ones still alive in the entire hall were him and his two warriors. Dagar was passed out at a side table from too much drink, and Olef was teetering on the bleary edge of insentience. Gustav, however, felt like he could stay awake all night.

Suddenly, he noticed Azulf standing in a doorway at the side of the hall. "What are you doing lurking there?" Gustav demanded as he sat up. He looked around for more ale, but all the nearby cups were empty.

The tall sorcerer merely stood there, saying nothing.

Gustav replaced his snarl with a smile. "Ah, well. I congratulate you anyway, on a job well done. Your beasts did their part, even better than I expected!"

Azulf looked around without expression. "This is no victory of mine. There is no honor in this."

Gustav threw his cup onto the floor amid the dead hounds, where it rattled for a moment before going silent. Silent, just like this hall. But Gustav had already decided he would make this his summer manor. He would bring in new laborers and servants, and make this place into a splendid retreat.

"Tonight was a vital step on the road to my eventual success," Gustav said. "With your powers at my command, I'll be jarl within a year. Then, I will rule over all those who doubted and derided me."

"Your ambition knows no bounds."

Gustav beamed at him, taking that as a compliment. "Indeed. In the coming weeks, I will secure the services of every freesword and hireling in— say, what's the matter with you?"

Azulf had turned away, and now had his head cocked slightly to the side, as if listening for a sound. "Something comes. Something—
"

The front doors shook from a heavy blow.

"—dangerous," the sorcerer finished.

Gustav frowned, feeling personally affronted by this interruption. "Banish your wolves, Azulf! We have no further need of them here."

"I sent them away. This is something else."

Gustav stood up. "Olef! Dagar! Get up! Your master has need of you."

Dagar merely snored louder. But Olef climbed to his feet, leaning slightly, and headed toward the doors with his axe out. Gustav watched anxiously, his mind filling with visions of a hostile army surrounding the hall. He had many rivals, and he cursed his own arrogance for not bringing more warriors on this sojourn.

Just as Olef reached the door, the broad wooden planks exploded inward. The warrior was knocked to the floor by the force of it. A cold wind howled into the hall and swirled about the corpses.

On the threshold stood a man in dark armor. Gustav squinted to see clearer and noticed the sword in the figure's hand, its blade as black as the armor. Upon the stranger's head was a closed helm, concealing his features. There was a crimson glow about the warrior, as if he had been rolled in burning ashes. He held something in his other hand, but Gustav could not tell what it was.

"Who are you?" Gustav demanded, trying to appear forceful.

The armored figure swung his left arm and tossed what he was holding into the hall. Gustav's blood ran cold when the objects rolled to a stop, and he saw the heads of his four other bondsmen, who had been stationed outside.

Olef rolled to his feet and charged at the intruder, swinging a mighty two-handed blow. Yet, the stranger was faster. His black sword shot out in a wide arc and cut the man down. A gout of blood spewed from the great wound across Olef's stomach as he fell.

The stranger started toward Gustav again, but Dagar came hurtling out of the shadows and delivered a fearsome blow to the stranger's head with his sword.

Gustav's heart leapt, expecting to see cloven metal and a spray of brains across the floor, but the helmet deflected the strike without even denting. Dagar swung again, but the stranger caught his arm and checked the downward stroke. Dagar was no feeble stripling. Gustav had seen him hew a man almost in half with that sword, but Dagar was unable to free himself from that grip no matter how much he pulled.

Dagar's mouth opened in a silent groan as the point of the black sword slid into his stomach until the tip came out his back. The stranger released Dagar, and the bondsman fell. The black sword was covered in gore when it came free, but then the blood vanished, as if it had been absorbed by the dark metal. Gustav shivered.

He looked to Azulf. The northern sorcerer was staring at the intruder like he was seeing his own death. "Azulf! Use your arts to send this foe to the deepest hell!"

The sorcerer raised his hands, fingers splayed in an alien sign. Dolorous words rang out from his lips, each striking the air with the force of a colossal bell's toll. The light in the hall grew dim. With the uttering of the final syllable of his incantation, Azulf collapsed to the floor like a puppet whose strings had been cut.

The intruder staggered as if he had been struck with a sledge. The tip of his sword dipped to the floor, gouging a line in the hard-packed dirt, and tendrils of inky smoke rose from the strange armor.

Gustav took heart at this, and drew his own weapon with the intention of delivering the mortal blow. Yet, before he could get around the table, the glow from the stranger's armor intensified. From this close, Gustav could see the many small runes in the dark metal, each one blazing like a hot coal.

The stranger straightened up, throwing off whatever enchantment Azulf had attempted, and resumed his approach.

"Begone from this hall!" Gustav shouted, as he retreated to keep the table between him and the assailant. "I command you. Do you hear? Get out of here!"

He came to where Azulf lay on the floor and kicked the sorcerer, but Azulf did not move. "Damn you!"

The stranger swung his fell sword, and the table split in half. Shoving aside the two ends as if they were kindling, the armored man came at Gustav.

Gustav lifted his sword, but then thought better of it, so he turned and ran. Or tried to. Before he had taken his third step, a terrible pain pierced him between his shoulder blades. He was driven to the floor by the force of the blow. His sword fell from his hands.

Gustav tried to turn over, but all his strength had vanished. A disturbing warmth was spreading down his back. He felt the trod of heavy steps coming toward him.

"Listen to me! I'll give you anything you want. My fortune is yours if you spare me."

Armored boots appeared on either side of Gustav as the stranger stood over him. The wound in his back flared with new pain as the blade was pulled free from his flesh.

With tears in his eyes, Gustav managed to turn onto his side. He looked up, pleading for his life. "Please, spare me! Please, I'll give you anything you want."

As he spat these words, Gustav pulled on his belt buckle, drawing the secret knife hidden there. "Please, won't you— die!"

Gustav stabbed up at the stranger's groin with all his remaining strength. The blade was tiny, yet as sharp as a needle. It slid between the dark scales and penetrated the flesh underneath. Gustav felt a moment of elation, thinking he might yet win free of this peril.

Then, the black sword came down, point first, through his mouth and out the back of his skull. He felt his front teeth shatter, a brief taste of cold steel, and then nothing at all.

The last thing he saw, as his life ended, were the stranger's eyes through the slit in the helm's face. Cold pits of darkness, without a sliver of remorse. Yet, somehow, they seemed familiar.

Geth looked down at Gustav Hidasson, lying dead at his feet.

He didn't know how he had gotten here. The last thing he remembered was walking up to the farm. Somehow, he had felt the presence of the men who had killed his family. Then, a red haze had filled his mind, taking over his thoughts. Until now.

He glanced around and saw the bodies of the merchant's bodyguards, saw the viciousness of their injuries. Had he done that? Geth didn't revel in their deaths. He didn't feel relief or vindication. Only anger, still burning under his skin like a fever.

He pulled the sword free of Gustav's skull, and watched as the blood and gray matter were slowly sucked into the blade. Part of him thought he should be terrified by that, but he wasn't. Just like in the dream cave, nothing scared him now.

Geth looked over to the bodies of his parents. They looked different in death, as if all the things that he had loved about them were gone, leaving only empty shells behind. It was his duty to bury them and perform the funereal rites, but just as with his fear, his duties to his old life were gone as well. He was no longer a son. He had become something far worse.

Gritting his teeth, Geth opened his hand and dropped the sword. It clattered with a dull ring on the floorboards. He pulled off the helmet and threw it down as well. He wanted to be free of this armor. Free of death, and the horrible ache that transfixed him, a hole he would never be able to fill.

He yanked off a gauntlet and froze, gazing down at the skeletal hand. It appeared so delicate, but he could feel the terrible strength in those fingers. He didn't know what he had become, but he knew he wasn't completely human anymore.

The voice spoke to him. "You are my champion, Geth, son of Ivek."

Dread filled Geth at those words. "I am no hero."

His own voice sounded odd to him. Hollow, like the echo inside a crypt.

The voice rasped harshly in his ear. "You have been saved from the edge of oblivion and sanctified in the blood of the guilty. You are my instrument in this mortal world."

Geth guessed the identity of his patron. "You are Morr, god of vengeance."

"Attend, my champion," the voice said. "There is more work for you. Much more."

A force compelled Geth to look to the east. He could sense that something awful was happening, far from this hall, and a rush of fury welled up inside him. He wanted to right this wrong.

Geth tried to fight these feelings, but violent images filled his mind. He saw people being killed by gigantic trolls, saw women and children being hunted in the night, smelled their blood as it was spilled on the cold ground. The anger burned fiercely inside him.

Geth, the Sword of Vengeance, took up the black blade and slid it into the scabbard at his hip. He put back on the helmet.

He paused a moment to gaze down at the corpses around him

through the eyeholes of the helm. Then, he stalked out of the hall. He would avenge the innocent. That was his purpose, forever more.

Perhaps, it would be enough.

In the hall, a pale hand reached out of the shadows to hover over the body of Gustav Hidasson. After tracing a series of mystical symbols in the air, the hand dipped down to clasp the talisman around the corpse's neck. A brief yank snapped the chain.

Azulf held up the amulet. Exhilaration flowed through him as he felt the return of his soul. He was whole again.

He left the dead hall. Striding out into the cool night, Azulf took a deep breath—his first as a free man in a long time—and started walking. Not following the grim specter trudging eastward – he wasn't insane enough to challenge *that* one again.

Instead, he headed south. He would pass through the woods and the mountains until he reached the sea, and then he would make his way back to home. He had many old scores of his own to settle.

JON SPRUNK lives in central Pennsylvania and has been writing fantasy stories since he was in short pants. He is a proud husband, father, lifelong geek gamer, and author of the SHADOW SAGA and BOOK OF THE BLACK EARTH fantasy series. More information about Jon and his works can be found at jonsprunk.com.

THE NORTH IN BONDAGE

CLAY GRIFFITH AND SUSAN GRIFFITH

Revna watched the boat slide from the mist shrouding the fjord.

Horns blared over the water to announce the arrival. Banners flapped from the mast. The drummer pounded the oar beat as the oars reversed and churned back the dark water. The boat shuddered in the foam. Heavy iron weights on thick cables went over the sides fore and aft. The oars lifted dripping and drew into the ports in the hull.

The boat dwarfed the sleek dragon-prow longboats in the harbor. She was wider and higher and had a blockish stern castle. This vessel was presumptuously built to mimic a galley of the once-great Gordion Empire. She reflected the haughtiness of the merchant who owned her.

Crewmen manhandled a small boat over the side and lowered it to the water. A stout man appeared at the rail dressed in a fine fur cloak and a cap that was likely silk. Clean-shaven and soft in a crowd of hard bearded men.

Erland Ulfsson, the master of this boat and the master of a good portion of the wealth that traveled this fjord from his up-country trading base. Usually just his wealth traveled; it was odd to see the man himself so far from the comforts of his home.

He carried a small wooden cask under one arm. At his side trudged a huge bodyguard fitted ostentatiously in full mail with a gleaming helmet and massive sword at his girdle. The cask was handed down to the small boat and then Erland Ulfsson was handed down too. The swordsman followed. When all were settled, the liveried crew rowed toward the dock. Even this little longboat had the merchant's outlandishly long banner hanging limp from the prow.

Revna watched as the little boat banged against the quay where a retinue of fur-clad men waited. There was much hugging and arm clasping, laughing and good-natured shouts of camaraderie. The men made their boisterous way up the quay.

Revna lost sight of them as they moved onto the planked lanes between the rude wooden buildings. She could easily presume their destination. Singandr Sinrisson, the Jarl of Jarls, had his hall here in Korjengard. No doubt the ermine-draped Erland Ulfsson was bound for the longhouse of the High King carrying the cask filled with shiny gifts as the prelude to a night of mead-quaffing such as only the richest and most powerful could enjoy.

Revna had to move now that the merchant was ashore. The water was calm. The treacherous currents caused by the spring melts hadn't started in earnest. She pushed herself to her feet and shook out her legs, trying to ignore the ache in her knees.

A small hand clutched at her tunic. A wharf rat, a child of the streets. Desperate hunger lanced his gaze. It had been a long cold winter. Pockets were empty and so were bellies. Revna reached into her pocket and pulled out her last coin. She tucked it into his pocket. His eyes widened and he fumbled for it. She jerked her head to the mead hall where the others had gone. He gave her one last long look of disbelief and scurried into the dark.

Revna held the simple pendant hanging around her neck. Silver with a glass center several inches across. The glass bulb contained a small tuft of blonde hair. Revna pressed the glass to her lips and secured the pendant back inside her tunic against her heart.

She sat on the edge of the quay and dropped her feet into the water. The cold shot up her legs. She slid into the frigid water. Her leather tunic and pants grew heavy against her flesh. She took several deep breaths, sending mist into the air, and started away from the dock with a measured stroke.

The strong current buffeted her legs and torso. Her chest constricted in the cold. She spat water through trembling lips. She forced her legs to kick despite the tingling in her muscles. Her shoulders burned. The water splashed over her entire face and she might have gone under. She struggled to maintain form even though she couldn't feel her limbs. If she started thrashing, she'd be done and just surrender to the cold.

Over the rasping of her own breath, Revna heard a new sound. Water lapping against something hard. There just ahead of her was a line of foaming white and straight planks of glistening wood.

The boat.

The high flat stern with two torches on the rail rose some twenty feet above. Revna also saw a patch of discolored wood where a name had been painted – a practice unusual for Norrønian vessels – now sanded away. Still readable though. The name was *Pernilla.*

A swell slapped her against the planks. Numb fingers scrabbled for grip before the rebounding wave could drag her back out. She found herself clinging to the wood like the rough barnacles under her hands. The rudder was to Revna's left, to her great relief. Three feet above was what she sought.

A rung. The bottom of four, a ladder fitted into the hull.

Revna worked numb fingertips up along the sodden wood. The water pulled at her without mercy. She knew if the waves plucked her from her tenuous hold on the boat, the cold water would not fail again to drown her.

Revna's breath rose like a cloud. Her left arm quivered from the pressure of holding her body up. She gave a desperate surge and hooked her fingers around the rung. With the burst of excitement that brought renewed strength, she immediately stretched and grabbed the second rung. She forgot the exhaustion and climbed to the top.

Hanging off the precarious rungs on the swaying boat, Revna felt along the hull, seeking something she knew was there.

Click.

A small section of the timber popped out a few inches. Revna worked her fingers into the gap and swung open a hatch three feet square. She climbed in and pulled the hatch shut behind her, listening for the snap of the latch.

She slumped in the dark, breathing, letting her heartbeat slow. The back of her bowed head pressed against the roof of the narrow little box. Her knees crowded against her chest. Water dribbled off her face and hair. Her sodden clothes dripped. Arms and legs felt thick. She blew lukewarm breath on her raw fingers thinking about how dangerous this would've been even when she was young.

Revna shuddered in the blackness. Her eyes flew open. She didn't remember where she was. Then she recalled the swim and climb. Had she fallen asleep inside the compartment? Had she just gone unconscious from the strain? How long had she been in here?

Revna put an ear to the interior wall. It was quiet. She flicked the second simple switch and an inside hatch opened. She quickly swung out, but her legs wouldn't hold her and she crumpled to the deck.

She pressed her hands on the floor and sat up. Revna heard voices and noise from the deck outside. The cabin was empty as she suspected, although she didn't know how long she had been asleep so she didn't know when the merchant might return. She had to work fast. Revna rubbed her tingling legs, forcing the feeling back. She dragged herself onto her feet.

Several bottles sat in a corner. They no doubt held a private mead that Erland Ulfsson had made for him by special brewmasters. Revna would've welcomed a warming draught of mead, but she had eaten nothing since this morning. She needed her head for the business at hand.

Thick tapestries hung from the bulkhead for both warmth and ostentation. The drapes boasted intricate needlework depictions of hunting and war. A newer tapestry hanging behind the bed showed a couple making love.

Revna shook her head. How pathetically typical for a man his age.

Near the luxurious carved bed stood a rack draped by a mail shirt. It was a beautiful, intricate shirt with hints of gold thread woven through. A wide steel belt hung around the waist. Thick leather and fur bracers hung by hide strips. Balanced atop the mail shirt was a helmet, as bright as silver and worked with scenes of bloody battle. A fine sword leaned against the wall with a magnificent corded steel hand guard and a huge emerald in the pommel. All of this war gear was foreign in make, but not the less impressive for that. It wouldn't look out of place on whatever god of war its creators worshipped. It was clear none of the armor had ever been worn and the sword likely had been drawn only for show.

At the foot of the bed lay a pile of furs. Revna tossed the pelts aside one by one revealing a large wooden chest. It wasn't locked. Theft was an unusual event in Norrøngard, perpetuated by only the most depraved or the most desperate. Revna hefted the lid.

Gold. Silver. Necklaces. Broaches. Clasps. Chains. Rings. Goblets. Plates. Daggers. Raw gemstones. Faceted jewels. Delicate gold filigree and intricately carved whalebone.

Revna could carry a few items. A ring or two, perhaps a thin chain or a few gemstones. Despite her fatigued arms and legs, and the daunting swim back, she needed to take something valuable to make the trip worthwhile.

Erland Ulfsson wouldn't miss it; he couldn't possibly know every piece in this chest. That was what Revna told herself every time she had stolen from one of the stalls his traveling merchants set up in the market, or when she lifted something from one of his caravans passing through Korjengard.

She always told herself that she wasn't a thief. Stealing weighed against you in the afterlife. Still, Erland Ulfsson was a selfish man who failed to serve his people. No one needed this much treasure. If taking a few pieces of gold let her fill the belly of that little boy on the dock, then Revna was content if it condemned her in the eyes of the gods.

A soft cloth bag sat atop the treasures. It appeared to be silk, a fabric rare in the north. She picked it up and unwound the cord. Inside the bag was a gold ring embedded with jewels with a flat golden disc inscribed with odd symbols. It was a script that Revna vaguely recognized but couldn't read. Around the ring itself, though, were Norrønian runes reading *The North in Bondage*. Inside the ring were more runes that showed the word *Norrøngard* and the Norrønian phrase for *Araland*, a land to the south, now a source of trade, but once a source of war. Revna returned the ring to its bag and pushed it into her tunic pocket.

Something milky caught her eye. She pushed coins and jewels aside and pulled out a silver ring with a glistening opal so large it was no longer beautiful, just remarkable.

Revna's heart pounded. The massive stone glimmered even in the dim cabin. She held the ring with thumb and forefinger, positioning it over one of her outstretched fingers. Revna lowered the ring until the tip of her finger penetrated the circle of silver.

With a hiss of disgust, Revna threw the ring down onto the treasure, but she still saw it glaring at her so she pressed it deep until it was hidden in the jumble of riches.

She slammed the lid with a thud. Clenching her mouth shut, she drew in long breaths through her nose. As she caught her breath, her gaze fell on the outline of a square cut in the middle of the cabin floor. A hatch so Erland Ulfsson could visit his wealth in the hold below? It merited a look.

Revna braced her feet and hefted the hatch. The scent wafted from below thick and foul. Not surprising for the hold of a boat. There could be uncured pelts or haunches of meat. Revna peered down into the darkness. She saw the faint outline of crates and bundles that were probably hides.

Something moved. Revna heard a faint sloughing sound and maybe even a slight metallic jangle. Live animals?

Revna placed a foot onto a broad-stepped ladder and descended into the dark hold. She crouched in the stinking damp. Under the thumping of water outside and the creaking of timbers, she heard a soft groan.

Something shifted just a few feet ahead of her. A shape lay in the dark. She couldn't make out exactly what it was. It moved like it was alive.

Revna shuffled toward the shape. There was a flash of pale skin when a large face turned. It seemed human but larger and twisted. Revna reared back toward the ladder. Huge gnarled fingers seized her wrist and pulled her down against the deck. She struggled, inches from the monstrous face. She smelled foul breath. Wide eyes glared at her.

Revna had seen such desperate glistening light in eyes before. She stopped fighting the strong hand that gripped her. Revna recognized the eyes of a child, alone and frightened, when she saw them.

"I won't hurt you," Revna whispered through trembling lips.

The eyes shifted. The shape moved with a humanlike grunt. Fingers tightened on Revna's arm.

"Stop!" Her breath misted.

The craggy shadowy face inched back with confusion.

Slowly, almost instinctively, Revna started to hum a lullaby. The memory of it came quickly to her lips though she hadn't sung one for a very long time. As the soft melody washed over them both, the expression on the strange child relaxed, the lessoning of terror. It took a few minutes, but the pressure of its grip eased.

"Let me go." Revna pronounced the words softly but distinctly while brushing the large hand clutching her arm. "Please."

Thick fingers slid away. Her arm throbbed, but nothing was broken.

"Thank you." Revna fought the urge to race up the ladder away from this thing. She watched it as it turned its head away from her and lowered its arm with a metal jangle. Its wrists were encircled by heavy iron cuffs attached to thick chains that ran to brackets high on the hull.

The thing was shaped like a man, but much larger, taller, and thicker. It curled up on the deck. Its pale flesh was visible on its naked arms and legs. It wore some sort of fur jerkin and breechcloth. With a surge of chilling exhilaration, Revna realized what she was looking at.

A frost giant.

Revna had only seen one such creature in her life and that from a distance while traveling in northern Raven's Wood. The sight of that huge thing tramping up a snow-blown ridge had sent her heart pounding. That frost giant was huge, perhaps twenty feet tall, while this male curled in chains was no more than ten. He possessed an otherworldly menace, but Revna felt more pity than horror.

"Can you talk to me?" She touched his large arm. The skin was rough. "Are you in pain?"

The frost giant kept his head turned away. Surely he understood her. Their languages were similar enough. One of the giant's hands remained pressed flat on the deck. From under his gnarled fingers spidery frost spread across the wood, gathering thin and white in the chinks between planks. His lips moved as he muttered under his breath.

Revna stared with amazement. Frost giants were said to have magic to control ice and snow. This was chilling what little moisture the timbers held, but it barely created a light frosting.

Revna took hold of one of the chains in her hand and followed it to the heavy bracket. The lock securing the chain to the bracket was massive. Revna grasped the chain in both hands, placed a boot against the wood and pulled. Surely the giant had thrashed and yanked on the chain and he hadn't been able to free himself. There was no hope for her.

The thought of Erland Ulfsson living warm and comfortable in his cabin above, knowing this poor captive was below caused Revna to pull the chains again, straining to the limits of her rage. She dropped to the deck, weak armed, and breathing hard, angry at her feebleness.

The North in Bondage.

Revna clenched her fists. This would not stand.

"I'll look for a key." Revna knelt next to the giant's head. She found herself stroking his oily hair.

Again, she hummed the lullaby softly. The frost giant's head turned toward her and watched her with wide expressive eyes, filled with despair but grateful for any hint of compassion.

His massive hand reached out with a finger extended, almost in curiosity. Revna froze, forcing herself not to cower back. The finger, the size of a sausage, traced the chain just visible about her neck.

Revna reached inside her tunic and drew out the pendant.

"This," she said, "is my son's hair."

The giant's head shifted. A large watery eye rolled up toward Revna.

Her finger touched the glass, wishing she could stroke the lock of hair trapped inside. She kissed the pendant before tucking it back inside her shirt. Then she looked back up at the frost giant with a smile meant to be reassuring.

"I will not leave you behind." Revna brushed a lock of hair from the giant's face and then went to the ladder, climbing up to the cabin to hunt for a key.

She flipped the thin mattress off the bed, running her hands over all the blankets and furs. The stench turned her stomach. She found a chest full of clothes, many of them silk and obviously imported through Araland. They were more suited to those kind and temperate lands than the heartless icy north, but they were luxurious and gaudy, two things Erland Ulfsson valued most.

After every piece of silk or ermine or velvet had been handled, after every inch of the rough wooden bulkheads had been scoured, after every dark overhead beam had been scanned, Revna turned back to the treasure chest. She knelt in front of it and dug in with both hands. Gold and silver and jewels spilled over the deck next to her. When she touched the garish opal ring once again, she threw it venomously across the cabin so she didn't have to look at it. Finally Revna's hands scrabbled across the bottom of the chest, scattering the last few coins and gems. No key.

Voices from outside. A horn blaring. Feet pounding the deck.

Revna leapt up. Erland Ulfsson had returned. She still had time to grab a few coins or gems and escape. She glanced at the hatchway in the deck.

She slipped into the shadows next to the door, partially hidden by a tapestry. She listened to the shouts of welcome.

The door swung open. Erland Ulfsson called out to someone behind him, his voice clear and sickening in Revna's ears, "There will be no inspections, as I knew. Jarl Singandr was pleased with my sweet words. Be ready to sail with the morning tide." As he entered the cabin, he muttered to himself, "We will be well shed of that fool."

The door closed. He shrugged off his heavy fur cloak with a groan of fatigue. Erland was alone.

With one quick step, Revna was behind him, her dagger to his throat.

"Don't speak!" she whispered. "Or you die."

Erland was taller than Revna by nearly a foot and much broader. Even so, he froze in stunned surprise. She drew a gem-encrusted dagger from his belt and tossed it across the cabin. She ran her hands over his tunic and then yanked a leather purse off his belt. Revna held the purse up in front of Erland and quickly took the knife away from his throat to slice the leather cord tying the bag. She put the blade back to his flesh before he could react.

Revna emptied the purse's contents onto the deck and used one foot to spread the coins around. No key.

"Who—" Erland began.

"Quiet!" Revna's dagger drew blood and brought a hushed gasp. "Don't test me. I'm content to loot your blubbery corpse."

She stretched her hand around him and ripped open his tunic. The sensation of his soft flesh caused her to shudder with horrific memories. She touched a thin chain hanging around his neck, grasped it, and pulled it roughly over his head, leaving a satisfying red welt.

Dangling from the chain was an iron key.

"This vessel is crawling with my men," Erland snarled over his shoulder. "Whatever you're thinking, you'll never get away."

"I got away before." Revna shoved him into the cabin wall.

Erland spun, hands flailing, expecting her to come for him with the dagger. When he saw her keep her distance, he stopped. Then he stared. Her features had aged, she knew, and her face was raw and red from the icy swim, but recognition did slowly come over him. The stunned disbelief in his eyes was worth all the effort.

"Pernilla?" he whispered.

Revna tasted bile, but she smiled. "I don't go by that name now."

"You've gotten old," Erland said.

"You look the same," Revna replied. "Still fat like a bloated walrus."

Erland glowered at her and gestured to the scattered treasure on the deck. "You were pawing through my things?"

Revna laughed bitterly.

"Why would you . . . wait." Erland eyed her with realization. "*You're* the thief of Korjengard? My agents told me how goods go missing here. That's been you? That's what you've become? You have lowered yourself to stealing from me?"

"I don't consider it *lowering* myself to use a fraction of your wealth for good."

"That's pathetic. I gave you everything." Erland noted her wet clothes. "Gods, you swam out here? I always knew you were unbalanced, but I didn't think you were stupid. How did you get on board without anyone seeing you?"

Revna had known for years about the secret entry where Erland had stolen goods and illicit women brought to his cabin. However she preferred to leave it all a mystery, letting him wonder.

"Let's don't dwell on my skills," she said. "I'm here to free the frost giant you've chained below."

"The frost giant?" Erland squinted in disbelief. "You've been driven insane by hatred of me. If you free that frost giant, you will die. Many others will die too, if you care about that. Those things are remorseless monsters, every one of them." He shook his head. "Stop your foolishness, Pernilla. You don't care about that frost giant. You just want to punish me. Surely there's something here you'd prefer. Your old wedding band is in here. Maybe you'd like that? It is quite valuable, you may remember."

"No, thank you." Revna motioned him toward the hatchway in the deck. "I'm just now getting over the queasiness from wearing it all those years."

"Do you imagine that you and that thing," Erland said, "will just swim away to freedom? How do you even know the creature can swim?"

"Then you will have your boat run aground so we can step off like decent folk. This night will end one of two ways. The frost giant will be free of you." Revna pointed the dagger. "Or you will be dead."

"By the gods, Pernilla, I don't know what sort of deranged play-acting you've been doing here in Korjengard," Erland put his hands on his wide hips, "but I assure you, I do not fear your childish threats. I know you."

"You didn't even know me when we were married, but the difference between then and now is, then, I only *wanted* to gut you. Now I *will*."

"If you are accused of theft," Erland summoned an authoritative voice, "the best you can hope for is banishment. Your life is in my hands."

Revna responded with a derisive snort. "You'll never see the jarl or anyone else if I wish it."

A weight thudded hard onto her shoulder. Something spun her to a face of half metal and half hair with dark empty eyes. A strong hand slapped the dagger out of her grip, sending it skittering across the deck. A towering swordsman gripped Revna as shadowy eyepieces sought out Erland for instructions.

"Don't hurt her," Erland ordered. "Close the door."

The swordsman half-turned to the cabin door. Revna hit his arm and lunged away. She heard fabric ripping and felt a tug at her throat. She ran for the hatchway into the hold. She didn't make it.

She crashed face first onto the wood. She was flipped onto her back. The swordsman held the tip of his sword a few inches above her throat.

Revna's pendant dangled from the swordsman's left hand. She instinctively clutched at her throat. Her tunic was torn from when she escaped him.

Erland appeared above her, gloating and victorious as if he'd had something to do with her capture. He pulled the key from Revna's hand.

"Accept fate for once in your life, Pernilla." Erland held out his hand to his bodyguard and took the pendant. He read the name inscribed on the edge with his mouth open. His eyes sank with surprising emotion.

"Manni," he whispered.

"Don't say his name!" Revna roared. "You don't have that right!"

"He was my son too." Erland's flabby face grew red. "You don't own the grief."

"You miserable cur," Revna said through clenched teeth. "You sent him to die!"

"He was doing his duty to me." Erland knelt beside some of the treasure on the deck, sifting through it and returning it to the chest. "Something he obviously didn't learn from his mother."

"You sent him across the sea to meet the Bear Folk while you stayed behind because you knew the danger. You knew he wasn't prepared. You knew he couldn't control your mercenaries. It went wrong just as everyone told you it would. Manni was killed in a fight he couldn't prevent! My boy died alone and far from home because you are a coward!"

The swordsman shifted his empty gaze from Revna to Erland.

"You're the coward," Erland told her. "Crawling around in the dark! Stealing from me." He scooped another pile of treasure and dropped it in the chest. "You sit here in your filthy clothes pretending you care about children when you ran away instead of giving me another son."

Revna exploded up from the deck. The swordsman pushed her down with his boot. She screamed and spat, tearing at the mercenary's leg.

"Calm down, Pernilla," Erland said over her shouting. He dug deep in the refilled treasure chest, searching for something, growing concerned. "Because you disappeared without having the decency to divorce me, I had to ask the jarl to dissolve our union so I could marry again and have a legitimate heir. But that jackass refused because he blamed me for the misunderstanding with the Bear Folk. He's so jealous of my wealth."

"I understand you now," Revna said. "I'll divorce you. You'll be free to marry again and sire a new one of you. I won't even ask for any of your precious wealth, which is my right, but I do have one condition."

Erland paused his sifting of treasure to listen.

"Free the frost giant chained below," Revna said. "Return him to his homeland and I will leave you free to marry again and create a legitimate heir."

Erland stared at her, considering her words.

"No," he said.

Revna tried not to show her surprise. She had dealt with his mercurial nature enough to know he never gave in if he thought he could gain more.

"Why?" Revna tried to assume a posture to argue, but the edge of the sword brushed her neck. She settled back. "How could that frost giant mean more to you than securing an heir and humiliating me in a single blow?"

"Where is it?"

Revna scowled at him, unable to grasp his question. Why was he being so obtuse? Was it just to annoy and exasperate her?

"Search her," Erland commanded.

The swordsman knelt on Revna's stomach. He ran his hands over her legs, shoving clothes aside, squeezing along her ribs. He felt a small bulge in her tunic and dug into a pocket. He held up the small silken bag.

Erland snatched it and opened the bag, pulling out the golden signet ring with a sigh of relief. He went to return it to the treasure chest, but thought better of it.

"Why did you take this piece in particular?" Erland slipped the bag into his silken robe. "Why not something far more valuable?"

"The north in bondage," Revna whispered through clenched teeth.

Erland squinted at her. "You can read. What does that prove?"

"It proves you're bound for Araland," Revna continued. "I know you. You would only leave your warm home for something earth shattering. You're taking your gaudiest vessel and you've brought all this gold and these jewels as gifts for some chief of that green land. That ring and that poor child chained are prizes too. Another chance for you to use a child for your own gutless benefit."

"A child? You soft-headed idiot. That thing is a monster and it practices the worst of dark magic. Even a pup like that could turn the blood in your veins to ice with a touch."

Erland took a large jug from the floor and poured mead into a glass horn. "Only the greatest of men would dare take a frost giant on a journey by boat surrounded by the sea! But I've made sure that monster is well away from water or wet timbers." He raised the horn to Revna. "That creature won't be my only living gift to the lords of

Araland now. When we were wed, I tried to teach you the simple fact of life that a person can choose to live in silks or in chains. You made your choice. So you may spend the voyage chained below with the monster."

"You no longer care about an heir?"

Erland smiled a unique smile, one that showed he did indeed know something no one else knew.

"After you ran away from me," he said, "I tried to find a way to undo the terrible thing you did to me, until I realized there was another way. A better way. I no longer require your divorce or your death. I will no longer need the jarl's blessing because his word won't resound much longer. A ruler with a wiser head will speak soon."

"No." Revna realized with disbelief the boldness of what Erland was planning in the twisted recesses of his mind. "You can't possibly intend to pay some warlord in Araland to attack your own homeland and overthrow the jarl? And replace him with who?"

Erland smiled at her.

"No." Revna gasped. She hadn't quite reached the depth of his audacity after all. "You? You think you can make yourself the jarl of jarls? Even you can't be that selfish and greedy. Or that insane."

"The jarl wronged me!" Erland screeched. He grasped the pommel of the pristine sword leaning next to his untouched armor. He drew the blade awkwardly and pointed it at Revna. "Only a great man such as I can prevent our frail and wasted leaders from withering the glory of Norrøngard! I'm saving our land. If I can use the wise men of Araland to do it, what's so wrong with that? I built an empire and it must continue unbroken! You can't understand that. You never created anything."

Revna glowered pure inexpressible hate.

Erland let the point of the sword drop to the deck. "My only wish is that Manni could be here to see you like this, and laugh."

Revna slammed a fist into the swordsman's groin and the pressure from his knee left her. She leapt to her feet. Erland shuffled back in stunned surprise. Revna roared at him, kicking the sword blade aside. She grabbed him by the tunic and pushed him against the wall. She had no dagger in her hand or she would have driven it into his stomach. Instead, she smashed Erland's head against the wall, taking savage pleasure in his terrified eyes and helpless soft flesh rippling under hands grown hard and strong in the years since she left him.

"Enough now, valkyrja," the swordsman groaned, taking Revna by the shoulder and pulling her off Erland.

Revna shrugged off the swordsman's hand and snatched the dagger in his belt before he could register surprise. She swung at Erland who cowered with a terrified hiss.

Revna didn't take time to relish his cowardice. She grabbed a jug of mead and ran for the hatchway. She raised the earthen jug over her head and hurled it into the hold. It crashed in the darkness below. Revna turned around and dropped the dagger.

She smiled.

"She's insane." Erland pushed off the wall, recovering his manhood now that his armed guard stood between him and Revna.

From down in the hold came sharp pops like snapping twigs. Frigid air rushed up Revna's back. The faint snaps became loud cracks that shot the length of the boat as if great trees were breaking in a silvery forest under the embrace of an ice storm.

"What's that noise?" Erland shouted. "What's happening?"

"Witch of Lotharr," the swordsman murmured. "Daughter of the Trickster. The mead. She helped the giant use his dark magic."

The boat shuddered. Planks buckled. The heavy chest tilted forward. Coins and rings and gems poured across the deck. Some of the loot slipped through the cracks into the hold. Erland scrambled to collect loose treasure.

"Help me!" Erland shouted at his bodyguard.

The boat listed. The swordsman scraped up a handful of coins and gems. He staggered to the cabin door and threw it open, stumbling out into the panic on the main deck.

Revna ran up behind Erland where he scrambled on his hands and knees for his treasure. Her fingers slid around his throat until she felt the small chain again. She snapped it, holding the key in her hand.

Shoving Erland to the deck, Revna ran to the hatchway and leapt in. She fell into shallow water flaked with ice.

The frost giant sat up with both hands under the water. His focus was beyond her, beyond this world, into whatever realm magic came from. Every ounce of energy and attention went into his magic.

His voice was loud now as he chanted, "Skapa kaldr skapa kaldr skapa kaldr," over and over.

Ice crept up the curved hull from every spot water seeped in. It moved like a living thing, growing along the edges of the wood, driving planks farther apart.

The moisture from the mead that Revna gave him provided enough to start an ice wedge in the seams of the hull. Once that first leak let water seep through, he had all the power he needed to work the ice magic that frost giants were fabled for. Revna wondered if he was able to snap the chains or crack the planks with the chain brackets.

No matter. He was focused on his magic and the water was rising. Revna had sought to key to free him. Now she had it and she intended to do what she planned.

"I'm going to free you," Revna announced though he likely didn't hear her.

The sound of cracking wood heightened through the hold as the giant drove more ice wedges between planks. Water gushed in torrents. The boat listed farther off its keel.

"You!"

Sharp pain sliced Revna's shoulder followed by a flash of fire inside her muscles. She rolled forward and landed against the frost giant who was as immobile as a statue.

Erland crouched at the top of the steps, his elaborate sword now tipped with her blood. His gaze focused on her alone, and there was a cruel simplicity to his intent that Revna had seen before.

"After all I did for you!" Erland managed to hold the sword straight. "I've always been too kind. It's time to be rid of you."

Revna fought through water to the bracket where one of the chains was fixed to the hull. Her shoulder burned from the stab wound. She fumbled with the heavy lock, trying to insert the iron key. The key shivered with her hand and then slipped into the keyhole with a soft clank. She worked to keep her footing as she turned the key.

Revna heard a loud grunt on her right. She ducked. A sword flashed past her head and sank into the frosted hull. She turned her head to see Erland pull the sword free and draw it back, tensing his flabby muscles to drive the blade through her.

A massive shape enveloped Erland. He started to scream, but his breath was locked in his chest. The frost giant dragged Erland away from Revna. He managed to gouge a deep wound in the giant's arm with the sword. The giant let out a ferocious roar, shoving Erland under the water and backing away, cradling his wounded arm.

The boat lurched roughly to the other side. Revna tumbled through the water until she rammed against the ladder. The water was up to her chest. The boat was sinking fast at the stern. She prepared to push off to the other bracket when she saw her left hand was empty.

"I lost the key," Revna gasped.

Floating debris slammed against her and she barely kept a grip on the ladder.

"Can you free yourself?" Revna called out to the giant with water lapping at her chin. "Can you break the chain?"

The frost giant pointed to the hatchway over her head.

"Go," he rasped.

"No!" Revna shook her head. "I won't leave you."

The giant took hold of her with the free arm that Revna had unlocked. His other arm extended behind him, still chained to the bulkhead. He pushed her up the ladder. Revna had to climb to keep from being scraped along the steps by his great strength.

She rose from the hatch and dropped onto the sloped broken deck of the cabin. The frost giant's face filled the hatchway, slipping in and out of the splashing dark water.

"No!" Revna screamed. "Let me help you!"

"Go," the frost giant gurgled at her.

The boat wallowed over. Water geysered from the hatch and when it settled, the giant was gone.

Revna lunged for the hatchway, but she was startled by the appearance of another face. Erland's head emerged from the water. He gulped, wide-eyed, nearly purple.

"Save me, Pernilla!" Erland thrust out his hand. "You owe me!"

Revna reached for him.

Large fingers curled over Erland's face like a weird spider. The giant hand closed on Erland's head and pulled him under.

The cabin surrounding Revna buckled inward with a roaring crunch. Water poured in great black torrents sweeping furniture and armor and treasure like trash in a storm. The flood bashed Revna, submerging her weak and helpless in the current.

She couldn't tell up from down. She had no idea where the surface was or how far. Her chest felt as if it would explode. Her hands swept through endless water. She was in the uncaring grip of eternity.

It would be so simple to relent to the power of the water, to draw the cold into her lungs. Maybe the gods would be merciful to her, forgive her thefts, let her slip peacefully out of this world so she could wake to see Manni again.

Then the stars appeared.

Revna opened her mouth, gasping in air and water, coughing and spitting. She flailed her arms and kicked her feet. The world righted itself. Distant lights were not Valhöll, but the harbor of Korjengard. In the distance, the prow of *Pernilla* slowly sank out of sight, leaving the surface of the water crowded with crates and masts and sails and rope, and men screaming, shouting, swimming for their lives.

Revna didn't have the strength to stroke for the harbor. She could barely manage to stay afloat while the current took her. Perhaps the gods would have her after all.

No. The will of the gods be damned. Revna would have to see her son another day. She fought the current. Her arms numb except for the fiery pain deep in her shoulder where she had been stabbed, she pulled the water. Inch by dreadful inch, she hauled herself away from rocks that would kill her and toward welcoming sand.

Revna's hand hit something. Her legs scraped earth. She struggled onto her knees, grasping handfuls of sand, dragging herself out of the water to collapse on dry land.

She lay breathing. She stared along the shoreline at the dirt and scrub plants, listening to the water lapping behind her.

Footsteps crunched nearby, but Revna didn't move. She couldn't. Someone knelt beside her. A heavy hand fell on her back. Another hand curled under her and gently turned her over.

The frost giant knelt beside her. Water drained from his tangled hair. When he saw she was alive, he smiled and grunted with a childish glee.

"You're alive?" Revna threw her arms partially around him. It was like embracing a mountain. He rumbled with what might have been laughter.

Revna pulled back, inspecting his wounded arm. The cut was deep but the blood was barely oozing now. Both of the giant's wrists were manacled. One chain ended in an empty loop. The other stretched to a bracket attached to a chuck of broken timber.

The frost giant settled onto the rocky beach next to her. He was exhausted near to death. Revna reached up to her neck for her pendant.

Revna remembered that Erland took it. It was gone. Her last piece of Manni lost.

Revna hung her head, too exhausted to cry. She sat next to the frost giant in silence.

"I'd like to help you get back to your home," Revna finally said.

The giant didn't react. He stared out over the fjord as if she hadn't spoken. She leaned on her upraised knees with a sigh.

An object appeared in front of her face. It sparkled in the moonlight. A silver pendant with a lock of hair in glass.

Revna gasped and took it. The frost giant stared down at her.

"Your son?" he said.

"Yes." Tears burned in Revna's eyes. She kissed the pendant. "Thank you."

The young frost giant huffed with satisfaction.

"Home?" he said.

"Home," she replied.

The chain was broken, so Revna held the pendant against her heart.

CLAY AND SUSAN GRIFFITH are the co-authors of historical fantasy such as the VAMPIRE EMPIRE series and the CROWN & KEY trilogy, plus superhero tie-in fiction *The Flash: The Haunting of Barry Allen* and *Arrow: A Generation of Vipers*. They have also written comic books including *The Tick*, *Kolchak: The Night Stalker*, and *Disney's Beauty and the Beast*. Visit them online at www.clayandsusangrif fith.com, on Facebook at clayandsusangriffith, and on Twitter @clayandsusan.

THE BUTTER CAT

RACHAEL SMITH

PART ONE

The stars in the huge night sky were twinkling brighter than ever, as the skald and the butter cat trudged the last few snowy yards to the broadside of Stolki's Hall. The dimly audible sounds of laughter coming from bellies full of sausage, cheese, sourdough, and mead made the two friends keen to get inside, but they were both aware that tonight's activity was not something to be rushed.

The skald leant his weary bones against the tavern wall and sunk down dramatically into a seated position in the snow.

"C'mere, old friend. I need to sort those flowers out."

The butter cat sidled toward him and lay down gratefully against his leg, looking up at its master with dull gray button eyes. The skald began to pluck several, withered brown flowers out of the tangled webs of yarn that made up the cat's body.

"This'll be the last tavern tonight, cat, I promise. Provided I can charm the barkeep into letting us kip on the benches, we may even be able to sleep indoors tonight."

The worn-out flowers were tossed into the frozen winds, and the skald carefully took a folded handkerchief out of his belt pouch.

"Managed to pinch some cornflowers from behind that farm we 'borrowed' lunch from yesterday...these should help with the smell for a few more days, eh?"

The skald had no way of knowing this: but the butter cat loved these moments more than anything in the world, and the flowers which the skald wove into its woolly fur were its most treasured of treasures. This changing of the flowers had become their weekly routine, ever since the butter cat had defied all odds and gone on existing past its one-day life expectancy. Out in the cold icy air of Norrøngard, it was fine, but indoors, this six-month old butter cat didn't tend to smell all that great.

Finishing with the flowers, the skald fished his lyre out of his bag and began polishing it with the now-empty handkerchief. The butter cat sat up straight and strained its neck around to admire its new decorations.

"Do you think it sounds more like a sing-song crowd, or a poetry crowd in there, friend?" asked the skald. The butter cat had no way of answering, but the skald never seemed to mind this. The cat merely looked at him, with what it hoped was an intense and serious expression. The skald laughed, kindly. "I agree! A few boisterous songs would offer some good distraction for you to sneak behind the bar and steal us some milk, yes? I might even get some coins tossed to me in the process."

The butter cat stood up obediently and lifted up its limp, yarn tail as high as it could manage. It was always happiest when the skald gave it a job to do, and it was always keen to get it done quickly. "Woah there, friend," chuckled the skald, "let me get this thing tuned first."

So the butter cat sat back down and patiently listened to each string of the lyre be coaxed into tuneful harmony.

"You go on lasting so long as I still have a quest for you, eh, cat?

Hopefully, someday I won't need to exist on stolen milk anymore and you can retire to the High Father's dairy parlor."

The skald laughed softly, and the butter cat put a tiny paw on his knee. The cat wasn't sure what a High Father's dairy parlor was, but it was certainly sure that it didn't ever want to go anywhere without its master.

The skald finished tuning and the two friends brushed themselves down, ready to enter the mead hall. The butter cat clambered up onto the skald's shoulder, and the skald threw the doors open.

They were greeted with an exuberant and rowdy crowd of farmers, fishers, and hunters, drinking, eating, hollering, but most importantly, *betting* on a flyting match that was underway in the middle of the hall.

A common farmhand was half-sitting-half-lying on top of a table and a wealthy-looking scholar was pacing drunkenly, yet defiantly, in circles around him. They were throwing rhyming quips at one another which were getting ruder by the minute, much to the crowd's delight. A rotund merchant wearing a heavy coin bag and obviously taking charge of the bets, was watching the match with calculated disinterest.

The skald turned to the butter cat and whispered, slowly:

"Your plan hasn't changed – but mine has. If I can win this thing, we'll be rolling in coin! To the bar with you. I'll whistle for you when I'm done."

So the butter cat jumped silently off the skald's shoulder onto a nearby table, and, as the skald approached the merchant to ask if he could take the winner, it scarpered away.

Meandering quickly around furniture and the legs of drunken patrons, the butter cat soon found the large bar, and crept behind.

The bar concealed a cacophony that was quite different from that of the flyting matches: Stolki's staff were almost falling over one another piling up dirty drinking horns and searching vainly for clean ones, orders were becoming muddled up and spilled, pieces of fruit, cheese, and bread were falling from huge platters as the folk carrying them struggled to get around each other. The butter cat squeezed into a cubby hole full of old, discarded bottles, and waited until it could see more clearly.

A harried looking woman bustled behind the bar, her arms full of dirty horns.

"That table of Karls are *still* waiting on their horsemeat!"

"What do you want *me* to do about that, you old bag?! Talk to the folk working the fire pit!"

"*They* told me they were waiting on *you* to give them—"

"*A new challenger for the scholar!*"

This announcement from the hall caused many of the staff behind the bar to forget themselves and drop whatever jobs they were doing to prop themselves up on the bar counter-top to stand up taller in order to see the newcomer.

"It's a skald! He's challenging that clever drunk fella!"

"He's quite dishy! He's got a lovely face."

"A lovely bum too...!"

"You're terrible!"

Now that the back of the bar area had been cleared of people, the butter cat could see the cold slab in the corner, housing the dairy products and–*ja!*–five jugs of milk. It made its move. Jumping between hanging metal pans it carefully made its way over to the other side of the bar. Once from atop a frying pan it saw a mouse run across the floor, but immediately turned its head away from it–this was no time to get distracted. It had a quest to complete.

"Ooh I really don't like that drunk one," the staff continued.

"I wish he'd stop stopping the match every two seconds."

"Yes. If you think someone's stolen a rhyme then wait until the end, surely?"

"Oh, what do *you* know?"

"I know *plenty!*"

The butter cat was within reach of the cold slab, but it would have nothing to hide behind once it was there. It would need to be quick. The bickering from the staff gave it courage, and it pounced.

Once on the slab the cat sank its head into the jugs of milk, magically emptying them into its yarn body, which bulged slightly and whitened with the creamy liquid. The cat managed to empty three of them before three things happened:

The skald cried out in pain, the kitchen maids screamed all at once, and a scuffle broke out in the main hall as someone was roughly apprehended.

"He's stabbed him!" shouted one of the staff.

The butter cat, forgetting all its stealth and careful vigilance, jumped down from the cold slab, and dashed straight across the straw-covered floor, in plain sight of everyone, to its master, and brought a gentle paw, worriedly to his face. The master looked at the cat and smiled.

"Things haven't gone to plan, cat. I'm sorry."

Stolki himself, having just arrived with two huge, freshly baked loaves of sourdough, had already taken charge of the situation.

"A healer will be sent for. Is there anyone who can help this man in the meantime?"

"I...I don't think we should *move* him," ventured one of the staff, shyly.

"Very well. Get him a drink then."

Two farmers were holding the drunk scholar and the offending dagger had been taken away from him.

"He used *two* lines from the famous Saislander playwright *Wilhelm Wavepole!*" cried the scholar, "The penalty for plagiarism in a flyting match is *death!*"

"That's...abso*lu*tely not true." sighed Stolki, pinching the bridge of his nose.

A tankard of mead was brought for the skald, but he was only interested in talking to his cat.

"Goodbye, my gentle friend."

Its master was saying goodbye. This didn't make sense to the butter cat, who had no intention of leaving him. It reacted by nuzzling the skald's cheek with its wet nose. Milk still on its whiskers brushed off onto the skald's face. Its master grinned, then grimaced.

"Go, my friend, go seek the milk of *human kindness* instead."

The butter cat realized that blood was pooling around its feet.

"*The milk of human kindness* is also a Wavepole adage!" spat the scholar, prompting Stolki to whack him about the head.

The skald laughed, bitterly.

"What an absolutely stupid way to die."

And his eyes closed for the last time.

The butter cat panicked. Its master was dead. It had a quest to complete. Yet it couldn't bring itself to leave.

Silence fell over the crowded hall as patrons and staff alike squeezed together to look at the dying skald. Then, the harried staff member asked:

"What should we do with his little butter cat?"

"*That's* a butter cat?! It's the mangiest thing I've ever seen! Toss it to the hounds! They like milk, don't they?"

"Perhaps we should give it to the Jarl...or the healer...as evidence?"

"Well, whatever we do with it, it can't stay here," said Stolki, "It'll stink up the place! 'Ere, boy, grab it for us, would you?"

The butter cat saw the young boy approach it but couldn't move. Its master was dead. It had a quest to complete...but its master was dead. It put a paw to the skald's already cooling face. This couldn't be happening. The boy, unsure of how to hold a stringy butter cat, clumsily grabbed at the wool around the cat's neck with his right hand. It came away loosely, so he quickly went to scoop it up with his left hand. The butter cat snapped out of its stupor. It would have to leave the master. And it would rather leave on its own terms. It had a quest to complete! It couldn't complete this quest if it were ripped to pieces by hounds! The boy yelped as the butter cat twisted itself out of his grasp.

"Stupid boy!"

"Catch it!"

"Argh! Wretched little thing!"

The butter cat was too quick for them all, and it nimbly jumped from floor to table to support beam and fled through a ceiling smoke hole into the frosty night air.

PART TWO

The butter cat awoke under a trestle table, next to a box full of cheese. Cheese was no good to it; it could only steal milk. All around, the butter cat could hear the sounds of a market being set up for the day's sales: sleepy "good mornings" and "how do you fares," stacking of pottery, glass, and metal goods, and prices being scribbled hastily onto wooden cut-offs. It wondered about venturing out from under the table but decided to gather its thoughts first.

Its master was dead. There had been a part of the butter cat that had assumed it would die when its master did. That had not happened. The butter cat looked down at its red-stained paws. If it had been able to sigh, then it would have done so at this moment.

Its master had also given it a final quest which the cat felt duty-bound to complete, but what did "the milk of human kindness" mean? Was it as simple as finding a human who was kind to it? Surely that would be easy! The skald had always been very kind to the butter cat. There must be plenty of humans like him. Encouraged, the butter cat crept out from under the tablecloth and, its button eyes shining in the sunlight, looked about for friendly humans. It was immediately hit with a broom.

"Ugh! What *is* that thing! Get away! Shoo!"

An elderly man was holding a precarious tower of cheese with one hand and manhandling a broom with the other. He looked very angry at the butter cat's presence. An elderly woman gently took the cheese from him and set it on the table.

"Looks like a butter cat, love. A very old one. Don't fret—they only steal milk. It won't want any of our stuff."

"Well it needs to go away! Scabby old thing's making the cheese smell off!"

The old man took a swing at the butter cat with the broom and narrowly missed it. The old woman frowned.

"How do you make *cheese* smell *off*, love?"

"I dunno, but 'e was managing it!"

The butter cat decided to move on rather briskly, but it didn't have much luck with the other market stall holders either. People seemed offended at its smell, its appearance, or both. At one of the glass stalls it had an entire mirror thrown at it. The butter cat managed to roll out of the way as sparkling shards shot everywhere.

"Are you out of your mind!? What d'you do that for!?" the stall-owner's assistant cried.

"Just trying to get rid of *that* thing!" He gestured at the backside of the cat, bobbing up and down as it scarpered away. "We don't need any bad luck around here!"

"How d'you know it was unlucky?"

"Just *look* at the filthy, smelly thing! It's hardly lived a *charmed* life, has it?"

The butter cat ran away from the market and into the forest. It needed more time to think. Perhaps this wouldn't be so simple after all. Perhaps the skald was unusual in his kindness. Was kindness not a thing most humans had? Thinking back over the past day or so there hadn't really been much kindness displayed by the humans the cat had come across...Stolki had sent for a healer for its master and had a drink brought to him...but had then not cared that his staff wanted to toss the cat to the hounds! The butter cat stood up, defiantly, its tail high in the air. No. There must be humans out there just like its master, maybe they just didn't live in *this* place. The cat must travel to a *different* place–that was it. Simple.

And so the butter cat picked a direction, held its nose high, and, for several days, bravely marched through the forest all alone. Rainstorms helped to clean the red bloodstains from off of its little paws, but also made a great deal of mud, which stained them brown instead, and caked to its underbelly. Swathes of rosebushes helped to scrape the worst of the dried mud off the cat's body, but the thorny branches snagged on pieces of its yarn, leaving it tattered and frayed. A small herd of rabbits let the butter cat curl warmly up with them while they slept one night, but in the morning had eaten all but one of the cornflowers from out of the cat's fur. Nevertheless, the cat got through the forest mostly intact and more determined than ever to find the milk of human kindness. Signs to Korjengard started to crop up on the sides of dirt paths, and so the butter cat followed them. It sounded like a kind and welcoming place. *Korjengard.*

Korjengard had lots of market stalls too, but the butter cat avoided them. Market people were not kind, it reminded itself. There were also mead halls, just like the cat and the skald used to play music in, but the butter cat avoided these places too. No one in the last hall had been very kind either.

Instead, the butter cat headed toward the farmlands. Perhaps humans that already looked after animals would naturally take kindly to an animal-like creature, it thought. Turning a corner past a barn full of cows, the butter cat ran into the legs of a young girl, tripping her over, causing her to drop the big bag she was carrying. The butter cat looked in shock as a dead fox and two dead beavers tumbled out of it.

"Be careful, girl!" A voice boomed behind them. The butter cat and the girl looked up to see a large, elegantly dressed man holding an ornately-carved bow. "I aim to sell the pelt of that fox! It'll do no good to scuff it up on this filthy ground!"

"Forgive me, Sir." said the girl, carefully scooping the animals back in the bag, "I tripped over this little cat...the fox looks fine to me." she added, nervously.

"When I want the expertise of a *thrall* I shall ask for it. A cat you say? You mean *this* thing?" The man prodded the butter cat with the end of his bow and laughed. "What's it doing out here?"

The butter cat sat up smartly, curled its tail around itself, lifted one paw by way of greeting, and looked up at the man with what it hoped was a friendly expression. This caused the man to roar with laughter.

"This thing is deranged!" he howled. "The magic on it has gone wrong, I warrant. Let's take it with us–it amuses me." And he walked on in front, leaving the thrall to collect the cat.

"Um." the girl, like the boy at Stolki's Mead Hall, was unsure how to pick up the butter cat, but the cat, eager to be taken home with this friendly-seeming man, helpfully climbed up onto her shoulder. The girl coughed at the smell but righted herself momentarily. "Right...Okay," she said, and like that, they walked home.

The man's home was within the harbor district, and so protected by 30-foot-high walls that the butter cat found very imposing. It was a grand longhouse, the biggest the butter cat had ever seen, but, other than the young girl, the man appeared to live there alone. The butter cat was also confused about the sleeping arrangements: the girl did not seem to have any personal space of her own and, for some reason, appeared to sleep in the hay with the cows in a small animal pen, despite there being plenty of benches in the longhouse she could have made a comfortable bed on. The man spent much of his time in a sectioned off area on the other side of the house. The butter cat wondered if the girl simply liked the cows.

Despite these little puzzlements, the cat was very pleased to have been invited into a human's home. Surely this was a step in the right direction to completing his master's quest. This man was certainly the kindest human it had come across so far. When it next saw him, the cat would try its best to be "amusing" for him, and perhaps then he will be granted some kindness. For now though, the man was resting in his sectioned-off area, and the girl and the cat were sitting at a large wooden table near the fire pit in the center of the longhouse.

The girl had opened a bottle of red wine and sat a glass next to it on the table. She noticed the butter cat watching her.

"Do you...understand me?" she asked.

The butter cat nodded.

"It's not for me, the wine, I mean. The master likes it to breathe in the bottle for a time before he drinks it."

The butter cat nodded, slowly. It was as if she was scared her actions would be misconceived.

"It's very expensive. An extravagance, really. The master usually drinks mead. He made a lot of money last week from selling fox pelts," the girl explained. The cat nodded again, it made no difference to the cat what was being drunk, but it listened politely all the same.

The young girl was now skinning the fox. She had removed the legs at the joints and was methodically peeling back the skin, revealing red and pink flesh. She sighed, looked over to the man's room, then, in a very low voice said:

"It would be nice to have someone here to talk to...but I would leave if I were you. I only stay here because I have to. He owns me, you know?"

The butter cat looked at her, wanting her to go on.

"He's just...after he's had his rest...after hunting...he's often in a bad mood. I wouldn't stay here...if I didn't have to..."

A tear had, out of nowhere, appeared on the girl's cheek and she went to wipe it away with her hand, then realized her hands were covered in the fox's blood. Instead, she awkwardly rubbed her face into her elbow. The butter cat didn't fully understand but could see that something had upset the girl. It hoped it hadn't been something it had done...or not done. The cat reached its head around its body. By the time the girl had cleared her eyes of tears, she saw that there was a single cornflower waiting for her on the table. It wasn't much, thought the butter cat, but it was all that it had. The girl picked up the flower and, after admiring it for a second, shyly put it in her hair, just above her ear. The cat was rewarded with a thin smile, which lasted less than a second. But it was something.

Suddenly, the man crashed noisily through the room partition and stomped over to the fire pit, holding his bow with one hand and clutching a bunch of arrows with the other.

"Right!" he commanded, "Let's see how fast this deranged little cat can move!"

And with that, the man clumsily notched an arrow and shot at the cat, who darted out of the way at the last moment.

"Pretty damn fast!" laughed the man, notching another arrow.

"I, um…I've almost skinned the fox. The fur is very soft, come see…" mumbled the thrall girl, in an effort to distract him from his horrible game. The man stumbled over to her and pulled her into an ungainly embrace.

"How's about I'll come see how soft *your* fur is later, *thrall?*" he slurred into her ear. He then noticed the tiny cornflower. "What is this!?" he ripped out the offending flower and crushed it in his hand. "Who gave you this!? Have you been out whoring!?"

"No, Sir! Of course not! You *know* I haven't!"

But the man's train of thought could not be stopped. He notched another arrow and aimed it at the girl, so close to her the arrow was almost touching her already. The butter cat looked on from the windowsill, in horror. This was all happening so quickly. What should it do?

"You belong to *me* and me *alone,* you whore!" the man hissed, then fell back as the butter cat threw itself at the back of his knee. The arrow flew diagonally, smashing the kitchen window. In shock and relief, the girl also fell back into the table. She tried to steady herself but her bloody hands slipped and knocked the bottle of wine all over the fox fur, ruining it. It was a step too far. The man's eyes bulged out of his face in anger. The cat couldn't tell if he was more angry about the fox or the wine. He was grasping on the floor for his arrows. If the girl didn't run now, he would kill her.

A flicker of movement at the window caught her eye. The butter cat was pushing the pieces of broken glass out for her. It had cut some of its yarn in the process, but it was still alive, still jumping up and down, still trying to help her. An arrow was shot just above the cat's head and then quickly another one, which cut through its ear.

"Run!" cried the girl.

The cat obeyed. It dived out of the window and ran. It had done all it could. It kept telling itself that.

The butter cat ran and ran until it came to a fjord, which it swam across, despite its exhaustion, very grateful for the opportunity to put a body of water between it and that evil man. Dragging itself heavily out of the water onto a stony beach, it lay down gratefully to rest and dry. As it rested, it thought of the young girl and hoped dearly that she had gotten away safely.

For two whole nights, the cat rested and regained a modicum of strength. Dry, brittle, tattered, but still alive, the butter cat stretched its tired wool limbs and wiped its face with a tiny paw. It tried to swallow down its disappointment about the man in Korjengard. It had thought its quest complete; that the man was a kind human. Instead, it had found the worst of the worst. It was also getting harder to stay determined. It was all out of flowers, and so smelled worse than ever, and its yarn fur was more tangled and tattered than ever before, the fur it still had left, that was—a lot of it was snagged on rosebushes or been pulled off on the arrow that pierced its ear. What would happen if it lost too much and came apart entirely? The cat tried not to think about that. But the only other thing to think about wasn't very nice either, specifically that finding a kind human now was going to be even harder, and it had already proved impossible.

No, thought the cat. It had a quest to complete. It had to keep going, for its master's sake. Its master would never have given up. The cold breeze and the slabs of ice on the water nudging the stony shore brought the cat back to the present: it was a fine day. Looking about itself, it saw it was near an old wooden dock, with a grand ship moored by it. A flash of movement told the cat there was someone working on the ship, so it padded down the dock toward the figure. As the figure's silhouette became clearer the cat stopped. It couldn't be...the man was the same height and build...could it really be the master? Back from the dead? But how? Had the cat's memories of him brought him back? The butter cat, had it been able to meow for joy, would have done so at this moment, as it ran toward the skald, as he climbed out of the ship onto the dock.

"What's this, then?" muttered the man, rubbing his head. The butter cat stopped running as its heart sank. It was not its master, only a man who looked remarkably like him. The skald had had a kind, friendly face and open-hearted demeanor, whereas this man looked closed and guarded, and as though he were haunted by something. He rubbed his head again and bent down to pick up a chisel from a small collection of tools laid out on a blanket on the side of the dock. "I've nothing for you if you're out begging for milk. Go back to the one who conjured you."

The butter cat's spirits raised, very slightly. This man wasn't his master, but he wasn't altogether bad. The cat could sense some gentleness in his voice. Was he a singer, a poet? Surely someone in the same line of work as its master could be capable of kindness? The butter cat took a few more steps toward the man.

"Argh! Be gone, foul-smelling creature!" the man bellowed, suddenly aware of the butter cat's unfortunate musk. He waved the chisel at the cat dismissively. "I have work to do! Let me be!"

In a final attempt to communicate friendship to the man, the butter cat pressed a tiny, woolly paw to the man's knee, looking up at him with intensity. The man sighed and went to push the cat away, but thinking better of it, picked it up instead.

"I already have one animal plaguing my life. I have no need of two!" And with that, the man threw the butter cat in a dizzyingly high arc right over the sail of his ship. It was a good throw, and the man actually felt in a much better mood after that.

The butter cat, however, was not in a good mood. It hit the water with such force that its yarn became dangerously loose and it very nearly lost itself entirely. It twisted around in the water to ravel up the remainder of its body and started to paddle clumsily in what it hoped was a direction toward land. With every desperate movement, the cat was reminded of how very, very tired it still was, and by the time it washed up on the shore it was almost unconscious.

A brown crab nibbling at the cat's tail brought it back to the here and now. It hauled itself to its feet and shooed the crab away with a paw. Dusk had set in, and the cat knew better than to be close to the water after dark, so it trudged slowly up the cold, soggy beach and up onto a wooden pier. Three fishers were starting to pack up their tools and the cat listened to them gossip and make plans for that evening's entertainment. As they walked by, the cat made an effort to sit up and looked at them hopefully. Perhaps one would take pity on such a pathetic looking creature and offer some kindness. Perhaps it could be that simple after all. The first fisher to walk by joked that they should kick the cat into the water. The second one tried to but missed. The third one just laughed. The butter cat pulled itself to the end of the pier, rested its head on the wet wood, and looked down into the black waters. It stayed there until night drew in.

The cat was so tired it knew it would never walk again. It had failed its final quest from its master. It no longer had any of its precious flowers, or even the red on his paws to remember him by. It had lost everything. A sea draugr had noticed the cat draped over the edge of the pier and was circling underneath, clearly wanting to pull the cat in. If that happened, the cat would surely become unraveled for good, and maybe for the best, the cat thought. And it pushed itself off into the water.

PART THREE

The butter cat felt the jaws of the draugr closing around it, and prepared itself for the ripping, tearing, scattering, and eventual, painful, tumultuous separating of its core into the dark, underwater world.

"Do you live?" a shrill, panting voice asked it.

The butter cat was not inside the jaws of a draugr, but instead was nestled in a pair of slender, girlish hands. It was also not in the water anymore; it could feel a soft, dry shawl draped over its head, and could hear soft waves lapping around the feet of the pier behind it.

"Oh, goodness, it *is* you! I'm so sure it is you! Please…be alive!"

The butter cat was very, very tired, but managed to look up at its rescuer, its button eyes still holding on to flecks of salty seawater. Shaking its head incredulously, the butter cat realized who it was: it was the young girl from the angry man's house. She was here. She had saved it. It wasn't possible.

"You live!" The girl laughed with joy and hugged the cat gently. "You saved me, you know. You saved my life. But, come…we must get you to the camp where you can warm up."

The butter cat felt a tug of shame, as it knew it couldn't possibly walk to a camp with this girl, as much as it wanted to, but then it became clear the girl intended to carry it in her shawl, and so the cat relaxed.

An hour or so later, the butter cat felt itself placed on a blanket, the warmth of a fire nearby fell comfortably on its frayed, tangled fur. Things were nicely fuzzy for the cat, at this moment, it felt people around it, and heard only snippets of what they were saying.

"– risked your life! For…for-what *is* that?!"

"–cat! the one I told you about!"

"–bit smelly isn't it? Looks *dead*-"

"Please, just for tonight? I really—"

"If you can do something about the smell, then—"

"Thank you!"

And so it was that the butter cat got to spend the night with the girl whom it had rescued only days before. As she untangled its fur and wove freshly picked buttercups into its body, she told the cat how, after she escaped the man, she found this group of völvur that had kindly let her stay with them while she figured out what to do next.

"I definitely do not want to go back to being a man's thrall. I am even thinking of training with the völvur to be a seeress! Imagine that! I'm very happy, cat."

Around them, the völvur sang songs and told stories and danced around the fire. Bread and stew and drinks were passed around, even a dish of milk was found for the butter cat, who did its best to look gratefully at its new friends. Late into the evening, the butter cat found the strength to lift its head so that it rested against the girl's leg. She reacted by lifting it gently onto her lap and spent the rest of the evening stroking it tenderly, being careful not to flatten its new decorative flowers.

The butter cat fell into a peaceful sleep, and when the girl looked down at her friend again, she didn't see a cat, but only a pile of yarn and two dull gray button eyes.

Not really knowing why, the girl turned her gaze from the butter cat's remains up to the huge night sky, where she noticed the stars twinkling brighter than ever above them all.

RACHAEL SMITH is an award-winning comic artist and writer. She has created many critically acclaimed graphic novels including *Quarantine Comix*, *Wired Up Wrong*, and *The Rabbit*. Rachael has worked for Titan, Image, Boom, and The New Yorker, among others. More information can be found at www.rachaelsmith.org.

THE TOWER AND THE RAVEN

J. DIANNE DOTSON

Hrafn Sjósson was a solitary man, known for his careful eyes, slate gray in color like the clouds before a winter storm; the eyes of a watchman, keen and alert at all times. For this, he held the position of sentinel in a watchtower overlooking the town below. It perched upon a high promontory on the far side of a fjord, where nothing could grow but for stubborn outcroppings of lichen. He held the town in his care, for his was the first watch from afar, and on a clear day (rare as they might be north and east of Wendholm), he could even see for miles in all directions. No one had better vision than Hrafn. He assumed his role in the tower as a volunteer. Any town would be so fortunate to have that quiet watch above, ready to light a beacon at a moment's notice.

But he was lonely. The ravens alone kept him company. He rarely interacted with town folk, only accepting the goods he kept on regular order in return for his silver. His words, to strangers, might come across as brusque. But to those few who knew him well—as well as anyone could, in his solitary existence, that is—his eyes could shift into a crinkled smile, and sometimes the thin mouth hiding in his fading ginger beard might curve upward as well. His laughter was rare but rich, and to bring it out of him brought joy to the few who could.

Friend to people and giants, avoided by trolls and haunts of the wood, he was reliable, loyal, stoic, and all the qualities one would want in a watcher. It might have been enough, the wind whistling about his tower, the ravens wheeling and dipping, sometimes landing, sometimes proffering their strong beaks for him to stroke. But sometimes he wanted more. And sometimes he missed a tale by a crackling fire in a mead hall, where he could lean back and watch the bustle and gaiety of a town, its locals and its wayfarers alike, with little interaction, but always with sharp eyes. He missed one particular brew; Dvergrian ale. Dvergrian ale was made by the dwarves in the Dvergrian Mountains, on the border of the neighboring country of Araland. This ale was highly prized, and the last time he'd had it was at Dragon's Dance.

Just now he gazed up at the heavy sky, as warm as it ever would be in the summer, but prone to rain showers, and spied Blárvængr, a raven of middle age. *Much like me*, he thought idly, as the great, sleek, blue-black bird dipped his wings and descended. With tiny, crisp flaps, Blárvængr landed next to him, and promptly lowered his head. Hrafn laughed softly and scratched the bird's head at the neck. The raven croaked, and extended his wings a bit, lifting his head upward; obligingly, Hrafn bent his head and touched the bird nose to beak. Blárvængr clicked and croaked.

But Blárvængr did not rely upon traditional raven speech alone; he was a remarkable bird that could speak as humans and frost giants could.

"What news of the air, friend Blárvængr?" asked Hrafn.

In his unique, rasping voice, Blárvængr said, "Snow is coming. But you did not need a raven to tell you that."

"Aye," said Hrafn.

"So is the anniversary of your hatching day, if the days are correct," remarked the bird.

Hrafn widened his eyes and exclaimed, "In a fortnight! But how would you know that, my friend?"

The raven ruffled its iridescent feathers, muted only by the dark clouds, yet no less striking. He said, "The shadows are the same, and the weather patterns, and all the things that you know, and some that we ravens understand that your kind cannot."

"So passes another year, soon, then," said Hrafn, and he sighed. "My bones tell me thus as well. I do not make the long walks to Dragon's Dance anymore.

The bird watched him with eyes sharper than those which brought him his renown and his position.

"What do you miss about the place?" Blárvængr asked him suddenly.

Hrafn's face twisted in surprise. He pulled his beard. "What a question! If a bit vague, friend Blárvængr. What do I miss about...what?"

"About your travels. It has been some time; we know this, as we keep our own watch and council."

Hrafn's thoughts darted immediately back to Dvergrian ale.

"Ah, a pint of the ale, the finest in all the land, the sea, and perhaps the halls themselves," mused Hrafn.

The bird clucked and grumbled in pure raven speech, and eventually flew off. Hrafn watched him go until he was out of sight; and given the strength of his vision, that was far away indeed. He felt a small stab of loneliness again and brushed it off, to scan the skies and gnaw upon a heel of bread in silence but for the swirling gusts about the tower.

Blárvængr wheeled and swooped and glided, by turns, battling the eddies of the changeable air flowing down from the mountains to the north. His blue-black feathers twitched and adjusted to each gust of wind. It would be a long flight, but he was well fortified. He spied with his dark eyes the ring forts of the humans below, which they called trelleborgs, and noted the sea to the south, the forests, and mountains to the north, and his ultimate destination lay beyond the horizon to the east: Dragon's Dance, where both humans and giants interacted; one of the only places where this happened publicly. Blárvængr did not fly there, however; he flew northeast and braced for the chill of the icy mountains. A raven can fly a long distance in a day, but all ravens must rest and eat. So, before he faced the challenge of the cold north, he swept down to the forest and spied a good place to roost: a tall pine, with fat nuts in its cones, just right to recover from the arduous flight. Tomorrow, his wings would carry him to the land of frost giants.

Late the next day, Blárvængr leaped from his roost and pumped his way skyward, away from the Raven's Wood. He wondered, in brief bemusement, how the great forest had been named after his kind. This was not something he had ever asked, as he did not concern himself with the names that the two-legged folk of the land came up with. He did, however, approve of the offerings for food in the tree-tops, such as fat pine nuts, and was glad for his wings, so that he did not encounter too many of the menaces beneath the canopy of tall firs and pines. He had heard plenty of tales of encounters with those kinds of creatures, and they rarely ended well.

He made the final stretch toward the Ymirian Mountain Range He was a keen fowl, keener than some. He beheld Gunnlod's Plateau and tilted his sleek wings into the cold north wind, beginning his descent.

Magnilmir retrieved some bottles of Dvergrian ale from his pantry and wrapped them carefully in rough-woven cloth. He had purchased a fair number of items, both food and drink, at Dragon's Dance, from a dwarf friend he traded with.

Magnilmir secured the bottles carefully in his pack, shouldered it, and left his home to set out on the journey to the far tower overlooking the fjord from the east. It was an arduous journey down the plateau, even on his long legs, to make it through the Raven's Wood. It would take several days but setting out now meant making it in good time...provided any obstacles he met did not divert him overly long. He would think about that when the time came to deal with it, for he knew that Raven's Wood teemed with all manner of creatures and spirits. And not all of them would avoid a frost giant, despite his impressive size.

And then there were the bandits...but no. He would not think of that just yet.

It felt good for Magnilmir to begin his trek. He felt light of spirit and looked forward to such a rare moment of simply traveling to see a friend. He spied Blárvængr launch from a tall fir tree, but the bird did not linger. It carried on and pumped its wings, presumably aiming for the fjord to the west. Magnilmir felt wistful for a moment, considering that it would have been nice to have the bird follow along. But he let that feeling go, and focused on his path, and sloped along the base of the mountains toward the dark horizon of forest that was the Raven's Wood.

It was an easy time of it, at first: the sky shone pale silver, like the shadow of a pearl, the clouds high enough that snow would not be imminent for a while yet. As the morning progressed, the sun struggled higher into the sky, and Magnilmir spent his time humming as he progressed along the edge of the tumbled stone between the mountains and Raven's Wood. Entering the tree line at last, he noticed one thing immediately: the silence. He knew and had experienced some of the many unsavory presences of the forest. Yet he chose to remain cheerful, as his deed was a noble one, a friendly gesture. Magnilmir claimed few human friendships; Hrafn he counted among them. Magnilmir thought fondly of the time he had traded with another human, Korlundr, at Dragon's Dance. This made him sigh, for that friend had suffered greatly, and his young son had needed to mature sooner than he ought.

This made him think of his daughter. With each passing step, he missed Thianna, his half-human child who had left home to explore the world and find more out about herself. And Magnilmir missed still, and forevermore, Thianna's mother, who was human. Although she had died many years ago, his love for his wife endured. But he also felt buoyed by the thought of taking a trip more or less for leisure...something uncommon for him, or for anyone else of that place and age.

His stature gave him an advantage in the forest in some ways, for he could see higher into the trees themselves. This became a negative aspect when it came to discerning what might be lurking behind tree trunks or rocks, and by and by, he grew wary, feeling eyes upon him as his great footfalls trod more carefully upon the soft pine needles. The air smelt of snow, and of a particular kind; a fine, flaked variety that would not coat much of the forest, certainly not the floor under the densest canopies. The farther he progressed into the Raven's Wood, the darker the forest grew. The sun decided to hide for the remainder of the day, and the clouds chose to cast soft flakes that he might only see in a clearing...and there were few clearings.

The sounds changed. The wind rushed through the highest treetops, sounding every bit like the rapids of a thawed and swift river. As the short day withered and the forest encroached, Magnilmir began to feel its presence more; he advanced enough that the mountains could no longer be seen at all. Only the tunnels of shadow remained, burrowing in every direction under dark evergreens. And he began to hear something strange. He dithered over his path, for it forked in three directions, and he looked up, hoping to see his raven friend; only a slate-gray sky met him. But there it was again! A whispering. It was no wind, he knew. And he felt then quite far from his home, even though the first day wasn't over.

He set down his pack and listened.

"*Come over here,*" a voice said, so quietly that he thought for a moment he'd imagined it. He swiveled his eyes all around, and felt for his club, touching the handle gingerly and only with his fingertips.

"Show yourself," Magnilmir called out, "and we can speak openly."

"*Come over here,*" the voice said again, and the giant turned in every direction to try to discern the origin of that haunting voice. Finally, he beheld something different from every other tree among the endless trees: something on one of their trunks, carven.

He approached and beheld what looked like a crone; the burls and knots of the pine etched a face.

"*At last, you see me, frost giant!*" said this wizened face.

"Ah!" exclaimed Magnilmir. "A hyldemoer, yes?"

The face twisted into something resembling a grin, and he was not sure whether he liked the expression; for it could easily have been a grimace.

"*What brings you into the wood, giant? Is not the mountain of ice and snow the home for your kind?*" asked the hyldemoer.

Magnilmir stepped closer and knelt before the tree-face, for the face was low for him; it would have been at eye level for an adult human.

"Aye, I am from the Plateau, and I do not wander here often," he told her.

"*Will you be making a fire?*" asked the hyldemoer.

The giant blinked for a moment and then laughed.

"Ah, no, fair forest guardian," he chuckled. "I've no need nor desire for a fire in these woods, as I am accustomed to the cold. If anything, I find it far too warm down here, sheltered under the tree-tops, away from the wind."

The hyldemoer seemed to consider this, and then asked, "*Will you be seeking to build with our wood?*"

Magnilmir thought about this for a moment, nodded, and said, "No, I do not. I seek passage through the wood unhindered. And I shall not hinder the forest, either."

A long moment passed, and he thought perhaps the tree spirit had fallen into slumber, but it opened its knot eyes and said, "*You must ask us for permission, should you wish to take from our number. Will you do that, giant?*"

"Absolutely," Magnilmir answered quickly. "I know these woods are sacred for you, and that any cutter of integrity would always ask before taking your trees."

He could swear he saw the crone nod within her tree-trunk visage.

"*That is wise and good, giant. Continue forth. But take heed! Damaging one of us would bring ill fortune upon you.*"

"I give you my word," Magnilmir assured her.

"*Peaceful journey to you, then, giant,*" said the hyldemoer.

Magnilmir gave a quick bow and set off on his way. He pondered the message and considered what wrath one might incur from a guardian of the forest. They preferred the largest and oldest trees, the old-growth portions of the forest, and he could see that he had entered a more entangled, ancient, gnarled contingent of pines and other trees. The corridors among them were dark indeed and smelled of stale air from an age beyond numbering. He decided to veer around this dark thicket, which sounded every bit as if it were whispering...to him, about him, he was not sure. He felt to his bones that he did not belong there, either way.

He continued until the sun sank and decided to make camp by a stream. The water funneled through a small waterfall into a broader pool, and from there cascaded down again through the forest. It was a lovely spot, a true respite, brighter and more cheerful, somehow than the darker woods he had traversed that day. Its beauty made him feel at ease, and he gnawed on a heel of bread while taking in the scene. He grew quite sleepy, and so he threw himself down upon the ground atop soft lichen and slept promptly. Yet by the stream, even while sleeping, he could hear the jumping and gurgling of the water, and it sounded, in his dreams, like laughter.

"What is it you carry through the dark forest, frost giant?" a voice, melodious and soft, said while he slept.

In his dreams, he answered, "I carry gifts for a friend, and provisions for myself. Whom might you be?"

"I live within the waterfall," came the answer, and the voice bounded and tumbled and gurgled like the waterfall itself. *"Do you travel alone?"*

"I do," Magnilmir's dream-self answered.

"Then I bade you take caution," said the bubbling stream, *"for my waters travel through darker halls than these, and they see and hear things that you cannot in the chambers of the wood. Your path may be hindered ahead."*

Magnilmir stirred in his slumber, reaching that point in a dream wherein one realizes they are indeed asleep; yet he was able to think through what the voice told him, and he answered in a murmur aloud, "I thank you for the warning."

He felt a splash of icy, clear water upon his face, and he shifted and sat up, just in time to see the slim figure of something dive back into the clear pool at the base of the waterfall. "A vættr!" he said, amazed.

Magnilmir bowed reverently to the spirit, and to its sparkling water home. He broke his fast then and found his food imbued with a richer taste, more nourishing, and he marveled. "The stories are true, then," he said aloud, "and I have been blessed by the vættr's presence. I honor this stream and will follow along for a little while in gratitude."

He refilled his flagon from the water and felt a crisp and vital current course through him. Magnilmir felt completely refreshed, then, and set back on his path ahead in good cheer. He did not forget the lesser vættr's words, however, and he kept his eyes alert. He glanced up and found the sky a muted gold from a feeble morning sun, yet no sign of the raven.

Onward he trod and the land sloped and rose, and sloped and rose again, and he heard distant calls of thrushes, the rustles of small woodland animals, yet no other giant nor human did he encounter. He began to think his journey might be easier than he had originally suspected, but by and by, he felt a chill, even in what, to him, was a warm land. Being a frost giant, that meant nothing like the pure air of the northern mountains whence he came. It was a chill in the spirit, a clouding *something*, and when he looked again at the filtered light above him through the dark fir canopy, the color of the very air had gone a muted blue. This seemed to him sinister, somehow, but he carried on, uncertain of what presence he felt. Eventually, he heard the distant howls of wolves and the wind among the tall pines. He stopped only to eat and to relieve himself. The Raven's Wood was not a place to dwell, for him; it was a shortcut to his destination, and he felt uneasy enough as it was, descending out of Ymiria into the comparatively warmer lands of the south.

Dusk approached, and with it, the cold malice of something continued to make him look over his shoulder. He took a drink from his waterskin and then listened, for something struck him as odd. The sound had stilled. He glanced side to side, and off to one side he could see something quite faint, something glowing: almost imperceptibly so.

"Foxfire," he muttered under his breath, and he stepped carefully of the trail to take a closer look. He found runestones. Frowning, he squinted into the forest.

And then he spied something in the distance, among the trees: a clearing that held a mound. He grimaced. Draugar, he was sure of it. Just as he turned to look behind them, one of them snarled and bound toward him. For someone of such large stature as he, Magnilmir deftly sprang away from the fell being, which, while much smaller, charged with extraordinary venom in its eyes. Then another appeared as though from nowhere, and another; and soon the giant was surrounded by savage draugar. He readied his club, Jǫkullbrandr, carved with intricate snowflakes and jagged patterns, prepared to swing, when almost casually, a much taller draugr appeared, walking slowly and powerfully, eyes dead yet blazing. In its hands, it gripped a battleaxe. Then all the draugar charged at Magnilmir.

He parried, he swung, he jumped. While he towered over them, the draugar were many and infused by such loathing that their slashes at him would take him down if he hesitated or faltered even for a second. They were relentless, being undead, and pulsing with rage and resentment at him and his living, breathing form, hale and strong and large.

"You dare enter my land," hissed their leader. He swung the battleaxe to and fro and Magnilmir could see its blade was aged yet stained with old blood, and likely guts as well, from some other unfortunate wayfarer through these parts. The draugr leader raised his hands at his minions. "This one is mine. You may have the pickings when I have gutted him and taken his head from his shoulders; a prize for this abomination who dares descend from your icy home into *my* land."

The axe swung, and Magnilmir leaped aside, and brought his club in an arc to the midsection of the draugr. This sent the creature sprawling, and he let out a hideous hiss. The other draugar then rushed at Magnilmir, and, thinking of his daughter, and of his friend who did not know he was even coming, he ran.

The draugar kept at his heels, though, and so he knew he must come up with another solution. Again, Thianna came to mind, and the tales she had told him of her adventure with the Norrønboy, Karn. What had she done? She had tricked draugr with landvættir, a spirit of the land. Would it work here? Could he find a mound of landvættir?

Fortune was with him as he ran; he spied a green mound, lush for the time of year, and he approached it, saying, "Should there be any landvættir here, know that I will not disturb you, and I will leave you an offering." He waited on the other side of the mound, and stayed quiet, counting on the draugar to crash through without regard for niceties, however, as they only pursued Magnilmir.

But the landvættir were not impressed by the draugar. They emerged like small, earthen men from their mound. They flew at the draugar, pummeling, snicking with their razor-sharp teeth, tearing at it with their claws, enveloping it, and then they multiplied, and Magnilmir halted in his battling and sprinting to watch in amazement.

They spun in a great battle of swirling snow and screeching and unearthly sounds, the sounds only the bitter dead can make, of all their perceived slights and resentments...and here they were again, kept from the object they wanted to make suffer.

Magnilmir whispered thanks under his breath, left some bread for the landvættir and ran as fast as he could away and out of sight of the melee, and on his long, giant's legs, he made it quite far before stopping. Only when he could hear an owl's hooting did he feel safe to slow down. He threw himself down under a thicket of scrub that formed almost a cave of boughs and thick, evergreen leaves, and finding it peaceful, he unfurled his sleep roll and fell asleep at once.

He awoke to see shafts of sunlight beaming down outside his scrub cave, and he crawled out to take in the morning. There would be little to no snow today, he reasoned, looking up between the tallest pines and watching the silver-gold morning sun filter through the screen of dark green needles, creating patterns on the forest floor that looked like watercolors.

He sighed.

"Well," he said to himself, "no snow today."

He ate some of the cheese he had brought with him, and some dried goat, and he began his journey. Fortunately, it was easier going that day; he heard more creatures than he saw. One of them wheeled high above: a linnorm, beating its wings, and he hoped there was no nearby lair. He was not in the mood, after the draugr fight, to come across one of the great winged linnorms. Particularly the kind that bellowed fire from their gullets. He had heard all those tales in his youth, about the great fire-breathing beasts, and they had filled him with dread, as many things related to fire had.

He shook off that unpleasant thought and moved on, occasionally keeping an eye on the sky. At one point, he thought he saw a small, dark shape above the trees, and wondered if it were Blárvængr following along on blue-black wings high above. If the bird did, it made no appearance that day, nor the next, nor the next; and for a fair number of days, Magnilmir passed through the Raven's Wood in relative peace.

He heard many wolves, spied reindeer grazing, and he set traps for game as his provisions began to wane. He kept close to streams and watched for any intruders every night until he fell fast asleep. One night, he awoke in his campsite in a clearing, and beheld the Norðrljós dancing silently above, high into the sky as if strung from the stars themselves: a maid with long and flowing skirts of ethereal green and dreamlike purple, arcs and curtains, and pirouettes of mystical light. This heartened him, as it made him think of home; he found it to be a good omen. He also knew that he would pass out of the best viewing range of Norðrljós once he reached Wendholm.

As he extended his reach into the Raven's Wood, he noticed the presence of humans from time to time, which told him he must be approaching the western edge of the great forests. The air shifted, and at times he felt uncomfortable with its warmth, but he knew he must forge onward. He had heard many tales of the Serpent's Gulf in the south and thought he might like to see that one day, but it was not quite the ideal place for a giant in any respect. He supposed that humans held an advantage over giants in that regard, to be able to ply the melted waters of the seas to the south. Then again, he had also heard talk of the kraken, beyond the relative safety of the

Serpent's Gulf. He might like to see a kraken, but certainly not up close, he reflected.

But more intriguing to him were the tales of the great falls at Wendholm. As he traveled under the whispering pines and firs above him, he tried to envision the legendary waterfall, one of the many defining features of that city. A tremendous old longship had been wedged into those falls, long ago, a relic of a long-vanished giant empire. The region had not been simply a human establishment, but also had dwarven history from ancient times.

Magnilmir pondered all of this while something slinked behind him. He halted and readied his club, Jǫkullbrandr. Filled with crawling unease that it might be more draugar, he turned slowly with a resigned sense of dread mixed with grim determination. He was not about to let another forest creature derail his journey again.

But there stood a cat. Or, for a moment, it was a great, ginger cat; from the corner of his eye, he thought he saw an impressive feline. But upon directly looking, it was a woman. Tawny of hair and gown, she stood among the woods, her eyes glowing amber. Her hands laced together before against her abdomen, and Magnilmir could see that her nails were incredibly long and sharp.

"Ah," said he to this strange woman, "well met, ketta."

The woman-cat nodded to him. "Well met, Ymirian. What brings you to the warmer lands of the South, giant?"

Magnilmir nodded, wondering what angle this stranger might want from him; ketta were rare as it was, and especially so in the Raven's Wood.

"I am Magnilmir, and indeed Ymirian. I travel over land and under tree to meet a friend," said he.

The ketta stepped closer to him; but he had not set down his carved club, and she regarded it with her almond-shaped eyes, their pupils vertical like a cat's. She spoke with a brogue to her words, as if each thing she spoke ended with a soft purr.

"I might ask the same of you, ketta," he said to her, looking down at her.

Do I trust this fey or not? he wondered.

"It is uncommon for ketta to roam these woods, is it not?" he asked her.

She purred, and brought forth her claws to pull her long, amber-gold hair behind her ears.

"We ketta roam as we desire," she answered silkily.

He tilted his head at her. She seemed rather imperious, but he found her interesting, and certainly several degrees less offensive than the draugar. So far. He tucked his club away, and she responded by letting her sharply clawed hands fall to her sides. If he needed to retrieve the club quickly, he still had the advantage of size.

"Feel free to keep roaming, then," he told her, "for I must travel on, and I do so in peace."

She responded with a guttural purr and walked beside him as he set foot back along his path to the west.

"This must be a worthy friend," she remarked, studying him with her luminous eyes, "for you to travel so far out of your way, and through warmer lands, to see him. Or her? Surely no giantess would choose to live in such a place?"

At that, Magnilmir laughed richly, one at the idea, for she was correct; also, for the very thought of visiting *any* giantess, which was the furthest thought from his mind.

"No giantess awaits me at the end of my journey, ketta," he answered, still grinning.

"Then what takes you to your friend?" she asked.

He considered her with a smirk. "You're quite chatty for a solitary cat person," he observed. "Is it not true that your kind are sought for information?"

At that, her face darkened momentarily.

"We know a great many things," she answered carefully. "And we have suffered mightily to spill such knowledge along with our own blood; I hope that is not a path you follow."

"No, indeed," Magnilmir reassured her. "I seek only the joy of companionship with an old friend, to celebrate another year."

The ketta visibly relaxed, tossing back the honey-colored mane of hair.

"I am glad to hear it," she told him. "I will leave you be, then, giant, and wish you soft footing and cooler nights, as befits your kind."

They bowed to each other then, and she slinked back among the trees. He glimpsed her in her amber cat-form, bounding softly on quiet paws deep among the gloom.

"The stories I shall tell about this one day!" Magnilmir mused aloud.

The Raven's Wood held no more fearsome creatures for him, and he was grateful for this, for his discomfort from traveling in such a warm land befuddled his wits a bit and fatigued him more than he cared to admit to himself. Still, he tarried forth, listening to the whispers of the great wood, dodging out of sight as best he could when he heard the voices of people, and keeping to himself.

He began to notice a shift in the air in the days that followed. A tangy scent of tannins, glacial runoff, and water upon the wind hinted subtle changes in the microclimates of the wood. He knew, then, that he must be approaching the far western bounds of that forest, and soon would reach the cleft of the land where Wendholm and its great falls lay. Indeed, the next day, he could see the trees thinning, and the land sloping down, and there before him was his destination, or at least part of it: the human city of Wendholm. From the south the wind carried a distinctly briny flavor, hinting at Dragon's Bay; and while he might have enjoyed a visit to it, he knew that his time afoot and afield had run short and it would behoove him to make his way to the tower where Hrafn Sjósson kept his watch.

The raven, Blárvængr, had indeed followed part of Magnilmir's travels from on high and on wing; and so, he knew that the giant approached

Wendholm. He therefore began a figure-eight journey a few times a day to check upon Magnilmir's progress, which amused Hrafn.

"Now, where might you be off to again, Blárvængr, my friend?" Hrafn asked the bird.

Blárvængr rasped simply, "I am patrolling, as is my wont, in aid to you, friend."

Hrafn watched the raven pace back and forth upon the tower wall, and he grinned to himself. *My friend is not telling me what he's about.*

"Aye, but what are you looking for?" he asked pointedly.

"Trolls, naturally," the bird answered, and Hrafn laughed.

"I welcome the patrol, but methinks you're keeping something from me," he said. "Very well! Keep your feathers tucked close to the chest, friend, and most noble and intelligent of ravens. Truly, there is none of your like elsewhere in the world!"

Blárvængr clicked his beak and set aloft again; and so it was that when Magnilmir broke through the forest, east of Wendholm, they spotted each other. The raven spiraled down from the skies and flew into a tree above the giant, and he croaked and preened.

"I am pleased to see you have left the forest behind you," croaked Blárvængr.

"It is good to see you, Blárvængr!" said Magnilmir, sighing in relief. "I trust Hrafn is well?"

"He is," answered the raven, "and thus far, he has not guessed that you're approaching, but I would not put it past him to figure it out! He's watched me keenly each day as I've patrolled. I did spy you from time to time and wondered if you might need help."

Magnilmir shook his head. "I had some moments of excitement. Enough to thrill listeners with the tales one day, perhaps. If I do not curse myself by saying so and invite a mountain troll to wreck the journey home!"

"Let us not tempt them by the suggestion!" cried Blárvængr.

"Certainly not," said Magnilmir, nodding. "Let us speak no more of that. Lead us to our friend and let us celebrate his day."

And so it was that Hrafn beheld an amazing sight late in his birthday, which until that moment he had spent in quiet contemplation, remembering years past, and assuming nothing of great import would happen upon the day. He had resigned himself to that, and was grateful for reaching the day, knowing full well his great fortune in surviving to his age. Yet his face broke as bright as the dawn at the sight of the frost giant and the raven, approaching his tower.

Leaning over the wall, he called down, "Have my aging eyes deceived me, or is that Magnilmir of Ymiria in the very flesh upon my doorstep?"

The frost giant smiled up at the man and felt glad of heart. His bag felt lighter, too, and Hrafn's surprised face made every step of the way worth it.

"It is indeed! Hello, Hrafn, my friend! Happy birthday!"

Hrafn clasped his hands together in delight. He descended and let the giant squeeze in, bowing to Magnilmir, and they climbed back to the top of the tower.

"My birthday it may be, friend," said Hrafn, "but the watch rests for no one and nothing; so, we must speak at length upon the tower, but keep an eye upon things out in the world."

Blárvængr awaited them and strutted upon the wall, looking triumphant.

"This is not your doing, Blárvængr?" asked Hrafn in disbelief.

The raven bowed and clicked and preened.

Hrafn and Magnilmir roared with laughter, and merry was the sound that rang down from the tower, such as no one had ever heard before.

"I will keep a watch while you converse," the bird said, launching up into the sky and joining his fellow ravens.

"There is none his like," Hrafn said, his eyes twinkling as the low sun's rays began to slide away into twilight. "Was this your idea, or his?"

"His!" exclaimed Magnilmir. "Although I did add one or two embellishments."

At that, he brought forth the mead, and Hrafn stared wide-eyed.

"That's not Dvergrian ale!" he gasped.

"It is!" Magnilmir answered with satisfaction.

Hrafn brought forth a horn. "Then we shall share it. I will take the horn and you take the bottle; since the only other cup of proper size for you, friend, would be a bucket...and I do not wish to share the one I have with me for that purpose!"

At that they both guffawed again.

"Tell me of the North," urged Hrafn. "What were your travels like?"

And so Magnilmir recounted his journey, and they spoke late into the night, pausing as needed for Hrafn's work, and to treat Blárvængr to some snacks as a reward for his cleverness and generosity.

"Well, my friend," said Hrafn, "you faced the beings of Raven's Wood with a deft hand and a sharp mind. I would expect no less."

"And here we are, a solitary watchman, a lonely giant, and a raven possibly more intelligent than the two of us combined," mused Magnilmir with a smile at the corner of his mouth. "We giants have a saying. 'It's a long, crooked walk to a bad friend, even if he lives close by. But it's an easy road to walk to a good friend, no matter the length of the journey.'"

Hrafn considered the giant, and he bowed and raised his cup.

"To friendship," he said.

"To your birthday," said Magnilmir.

"To Dvergrian ale!" they both chorused.

J. DIANNE DOTSON is the science fiction, fantasy, and horror author of *The Shadow Galaxy* collection (March 2023; Trepidatio), *The Inn at the Amethyst Lantern* (October 2023; Android Press) and *The Questrison Saga®* space opera series. She is also the author of several short stories across genres. Additionally, Dianne is a science writer and artist. She holds a degree in Ecology and Evolutionary Biology with an emphasis on Zoology, and is quite fond of birds, hiking, and journeys. Visit Dianne's website at jdiannedotson.com or follow her via Twitter/Instagram: @jdiannedotson

THE BEAR SON'S TALE

JONATHAN ANDERS

Hark ye heroes || hale and wise-hearted
I would weave for you || the lay of illustrious Bothvar
And Ingeld Spear-point || Splendid heroes both
They met with a wretched fate. || Their story unveils
The lot of men || who contend with jealous foes.
Ingeld son of Ingweald, || skilled at swords'-dance
Witty-wise at word-play || wanted a mead-hall of
*   his own.*
So he departed Harthbor's hold || left the confinement of
*   stern walls.*
The petty lord's laws || did not restrain his steps
Into the wilderness he went || looking for allies.
In the wilds, where || valor is better than gold
He won many friends || among warriors wandering
Away from deathless lords; || wolf-lipped vagabonds
And spirits with hollow backs: || the hallowed Huldrafolk.
Most famous of his followers || are Brunhilde Dragon-
*   Hide ,*
And Alithie[1], a seer forsaken || exiles and outcasts all.

From six deep pools || Alithie surveyed the world
Each of her two eyes || was thrice-split. Three pupils
Silently shone, new moons || upon a silver sky.
Brunhilde bore a breast-plate || carved of linnorm-scales
Axes shattered against it || Her battle-song inspired
Beautiful deeds of valor. || Ingeld fought first
In every fray || and first dispensed gifts
They loved him deeply || their wandering jarl,
who risked his life || alongside his fellows.
Alithie saw the place in a dream || where Ingeld's mead-
    hall would be
It was fat with foul-spawn: trolls and dire-wolves
Wicked fey and enchantments. || Nothing daunted Ingeld
He led the charge into the forest. || For days they blazed
    a path
Hungering for victory more than meat. || The slaughter-
    path had been simple to steer.
At last they discovered the spot || Where Alithie had
    dreamed Ingeld would build
A mighty mead-hall. || The gift-giver, first in the fray,
    pierced the earth
Planted his iron-leaf'd tree in that place. || He called to
    Aurvímnir
Chief of gods, || who delights in deeds of boldness
To bless his endeavor. || The all-father heard him,
Bestowed his boon || upon the spear, it blossomed
taller than any other tree || A shining giant,
bark-boned and brilliant-green || In its shade Spear-Point
    hall was built.

After many bold deeds || fighters need a feast
To boast before beautiful eyes || and seek hearth-
*   companions*
To share spoils and stories. || And so the Jarl declared
A holiday to mark the making || of Spear-Point hall
Their tales of triumph || Voyaged on valkyrja wings;
Fell swiftly into the ears || of thrall, thane, and jarl.
Guests arrived from Harthbor's hall, || Beard-blessed
*   dvergr-kin came to see.*
Curiosity compelled them. || They had heard that Ingeld
*   was no miser.*
Gold and gifts || flowed from him freely.
Friendship with such a lord || was sure to bring boons.
The mead-hall glowed. || The warrior hosts gathered there
made music to the gods || swapped tall-tales and songs.
Flame-light flickered || from the great hearth,
Where wild boars roasted, || and danced from shining
*   shield*
To scabbard and sword || so that the mead hall seemed
Full of silver stars. || Ingeld addressed the gathered hosts
"Friends, Spear-Point hall || is open to every noble soul.
A true Norrønur knows || that valor is the measure of man
if he carries himself well in combat || if he stands fast by
*   his friends*
He has no cause for shame. || I give you these gifts
As a token of good intent. || If you abide by honor
our riches shall increase || and we shall have no cause to
*   quarrel"*
The lords were glad || to listen to Ingeld's counsel
They took the gifts || and made promises of future
*   friendship.*
All except Harthbor || who now stood up and addressed
*   Ingeld*
"Art thou that same Ingeld || who for faintest slight

Didst draw daggers || in a peaceful place,
Laying five harmless men low? || Anger unchecked
Is no mood for a mighty lord. || Thy bloody deeds
Speak stronger, it seems || than well-formed phrases.
Ingeld held his word-hoard ready || waiting to deliver a
  stern reply
"Harmless men, thou sayest? || Those villains got what
  they deserved.
Ale-strong ruffians assailed me || in a place of peace
And met the end the gods hold || for desperate conduct.
From my youth, you all know || I have held to honor.
Have never broken a vow. || My friends have no cause
To call me greedy. My gifts || are proof of my word's
  purity."
Harthbor had ready no witty reply. || Then Ulfri, stout-
  strong dvergr-kin
Applauded. A war-like anthem || echoed in Spear-Point
  hall.

Some warriors slept || minds mead-clouded
Others stumbled in each other's arms || snatches of song
Escaping from drunken throats || Flame-light out-flew
From that famous hall, || flicker'd on whale-roads
It reached over waves. || Afar from his cavern
Scithved beheld the fitful light || the troll had received no
  invitation.
Forgotten monster || great was his grief to see
Such shining warriors || sharing brother-bonds.
Jealousy drove him || from sluggish slumber
He walked the night-veiled way || toward Spear-Point
  hall on the hill.

*Scithved's envy matched his might || Terrible troll,
    his kind*
Seldom now wends the shadows. || Night had gifted him
To swim through darkness || shark-like in search of flesh.
*Silent, unseen Scithved strode || through the hall's open
    doors.*
On shadow-steps || sight-safe by sorcery
*Night-troll stalked; gloom-stepper || Twice-tongued
    troll-kin*
He knew naught of honor. || He wound among
The shield-maidens, || strongest in Norrøngard.
Selected from Sleepers || one who seemed fittest.
*Scithved brought his bulk down || upon Brunhilde's
    breast-plate.*
*Burst her blood upon the ground || he made a meal of the
    ruined warrior.*
*Speedily gobbled down bone || smacked sinews and flesh.
    At last*
*Slurped down ruby drops of blood. || His envy for now
    sated*
*Scithved fled unseen into the night. || The sun rose in
    sorrow*
*Upon the scene of slaughter || Ingeld, incensed, called
    loudly*
For revenge. Made a solemn oath || he would slay Scithved
Upon the next night || Alithie withheld her weeping
But stood soul-shaken. || Brunhilde had been closer
*To her than sister or shieldmate.|| To her shame she hadn't
    foreseen*
*Scithved's coming. The troll's sorcery || had shielded him
    from her sight.*
Brunhilde's passing made her bitter. || She cursed her gift
*And gave her heart to vengeance. || Troll's blood alone
    could slake*

Her freezing thirst. || The hosts waited for gloom-fall.
They were well prepared || to slay Scithved in battle.
Pay back blood for blood. || The hall's fires blazed hot.
Swords quivered at the ready. || Scithved saw once again
The flickering fitful light. || His envy swelled. He
    summoned
Shades to hide his steps || and foul vapors to keep the
    warriors slumbering.
Shadows opened a door for him. || The awaiting warriors,
He sent to sleep. || Undisturbed he approached Ulfri
Slumber-sunk, dream-drowned || the beard-blessed
    dvergr-kin
Died without honor || under the troll's rotten teeth.
Once more did Ránar's flaming rock || sail over a wretched
    sight.
The Dwarves made great moan; || Shield-siblings
    lamented
They cursed themselves || that the troll had slipped their
    vigilance.
But among the guests gathered || and even among Ingeld's
    men
Doubt's bitter root had taken hold. || They whispered
That Ingeld was false: || perhaps the feast had been
    prepared
As a lure to slay || the lands' rightful lords
To bait the butcher-troll || with the scent of beating-blood.
The guests were gone || eager to exit that tarnished place
Ingeld's company, crushed || solemnly sang dirges into
    darkness.
Scithved, however, was not sated || Under crepuscule-
    cover
He killed a third time || Ingeld's anger on the morn
Was matchless: his shout shattered || the very stones. None
    dared speak

When Scithved slew again. || The following day saw a
  fresh corpse.
For three ten-days Scithved ate, || uninvited, the flesh of
  Spear Point hall.
Ingeld was impotent to prevent || the massacre of his men.
His followers left him || seeking fortunes untouched by
  troll-curse.
Alithie remained and a few others || steadfast to the end.
They departed the mead-hall || hearts leaden, to shelter in
  the forest.
Spear Point hall surrendered || to Scithved shadow-troll.

Ingeld son of Ingweald || skilled at swords'-dance
Witty-wise at word play || Fell into a great despair.
He lost his will to live, || Who lived so fiercely:
His heart heavy-clouded, || vile visions tortured his rest
He sat stricken || as a father who sees his son
Swing from a scaffold-tree. || Words could not rouse him
Nor blows shake him from his stupor || An empty field
  stretched before his sight
Frigid, pale, and lifeless || He wandered in dream
Endlessly across the frozen soil || The frost followed him
filled his footsteps with snow. || Swallowed his trail
he knew nothing but cold || and he was naked.
The Norns seized Alithie. || She could not easily forsake the
  fated gift.
Second sight was ever hers. || She beheld Bothvar in
  dream.
A wild warrior || a glorious doom inscribed upon his brow.
He of all men || had might to match the gloom-stepper.
Alithie came to Ingeld. || He lay without light in his eyes,

Spoke to him of her dream, || "I saw by my cursed sight
A man, Bothvarr by name, || he bears no shield shining
Nor spear nor sword || from hauld or jarl
But the forest-father || provides for him freely.
Among the honey-eaters || he grew to great might
Knows their names and speech, || Borrows bear-brawn.
The spirits whisper to me || that he can't be bested in
*　　battle.*
Send me to seek him out || My jarl, to ply him
With gifts and wise words || that he might join his might
*　　to ours,*
Cleanse Spear-Point of the rot within, || Slay with forest-
*　　force*
What mere muscle could not." || Ingeld agreed. In truth
He cared little for anything. || He desired now a speedy
*　　death:*
To walk along forsaken Myrkvegr || and await nothing-
*　　ness in Nethahellir*
Alithie departed, sought the coast. || She found a ship
*　　ready to sail.*
Her sight instructed her || to travel northwards.
The wood-wreathed boat || steadily swam
The ways the sea-fowls fare. || The second day of travel
Brought stormy skies. || Wodagr whipped the waves,
Whistled to the winds. || The Ship danced
Drunk on saltywine. || The drowned lord
Had prepared a grand repast || for the sailors of the
*　　doomed vessel.*
When the keel cracked || they heard pipes playing
Over the waters' roar || and swiftly sank
To sleep in Njunn's quiet city. || All but Alithie, yet afloat.
She set her will against the sea. || Spear-Point's survival
Hinged upon her life. || Yet sea is stronger than desire.

Alithie screamed her dying defiance || sinking at last, salt-
water in her lungs.

Her soul struggled || with wave-battered body
Her leaden limbs, || storm-swallowed, sank deeper
To the darkest depths || past coral-cathedrals
To rest on a throne || of azure rock, wave-hewn,
Awaiting a warrior to enwrap || in stony embrace.
The throne was Njunn's doing || an enchantment to claim
*   the warrior's corpse.*
Before her salt-sealed eyes || stretched a host
Of splendid skeletons. || The ocean had glamoured them
*   richly:*
glued bones with gold, || Grown a garden of rubies
In tempest-dashed ribs. || These were Njunn's quiet
*   company*
Wealth beyond dreams was theirs || Yet no song issued
From their foam-filled throats. || The coral table held a
*   feast:*
Food floating before empty skulls. || Centuries of
*   shipwrecks*
Had filled Njunn's hall || With hungerless husks.
They only taste salt. || Njunn had desired,
That forsaken queen, || to welcome a warrior
Whose might would rekindle || the sea-soaked hearth.
She wanted a warrior || hale and wise-hearted
To raise a song || Around the silent hall.
"Sweet one, I welcome thee" || spoke Njunn Unfathomed,
"By great good fortune || A fine breeze brought thee here
"To mine own gilded hall. || Here thou mayst find friends

"Gathered from all the world || Do not despise our
 fellowship
"We beg humbly of thee." || Alithie was deaf
To the Drowned Lord's welcome, || Her ears sprouting
 seaweed.

When Alithie's fate || had become unfastened
From the World-Tree Evergreen || Aurvímnir All-Father
Sent Sigrid || to retrieve her for Valhöll.
The Valkyrja hunted happily || the scent of the warrior's
 soul;
Divined despite the salt-stink || the trail it had taken
Down to the coral throne. || Sigrid pursued, plumbed
Delved to darkest deeps || Came at last to Begjasborg[2]
Where the drowned lord kept || inscrutable counsel
With her silent hosts. || Sigrid saw the skeletons,
Sea-shining in water-rich rags || Heard Njunn's
 entreaties
To Alithie ill-fated. || The battle-sprite then beheld
A wonder of wryd: || A Fate yet fought
For life within || the broken body.
Foam-glued lips yet struggled || to utter a prophecy.
Njunn had no right || to encage a soul
Driven by so fierce a Fate. || Wrath rose hot
In Sigrid's heart || The High-Father would will battle
For this foul offense. || "No kelp-cloaked keeper
"Of drowned men || must unwind wyrd.
"This shatterless spear || shall shake thy grasp
Upon yonder warrior's will." || So saying Sigrid charged
Turning too late toward || the Valkyrja's onslaught
 sudden

Njunn met Sigrid's full mettle. || Her barnacled breast-
    plate
Bore the brunt of the blow. || Her spine shook against the
    steel
Her teeth clapped shut. || Reeling, she retreated three
    steps.
"An intruder disturbeth our dinner!" || Spoke Njuun,
    shuddering
"Unkindly knocking || at my steel-shielded bones
"But these plates, cleverly contrived— || even Valhöll-
    spear can't pry them apart.
"Smash as thou wishest || I shall not surrender
"My sweet warrior, there, || to Aurvímnir's spear-pup."
Now the conflict fierce || spurred by shared hatred
Lasted a long time. || The High-father wondered
What had delayed Sigrid. || So he sought the heights
Down-peered from god-perch. || Sky-sight was his
Loftiest of gods. He looked || at the earth sheet-spread.
His eyes unveiled the battle: || Sigrid locked in strife
With Shipwreck-queen. || He saw also Alithie
Whom Njunn had imprisoned. || As soon as he saw them
Aurvímnir mounted the wind. || Rode storm-steeds swiftly
To Bejasborg; bellowing || that Njunn had made a
    blasphemy.
So strong his outrage || that tempest-sprites drawn
To his bright-flashing ire || galloped at the god's heels.
Lightning-lances flinging in his wake, || raising peals of
    thunder-wrath
To announce Njunn's sacrilege || to the earth's far corners.
Nethis heard from afar || exiled queen of all dead.
She bore no great love || for Aurvímnir or Njuun.
Arrogant gods both || they meddled in matters
Outside their concern. || Nethis sped along Myrkvegr
Wended hidden ways || Only her feet could trek,

Came suddenly into the sunken hall.// "Cease your sense-
     less conflict,"
Spoke Nethis. "This contested soul // By law belongs to
     Nethahellir:
"Those who have suddenly died // who have faded away
"From old age or wasting disease— // These must tread
     the darksome way
"Through perils and travails // and arrive at last at
     Enðavegr
"Where they are granted rest. // This one died at sea
"Through sudden accident // Your fondness for fighters,
     High-Father
"Leads you to bend taboo // For by her very death
"She is marked as mine." // The High-Father prepared
To make reply, when rang out // a voice as yet vexed
To utter through seaweed seals // its tremendous prophecy.
"You are all wrong O gods!" // The voice enveloped them
     there.
"Alithie's fate lies in fact // with me: I am her Gift,
"The second-sight ever with her: // It is I who provoked the
     völva
"To a quest greater than you gods // can suspect." The fate
     yet fighting
Had at last severed the spell // that kept it tongue-tied.
"I am sent from Ingeld // son of Ingweald, surely
"You recall him High-Father? // How he planted in
     poisoned ground
"A spear you hallowed? // Your Holy-place lies now ruined
"A shadow-troll has taken // residence in hall raised
"In your name. The troll has eaten // fighter-flesh for
     thirty days
"How can this be // that you allow your thanes' honor
"to be tarnished so terribly? // I seek Bothvar Bearson
"His fate is fastened // to your fate, High-Father

"He is the mightiest among || both man and beast
"I know for certain || that he shall expel
"Scithved the troll || from Spear Point hall
"If I am permitted, that is || to fulfill my fate.
"Unbind me from this body || Let me fly northwards[3]
"Bear my burden || to Bothvar, wood-dweller
"Urge him to grasp || at his golden destiny.
"He and Ingeld will build || a shining city
"Heroes hale and wise-hearted || will gather from across
    the world
"To shatter mead-cups || in mirth for Aurvímnir.
"To join shields together || in matchless might.
"A noble sight it would be || if my path were not
    hindered."
The gods gathered there || sat in silence, considering.
Not one dared || to impede the prophecy
The weave of wyrd || binds all beings together
Even gods cannot escape fate. || Nethis acknowledged
That Alithie's fate spoke truly. || Aurvímnir after long
    thought
Said he would allow the Völva-soul || Bothvar Bearson to
    seek.

Among the wild woods || Bothvar honey-hunted.[4]
Bruin and Bjorn, bear-brothers, || wise in wood-ways,
had taught him to taste || on the wind's wings
The faintest perfume || of corpse or creature.
A sweet scent || was entering his nostrils.
He followed the odor || swiftly along forest-tracks
The smell led to a stream || singing softly in sunlight.
Seated, it seemed, upon the air || A smiling spirit

Was out-pouring the perfume || that drew Bothvar
    thence.
The dís dripped with scarlet || Each of her two eyes
was thrice-split. Three pupils || Silently shone, new moons
Upon a silver sky. || Alithie's fate had found him:
Bothvar Bearson || The ruddy warrior recognized
The seer's-eyes: || it was the same enchantment
That guided gloombirds || to glimpse where their prey
    would be
The forest knew future-sight || "Who are you"
The Bearson barked, || "And why do you smell so sweet?"
The dís made reply: || "I have no proper name myself
"I am the Fate of one warrior || called Alithie Curse-
    Sighted
"And I drip with the blood || of Vile Scithved the Troll.
"Listen, Bearson || he is your fiercest foe
"And the foe of all the forest. || His blood smells sweet
    to you
"Because his destined death || has been too long delayed.
"I herald a great hunt || And your prey is ripe, Bearson
"I can say with surety || that if you are triumphant
"Then Among jarls and lords || and among outlaws and
    outcasts
"And among the many beasts || All will know your
    name.
"Lays will be sung || of your valor and victory
"Do not delay, Bothvar || but speed over oceans
"To deliver aid || to Spear-Point hall"
The Bearson spoke || "Slaughter-sweet spirit
"Your war-like words || make music in my ears!
"This Scithved you speak of || seems a fine foe
"I shall follow you || to where the troll dwells
"But first I must || bid farewell to my kin.
Then the Bearson sought out || Bruin and Bjorn

He told them a great hunt || awaited him over the
     horizon.
His brothers in the beginning || would not let him leave
They would not release him || beloved bear-brother until
Bothvar had bested them; || in battle-sport shown
He was fit to face || and slay Scithved the troll.
"So be it!" spoke Bothvar || His limbs swiftly moved
In the snap of a bowstring || Bothvar locked Bruin
In unbreakable embrace. || He wrestled his roaring
     cub-mate
Into stillness, the bear submitted || to his brother's greater
     brawn.
Next Bjorn slowly circling || approached on
     earth-study paw.
Eyes seeking a weakness || his teeth sudden out-flashed.
The iron maw sought || to enclose Bothvar's chest.
Slipping snake-like away || the hardy hero stepped under
The plunging bite, and grasped || at Bjorn's neck, exposed.
He slammed his sibling down. || Bjorn and Bruin had
     been bested
The victor's kin knew || that Bothvar was battle-ready.
"Ere you leave, sibling" || spoke the bruised Bjorn
"Seek out our mother: || she sleeps in yonder cavern
"She may mete out || wise words for you
"As you venture from the wilderness." || Morbjara bear-
     mother slept
Weary of winter-frost. || Her den was dew-damp
With her hot heaving breath. || Swollen with summer's
     spoils,
Her body filled the burrow. || Though asleep, she knew
     her son
Bothvar stood before her; || had heard in dream
Bruin and Bjorn telling || Bothvar to seek her counsel
She shifted in her slumber, || moved a massive paw aside

Uncovered a rare treasure: || it was a honey-comb,
    glowing faintly gold.
Bothvar little understood || what use such honey might
    serve
Still it was better || to take the honey-comb
Rather than risk || his mother's umbrage.
Bothvar returned || to where his brothers waited
Bruin approached; placed his paw || into the hero's hand.
"Brother," said Bruin || "I give you the gift
"Of my crushing claws." || "I accept your gift"
Replied Bothvar || "as it is given."
Bjorn approached; placed a kiss || upon Bothvar's lips.
"Brother" said Bjorn || "I give you the gift
"of my bone-breaking bite." || "I accept your gift"
Replied Bothvar || "as it is given."
And so Bothvar Bearson, || bade again goodbye
To his brothers || standing watch upon the shore.
The dís then cast || a puissant spell.
Called on Aurvímnir || and Sigga great Huntress,
Dipped her bloody garb || Thrice into the sea.
Before Bothvar's feet || there blossomed a trail
Scarlet and shimmering. || Southwards it stretched
Over the vast ocean || blood-bridge blooming
Above the wet miles. || Bothvar boldly followed
The scarlet trail[5] || left by Alithie's fate.
Seven days he strode || and on the eighth alighted
Upon the beach below || the steps up to Spear-Point hall.

That Great Tree || hallowed by the High-Father
Writhed with rot. || Its roots drank deeply
From death-stained soils. || The bark-boned giant,

Once sprung from Ingeld's spear, || stretched skeleton-
    fingers
Across the sky. || Troll-Sickness seeped
From barren branches || down on the mead-hall.
Bothvar took care || to make no murmur
As he crept quiet || up the steps.
If the troll was as terrible || as the dís had told him,
Bothvar thought it better || to take every advantage.
He approached Spear-Point. || Slipped unseen
Under the doorframe. || Stealth-shrouded, Bothvar
Looked for his quarry. || The whole hall
Was drenched in shadow. || Shades hung thick
Across mangled carcasses || Scithved was unseen!
Stench-choked air || Held no hint
of Scithved's scent. || Bothvar favored hunter
Had lost the trail. || Unbidden fear rattled
At the latches || of his hero's heart.
Scithved stirred. || He heard his prey's heart pumping
The troll tasted also || the honey that Bothvar held.
Slowly he stalked || Taking the measure of him
Who had disturbed his slumber. || He would waste no
    strength
On this one warrior, || would approach and wait
For his heavy scent to send || the frail fighter sleepwards.
Bothvar perceived the poison. || The forest's-child natu-
    rally knew
Such air was bad to breathe. || Bothvar held his breath.
Then Scithved snapped || shade-cloaked claws
Intent on stealing || the precious portion.
Bothvar swept the grasp aside. || The wind whispered
When Scithved's claws || came too close to flesh,
But the Bearson staggered: || he had barely beaten off
That first attack. || Without sight or scent
Bothvar had little time || to fight Scithved's onslaught.

It came crashing || with redoubled deadliness down
On the hero's head. || Blow followed blow.
But Bothvar held him back || Scithved struggled to break
Bruin's gift. The crushing claws || fended off the foe
For now, but wouldn't remain || firm forever.
If the troll desired to drink || the hunter-hallowed honey
Bothvar thought it better || to quaff it himself.
The golden honey faintly glowing || had no sooner passed
    his lips
Than the shadow-dark hall || shed its gloom-garb
    suddenly,
Burst into brightness || before the Bearson's eyes.
Bothvar knew now why || the troll had sought to steal
The gift from the great mother. || He saw through
    Scithved's sorcery.
The proud warrior laughed || Lunged at the gloom-
    stepper
Hammer-fists resounding || in tremendous thunder-crash.
Scithved clattered over chairs || overturned tables, crashed
Into the wall's sturdy timber. || Astonishment seized the
    troll
He didn't expect his prey || to pierce the shadow-shroud
That concealed his bulk. || The poison he produced
wasn't enough to subdue Bothvar. || Fear gripped his
    throat.
He hesitated. Too late to see || Bothvar charging.
The warrior crashed || with a bear-worthy roar.
Ribs bent and broke. || Bothvar's claws cleaved
Through hideous hide; || started rooting around
For the troll's over-ripe heart. || Suddenly desperate,
Scithved shrieked, || struggled greatly against
The proud hero pinning him || his cries resounded
Around for miles, reaching || the grove where Ingeld
Dwelt for a time. || Hildred, faithful follower,

Heard the hellish howling, || supposed some beast to be
Caught in troll-talons. || He left his lord
Intent on investigating || the tremendous tumult
Ingeld, still sunk || in deepest despair,
After awhile || beheld his friend dashing
stag-swift toward him. || Hildred called to Ingeld.
Excitement locked || the warrior's wordhoard.
Hildred could only call || for Ingeld to follow.
Ingeld had scarce stepped || to the mead-hall's threshold
Before he heard the troll, || Scithved shriek his last;
Beheld Bothvar close his claws || around the troll's heavy
    heart.
The corpse-bloated belly || swiftly began to swell
Shadow-smoke coiled || from the putrid lips agape.
The Bearson couldn't step || entirely away ere
The carcass exploded || in foul profusion
Slinging gore-shadows || and slaughter-stench
To every wind and way. || Bothvar withstood the burst
Charcoal-black blood || Clung fast to his flesh.
Great then was Ingeld's gladness. || His grief fled from him
Like frost before a flame. || He jumped for joy,
Raised a hearty shout || Ran to embrace the champion,
"Before me you stand, Bearson, || bathed in the blood of
    my foe.
"Foolishly I questioned || my seer's visions
"But I know now || that the High-Father doesn't forget
"His favored warriors. || Henceforth we shall be siblings.
"I shall honor you in my heart always || forest-born
    warrior of noble soul.
"Do not scorn my fellowship, I pray || but abide by me
"And become the shining shield || of our new Spear-Point
    hall."
Ingeld then declared || that the defiled bodies be
    gathered.

They placed the carcasses upon a pyre, || made merry
    around the roaring flames.
Their shieldmates' spirits || at last could be at rest.
Aurvímnir from god-perch peering || with powerful thun-
    der-peal
Opened a path for Valkyja to travel. || The few warriors
    around the funeral fire
Raised a great cry || to herald the heroes' return home.
The Valkyria plucked || the awaiting souls from the flames
Welcomed them late into the Enduring Hall. || Scithved's
    magic no longer impeded them.
One spirit stood aside. || Alithie wouldn't ascend
The pyre-steps upwards || though Brunhilde's battle-
    shade beckoned.
She yearned to join her shieldmate || in joyful war-feasts
    forever
Yet she was bound to Bothvar still || for she foresaw his
    final moments.

And then, freed from troll-foulness || the blessed
    Spear-Point Tree
Shook the shadows from its boughs || bloomed in brilliant
    bursts
Shot branches skywards. || The loftiest scratched the clouds
Light from the blossoms || it is said, could be seen,
By ships far out at sea. || Many beheld that splendid glow
And went, wondering, to witness || the flowering titan-
    trunk
Dverkin beard-blessed, || and men from Harthbor's hold
Even the Svartálfar traveled thence. || Upon seeing
    Aurvímnir's might

Those gathered there were eager || to support Spear-Point.
Some with Ingeld worked to rebuild || the mighty mead-
hall.
In time it grew great || hundreds sheltered under its sturdy
shadow.
To Ingeld's rare delight || the High-Father had seen fit to
bless
His hall with hallowed honey. || The same sweet comb
Whose magic had helped Bothvar || to pierce Scithved's
darkness
With each summer dripped || golden blood over the eaves.
Ingeld made a mead out of it || that set his warriors' eyes
ablaze.
Other warriors with Bothvar went. || The fierce hunter
disdained idleness
When prey yet roamed the wilds. || With a band of boldest
fighters
He cleansed the lands around || of filth and deadly threats.
Nights were seldom without music || mead flowed like
water.
Plentiful were the times || when Ingeld wisely led the way
To Spear-Point's prosperity. || With all folk of the land
Ingeld and Bothvar enjoyed friendship. || Bothvar's
matchless might
held back the beasts. He hunted them all. || Soon no
monsters remained.
His fame grew as the dís prophesied. || Jarl and rogue held
him in reverence.
He was pleased to see || his strength widely celebrated.
He loved to listen || to his name chanted in poetry.
His fame was well-merited || yet Bothvar, in time, forgot
his brothers
Bear-language slipped from him. || He came to prefer the
company of men

And so spent his days || in boasting and feats of
    strength.

Bothvar's boasts and the renown || of that famous
    mead-hall
After long years reached || even the ears of Niðaug the
    dragon.
The wizened wyrm plunged || in profound century-sleep
Stirred. She felt the woods, erstwhile hers || slipping from
    her grasp.
In vision she beheld Bothvar || purging the forest of the
    last monster.
Death at his hands was hers || if she let the man-cub
    continue
So the dread dragon arose || from glittering gold-heap,
Shook slumber from her limbs || stretched her wings ten-
    fathoms wide.
Her roar upon awakening rent || the stones asunder, they
    broke
Like shipwrecks. The sky shivered || and assumed a somber
    cast.
The watery whale-ways || storm-seethed, anticipating
The dragon's wrathful return. || All of nature remembered
    Niðaug.
The winds uplifted the ancient wyrm. || She scorned the
    soil,
Rose on hurricane gusts, || Soared toward Spear-Point.
Niðaug's jealousy upon seeing || the brilliant titan-tree
Cankered at her stomach: || the arrogant gods again
Intruded upon her domain. || Aurvímnir, false-father,
    had invited

Men-insects to invade her peace, || to plunder her riches
    immense,
To slay her subjects. She lunged || in rage against the
    bark-boned giant.
The Serpent embraced || the blessed tree-trunk.
Spear-Point hall shuddered || Under dragon-shadow.
Niðaug's clasp was ages strong || the bark cracked
    and bent
Beneath the wyrm's foul coils. || Bothvar, hearing
    affrighted cries,
Rushed out of doors; beheld || Niðaug rage-rending the
    sacred tree.
Bothvar wasted no time || in calling his war-company:
The protectors of Spear-Point hall || locked shields close
    together
Bent their bows skywards, || unleashed a rain of arrows
Against the wicked wyrm. || The sharp steel shafts
Clattered like sticks upon || Niðaug's shining scales.
She drew her coils in closer || pressed the bark with fren-
    zied force.
Horror seized the heroes beneath. || They were powerless to
    prevent
The titan-trunk from falling. || With tempest-crash it
    scattered
The fleeing fighters. || The stoutest of them couldn't
    withstand
The dragon's immeasurable might. || Only the Bearson
    stood firm,
On earth-steady step advancing. || Niðaug's fierceness did
    not affright him.
Wind-borne huntress, bane of heroes || she swooped with
    sword-wings down
But could not cleave || hare-nimble Bothvar, deftly
    dodging.

The whirlwind in her wake || shook the Bearson's bones.
"I have never faced a foe || as deadly as you, dragon.
"Yet forest-force is mine || And I will slay you as I slayed
    Scithved.
"Spear-Point hall shall not succumb || While Aurvímnir's
    chosen , Bothvar Bearson, stands!"
Evilly Niðaug laughed || "What care I for such exploits?
"A wyrmling could easily match || so small a feat: to fell
"That sea-stinker, muck-crawler, || scare a century old.
"My elders were old || when the stars were sired.
"My fathers were there || when the world-waters receded.
"I remember Aurvímnir || how he slaughtered Otar ice-
    eyed.
"And treacherously ruled || the feeble, fawning gods.
"I relish the chance to devour || a champion chosen by that
    false lord.
"Your strength does not suffice, Bearson || To tame the
    elements I command.
"The gales recognize me and obey me || Behold! they
    sweep your dwellings away!
"The earth trembles at my touch || Behold! It swallows
    your shieldmates whole!
"The oceans seethe at the sound of my roars || Behold!
    They arise and sink your vessels!
"And the fires were mine from the first. || Behold, Bearson,
    the flames that bring your doom."
So saying, the dragon spewed || her burning breath.
The rain-parched timber burned first || then swiftly passed
    the fire
From tree to tree. || The forest flared.
Bothvar's armor had melted away || from his skin,
    serpent-scorched.
He crouched unclad amid the ashes. || Niðaug arced back,
    swooped again.

*In his shock the Bearson couldn't step aside. || Moments
    from his doom he remembered*
*Bjorn's gift of tearing teeth. || As Niðaug's foul fangs
    enfolded*
The hero's chest, he lashed out || with bone-breaking bite.
*His teeth found the wyrm's throat. || He tore it out.
    Niðaug crushed his frame.*
*The two of them death-stricken || plummeted upon the
    ruins of Spear-Point hall.*
*Niðaug bled a river of blood || before perishing. Razed the
    entire place*
*In her enraged death-frenzy. || Battle-battered beyond
    healing,*
*Bothvar yet struggled to grasp at life. || He refused to
    relinquish*
His bonds with his brothers, || Or with Ingeld or Alithie.
*Earnestly he desired his shieldmates || to soothe his
    suffering.*
His heartbeat became soft, || his breath in ragged bursts
*Escaped from wyrm-lashed lungs. || The barrows
    beckoned.*
*Yet Bothvar disdained true death. || Fate still fastened him
    to the famous mead-hall.*
While Spear-Point stands || Bothvar cannot walk the way
*to Vallhøl. He sleeps the long sleep || of the dream-bears of
    Draumheim,*
*His spirit in dream-worlds wandering. || Alithie stands
    ready still*
To urge the forest-fighter || to bold and warlike deeds
*Should foul foes again || threaten the peace of Spear Point
    hall.*[6]

J ONATHAN ANDERS is a linguist, poet, and musician with a fascination for the uncanny and the arcane. He has written scholarly commentaries on the works of Jean de LaFontaine, Richard Wright, and William Blake, and has devised a conlang for Meta. His favorite piece of fiction is *Moby Dick*, which he contends is a work of High Dark Fantasy. He is in fact currently working on a sequel to *Moby Dick* set many years in the future on the saltless seas of a far-distant world. In his free time, he can be found free-styling on his electric piano, playing RPGs, and ranting about linguistic prescriptivism.

---

1. According to Liffir Olandsson, first skald of present-day Spear-Point Hall, the Bearson poem drew from other contemporaneous oral sources. Brunhilde would have been known to audiences from the *Drakkwif Saga*, in which she wove together her armor from the shed skins of her husband, who was transforming into a linnorm. There are no known surviving poems that mention Alithie explicitly, though tales of wandering vølva were common at the time the Bearson poem was composed.

2. Derived from Old Norrønian. A combination of the verb for "to be silent" and the noun for "city."

3. Westwards is some versions.

4. We find the most disagreement between the Norrnian and Swithemarkain variations of the poem in the chapters detailing the adventures of Bothvar. In the chapters previous, the main differences between the texts were regional variations on the gods' names (e.g. *Norr.* Aurvímnir vs. *Swith.* Aubíamnír) and slight grammatical differences. The Swithenmar version contains a whole other passage that modifies Bothvar's motives for coming to Spear-Point hall. While in both versions Bothvar and Ingled collaborate to establish Spear-Point hall, only in the Swithemarkian version is this idea credited to Bothvar himself. This divergence has led the scholars of Qualth to propose two hypotheses for the lineage of the Bearson Poem. The similarities between the two versions seem to indicate that they both derive from an earlier source, which was subsequently modified. However, some scholars point out that the Norrøngardian version displays grammatical structures of greater antiquity that the Swithenmarkian version lacks, not to mention that the Swithenmarkian version seems to add passages. There is reason to suppose then, they argue, that the Norrønian version is the original. Unsurprisingly, the wise men of Swithenmark accept the first hypothesis. Furthermore, in a variant of the saga, Bothvar actually hails from Swithenmark, but this version of the epic was employed as partial justification for Swithenmarkian rule and is understandably less popular today.

5. From the description, it seems likely that the dís cast the spell known as *Bloodwalk,* a powerful divinatory sortilege, whose secret has been lost to time. It permits a hunter unerringly to find their quarry, though mountains or oceans should stand in their way. There is mention of this spell in the *Sagar Jarlis Halvaldar Fylgja* (618 AG). The priests of Sigga, goddess of the hunt, claim it as a divination of that goddess's domain, though they are unwilling or unable to explain it further.

6. Spear-Point hall stands to this day, where the Skalds of Oslendholm yet sing Bothvar's deeds. The divine tree no longer stands; indeed, there are scarcely any forests left for miles around Oslendholm, as the timber is needed to accommodate the needs of the prosperous and expanding city.

RUNEFALL

CHRIS WILLRICH

How did I come to tumble out of the sky? De-Zhen thought. *For that matter, how did I come to tumble out of the sky over a land of smelly hot-headed barbarians? Yes, good question, Me, well done. Let's think it over, as if writing for the Government Examination …*

Junior Mapmaker Chen De-Zhen had signed onto the Foreign Expeditionary Aerial Armada out of duty, yes, and pride in her cartography, indeed, and to further her career as a sky-sailor, absolutely; but mostly she had come to see the clouds race over unfamiliar lands, like these evergreen-covered surges of craggy hills and plains like pale jade, all framed by the cold blue of rivers and inlets and the vast lake up ahead, looking, viewed from the west, like a huge turquoise tablet.

She had most assuredly not signed on in order to do battle with ghost-pale, black-clad, pointed-eared assailants like the ones who'd screeched aboard the sky-ship *Changning* riding nightmarish giant bats.

There were at least twenty of the boarders. The ship was in trouble. And hers was no Treasure Ship proper but a scout sent from the main fleet to overfly the less hospitable regions of this continent. They'd only a crew of fifty, and all were needed to repel boarders. De-Zhen, belowdecks in the many-windowed navigation room, had been startled by the alarm. She'd known they were on alert, seeking an auxiliary cloud incubation device stolen when they'd last landed. But the attack had come as a shock. She'd dropped her pen and hastily donned her furred armor, sword-belt, safety-line, land-kit, and parachute, knocking over her porcelain inkwell in the process, blotting out half her carefully-observed map of southwestern Norrøngard.

Senior Mapmaker Kang would have lots of words about that, if they made it out of this alive. So would De-Zhen's mother, if they ever made it home. *You could go far!* Mother had shrieked in delight a year ago when De-Zhen had showed her the Government Service Examination score, with the honors for Penmanship. Then when De-Zhen had handed her the certificate for Fleet Training, she'd shrieked in dismay, *I didn't mean like that! You are only seventeen! Do it when you are twenty-seven! Or seventy! You are such a beautiful girl! A bit tall, to be sure, and a bit over-muscled, but such lustrous hair like a moonless night and eyes like autumn. Serve the Emperor at home, where you can find a good husband!*

But there was no time to think about anything but battle now. It had raged what seemed like an hour as *Changning* shot at maximum speed away from the mountains where the bats had ambushed them. And a good thing too, De-Zhen thought as she drove away one of the short humanoids with her double-edged jiang longsword. There had been a whole cloud of the giant bats in the sky, twice again as many as the ones that had gotten close. Luckily *Changning* had outrun the bulk of the wave and shaken off most of the ones that had alighted. But there were still three of the winged monsters occupying the stern and they'd entered the fight beside their humanoid masters. Worse, many of their fellow bats had deposited riders on deck before falling back. De-Zhen's group of defenders had needed to retreat once already, reattaching their safety lines at the rearward mast.

A few of the boarders were down, at least. The ship's resistance was hardening, and standing beside two officers of the line, De-Zhen found her lackluster swordsmanship was less of a problem.

Then she saw something that was much more of a problem. One of the pale attackers had climbed back into the saddle of a bat and was readying to launch.

"Look!" she said between thrusts of her jiang. "We should stop him."

"Don't worry," said the officer behind her, breathing hard and speaking between swipes of his dao saber. "Wind'll knock them backward — as soon as they're — airborne."

But De-Zhen was a good observer. Her Examination scores showed that. Good at painting from life, excellent with cartography, superb with languages. But she didn't need to know the bat-rider's language to read the smug sardonic look on his face. He had a plan.

She followed his gaze and guessed his plan at the last moment. At their current speed the sails were bending backward, and maybe the bat could, with a combination of leg- and wing-power, reach a sail before the winds blew the animal clear. From there the bat-rider might claw and leap past the defensive line and wreak havoc, maybe even reaching the pilots at the bow.

There was no time to explain. It was easy to imagine her mother shouting curses at her as she detached her safety line and ran at the bat.

The pale pointed-eared folk seemed so startled by her charge that she made it past them just as the bat took off. She plunged the jian deep into its throat and its leap went wild. Bat, rider, and De-Zhen tumbled out past the stern as the wind caught them.

De-Zhen's grip on the sword was all that prevented her from plunging into mid-air as the mortally wounded bat flapped futilely to regain the sky-ship and its rider swore venomous gibberish at her. He leaned over with his short sword.

Shoving against the bat with her legs, and tucking her feet into its saddle straps, she wrenched the jiang free and blocked the rider with a beautiful parry she wished her captain had seen.

Then momentum flipped her over and she stared down at the distant ground, suspended only because her feet were lightly twisted into the saddle straps of a wounded bat.

The rider cackled at her, scooted onto the bat's neck, and loosed the saddle straps. De-Zhen tumbled free. The cackling grew louder as she fell but quickly tapered off as she and the bleeding bat spun away in different directions. Spinning in free-fall she clutched tight on the jiang and saw *Changning* once more, a distant wedge looking like a toy ship ...

... A broken toy ship. The other two bat-riders had succeeded in their leaps, and they had not only reached the navigators, they'd left mangled sails in their wakes. Worse, levitation mist was venting. The ship was veering out of control and dropping toward the grim-looking shadowed forest beyond the great lake.

Her own spin intensified, and the world was half green, half blue, and whirling like a child's tsa lin spinning top. She knew from her studies that the icy cold air wasn't really an invisible beast attacking her face, that her own heat was flying treacherously from her body. But it still felt personal. She couldn't let it get personal. She had to stay calm and feel no shame at her failure and keep a death-grip on the jiang and wait for the right moment to deploy her parachute. Then she'd worry about being marooned on barbarian soil.

And that, honored proctors of Heaven, is how I came to tumble out of the sky.

Postscript: I sure hope my chute works.

Before his life changed like a river diverted by a falling mountain troll, Havtor Runeson was loitering in a warm furred cloak on the western edge of the little plateau of Fornuppsalir with only squirrels for company, trying to get a new rune perfectly scratched into wood before lunchtime and, what was perhaps harder, scratched into his brain.

For this task Havtor had a carving knife and a curved section of tree bark about twice as big as his hand. He was to inscribe the inside with the Mannaz rune — ᛗ — and not stop until he'd produced a perfect one. Then he was to show it to his father, the head gothi of these parts, and probably the most important gothi of all Norrøngard, and expound upon the mystical meaning of Mannaz in a clear voice, without his attention wandering once. Then he was to write several words beginning in ᛗ, for the runes also had their mundane use as an alphabet.

He'd slipped out of his study nook to clear his head, but his bark was covered in quite imprecise scratches, and his mind was already wandering. He'd brought some nuts to eat but by now he'd given them all to the nearest squirrel, a maimed fellow with a bad leg he'd taken to calling Ratatoskr. He watched Ratatoskr eyeing him hopefully. Havtor laughed.

"Sorry, my friend, see, all I have in my hands are this knife and bark — Naði's fangs! Get back to it, Me." He grinned, chagrined. Surely no one else in the world, he thought, talked to themselves like that.

They used to say he'd grow out of his inattention and his shaky hand, but here he was, just turned sixteen, still struggling to focus and carve. His surroundings helped, though. He'd picked this spot for its view of the plateau's vast stave temple, big enough to have separate levels for the three gods it honored. It had a number of runes carved into the sweeping wooden tower, and Mannaz was one of them, visible just above the reddish-golden magical chain that wrapped the temple at its middle story. Visitors to the temple would be far more interested in the chain, which was of the unearthly metal orichalcum and supposedly unbreakable so long as the temple stood, and whose magic in turn protected the temple. His father often used the chain as a metaphor in speeches: *Each of us protects one another, like the chain and the temple protect each other.* But Havtor just wanted a visual reference for his carving.

His chosen spot had a down-side however, quite apart from the fatal plunge he'd suffer if he wasn't careful. His rune-work was hard enough in undistracted times, but this was — for the Temple at Fornuppsalir, and for the village nestled down below, and for the ring-walled town at the nearby lake, and for Havtor "Fidgetstick" of the easily rattled head — the most distracting time of the year.

It was the Festival Week in honor of Beysa, goddess of the Summer. It wasn't Summer yet of course; you didn't need to invite the goddess of Summer when she was already here. Winter wasn't quite gone. It still snowed a little most nights and patches of white lingered on shadowed ground. Up here on the plateau there was snow crunching underfoot all day. But down below there were girls like Britt Bjornsdóttir and her gang, wearing bright dresses and flowers in their hair; Havtor could see them from up here. There were meats roasting on spits; Havtor could smell them from up here. There were men holding mock duels and some not quite so mock; he could hear the clangs and the shouts from up here.

Maybe worst of all he could see the clear waters of the great lake, the Mikillvatn, with ice clinging only to its edges. He could readily imagine running to the little faering he regularly rented from Trygve the Trustworthy, one of the jarl's housecarls and a man too busy most days to enjoy the waves. Havtor was a great runner and an even better sailor, at least on the lake. He'd never been to sea, and at this rate, stuck as apprentice to his father Rune, he'd be an old man before he even made it far as Korjengard —

"Do the girls down there hold the secrets of the Mannaz rune?" a gruff voice startled him.

Havtor Runeson was of the opinion that no man in the wide world of Qualth was better-named than his father. Not only was Rune the gothi utterly fascinated by his namesakes, he had a sort of runic flavor to his dealings: sharp-edged, precise, stern, and a bit cryptic.

Rune's face, like Havtor's, had an angular look to it, and they had the same dark brown hair and cleft chins. Aside from age the chief difference, Havtor had overheard the village girls say, was their eyes. Havtor had his late mother's eyes, green like growing things. Rune's eyes were an icy blue. Havtor wasn't idiot enough to think that eye color really showed your personality; he figured it was the intensity of Rune's stare that made his eyes look cold. As for his own, well, he was notoriously fidgety, like a tree in the wind.

"Sorry," he murmured.

"'Sorry' can earn you mercy, my son, but it can't earn you respect." As Havtor reddened, Rune went on: "There's time enough for girls when you've established yourself."

Havtor wanted to object that he hadn't been thinking *only* of girls. He was a much more well-rounded person than that. But the thought of well-roundedness made him think of Britt Bjornsdóttir, which got his thoughts in a tangle, and he thought then of flowers and meat and sword fights and waves and his hand made a wavy motion and his carving, which had been going relatively well, slashed all the way off the wood.

Rune grunted. "I know you have more difficulty than most boys forming the runes. Your mother noticed your trouble with fine work long ago —"

"Most boys don't do fine work," Havtor said, cutting him off, bitterness sweeping into his voice as inevitably as bad weather. "They farm, or fight, or sail —"

"And you're also highly distractible," Rune sighed, "even for a Norrønir."

"You don't get distracted," Havtor said. It was almost an accusation.

Rune shrugged. "I am a strange Norrønir, Havtor. I admit it. When I focus on the sacred knowledge it's as if the world goes away."

"I'm like that when I'm sailing."

"We've gone over this ground."

"It's not the ground I want. Other boys go roving."

"The high king forbids raiding."

"I didn't say raiding."

"You're a gothi's son." He didn't say *the* gothi's son, but Havtor heard it. *The* gothi. *The* son. "I can't prepare you to be a farmer or a warrior, but the gods need good servants." Rune had his orator's voice on now, as if he was addressing worshipers in the stave temple. "Especially these days when the high king bids us keep the best traditions and leave the worst —"

"Maybe you should prepare somebody else. I think almost any other boy in Neðarheim or Herkeby could be a gothi's son better than me." It was as if both his mind and his hand rejected scholarly work, and he had only his own stubbornness and his desire to please his father to tame them. He didn't mean for it to be this way. It would be far easier for him if it wasn't, but it just was.

"Not true!" Rune said, as if eager to attack something that wasn't Havtor. "You're sharper than the lot of them. Your memory is keen. You have mastered the basic blessings. You have an analytical mind and ask excellent questions. You're good-hearted. But —"

The blizzard of praise, perhaps meant to soothe Havtor, did the opposite when that *but* arrived at the end. It felt like a bundle of demands, not compliments. "*But* I fail to apply myself, Father. So I need to practice now." Havtor made a determined fist. It looked stupidly serious, like something from a saga, but he kept it there. "I only have till noon, correct?"

Rune looked as if he'd been struck. "Correct," he said coldly. He turned to go, but hesitated. He looked for a moment as though he'd say something heartfelt. Then his expression hardened. "I'm performing a ceremony up here soon, with the other senior gothar. You can stay there, but don't disturb us." Rune stared at the temple, scratching his beard, watching temple servants haul bushels of hay into the temple's storage room. "That's an odd thing to be putting inside the temple," Rune murmured. "Perhaps it's to do with the festival."

He shook his head. In a stern voice he said, "But I've no time to worry about that. Or you. That old fool Bendik has always resented my claim as senior gothi. He could make trouble. Same with that goat Gundar, since we both serve the High Father in particular. He'd love to claim my place. Nor can I entirely trust Svein. I swear he'd bring back human sacrifice if he could, wringing his hands about the necessity. I always feel he's up to something." Despite his authority, Rune was always cautious about the other gothar at the temple. They were more traditional than he and if they united against him they made his life difficult. Rune's own son's concerns, Havtor thought, came second to temple politics.

"Of course, Father. I aim to please."

Rune snarled something under his breath and stalked around the corner of the temple. Good, Havtor thought, attacking the runes with warm fury. *If I'd had any other father between Dragon's Bay and the Serpent's Gulf, any at all, I'd have had a life better suited to me. I might not even know I was different. Does anyone care if a herdsman can do delicate things with his hands? Does anyone care if a berserker is distractible?*

"Havtor Runeson?"

He almost lost the bark and knife he was so startled. He nearly started again as he looked up and found that the morning mist had crept in as though it were dawn again. The sky overhead was blue but the plateau was wreathed in fog. The temple was now a shadowy suggestion of triangles and rectangles, as though it was creation's dawn and the gods had almost but not quite invented geometry.

The speaker, whose red-bearded face had an expression of cruel humor at Havtor's startlement, was Svein the Scowling. He was the gothi of the goddess Lotrisa, whose realms were love, passion, fertility, and fighting. Svein, perpetually ill-tempered, seemed suited for only the last quarter of those responsibilities. "Runeson, we are about to perform a brief fertility rite on the opposite side of the plateau, in honor of the Spring. It touches on old mysteries. It is best if you don't observe. Can we count on you to continue ... whatever it is you are trying to do?" The scowl turned mocking.

Svein really wasn't called the Scowling except down in the village. Nor was Bendik, the gothi of night-goddess Naði, really Bendik the Bungling. Nor was Aurvímnir High Father's gothi truly Gundar the Greedy, or his superior, Havtor's father, Rune the Relentless. But there was truth to each nickname.

Gray-bearded old Bendik, for example, who was now emerging from the mists beside Svein, had the manner of a clumsy, absent-minded fellow whose days of walking among dark trails were done, and who was content to finish out his life as the doddering gothi of the night-goddess until night claimed him. Nevertheless, as long as Havtor could remember old Bendik had resented Rune's primacy.

Gundar, meanwhile was a fierce-eyed yellow-haired man in his thirties who clearly felt that as the High Father's specific servant *he* ought to be in charge. Gundar dressed wealthily, Rune shabbily. Gundar wore a fancy holy sign of the High Father (twin obsidian ravens looking in opposite directions with golden eyes), yet Rune never made his visible. Gundar was a favorite of women, while Rune was content to remain a solitary widower. Rune, Gundar hinted, could go off to pasture any time he liked.

None of the three senior gothar seemed to like Father's emphasis on charity and mercy, and facing them Havtor felt his anger at Rune turn to sadness. He wished he was making a better showing, in the face of these people. "I won't go over to the eastern side," he told them. "Don't worry."

Svein smirked and turned away. He spotted Ratatoskr, who was eyeing the newcomers in hopes of new food, and aimed a kick at the squirrel.

Havtor shifted immediately between them. Svein, a bit off-balance now, glared at Havtor in rage. "My apologies, gothi," Havtor said evenly. "The squirrel is named for the messenger upon the world tree. It might be unlucky to kick him off the cliff."

Gundar said, "Enough, Svein. This is irrelevant." For the first time

Havtor realized the self-contained and elegant Gundar smelled of alcohol this morning. Gundar glanced toward Havtor and the squirrel and half the world as though looking straight through them. Svein scowled, grunted and walked off with Gundar. As the two of them disappeared into the mist, however, Bendik lingered.

Bendik pulled out a dagger, and for a moment Havtor felt a surge of fear. But the old man who'd once run with berserkers held it out to him hilt-first. "Not everyone can stand up to Svein. I see your strengths, Runeson, and your struggles. There is no shame in using a better tool for your rune-work. This blade was made by Toke the dwarf over in Herkeby. You are welcome to borrow it. Pay special attention to the hilt."

Havtor's eyes were like boulders as he took the weapon. Toke's runic name was engraved in runes upon the blade: ᛏ ᛟ ᚲ ᛖ. Everyone knew Toke was the finest smith in Norrøngard. He could even enchant his work when he had a supply of the precious orichalcum metal, like the stuff of the temple's chain. Havtor couldn't immediately see anything special about the hilt, but it would be churlish to say so. "Thank you," he said instead.

For a moment something seemed to clarify in Bendik's face, as though the sun were burning away mist and revealing ... Hope? Fear? Havtor couldn't read it. Bendik said, "I am not what I once was. I seem to lose abilities by the week. I have sympathy for your difficulties."

"The rite, old man!" Gundar called out from somewhere in the fog.

Bendik nearly slipped on a patch of ice as he vanished into the white.

Havtor tried the knife. It cut smoothly. It didn't remove Havtor's difficulty with precise hand motions, but it did make things easier. Wondering at this sudden generosity, Havtor studied the glinting blade in the sunlight a long time before he realized Bendik hadn't thought to give him the dagger's sheath. He didn't feel right going after the old man, not after he'd been warned away. So he decided to go over to his old friend Mótmeiðr, the great tree that grew beside the plateau and surpassed it. He had some favorite resting spots in its branches and he'd still be out of sight of whatever rite the gothar were planning.

He wondered what sort of tree it would manifest as this time.

After she deployed the parachute De-Zhen had thought her problems were simple: reach ground safely while tracking the fall of the sky-ship. She hadn't counted on any distractions on the ground.

Still high above she spotted four diminutive, fog-obscured figures in furs at the edge of a small misty plateau. Rising through the mist was a big wooden building reminiscent of a pagoda. There was also an unnaturally huge Tree of Heaven rising beside the plateau. The figures — grown men, she decided — were in a group at first, and then dispersed. One was engaged in creating some manner of symbol at the cliff's edge, in barley. Another seemed to practice fighting moves. The other two seemed engaged in private mediation. The men below were so intent on their own business that they seemed not to have noticed the aerial battle or De-Zhen's descent. One could almost take offense. Perhaps it was the fog.

She looked up to track the descent of *Changning*, and saw it disappear into the dark forest beyond a vast lake. She did her best to memorize the lay of the land. Looking back down she saw that two of the figures had converged upon the barley-symbol on the cliff's edge, while the remaining two were off in separate locations in the fog. She could not say now which were the symbol-drawer, the fighter, or the meditators.

Suddenly one of the pair at the precipice seized the second and shoved that person off the cliff.

There was no hope of even landing upon the plateau, let alone saving the victim. There was nothing she could do but watch. Such was her duty. She was a keen observer but she was too high at that point to be sure who was whom or what exactly was happening.

But surely there was no country upon the globe where throwing somebody off a cliff was anything but murder.

Legend had it that no two individuals could see Mótmeiðr as the same kind of tree. Sometimes even the same person would see it as different trees on different days. Havtor's father, unusually analytic for a Norrønir, decided to test the limits of this mystery one Midsummer Feast, paying one egg to each of a hundred people who would declare then and there what manner of tree they saw in Mótmeiðr. It had taken Havtor a week of traveling the nearby farms to gather the eggs for this experiment.

The obvious types, your firs and hemlocks and pines, had gone first, and with all the variations thereof, it had been twenty-three observers before the more foreign varieties showed up, like chestnut, cherry, olive, orange. Eventually came the ones no one had ever heard of but which each speaker was quite sure of at the time, such as palm, banyan, eucalyptus, redwood. The last set named were delirious-sounding things, a barnacle tree, a lotus flower tree, a man-eating tree, an ever-burning tree. When the hundredth person had spoken of a nameless golden tree with a linnorm weaving among the branches, Rune paid him off without ever announcing what he himself had seen that day.

He hadn't asked Havtor, and it was just as well because Havtor had seen a tree with sprawling branches and dark green bladed leaves, and a voice like whispering branches had seemed to say something to him in a language he'd never heard. But at the same time the light flickering between the branches had for a moment sketched something like and unlike runes. When he'd tried to sketch it later his rebellious hand had needed to spend a whole sheet of paper on it so the sweeping motions could be large enough. He'd hidden it later so Father wouldn't rant about the waste. It had looked something like:

臭椿

To Havtor, today, Mótmeiðr was a spruce tree with roots of a wavy, flowing appearance like a gray frozen river delta on a steep slope. Its trunk was spotted with sunlight broken by jabbing, splayed branches that were almost foaming green with thousands of needles. He was nestled within its branches to practice the runes because something about the tree's presence, with its branches quietly rustling, stilled some of the "wild weather" inside him and helped him concentrate. Even having Ratatoskr nearby wasn't too distracting.

He needed all that concentration. He was getting so that he could form the rune-shapes successfully if he bent his entire attention, mind, eye, and hand, toward the problem. Any interruption, any at all —

There were screams and shouts down in the village. The only words he could quite make out were "The sky!" And so he looked up.

In hindsight, much later, it occurred to him that he was as influenced by what he couldn't see as by what he could. The branches of the great tree hid from him the reeling sky-ship and the plummeting giant bat — he would only hear about those later. But they did reveal the person drifting toward the lake like a human dandelion seed. He didn't know what to make of it, but his brain, like a tree transfixed by lightning, fixated on the sight. It seemed to him this person was trapped within physical bindings, just as he was trapped by immaterial ones. It also seemed to him that the person would eventually intersect the lake.

He didn't think there was time to explain it to anyone, but someone had to help the stranger. He might just manage it. Just as earlier he'd leaped to help Ratatoskr, there was no hesitation.

Getting down the plateau was a challenge, but Mótmeiðr had accommodated him many times before, and did again today. There were many knot-holes where branches had split and the trunk was otherwise smooth. There were even creases in the trunk that were practically slides, and he couldn't shake the notion that the tree was watching out for him. Thus Havtor could slide down when needed and stop when called for. It took several minutes but it was better than taking the long stairway from the plateau.

He got his bearings, spotted the tiny person under the blue canopy, just east of the plateau. He was right about the direction. He dashed toward Herkeby and the lake.

Behind him came shouts and screams, not just from the town but from the temple. If he'd stopped to think he might have heard the dismay in those sounds. But he was afraid it was his father calling him back, and until he was sure it was, he could pretend he hadn't heard.

Havtor had been a message-runner for the temple almost since he could walk. When allowed to compete at festival games he always placed at sprinting. Thus he was short of breath but still at a jog when he at last circled the wall of Herkeby and came round to the docks.

People were pointing, not at him but upward.

"By the gods!"

"Never seen such a thing!"

"Boy, do you see?"

"Yes," Havtor called without looking, "yes, I do!" He leaped into the oared and sailed faering, cast off the line, and rowed out. A few heads turned his way in surprise, but he'd borrowed the craft from Trygve so often they shrugged it off.

He wasn't going to catch the dandelion-seed-person, not before they hit the water. He didn't really think this was a dandelion-seed-person of course, or that there was such a thing. It was someone who'd found a very clever way to take to the air. Maybe they'd jumped off a mountain. Maybe it was a Svartálfar; the dark elves had a reputation for cunning devices. It certainly didn't look like a dwarf. Indeed it was starting to look like a young woman. Havtor rowed harder, got into the deep water, and unfurled the sail.

The wind was in his favor and he made better time.

As the drifting woman (girl, maybe — she looked close to his age) fell closer to the water she began shedding armor. Wise, Havtor thought. You wouldn't want to be weighed down by metal in the Mikillvatn. But as he got closer he wondered if he could help best by recovering the gear. He managed to snatch a breastplate and greaves but lost the rest. They were intricately decorated with linnorm-like shapes around the edges.

The flyer splashed down. She flailed as if the impact had taken the wind out of her, and she seemed to be getting caught in the lines that connected her to the blue canopy that she'd ridden down. It didn't help that she refused to let go of a double-bladed longsword. He nosed the boat in close. Careful not to let the whole works tip, he offered her a line. She clung thus to the edge of the faering for a time, breathing hard, and began using the sword to cut her way free of the canopy. Her leverage was poor and she made little headway, so Havtor helped her with the dagger from gothi Bendik. At last freed she climbed on board, shivering. Havtor found her a blanket from the wooden utility chest Trygve kept under the bow. She gratefully accepted it, saying something that sounded like "Shay-shay."

Only now did it occur to him that this was a person from far away, not a Norrønir, nor a dark elf or a dwarf, not even someone from Araland or Swithenmark. Her wet hair was midnight dark, her eyes a mead-like brown, and her skin had a hue that reminded him a bit of sunsets. Even dragged from the water she seemed to him startlingly beautiful, and he forced himself not to stare.

"You're from far away," he said out loud. "You probably can't understand me. We'd best get you to shelter."

She coughed and said, in strongly accented Norrønian, "In truth I am from about one *li* overhead. And I know your tongue, Norrønir." When she spoke the *r* sounds came out more like *l* sounds, so that it sounded as though she said *Nollonil*. But he could understand her. "Thank you for helping me from the water. Now I have a job to do."

"What is it?" he said, startled that she knew his language so well. Although Havtor piloted the faering he immediately felt out-ranked. She seemed a bit older than him and a great deal more experienced. It was somewhat off-putting but also energizing. He was ready to escort her wherever, gallantly. The hard part was surely done.

"I have to report a murder."

After she'd been distracted by the barbaric violence at the plateau, De-Zhen had encountered a more personal problem — the lake. She'd been so preoccupied with the murder and the crash site she'd lost any chance of steering toward land. She would plunge into the water beyond the circular-walled town passing beneath her.

Yet somebody in a small, sailed boat looked to be trying to intercept her. He'd taken note of her despite her blue clothing and blue chute, camouflage in case of landings in hostile country. She hoped he'd prove a friend in this murderous land. She was going to come down hard ...

Her armor! By all the demons of the seven skies she was a fool! She'd landed in practice but not over water. The armor would be a liability. Frantically she removed the pieces just before the impact.

The water looked smooth as blue silk and hit her hard as ice. She connected as glancingly as possible but still saw fireworks as she flailed in the cold lake. She'd grown up in an inland village where her only swimming experience had been during crew training.

The local peasant (a fisherman perhaps, though he was just a boy) showed up just in time. He rescued her and some of her armor from the water. Sputtering and shivering in his boat, she informed him of the situation.

"I have to report a murder," she repeated to the fisher-boy, who she feared might be some kind of simpleton. He hadn't, it seemed, even brought nets. Despite her many difficulties, she was grimly proud that she hadn't lost her jian. She pointed it at the town. "We must go to your people." Next she pointed at the woods. "Then I must reach my ship."

The barbarian boy, pale enough to seem ill but pleasant-looking for all that, stared in a somewhat rabbit-like way. She rather enjoyed discomfiting him. Half-drowned fallen sky sailors, she reasoned, have to take what pleasures they can. He seemed to not know what to say, and responded by fetching a hunk of bread and offering it to her.

"Xiexie," she said. "Thank you." She added between nibbles, "I can pay. Though I do not know if your people will take my yuan. We have rarely come to this land. There may not be trade in the future."

"I will take your money," he seemed to blurt. After a pause he said, "In an honest way. Not like a thief. It would be interesting, to see your money." Another pause. "A murder, you said?"

"Please. I am bound by honor to report. I am a witness. After that, my duty is to find my ship."

"All right." The boy angled the sail. The wind was against them but by tacking he made progress. "My name is Havtor. Havtor Rune-son. What is yours?"

"Chen De-Zhen. You can call me De-Zhen. I am a sky-ship mapmaker from LongGuo."

"Sky-ship. Is that what made the big crashing sound earlier?"

"You did not see it?" That was almost as shocking as the attack and the murder.

Havtor shook his head. "Sometimes I get very focused on things. I wanted to make sure I reached you and that you were okay."

"Why?"

He blinked as if puzzled. "It is the right thing to do."

"I mean, why you? Is it your job to rescue people?"

"No." He laughed. "My job is to be the worst scribe on the planet."

"I do not understand."

So as they sailed he told her something of the local temple. Much of it was confusing, for all that she'd studied this land as much as anyone on her ship. She knew the names of many local gods, but they were mostly just names. They did not seem to fit together into a cosmic bureaucracy like the deities of home. More like a cosmic shouting match.

Some of it was familiar, however, especially how he needed to learn much lore and become skilled at drawing characters, and that he did not feel he fit in, and that he wanted to please a demanding parent.

She told him, "My mother was not happy I became a sky sailor. I keep thinking what she would say now." She told him about the aerial attack, and was just getting to the murder when he interrupted.

"Look! A boat from the town." They'd swung around the huge black island he'd called Bitter Rock Barrow and came upon the small town harbor. It was crowded with people and with boats casting off.

"This is ... Herkeby, yes?" she said.

"Yes, Herkeby. You're very knowledgable, I —" He swore something she couldn't translate. "That's Inga the Undaunted's boat! She's the jarl of the town. The leader. It's a real ocean-going longship, you know. She bought it in Korjengard and actually had a bunch of men carry the thing here from the nearest navigable river. Crazy, but they gladly did it for Inga."

Havtor laughed and waved. She understood. He felt like a hero. But De-Zhen knew at once this was no time for laughter. The men in the boat looked worried and somber-faced. One of them, an older man, greatly resembled Havtor.

"Father!" Havtor called out.

"Havtor! Thank Aurvímnir you are safe."

The boats maneuvered so that they drifted ten feet beside each other. Sound carried easily over the water; even the people in other boats or on the piers could hear them.

Havtor's father said with mingled worry and frustration, "What possessed you to come over here and steal Trygve's boat?"

"I didn't steal it!" Havtor objected. "I borrowed it!"

"I'll be the judge of that," said a second man, his age between Havtor's and his father's. The man was smiling but there was an edge of consternation to that smile. "Just be glad Jarl Inga's busy right now. It's all right, kid. I figured out you were making a rescue."

Havtor pointed at De-Zhen. "I saw her fall into the water."

"Is she from the sky-ship?" asked the man, whom she decided must be Trygve.

"Yes! Her name is De-Zhen! She says she has to ..." His face fell. De-Zhen realized why. *Report a murder* should be his next words, and though it must be said there would be trouble. As she gathered breath to speak in Havtor's stead she was pre-empted by Havtor's father.

"Son, I have to tell you. There was an accident at the temple. Bendik, gothi of Naði, saw the sky-ship as we prepared for the Springtime rite. It startled him so much he fell from the cliff. He had gotten very clumsy in his old age, but this ..." Havtor's father shook his head. "Then you disappeared and I feared the worst. I had to come see if the person who ran away and took the boat was you ..."

Suddenly his voice broke off, as he stared at his son.

Shocked, Havtor had raised the dagger he'd used to help free De-Zhen from the parachute. She didn't know why he did so. Aside from its fine quality it meant nothing to her, but it did mean something to Havtor's father.

"That's Bendik's," he said.

"I know. He loaned it to me before — before —"

The man Trygve, who had been so friendly before, frowned and clenched the edge of the longboat. "If he loaned it to you, where is the sheath?"

"I didn't steal it," Havtor said.

"I didn't say you did," Trygve said, "but you're using that word a lot lately. Is there more you're not telling us?"

"Yes!" De-Zhen called out. "I am Chen De-Zhen of LongGuo's Treasure Fleet, and I must report a murder." As they all stared she pointed. "Someone pushed someone else off that plateau."

"What?" Havtor's father said. "No ... ah, esteemed foreign visitor. I am Rune the gothi, of the temple yonder. I tell you my friend fell by accident."

"Did you," Havtor said, "see that personally, Father?"

"No. There was a fog about the plateau. I only heard the scream. Poor man. I can see, visitor, how it might seem to be a murder, but —
"

"Not 'seem,'" De-Zhen insisted. "I am a good watcher. I saw it. The person was pushed."

Rune turned to Trygve. Trygve pounded fist to palm. "Drown me in Gjöll. This thing's a mess. Too many oddities. Kid, lady — I think we'd better settle this at Inga's Longhouse."

"Good!" De-Zhen said. "Let us settle it!"

"All right ..." Havtor said, less certainly.

But his voice was overwhelmed by the roar of a huge wave that suddenly sprang into being between their craft and the longboat. It was so big it hid the harbor from view. Havtor immediately seized the tiller and struggled to keep the boat from capsizing. De-Zhen grabbed the oars and tried to give them some forward momentum. Glancing over her shoulder she could just see the harbor again as the wave rushed down; it seemed to her none of the other craft, not even Inga's, experienced more than gentle ripples.

Between them they managed to ride out the wave. At last the watery tumult began to ebb and their boat rocked wildly at a parade-field's distance from Inga's vessel. "Magic!" Havtor cried across the roiling waters. "You know it, Father!"

De-Zhen snatched a look behind. Rune, Havtor's father, scratched his beard but said nothing.

Suddenly Havtor reached a decision. "Keep rowing, De-Zhen!" he called, and adjusted the sail. It seemed his new goal was to get away from here. Soon he'd caught a strong wind.

But the hostile magic was not done with them. A whirlpool suddenly manifested ahead. Havtor's hands flew between tiller and sail like hummingbirds and De-Zhen's arms flexed like eagles' wings. They escaped the whirlpool's edge; it even gave them a burst of speed. But now a surge of water seemed determined to crush them into a rocky shallows ahead. Havtor nimbly steered them around. If De-Zhen were feeling paranoid, she'd have said the lake itself was trying to kill them. But she suspected the source was a human being. A human being who could be fought.

"Why do you run away?" she demanded. "Do you not have friends and family back there?"

"These effects — it's gothi magic! Priestly power! I have a tiny bit of it. I can make spoiled food healthy. I can make you a bit luckier in a fight. A few other things. But that's nothing to what the three main gothar of our temple can do. They were all there. Rune the Relentless — my father. And I saw Svein the Scowling and Gundar the Greedy on the docks. They could have heard you. One of them is a killer, and he doesn't want you to give him away. Without you there's no counter to the story that Bendik was just clumsy and unlucky."

The disturbances in the water continued to chase them. An unnatural rift, like a small gorge made entirely of water, appeared behind them. The skiff shook. Both De-Zhen and Havtor cried out as the boat lurched. But whoever had commanded it had miscalculated their speed — speed that had been enhanced by the magical wave, whirlpool, and current. Had they been only a little slower they'd have been caught in the trench. Yet soon they steadied and the harbor fell fast behind them and the waters ahead were calm save for ripples raised by the winds. Havtor had helped De-Zhen escape drowning several times now and the day wasn't over. She was impressed.

"We'll go back under dark and make contact with Jarl Inga," Havtor said. "She'll sort this out."

De-Zhen took a few minutes to think about that. "No," she

decided. "Your people are crazy and violent." It was not diplomatic. But she couldn't find softer words in Norrønian.

Havtor looked a little stung. "You're not seeing us at our best. But you're not exactly wrong. You want to find your ..." He seemed to struggle with the concept as he spoke it. "... Sky-ship?"

"I did my duty. I reported a murder. Your people attacked me. Now I return to my regular duty." She gave a sharp nod, sealing the decision in her mind. "I can't compel you. You can take me as far as you want and then I will do my best. Maybe we can go back with soldiers so they won't dare kill me."

He stared at her as though she was some sort of mythical being. For a moment she thought he'd shout at her, but he surprised her and said, "I'll get you as far as I can. You can pay me if you like. I know this lake better than anybody." He looked back over his shoulder and said, "But we're going to need a lot of luck."

Luck was with them. The afternoon winds were fast and changeable today. Havtor hadn't been bragging about his knowledge of the lake. It was as if he could sense the change in the wind before it began. Inga's longboat was a fine craft and in changeless weather it might have won the race. But bit by bit Havtor's tacking put them far beyond the longboat. He had a few tricks to help. Longships had a small draft, but the faering's was smaller; he slipped across mudflats and reed beds impassible to the longship. The faering was lighter as well. Had the wind died the rowers of the longship would have overrun them, but the wind proved a friend.

One more bit of luck, and one that De-Zhen didn't agree was lucky: a downpour began once their lead was well established and the longship was a distant fleck behind them. The wind was still gusting but water and mist filled their vision and even Havtor had some uncertainty as to where they were. At least the longship would be even more uncertain.

After hours of cold and wet, the mists cleared ahead but not behind. Havtor saw the hills of the southeastern shore through a gray haze, beyond which plumes of mist, pink in the late afternoon light, rose in half a dozen places like the smoke from fires.

At last the rain eased, and in blood-colored sunset mists, they pulled the faering onto the southern shore. Havtor had chosen this spot because it had especially thick clumps of trees and a smooth enough shore they could drag the faering well out of sight. Once they'd done so, they slipped back to the treeline to look back.

The rain had stopped, leaving the air clear as the polished windows, glass all the way from Oslendholm, in the temple at Fornuppsalir. The sun had set on the Herkeby side of the Mikillvatn, and below the fading salmon-pink glow outlining the mountains the town was only visible by the roughly circular pattern of firelights, like a herd of corralled torches beside the faint reflected sunset glow of water the hue of a faded rose. It seemed to Havtor there were more fires than usual. The town was roused, and there were probably men sailing in the dark, or following the trails around the lake, to find the fugitive.

Fugitives, he corrected himself. He'd become one now.

"We'd better get back under the trees," he said to De-Zhen. "I don't see the longship, but it could be just around the big curve in the southern shore." They raided Trygve's well-stocked trunk so they had cloaks and blankets, and some dried meat and fruit, bread and cheese. But Trygve used the faering for jaunts, not long expeditions, so they could maybe last a couple of days. Hopefully they'd find the sky-ship by then.

Havtor said. "I hate doing this to Trygve. I'm going to be owing favors to him for years. If I'm not exiled." He gulped. *Or killed*, he thought. *Well, you wanted to prove yourself at something other than scholarship. Congratulations, Havtor.*

They traveled just inside the tree-line for a while. In the evening shadows Havtor didn't think they'd be seen. Beyond the trees the sky had gone a pale, almost silvery blue and the smooth lake was of a like color except where it reflected the somber dark green of the shadowed hills.

"Surely they would not kill you," De-Zhen said abruptly.

"Probably not," he admitted. "Unless their tempers are up. But it looks bad. I have the dead man's dagger, and we ran away."

She shook her head, at him, at the forest, at the lake, at everything. "If they suspect you of wrongdoing, that means they now suspect there is something wrong with the story of a simple accident. And the real murderer had them convinced of the accident story. We are dangerous to him now. That is why he magically attacked us. Could he have used such magic without revealing himself?"

Havtor mulled over her words. He was becoming used to her accent, and was finding her better spoken than many a Norrønir.

"I think so," Havtor replied. "I've seen my father use that power before. He had to make small gestures and speak a quiet prayer. There was a bit of water and dust he had to mix. You can carry things like that in pouches or small vials. I think in all the excitement it wouldn't have been too hard for a gothi on a boat or on the piers to do it and not be noticed."

De-Zhen thought about it. "But everyone would know it was a … gothi … yes? Even if they did not know which one?"

"They might blame it on us. They wouldn't expect me to have such power but they don't trust me completely now. Maybe they'll think I have hidden strengths. Now that's funny! And they don't know what you're capable of. Also, there are magical beings of various kinds around this lake; one of them even likes to visit Bitter Rock Barrow. I don't think commanding the waters is something old Bror can do, but who can be sure?"

"But *you* do not think it is this … Bror."

"No. Between what you've said and what I've seen, I think it really is a gothi."

There were a lot of unknowns in De-Zhen's account, he mused. Yet he trusted it. It was absurd to think a castaway would make extra trouble for herself by lying about what she'd seen. And Bendik *had* unquestionably fallen off a cliff. It was chilling, to carry a dead man's knife.

And that realization led his thoughts down still darker paths. A gothi was involved. One of the powerful ones. There was no one else like them for scores of miles. On the water voices would carry easily; the murderer could have heard everything from anywhere in the harbor. Svein the Scowling or Gunder the Greedy.

Or ... Rune the Relentless. The idea seemed impossible. Angry as he might be at Father, he found it madness to imagine Rune as a murderer. Father was forthright, grim, direct. Even in a deadly rage he'd surely confront a man from the front, allowing the other to defend himself with word or weapon.

And why would *any* of them kill Bendik?

The landscape diverted his thoughts. He welcomed the distraction. They'd been meandering west, but a rocky region obliged them to turn south and they stumbled deeper into the forest. There were two kinds of obstacle — thick bushes and small plants between the trees, and barriers of needled tree branches crowding into the undergrowth.

Havtor tried using the dagger and he found it cut well, at least against thorny bushes. But De-Zhen insisted on taking a turn, hacking at bramble and tree limbs with her sword.

He watched her determinedly muscling through the undergrowth. He became even more certain he trusted her. Strange visitor though she was he was sure she was no fool or liar. Liars usually lied to smooth things over for themselves, and she brought too much trouble on herself. Mistaken? He doubted it. He'd known people at the temple so brittle in their opinions that they had to be right about everything. De-Zhen didn't have that manner. Witnessing murder was a complication in her already dismal day.

He saw her shiver. He cursed.

"I'm being an idiot," he said. "It's getting late. Come this way."

Close beside the tree trunks was some respite from the under-brush. Here the dense branches overhead choked out sunlight and prevented the growth of other plants. These places were dark and dry and a bit warmer, too.

"We should use the blankets to make sure we're completely dry," he said. "It will get cold at night and any wetness will bring on a chill. It can kill you. My mother used to say, *The weather can kill you just as surely as any berserker, and it's better at sneaking up on you.* You can go first. I will look away."

De-Zhen simply nodded. As he turned away, he wondered at her matter-of-factness. Her command of his language was excellent but he supposed it wasn't easy for her to simply make small talk. And she was a soldier, of a kind. Havtor had no experience of soldiers, though he'd heard of them. In his experience there were warriors, yes, but they usually had ordinary lives as farmers or herders or craftsmen, and only fought at need. The closest thing to an army in Herkeby were Inga the Undaunted's housecarls and guards, and even they had other duties running endless errands to keep the town running smoothly. There were mercenaries but they were half-vagabond. The closest thing to a real army was in the city of the high king, where you'd find men who fought and nothing else. But Havtor had never been there.

"How many on your sky-ship?" he found himself asking.

"State secret," she said. Then she laughed and said, "Let us say between forty and sixty people."

"You must be packed like a bucket of fish."

"You mean it is cramped? Yes. We sleep in bunks on *Changning* — the ship — except the Zhǐhuī shī, the one in charge, and his top people. We get to stretch out on deck. And the navigation room is nice. You need space to set out maps."

"You said your job is mapmaker?"

"Yes. I am good at it. I also join groups to talk with local people.

And I do simple ship jobs." She chuckled. "I am not good at wandering through trees."

"Not many are. Even here! Some people boast a lot about traveling in the wild, but they usually mean being away from towns, traveling good paths between farms. Your ship won't have landed on a road, though. Can you sketch a map of the area where you saw the ship go down?"

"When I am done I will use a stick and the dirt, while you get dry. I will not look," she said with a little laugh. He wasn't sure how to take the laugh. But at least they were on good terms. Right now she was all he had.

When they were both dry and she'd sketched a remarkably accurate map of the lake, he judged from the position of the X marking the crash site that they needed to head deeper into Raven's Wood bearing east-southeast. The faering lacked a compass but De-Zhen had one as part of her usual gear. She sighted along it and pointed. "That way."

He scratched the day's stubble on his chin. (Mother had never liked the look of his beard so he'd been clean-shaven. He supposed that ended now.)

"Twenty miles," he said. "Twenty miles through the Raven's Wood."

"On a good path we can do it in a day," she said. "Will we have a good path?"

"Ha! No. There are trails running around either side of the lake, and a few farms. I think we'll have to chance them. But Inga, our jarl, she's going to have people riding those paths. They'll be looking for us, and spreading word."

"You have gotten into a lot of trouble for me."

He tried to sound grim, but his voice squeaked a bit and betrayed him. "It was the right thing to do. The gods value courage, and they see all, or most all. Anyway, even cutting along the path I'd give it two days. Our food will run out in a day, but we can go hungry for a while. Hopefully your friends will have food. And there are berries, and mushrooms. Maybe we can kill game. Maybe there'll be a merciful farmer. We'll make it."

He wasn't sure he believed it himself, but it sounded well-said. He hoped.

De-Zhen woke during the night and saw a strange glow in the dark. There was a trail of little glowing mushrooms leading out from beneath the tree, up to where De-Zhen herself slept.

She shook Havtor. "Wake up." Once he'd done so, mumbling things about Rune or runes, she pointed. "What is that?"

Bleary-eyed, Havtor stared at the trail of glowing fungi. He blinked a few times. "The Underhand," he murmured.

"What? What about a hand?"

"Underhand. It's the name of a band of alfar, or elves. Dark elves in particular, Svartálfar. We call them that because they're usually deep underground. Short, pointed-eared people, very pale —"

"We fought them! They attacked the ship! This is from them?"

"I've heard of this. It's in a couple of chronicles." Havtor's difficulties in writing had no effect on his ability to read, for which he thanked the gods, unless his studies had piled up. "Underhand agents can attach special mushrooms to people they want to track. The mushroom drops spores that grow into these luminescent things. Leaving a trail."

She punched the ground. "That little goushi must have left this behind when we fought in the air."

"Goushi?"

"Dog shit."

"Huh. Could the dog shit have survived?"

"I did. His bat might have lasted long enough. He might want revenge."

"Or he gave up, or he's dead."

"I need to find this tracking mushroom you speak of. Help me look." Together they scrutinized her clothing, armor and gear. She was grimly amused by Havtor's diffidence in examining her garments. He seemed shy of being this close to a woman. *Good!* she imagined her mother saying. *But be ready to chop his head off if he tries anything!* She rolled her eyes.

The tracking mushroom turned out to be in one corner of De-Zhen's breastplate. She ripped it off, stalked out from under the tree's branching canopy, and threw the mushroom as far as she could.

"The moon and its child are up," she said. "We have light. We should move."

"I suppose you're right. But it's easy to get lost, traveling at night. Actually it's easy to get lost traveling by day, in Raven's Wood."

"I am not waiting for that sneak to stab me in the dark. We can check the luópán — the compass — every so often."

Havtor led the way at first, on the theory that he knew the country, though he admitted he'd rarely been this side of the lake. It was a cold journey to the lakeside path, and in this area the path was well inland. It took a diǎn, what Havtor would call about half an hour. In addition to the old snow that had become slush and now re-frozen, and the leftover snow clinging to tree branches that sometimes slid onto them as they pushed past, there was also a scattering of freshly-falling snow drifting onto them in the moonslight. De-Zhen's hands and face did not find it an enjoyable journey, but her eyes did, for the moonlit snowy forest was a place of wonder; nor was it unpleasant to study the young man's strong shoulders and — *No, be professional, sky-sailor!* she chided herself.

At last they stumbled into the path without quite realizing it was there. It was just a meandering track of frozen, crunchy mud between two walls of evergreens, with the light of the the moon and its own satellite silvering the patches of ice that lay here and there. There was no sign of pursuit.

Havtor looked around. "If Inga sent horsemen then at least we'll be harder to spot now than by day. I think we should walk for a time along the path. But we should be alert for riders coming in either direction."

"That is good," she said. She took a sighting on her compass and walked beside him. "What else is there to fear, Havtor?"

"Any number of things. Trolls. Draugar. Angry farm dogs. But I think the path is pretty good for now."

"And your father? Do you fear him, Havtor?"

Havtor said nothing. He just walked, staring straight ahead.

"Did I offend?" De-Zhen asked.

"No. I ... I get so angry at him. And I fear, not him, but his anger. I feel like a bird tossed by a storm when he's angry."

"Is he a cruel man?"

"No. He never hits. Hardly ever yells. But his disappointment feels like fire." He was silent again. De-Zhen wondered if anyone had ever asked him such questions. After many minutes he said, "Maybe it's because my mother died when I was very young. It made me stay awake at night thinking how anyone could die, at any time. I found I couldn't defy my father. I was afraid of losing him too."

"I do not know what that is like. My father died before I was old enough to remember. My mother made me the center of everything. Like the center of a map. That is hard sometimes."

They continued along the path. Sometimes it widened until it was almost a road; other times it compressed until De-Zhen was afraid they'd lose it. Occasionally they ran into a snow-covered stump where someone had decided there was no help for it but to fell a tree blocking the path. Stepping over such a stump Havtor suddenly spoke, as if the small change in altitude had broken his diffidence. "Do you have brothers and sisters?"

"Three brothers. None of them passed the Examination." She smiled in satisfaction. "But they aren't so bad. One has the family farm. One is a sailor — an ocean sailor. One became a ... I do not know your word for it? Someone who takes a vow and wears a robe and lives in a special place and prays for the health of the world."

"We sure don't have anybody like that here. There are people called 'monks' in Araland. They sound sort of similar. How ... how did your mother feel about you going far away?"

"Ha! She hated it!"

"Oh."

"But after a while she spoke to me again. I think she is proud of me but won't say it. She doesn't want me to get too big-headed."

"You don't seem big-headed at all. You are handling falling off a sky-ship much better than I would."

"Thank you."

"I mean, I'd go splat!" He mimed an impact with his hands.

She chuckled. She actually felt flushed and embarrassed by his admiration. She who had fought Svartálfar. "It is good not to be alone. Or go splat."

They came around a bend and spotted candlelight in a farmhouse. The house was set back a bit into the forest, off the trail, in a large clearing, the fields beyond glinting pearly in the moonslight. The house had a thatched roof that caught some of the silvery glow.

"This is a chance to get warm," Havtor said.

"That would be good," De-Zhen said. "This land is like a line by my favorite poet: 'the north wind was cutting through them like a sword.' But have they been warned about us?"

"Maybe. This is a strange hour for them to be up and about. Maybe they are watching for us. But I've never been a farmer. Maybe some rise exceedingly early."

They stood there in indecision.

"When in doubt be bold," said De-Zhen, stepping forward.

"Are you sure you're not a Norrønir?" Havtor said close behind, and she grinned.

A number of things nagged at Havtor as they approached the farmhouse. For one thing, although he hadn't been this way in years he didn't remember any steadings that looked quite like this. For another, the clearing of the trees seemed haphazard. The house itself looked at first glance like a proud miniature longhouse with a cheerfully open front door. But as they approached the thatch looked withered and the wood looked rotten, as though the moaning wind might blow the works over.

At that moment they heard hoofbeats and turned around. On the path a rider passed by. Havtor couldn't tell who it was in the darkness, but the moonslight glinted off a helm as the rider passed from the direction of Herkeby off to the east. The helm did not turn; the rider did not so much as glance at the farmhouse.

Although glad to have avoided the rider, Havtor thought the lack of notice strange. Some instinct warned him not to approach the front door. "Let's check around back and see what we can see."

"All right."

The stroll earned them another surprise. The farmhouse was only a farmhouse in front. The back of it was a shambles, as if a giant sword had cloven the building in two. The break was right down the middle, slicing the main hall and the fire-pit. Of the missing half of the house there was no sign.

A blue-gray cat was sitting on the edge of the halved fire-pit, and the glow from the embers was green.

"I think this is a bad place," De-Zhen said, her sword out.

"A half-house?" Havtor said, his flesh going clammy as he remembered old stories. "It reminds me of the half-ships the draugar are sometimes seen in."

"You said that word before. Dra— what?"

"Draugar. When bad men die, they may not go on to the places of the dead but linger to trouble the world. They become draugar. They mostly lurk in their barrows or ships. But sometimes they attack the living out of malice."

Out of vengeance, something replied. The voice was in their minds but also seemed to belong to the wind in the trees. *Vengeance against the arrogance of the living. How dare you selfish children hoard your life-blood.* The cat was licking its paw, but it gave the oddest impression of covering up a laugh.

"Did you hear that?" De-Zhen asked.

"Did it come from the cat?" Havtor said, watching it.

Yes, came the voice. The cat looked his way, and even though it faced away from the emerald fire its eyes glowed green.

"I was right," De-Zhen said. "This is a bad place."

I can make it better, traveler. A mist flowed in like the aftermath of heavy rain, and when its green and silver reflections had parted again the moonlit farmhouse was different. The roof was made from tree trunks smaller than those nearby and it curved up at either end like the prow and stern of a boat. Inside the cleft structure there was no fire-pit, but there were hanging scrolls of intricately painted land-scapes, and tables and chairs that looked to have an elegant square pattern repeated in the wood.

"Mófǎ!" said De-Zhen. "Magic! It is my mother's home come to life."

Havtor shivered, but he stood his ground and said, "I have heard that the after-walkers can have many powers, but I did not know illusion was one of them."

The illusions are not mine, came the whisper, and the cat hissed.

The mist returned and now the trees closed in and they beheld a grassy mound with a small hut on top, a gash within the mound leading into darkness, and the cat pacing languidly in front of the gash. A group of four transparent, pale figures seemed to stand in a half-circle around the hut. They were a woman and three children, the oldest one tall as Havtor, the middle perhaps eight, the youngest a toddler. Their eyes glowed like moonslight. They did not move.

Havtor's legs were shaking but he called defiantly, "Name yourself!"

I have forgotten my name. I left fighting for farming hundreds of summers ago. But when the Fimbulwinter came, I found my greatest foe was the weather. Summer hid her face, so I strangled one of my daughters as an offering to the High Father.

The wind picked up and Havtor almost thought he caught the sound of a distant scream.

But it was only she who escaped. For my wife struck me a mortal wound. Dying, I went berserk. She and the other children are still with me, as you see. They do not understand what happened. My family's longing for home and safety touches the minds of travelers and sometimes brings me prey.

"We'll be going now," Havtor said.

I think not. You are both young and strong. I have not fed in many moons.

"We mean no harm!" De-Zhen replied.

That makes it easier.

That cat leaped upon Havtor. It hit him like a bale of hay. Havtor fell over into the snow.

The cat's eyes gleamed, twin moons made of emerald foxfire. Havtor felt something leaving him. He only knew it by its absence; its departure made him feel there'd be no more throwing snowballs or climbing trees or pulling sails tight or smiling at girls or feeling spirits burn down his throat. Somehow the cat was drinking all that in, leading Havtor closer and closer to the straw-death that was the fear of most Norrønir, a dwindling into infirmity and helplessness, beyond any hope of great deeds. *You will dwell forever in the half-house,* hissed the cat in his mind. *That is fitting, for you are half-people, each torn between two destinies, the hearth or the road. You are like me, not truly alive nor truly dead.*

"It takes more than one night to freeze a river," said De-Zhen, and stabbed the cat through the middle.

Before the cat yowled, Havtor had felt he was falling down a long well. But at the bottom of the well a rune suddenly blazed the color of sunlight: ᛉ. As the cat screeched in pain Havtor snarled, focusing all his energy on the image of a fluttering white sail lit by the sun. He shoved the cat up and off him.

De-Zhen helped Havtor up. He was shaking like a man in a blizzard. But the straw-death hadn't gotten him yet.

The cat got to its feet, a huge gash in its side revealing pale ribs and blue flesh. It did not bleed. Before their eyes the cat swelled into an armored man, but not truly a man, for his armor hung in tatters, and his skin was a sickly blue.

Your paths lead to death, fools, whether here or deeper into Raven's Wood. Surrender to the shadows now.

Havtor pulled out a small vial, poured water onto his hand, and sprinkled it in the air over his and De-Zhen's heads. She flinched. "What is that?"

"Rainwater I collected from holes in the great tree. For luck." He crouched and with his wet fingers drew a design in the snow.

"Now what are you doing?" De-Zhen said. "Preparing your grave?"

"It's the Dagaz rune," he said completing it, focusing all his hope and fury on it. "Meaning 'day!'"

The draugr flinched and hissed.

Nothing else occurred. Dagaz was just a drawing in the snow. Havtor had not mastered the power of this or any rune. Nor could he be sure that the blessing of the rainwater had any effect.

But the distraction allowed De-Zhen to swing her sword with a snarl and chop the head off the draugr.

They ran into the woods at once, faces smacking into snow-covered evergreen branches. Havtor risked a glance behind him. The draugr's body had snatched up the head and was poised for a throw. "Come on!" he called to De-Zhen.

The draugr head sailed above theirs and tumbled down branches into the snow ahead of them. It hissed like a cat and transformed into one, albeit much smaller than the first. The ghastly eyes were the same, however.

"Begone!" Havtor yelled, terrified but also furious. He held out a fist. "In the name of Aurvímnir High Father, I condemn you, I who am son of his gothi!"

The cat growled and hissed. De-Zhen said, "I also condemn you in the name of the Emperor of LongGuo! Whose daughter I am not! I would not be so presumptuous as to claim that!" She added, "We do not fear death!"

You should, came the rasping voice. *You should fear it more than anything.*

"I see!" De-Zhen said, "That is your fear! You fear admitting your own death! Fear made you a monster, before you even became this beast you are."

The creature made to spring, and Havtor could hear the thumping of the rest of the draugr's body running up behind them. He and De-Zhen pressed together back to back to make a stand.

But there came a new sound, a flapping from overhead, and a white shape flashed in the light of the moons. It descended, hovering over the snow, and Havtor beheld a magnificent young woman in chainmail and helmet, bearing a spear and a shield. Her red hair flowed in the wind, as did the swan-like wings emanating from her back.

The cat yowled at her in recognition. *Have you come at last to claim me, eldest?*

That day, Father, will never come, said the winged woman. *I come only to aid your victims, for they fought you valiantly. And to once again try to call my family to their reward.*

It was the winter who made me this, not I!

Then make your plea to the winter; I will not hear it. She swooped down and skewered the cat on her spear. Then in the same motion she flew past the gaping Havtor and De-Zhen and slammed the spear into the headless dead warrior that had just caught up with them. She spun in mid-air and the cat and headless warrior were flung into a tree. They toppled down and blurred together and were one entity once more. The skeletal jarl leaped forward and grappled with the winged woman. Together they rose into the moonslight, struggling.

Run, travelers! the winged woman called. *This battle is not for you!*

You will have your share in the future. Sight your way through the light-ning-riven tree.

Havtor and De-Zhen ran, their footfalls crunching on the hard-packed snow and frozen earth. It seemed to Havtor at one point that spectral figures, three children and a woman, ran briefly beside him, their faces transfixed with both sorrow and joy. They dispersed like mist with a dawn-wind at their backs. And Havtor and De-Zhen ran until a slice of the sun had made a crown upon a distant eastern hill and lit their breaths so that they both seemed like walking chimneys.

They stopped. De-Zhen leaned over and Havtor fell to his knees.

"What ..." De-Zhen finally gasped, "... what a mad country this is!"

"That ..." Havtor said with a great wave back the way they'd come, "was not what I consider my country!"

"He was your countryman."

"Was. Was, was, was. He's dead now."

"Death is not the same as leaving the country."

"Well, it ought to be! When people die they're supposed to descend the great path toward the realm of the dead."

"Strange. Our dead are said to ascend to the spirit world where they watch over their descendants."

"Well, if ours are lucky they get chosen for one of the realms of the divine warriors instead. Like the one who saved us. Either way, spirits aren't supposed to stick around in their old bodies."

"Agreed!"

"Though the bad ones sometimes do."

"There are more like that one?"

Havtor sank backward into the snow. He'd regret that later when the bits of snow melted down his neck and back, but for now it was a relief to just lie down. Staring up at the deep blue morning sky he said, "The draugar aren't everywhere."

"Good."

"Maybe one or two near every town."

"One or two!"

"But they're enough of a hazard that most people don't blunder around near barrows late at night. Just in case. Occasionally people explore barrows and get rich from old treasure. But some of those explorers just disappear sometimes. Anyway, I'd never have gone near that place if I'd known it was a barrow."

She laughed, a bit harshly. "Fine native guide you are."

"At least I kept us from going inside!"

"True. Well, I don't feel like sleeping, do you?"

"No." He sat up. "I've lost my bearings."

"So have I." She took out her compass and pointed east-south-east. "I know the directions but not where we are. That winged spirit said to find a tree hit by lightning. Can we trust her?"

"The Choosers of the Slain are sent by the gods. The only bad thing about them is they sometimes drag off the living before their times."

She made him repeat that and explain it and then said, "That is not very reassuring, Havtor Runeson."

He decided to change the subject. "The draugar don't like daylight, so it's said. We should be safe enough. But let's find some higher ground and then we can camp and maybe spot that tree."

It was easy enough to find an upward slope in the woods, because the fractured morning sunlight was replaced by green-brown undergrowth or ruddy soil. The harder part was finding actual high ground. Their first two ascents led only to minor ridges. But their third brought them to a rocky spire with just a few proud-looking trees lofting above their fellows. They were exhausted as they reached the cool shadowy spot between the three trees. From here they could see the lake in the distance. The fallen sky-ship remained invisible but they spotted a tall tree half a mile downslope split like a wishbone, streaks of exposed wood revealed like red-orange scars. Looking through the span sighted them toward an even thicker stretch of Raven's Wood.

There was no chance of their continuing, however. They had

slept badly and expended their strength in the fight. They collapsed and slept where they lay.

De-Zhen dreamed she was sitting the Government Exam again. Only this time she was doing it beside the temple she'd seen back near Herkeby. The chairs and tables were fashioned of the dark wood she remembered from home, but they were arranged at the cliff's edge where she'd seen the man fall. Havtor was taking the exam next to her. She saw that he was forming the language of LongGuo with great skill, while she was having trouble drawing the day-rune he'd formed in the snow. Her hands refused to make neat motions and straight lines. The proctor walked up to her, scowled at her page, and flung her off the cliff.

But she caught hold of an exposed tree root, one that jutted out from the rock face as the tree proper blotted out the sun. She struggled. She saw Havtor climbing down to get hold of her. He reached out and was beginning to help her up when lightning struck the tree and left the same rune burning in its trunk.

The tree toppled forward and she and Havtor went with it down the cliffside.

"De-Zhen!" Havtor was whispering in her ear. "Wake up!"

She awake at once in the chilly air and bright sunlight, reaching for weapons. She was sweaty and uncomfortable, having slept the morning in her gear. "What?" she began.

"Sh!" he said. "There's something down there."

They crept to the edge of the hill and saw something disturbing the undergrowth down among the shadows of the forest floor. From the sounds it was a large animal, perhaps a deer or bear. They got a glimpse of what appeared to be white fur. After a time the creature moved on to the west and they heard it no longer.

"What do you think that was?" she asked Havtor.

"Probably an animal," he said. "That draugr wouldn't be out by day. But there are strange things in Raven's Wood. Trolls. The small ones are mischievous, but bigger than that they get cruel and tough. At least the ones a bit larger than man-sized are. I don't want to think about the ones bigger than that. And there are ketta, huge fey cats. And vættir. They're nature spirits and they're not always nice." He frowned, as if he wanted to say more but wasn't certain of it.

"Do not keep your knowledge to yourself," she urged. "I only know this land by hearsay, or from high up, or on a map."

"So. As you've seen, my father is a gothi, a holy man of our Old Custom. And I'm a gothi in training, a very weak one. And that wave that hit us near Herkeby — I'm sure a strong gothi did that. So you see that they have power. Well, my father Rune can do more than the others. At great need he sometimes lays a compulsion on other beings, so they will serve him. He can do it to people, but also to magical creatures, at least some of them. He could track us that way."

She thought about that, sifting through the difficulties of his language. "So you fear some creature is following us. Would your father command it to attack?"

He took a long time to answer. "I don't think he'd ever hurt me on purpose. But if he thought I was up to no good ... I don't know. Family honor might be at stake. But he would not simply kill us. He would have questions first."

"So his servant might block us but not kill us, yes?"

"Maybe. But if he leads the other gothar to us, then one of *them* might kill us. The one who killed Bendik, I mean."

She looked at him carefully. There was a question she needed to ask, but she wanted them moving first. "We should go. My crew can help." *If they are still alive*, she thought but didn't say.

They gathered their things, an easier matter since they'd collapsed rather than camped. Her trainers would be dismayed. So would her mother. De-Zhen wished for a bath, even in freezing water. But in training she'd learned to ignore feeling dirty, sweaty, tired, sleepy, grumpy, aching, and lonely. At least she wasn't lonely. Though she still had to ask the question that might drive her new friend away.

As they descended the hill, however, he asked one of his own. "De-Zehn? Why are you so good at our language? Did everyone on your ship know it this well?"

She hoped he didn't think she was some kind of spy. She wasn't, of course, unless you considered any kind of scouting spying. "We all learned a little. There was a traveler, a countryman of yours, Frode the Footsore, who spent many years in a desert outpost, far from this land and far from mine. The Treasure Fleet recruited him to instruct our crews on languages, for he knew several. We have many such language experts."

He sounded a little suspicious. "I've never heard of anyone from here going so far. Nor of this Frode the Footsore."

She laughed. "I may never understand your people, Havtor! You go off and take terrible risks, travel far, have adventures. But you hardly ever write anything down! If half of what Frode said is true he is one of the great journeyers of all time. And you don't even know him."

He looked suddenly ashamed and she wasn't sure why. He said, with a bit of heat, "We are a people who believe that death is to be accepted. Not passively, like cattle. Boldly, like wolves. We seek out exciting deeds under the eyes of the gods. It is really for our own sake, not for the amusement of the idle and the curious. Sometimes we wander far, and only the gods know what we've accomplished."

"Like you," she said.

Now he looked angry. *De-Zhen*, she thought in dismay, *you may be good at languages, but you're a terrible diplomat!* She could imagine her mother saying, *See? You don't belong out there among crazy barbarians! They are like lit fireworks!*

Havtor said, "What do you mean?"

She held her hands palms-up. "I mean, you have risked much. For me. I am grateful. But ... it is for glory too, yes?"

That hit home, she realized. For a time the snow and frozen mud crunched under their feet. "Yes," he said. "I think you are right. It is a little bit about glory. Sorry I got mad there."

They entered the thicker body of trees. They crossed snow where the sky was open, dirt where it was not. He said, "In normal times I'd never wander this far. I used to, with my mother. She was a farm girl before she married my father. But she also hunted. I hiked many places with her. I didn't learn much about hunting, but a little bit about the woods. At least the woods on the other side of the lake."

"You miss her?"

"Sometimes. But it is hard to remember her too. It is easier when I'm out here. The temple is Father's world."

"She died, yes?" At his fresh look of hurt she added, "Forgive me, Havtor. I don't have all the words to say it gently."

"No, it is all right. Yes, she died of a sickness that passed through Herkeby a few years ago."

"That is how my father died."

"I am sorry."

"It was twelve years ago. I don't remember him well, either. The thing I remember most is him carrying me around his workplace. All the ink and paper and documents and maps. He was a clerk. Like you. He scribed for our village mayor."

"Why do you say, 'like me?'"

She looked at him sidelong. "Are you going to get mad again?"

"I'm not —" In his silence De-Zhen could hear a group of birds in a tall tree screeching about their approach, as if the tree were a ship about to repel boarders. "I ... I won't."

De-Zhen strove to put heart into her voice. "Your country is very different. But you are one of the people who learns things, and knows things. You are not a ruler, but you have much knowledge of the world and your gods, and you are training to help the people, yes? So, you are something like my father was. Where I come from, that is a very honorable thing. People compete for roles like that."

He sounded bitter. "That is very hard to believe."

"And you would be considered very brave. A scholar who can fight too."

Something seemed to clarify for him. "Like you."

She flushed and studied the snow. "I am not brave."

"You're braver than anyone I know," he said in a rush, "man or woman." He withdrew into himself again then, bundling himself with his own folded arms, and whether he was abashed or trapping his heat it was hard to say.

It was not a good time to ask her question, but it was probably the best she'd get. "Havtor. Hear me. You think one of your holy men tried to kill me. Because I saw him kill another holy man."

"Yes."

"I could not tell you who, except that it was a man in furs. But all three men who could have done it wore furs."

"All three." He seemed to chew the words.

"Three men outside on the plateau, in the fog." She tried to recall all the names. "Svein. Gundar. And Rune."

"And you suspect my father?"

"Not any more than the other two. But tell me, did he have reason to hate the dead man, this ... Bendik?"

"No!" Havtor thought about it, however. He seemed the kind of boy who could not help thinking about things. "Well, perhaps ..." The words seemed pulled out of him like an anchor from the depths. "If you stretch things. Bendik thought of himself as the rightful head gothi at the temple, because he was oldest. He wanted Father's job. It drove Father crazy. But Father would never kill him!"

"And the other two? Why would each of them do it?"

"Svein might do it out of sudden rage. He was always a fierce one. He'd pick fights and hurt animals. And he didn't like Bendik. I don't know about Gundar. But he's ambitious. Young and flashy. He'd like Father's job but with Bendik out of the way Gundar would be the obvious second in command, being the junior priest of the High Father. Maybe that would suit him."

Something about the situation nagged at Havtor's memory.

"They were going to do a ceremony of some kind. A fertility rite. Did you see any signs of that?"

"One of them made a symbol on the ground, I think," De-Zhen said. "He spread plant matter to do it. Grain or barley or rice. Like this." She stopped to draw symbols in the snow with a stick.

ᛋ ᛗ ᛋ

Havtor stroked the stubble on his chin. "That rune combination can mean 'harvest man.' In the past it could mean 'human sacrifice.' It's a little ambiguous. But Svein's been wanting to do a human sacrifice for ages. He thinks we've fallen from the true Old Custom by not doing it. That attitude's still around here and there." De-Zhen, shivered, remembering the draugr's tale. Havtor continued, "He's forbidden from snatching anyone for the purpose. But ... what if he arranged an accident? For a man he didn't like? Was Bendik in the symbols when he fell?"

"Yes. How horrible!"

"So, maybe Svein's motive is dislike plus human sacrifice. Gundar's is ambition. Father's — his would be self-protection, to remove a threat. I don't believe it, but that's what it would be. I think it's Svein."

She put kindness into her voice. "The truth is, my friend, you do not have enough knowledge to say for sure whether it was Svein, Gundar, or Rune. Regardless, I want my captain backing us before making any accusations."

Havtor, despite it all, seemed to stand taller as she said *my friend.* "Agreed," he said.

Havtor led them on through the woods. Snowy beard-like moss was everywhere in this area, as though the trees possessed grave elders' faces. Seen from below, the crowns of the trees, bathed in light, looked like green sunbursts. They encountered a river. Havtor hadn't expected this. But except for its reputation he didn't really know Raven's Wood, only its westernmost stretches. The river surged down from rugged hills to the east. Three waterfalls were visible from where they stood overlooking the flow. More falls might well be hidden by the trees, judging from the roars.

"Are you looking for something?" De-Zhen asked.

"A way across," Havtor said, for although it was only a little wider than the range of a good jumper, the river was one of those swift, rocky affairs frothing with whitewater and prone to treacherous hidden depths. Rocks and boulders looked like misshapen ships making headway against a narrow stormy ocean. One might, with icy resolve, pick one's way across the rocks. But a misstep could be fatal. And he didn't know how long it would take to find a safer ford.

"I'm also looking for nøkken," he admitted.

"That is a word I never heard from Frode the Footsore."

"They're fey creatures who live near bodies of water. Some of them love waterfalls. They play weird music that lures people to their deaths. There's a nøkken who shows up on our side of the lake now and then. I mentioned him before — Bror. Everyone gets warned about Bror, but he still catches people off guard." Satisfied there were no nøkken today, he said, "There's that fallen tree a little downstream — see it?"

"It looks ancient and covered with moss."

"It'll hold. And it means we only have to balance on one thing, not a dozen."

"So brash, your people."

"Are you up for it?"

"Of course. I have climbed a sky-ship's rigging in flight. It is just that I am not brash."

The fallen tree was so moss-covered that the only visible wood was in the bare branches that jabbed out everywhere like a badly-organized armory, and the snake's-nest of roots they had to haul themselves over to reach the trunk. Once on it their feet felt secure enough, though the upper layers of bark caved in like dry cornmeal. They inched across, occasionally obliged to hold hands. Those moments felt awkward and formal, making them both laugh nervously.

There seemed to be an unspoken law, Havtor reflected, that people crossing a span must stop halfway to regard their progress. They looked around and gasped.

Away from the tree-cover the rugged country upstream revealed itself as a tangle of stony bodies as big as stave temples. The effect crept up on the observer little by little — a brow-like ridge here, a grimace-shaped fissure there, a stony elbow entering a half-shattered tree, five boulders in the river suggestive of upturned toes — then all at once. Dozens of vast stony figures lay asleep in a dog-pile as though exhausted by some long-ago free-for-all, so long ago that grass, moss, flowers, and saplings covered the combatants and waterfalls stood in for their snores.

"Please tell me," said De-Zhen, "that this is the work of a mad sculptor."

"This is the work of a mad sculptor."

"I do not find you convincing."

"Let's get across."

It was as they moved that the music began.

It was the sound of a fiddle. It had the haunting and slightly eerie, to Havtor's ears, resonance of the eight-stringed fiddle popular at dances and weddings around Herkeby. Four strings would be sounded by the bow, with four more resonating beneath. Havtor even recognized the song because he'd danced to it with Britt Bjornsdóttir once (along with twenty other people, but still) and he'd have found it beautiful except that he caught sight of the player downstream. This was a pale, winsome man with white hair, standing without a care upon a boulder in the rapids' midst. He smiled at them as though sharing an unspoken secret.

"A nøkken," he whispered. "But the tune isn't calling us to our deaths by drowning."

"Do I hear a request?" called the bright mocking voice of the nøkken. "But alas, Havtor Runeson, I am otherwise engaged. My music is for the trolls yonder." The tune broke into the rushing cadence of a song called, appropriately enough, "The Hall of the Troll King." Havtor had used to love that tune. Right up until this instant, in fact.

And the vast mass of stone upstream vibrated and made the moss shiver and the saplings shake; and the roar of the waterfalls gained an undercurrent of rumbling, and lip-smacking, and gravelly half-formed words.

"You're waking them up?" De-Zhen demanded.

"Yes," said the nøkken. "It is time for them to resume their tumult. Unless …"

"Unless?" Havtor yelled.

"Unless you turn back and rejoin your father."

"Not until my friend is back with her people!"

"Let us make haste, friend," hissed De-Zhen. "And thank you."

The nøkken smiled. "Wrong choice, but it matters little enough to me." He redoubled his efforts. All on his own he sounded loud as a whole fair-full of fiddlers.

The trolls responded. It was as though an earthquake struck Raven's Wood. Almost as bad, the rhythm of the fiddle was distracting, even if it wasn't directed at them.

As they neared the opposite side, three trolls lurched up, sending a blast of water their way. Havtor offered De-Zhen his hand and helped her onto the far bank just as the wave dislodged the log and sent it thudding into the river. The tree-trunk jammed against the boulders, and a mountain troll, head halfway to the crowns of the tallest trees, stumbled forward to grab it. The nøkken was nowhere to be seen.

The mountain troll snatched up their log bridge as if it were a fire poker and swung it at them. The ground shook and the snowy duff of the forest floor sprayed in every direction in a splattering, crumbly hiss.

It glowered down at them. "MORE MUSIC!" it bellowed. "MORE!"

A second troll grabbed at the log. "NO MUSIC! NO!"

"ARGH!" The two trolls wrestled for the tree. It shattered in a shower of spear-like splinters.

By now Havtor and De-Zhen were running for their lives. The first two trolls had lost immediate interest but there were plenty more surging up.

In between dashes, as they gasped for air, Havtor attempted every gothi trick he knew. He prayed to Aurvímnir to grant De-Zhen presence of mind and alacrity of action. He sprayed the holy water from Mótmeiðr over their heads. He handed De-Zhen a little doll's cloak. "Stuff it in a pocket," he urged. "It will bring the gods' affection." She took it dubiously.

"MEAT!" bellowed a troll. One of his gigantic gray hands bent a tree aside; the other reached down to break his fast. Havtor and De-Zhen screeched and drew weapons, dagger and sword.

Time seemed to hover like a hummingbird. Havtor slid into memory. A year ago he'd strayed long on the lake and had walked from Herkeby back to the temple after dark. No draugar had menaced him, but he'd run afoul of wild dogs — not wolves, or they might have finished him, but dogs gone astray and organizing themselves like their ancestors. Their growling leader had dashed up to Havtor and bitten him on the leg. If he'd fled things might have gone worse. Instead a forge-light of fury, something sealed in the pit of his soul, burst out. Fists raised he'd faced the dog and shouted, *"Back off!"*

Just as the dog, surprisingly, had turned tail, so too did the troll flinch and let go the bent tree. For Havtor had just cried the same words.

The tree, released from the troll's grip, whipped up and smacked him across the face. The troll bellowed its rage at all of non-troll existence.

Havtor shook his dagger at the troll. "Yeah!"

De-Zhen's hand came down upon his shoulder. "Run."

"Yeah!"

They darted like mice amongst the thickest trees, for on open ground they'd be troll-treats. As it was, the mountain trolls stomped and smashed and kicked the trees in their wake, and it was only the obstacle course of the deep forest, plus the trolls' slowly dawning antipathy for each other, that allowed Havtor and De-Zhen to escape.

The sounds of the troll fracas seemed to follow them for hours. Clouds of birds and hordes of deer scattered along with the two humans. At last, with a stitch in his side that felt like a small animal gnawing at his left lung, Havtor called a halt. They nestled in the exposed upper roots of an enormous nut tree of some sort and gasped.

The sheer pleasure of *not running* and *not being eaten* filled their minds for a time.

By the time they could think of anything else, their stomachs were groaning. Their meager rations were nearly exhausted. Havtor picked the mysterious nuts, offering thanks to the tree (some trees appreciated that) and gathered water from a nearby stream. Then he invoked Aurvímnir in a way that he hoped would remove any taint from the food. It proved not immediately poisonous.

De-Zhen chewed thoughtfully. "You have used much magic."

"Have I?" He shook his head and smiled. "I'm not trying to be difficult. I'm not always sure my blessings really make much difference. It all seems plausibly deniable. Maybe I can make food and water pure — or maybe I just get lucky in what I forage. Maybe the holy water improves our chances, or maybe it's just the idea of the thing. Sometimes my father deliberately makes elixirs that are more tasty than potent, and performs rituals that are more showy than magical. He says that can be surprisingly useful, even if it's a bit dishonest."

She took a minute to digest his speech. She said, "But you were honestly brave. You commanded that troll to flinch. I think that was an act of power."

Havtor remembered the wild dogs. "I can't really be sure. I've never done anything that couldn't be explained away. And I'm no good mastering the runes, even just using them as an alphabet. My father, now — you saw his power there. He has that nøkken, that fiddler, working for him."

De-Zhen just looked at Havtor thoughtfully. It made him feel a bit uncomfortable, and a bit flattered at the same time. "We had better move, then," she said.

They walked for hours through increasingly dense woodland. Maybe it was the effect of the troll battle but Raven's Wood seemed free of things trying to murder them. They relaxed a little, and they spoke of what they'd seen of life. Havtor enjoyed hearing De-Zhen's tales much more than he enjoyed sharing his own. It seemed to him he'd done little of interest besides sailing, and she'd seen that for herself. But *she* had tales of crossing the north polar region of Qualth, and exploring lost ruins of the Gordion Empire, and charting the coast of the Wilderness of the Bear Folk across the Cold Sea.

"What are the Northern Lights like?" he asked.

"You don't know?" Her tone made him feel as if he were a poor excuse for a Northman!

He quickly said, "You only rarely see them south of Wendholm. Hasn't happened in these parts in my lifetime." He coughed, realizing that that wasn't many years to speak of. "I'd love to know what they looked like. To you."

She thought about it. He liked how she chewed her lower lip when she concentrated. Part of his mind was suddenly, acutely aware of the curves of her silhouette even under armor, and another part told him sternly to be honorable in thought and deed. He'd sensed from the start that both their cultures prized honor, albeit in different ways.

"Nothing has ever made me feel smaller," she was saying. "I have seen gigantic glaciers dwarfing all the country we've just traveled. Imagine a block of ice that big! Bigger! I've seen the Cold Sea go on and on and on. Back home we have vast walls, the work of centuries, to keep out nomad barbarians. None of those things made me feel small like that. You look up at the sky and you come to expect certain things of it. The sun. Clouds. The stars. The big moon, and its own moon. But those things don't fill the sky like the Northern Lights do. And at the same time that it makes you feel small it makes you feel ... clod-like. Like a lump of dirt. Because it's so fragile-looking and beautiful, weaving here and there like something alive. Like the whole world is just the playground of this lovely thing and you're simply down here by accident, like a bug."

"I don't think you're like a bug," he said, staring. She looked away, smiling a little, and finding it necessary to adjust something about her hair. He realized just how rapt he'd sounded. Listening to her made him feel almost like he'd been there beside her, or could be there yet. Out there. With her. Either. Both. It all seemed to go together. He realized he'd gone silent and added, "Even if you are here by accident."

She laughed a little loudly. "What is the most amazing thing you've seen?"

"You've seen it already. It's the great tree by the temple. Mótmeiðr. It looks different for different people."

"How did it look to you?"

"Different things at different times. My father did an experiment once ... wait, hold on." He stopped. "I've spotted some of your writing, on your gear. It reminds me of something."

He scuffed away pine needles with his boot to expose dark bare earth. Then he took Bendik's dagger and drew, with extreme concentration. He drew upon a memory of characters written in light through the branches of Mótmeiðr. It was difficult. He had to correct his recollection or his rebellious hand several times. But at last he'd written, more or less: 臭椿.

"'Tree of Heaven!'" De-Zhen said. "At least, I think so. How did you know how to write that?"

"I think Mótmeiðr showed it to me." He laughed. "I've been waiting a long time for someone to tell me what it meant."

The thoughtful look had returned to her face. "I wonder why the tree wanted you to know that."

But he could not answer, for he had just noticed something strange about the dagger hilt. He nudged at it idly, still listening to the rich sound of her voice.

She said, "When you speak your mind you reach everyone. When you write it is more difficult."

"Tell me what I don't know," he murmured, peering at the dagger.

She laughed. "That is surely a good reason for telling someone something."

"No, it's ... it's an idiom." He fidgeted at the hilt, feeling nervous about this conversation. "Don't worry about it."

"But Havtor, I see you *do* succeed, given time. Why are the runes so hard?"

"Any writing is hard for me. I think it's something about my brain, and my muscles, together. But the runes, they're special ... they come down from the High Father himself. Each one represents a gift of power. Like the one I worked on just before I met you ..."

Leaving off his examination of the hilt, he drew a ragged version of: ᛗ.

"That's Mannaz. It stands for 'man.' People. Humans. And the 'm' sound. But if you really connect with the rune it can become a form of power. It can compel truth in the people around you, for one thing."

"That is wonderful! With that you could reveal the murderer."

"The trouble is, to master a rune you have to go through an ordeal. The High Father himself nearly got himself killed before he could fathom their power."

"You have nearly gotten killed at least twice recently."

"That doesn't seem to be enough."

"I'm not sure," De-Zhen said. "I think you did command that troll. I think some of the same spirit may help you master the rune."

"Are you offering to almost get me killed?" He waved the dagger at her jokingly. "Ah!"

"What is wrong?" De-Zhen said.

"Now I understand something that's bothering me about this dagger. There's a little compartment in the hilt." Havtor slid open a small hatch at the base. "There's a small bit of paper in here. A little scroll. Lóðarr's nuts! I'm a fool, De-Zhen. Bendik gave me this. Maybe this message was meant for me." He frowned. "It looks soaked. From that wave on the river, no doubt." He made to pull it out.

"Havtor, wait! Trust someone who handles paper a lot. We want to dry it out before you try to remove it." She looked around. The sunset light seemed to fill the lower trunks of the trees while the crowns rustled against deep blue, as though a forest blaze raged that only hungered for roots. "We'll need a campfire."

They found the best spot they could on short notice, a low rocky ridge curved like a crescent moon and free of animal dens. De-Zhen worked with her fire-starter (a copper tube she blew on to produce a small flame) on a handful of sticks while Havtor gathered more. She soon had a blaze going. They set Bendik's dagger hilt-first beside it. De-Zhen pulled out another metal tool. "It's for gently extracting things," she said. "Sort of like kuàizi." Then she had to explain chopsticks.

"I'd like to see my father try that," Havtor said eventually. "He thinks eating with knives is a little fussy. Tearing food with your hands ought to be good enough for anyone, he says."

De-Zhen laughed. "He is very strange! Forgive me."

"It's all right."

"He is a scholar! He wants you to be a scholar! But he seems like such a rough person."

Havtor thought back. "My mother told me once that Father's own father forbade him from being a gothi. Said it wasn't really fitting for a man. The wandering women priests, the völur, were sufficient. Men should fight. They lived all the way up by Umsborg on the Cold Sea. Rough place. Father came looking for gothar to study with because he felt called to it. But he had to roam for a while to do it. And he got into plenty of fights."

De-Zhen looked thoughtful. Under the deepening blue sky, flames danced in her eyes. "My mother didn't want me to join the Fleet. She wanted me to be a nice safe official. But the funny thing was, *she* was a wild girl. She was climbing rooftops and getting into fights when she was younger than either of us. She served in the village militia before she married my father and got distracted with us four kids. But she never lets on about all that. My father had to tell me. *She* just went on about being respectable."

"My mother said when my father got older he got wilder, because some part of him still wanted to be what his own father wanted." He rubbed his forehead, remembering. "She said it's strange ... but we sometimes want to please our parents most when they're farthest away. Or gone. When they can't ever know about it."

"I hope my mother would approve of me now." De-Zhen laughed. "Sharing a campfire with a strange young man! Sharing life and death!" Her look turned serious. "I see a ... what is the word? Contradiction? About your father. The runes can't truly be earned except when facing death, yes? And your father knows this?"

"Yes."

"But he is determined you have no danger. There is the contradiction. He says he wants you to learn. But really he wants you to be *safe*. But he won't admit it. Maybe he can't admit it."

Havtor stared into the fire. "I never thought of it like that. I guess I always imagined I'd find another path to rune-lore. It does happen occasionally. Someone learns through a dream or fasting or even wishing hard enough. I suppose I thought Father believed I could do it that way. But I never asked, and never questioned. You're right, it doesn't make much sense." He shook his head. "What was he thinking?" He stared at De-Zhen and impulsively took her hand. "What was *I* thinking? You don't learn anything without going out and experiencing it."

Without quite realizing it he had leaned closer. He blinked, imagining De-Zhen would pull away now. Britt Bjornsdóttir surely would have, after saying something witty to make her friends laugh. But De-Zhen only smiled, staring at him in a way that made him almost feel like he was on the end of a spear. They both leaned forward. They brushed lips — but also noses.

She laughed a little, still transfixing him with her eyes. She said, "I think one of us has to tilt a little. I'll do it."

"No, let me."

They smashed noses again. They both laughed. "It's not fair," he said, but not bitterly. "I'm only supposed to be bad at writing."

"You're not bad at this," she said. "Let me show you."

She did. When she pulled back, a few seconds and a whole book of sagas later, she said with a shy-looking smile. "Let's have a look at that paper."

"All right," he said, staring out into the darkness as she got her metal tool ready. "Gently now. Gently..." Worries and hopes flickered excitedly like sparks rising into the deepening blue. Was he bad at kissing? Was that why she'd stopped? But she didn't sound upset. His stomach felt like it was on a sky-ship under the Northern Lights. He imagined he saw shooting stars ...

No, wait. He *had* seen something. Not shooting stars. Something that seemed to create, with a *boom*, a series of distant red sparks.

"De-Zhen ..."

"I heard it!" she said, up on her feet. It happened a second time, a flaming ribbon rising and bursting into dozens more. "Baozhang!" she said, and to his confused look she added, "A fiery signal. Your people don't have such things. It is my ship, and not far away. We must move!"

It happened a third time. And in the flickering light Havtor saw some white-furred thing out in the woods, nearly in the direction of the sky-ship.

He picked up the dagger and sealed the hilt. "We'll have to read that later. There's something out there."

"We'll face it together, Havtor."

They advanced, and Havtor braced himself for a cat-like creature, or a bear. He should have known better.

The haunting fiddling began. It sounded like a rendition of "The Bear Son's Tale," a lively and somewhat menacing song based on the old epic. It made Havtor want to follow it, as though the racing notes and his own footsteps had become as one.

"Havtor, where are you going?" De-Zhen said as though from far away.

"The linnorm's lair," he murmured.

"What?"

But he could not explain. The music and the old tale had seized him, grabbing the part of his mind where distraction and focus wrestled like mountain trolls. There was a kind of itching, intolerable unless he bent all his will toward scratching it, and in this case scratching the itch meant following the tune.

"Havtor, stop! This is that — that creature — that nøkken!"

The strange thing was, he even knew it. But the fact was not relevant anymore. The music had to be followed, just as a puzzle had to be solved, a path cleared, a dance mirrored, a rune drawn.

De-Zhen tried to drag him backward, but there came sudden silence, and he stood there in a daze as the compulsion fled him. But before he could flee himself, a white horse exploded out of the underbrush.

It sideswiped him. A supernaturally sticky quality of the horse-hair held him fast and wrenched him off the ground as the horse galloped away from De-Zhen. Her grip on his hand was broken. He was dragged along upon the creature's side, and this was a dangerous position for any horse rider to be in; but this was no real horse, and he was not really riding.

Havtor knew a nøkken could take a horse form, and for all that he kept hitting bushes and rocks this one seemed to want him alive.

All he had to defy his fate with was the dagger he'd gotten from a dead man. He realized he still hadn't read the message within. He hoped he'd get the chance before the murderer from the temple eliminated him.

Move on, he silently willed De-Zhen. *Please. Get home. Forget about me.*

De-Zhen stared after the nøkken. All her honor, and much besides, wanted to chase them. But she had her duty as well. And beyond that, her brain. At that speed Havtor could be dragged several *li* away before she could even cross half of one. She was terrified for him, but her best hope was to behave as ship's crew and reach *Changning*. There she could get help.

She took more chances now. The fireworks had stopped, but from them she'd judged the ship was no more than a single *li* from her. She might be able to gather a rescue party if she moved fast. True dark had fallen and the moon and its child were only just up, so the land was a silvery domain of tall shadows. She proceeded at a jog.

A sudden sound prompted her to look back. Had that been a disturbed branch? She saw nothing. De-Zhen drew her sword and proceeded more slowly, looking back often.

A snapped twig alerted her at the last moment and she spun to block the short blade of the Svartálfar bat-rider. He jabbed once at her wrist, leaving a shallow cut, but she pressed him and he reeled back.

"What is the meaning of this?" she demanded in the Norrønian tongue, not really expecting an answer; but before he closed again he laughed and gave her one.

"Self-advancement and revenge," he answered in the same language. "You slew my mount Akreesha of the Vaunted Fangs. I will parade your head before my comrades! Let them tremble at my tenacity!"

The Svartálfar's speech was so embroidered De-Zhen struggled to understand it. She blinked and answered, "We only defended ourselves."

"Irrelevant! Fortune smiles on the vengeful! For in tracking you I espied your ship, with my comrades imprisoned within. By lighting its fireworks I crafted a distraction and liberated them. But slaying *you* remains my obsession. I waited, but it appears I did not need to wait long."

"But why attack us?"

"Why not reveal it? The poison has bit. My people are rightful rulers of these lands but we need resources to claim them. A Norrønir traitor offered a vast supply of orichalcum. We assembled in the mountains to attack the place of the treasure when we beheld your ship, and our target list swelled."

She began to feel dizzy and knew she needed to end this. Perhaps she was poisoned indeed, but if she could finish the assailant swiftly she might stagger on toward help — if her crewmates yet lived. Yet even as she advanced she gambled for Havtor's sake. "Who is the traitor among the Norrønir?"

"One of the high! But enough! Vengeance for Akreesha!"

They slashed at each other, the impish pointed-eared figure laughing at her. She had stature and reach, and he was limping; but her strength was ebbing fast. She had one gamble. She was good at imitating sounds; it was part of her skill with languages. She remembered the dying shriek of the bat.

She screamed the sound as loudly as she could.

The dark elf flinched in horror, even as De-Zhen drove in hard during the split-second of his distraction. She gored him in one lung.

He chuckled and gurgled and coughed scarlet. "Very deceitful ... you ... are one of us ... in spirit." He fell, and she finished him with what she hoped was a merciful strike.

She wobbled and knew she was about to succumb. Remembering how he'd first tracked her, she searched through his gear for anything resembling a mushroom. She found three. She crushed them together and scattered the remnants in great clouds. With luck someone would find her, for good or ill.

De-Zhen also found a holy symbol, and she did not think it a thing made by the Svartálfar. She clutched it tight as she fell into darkness.

The nøkken had a reputation for drowning their foes. The one that dwelled in the lake near Herkeby had made a long list of victims over the years. But this nøkken passed the river, and a small pond, and continued to proceed among the trees, careful to never trample on Havtor's legs. The fey being was treating him none too gently but it clearly sought to deliver him somewhere intact.

Thus he was not entirely surprised when the nøkken halted and shifted form to the white-maned humanoid they'd seen at the river, allowing Havtor to slump to the ground. "Rune," called the nøkken. "I have brought him."

"Took you long enough," came his father's gruff voice.

"He has a knack for escaping things," said the nøkken.

"I know. Responsibility most of all."

"I care not for your human dramas, unless you set them to music. I claim my freedom."

"Begone, creature."

By the time Havtor rose listing to his feet the nøkken was gone. That did not make the glade empty. Ten men stood beside Rune under the moonslight. Among them were the gothar Svein and Gundar. Trygve the Trustworthy loomed beside them. A large raven perched on his shoulder, probably the bird belonging to Jarl Inga which reputedly whispered secrets to her daily. Four of the remaining men were housecarls serving the jarl, but the remaining two were wearing wolf-hide coats, marking them as Wolf Warriors, sacred to the night-goddess. Although not all Wolf Warriors worshipped Naði as such, they were surely grieved at her gothi Bendik's death.

Havtor confronted them all, searching for his voice. One of these men was a murderer. It might even be (*face your fears, Havtor*) his father. But the rest might be swayed depending on what Havtor did. It was like the wild dogs again. Havtor realized, without the feeling even crystalizing into words, that he had to remain calm and focused or this search party would turn against him. And remarkably, for someone told all his life he had poor focus, he had no trouble seeing this truth or maintaining his clarity. He felt as though De-Zhen were by his side, telling him he could accomplish this thing.

All his senses were awake, and they drew a picture as sharp-cornered as any rune.

He held up Bendik's dagger. The eyes of the Wolf Warriors in particular glinted at it. "You have questions, no doubt. So do I. A man pushed Bendik, the owner of this dagger, off the plateau of Fornuppsalir."

His voice was calm and ringing, and he saw his father Rune's look of surprise. Havtor would only think the matter through later, but he thought he owed his determination to his mother. He'd never really learned the tricks of bonding with a group of men. He didn't participate in group sports like the Knattleikr ball game, preferring board games like Thrones and Bones. He hadn't been part of a hunting group or a sailing crew, or even a house-raising or timber-felling team. His own father hadn't gone in for those things in decades, and indeed it was his mother who'd taught him what he knew of the outdoors. He could speak well enough with men or women in small groups, but a large batch like this left him at sea. Yet he must keep his composure or all was lost.

And he was doing so.

"We would see that dagger!" said one of the Wolf Warriors, and "How did you come by it?" said the other.

He held their gazes. "Bendik himself gave it to me. And I will gladly give it to the Wolf Warriors, but first I will share his last message." He opened the panel in the hilt and extracted the paper.

He certainly had everyone's attention. It was as if he'd been captured on purpose, to stage the reading of this mysterious note.

His mother had told him, *Outdoors, ready to take action, you are as tough as anyone, Havtor, even the jarl. It's only the work of the temple that challenges you so. I admire you for doing it. But always remember, you are as good as anybody in the land.*

"What is the meaning of this, Havtor?" Rune said, but his tone was more quizzical than threatening.

"Let us find out." Havtor pulled out the paper as carefully as it could. It was much dryer now, but he thought it would be a very Havtor Fidgetstick sort of moment if he tore it apart now.

"Is this some bluff?" Gundar called out.

"Let another man read it!" Svein demanded.

"No!" Havtor said. "You may verify it afterward but it stays in my hands for now."

"That is fairly spoken," Trygve said, and the raven squawked.

Havtor read:

Runeson,

I know you and your father have little liking for me, and we have had many disputes. As eldest gothi of the temple I deserved pride of place. But let it be. I am stepping down after Beysa's Festival. With the approval of the Wolf Warriors I will choose a replacement. I have told your father this. You may wonder why I am telling you. When one of my assistants is elevated to my role there will be room for another to enter Naði's service. I would like you to consider it. I have seen you struggle, you see. Perseverance is a trait Naði admires. Do think about it. You may carry this letter to prove my good wishes — if of course, you've the wit to find it! Live well.

Bendik the gothi.

Havtor met his father's eyes like a compass needle drawn north. Both were thinking through the meaning of Bendik's words.

"I would see that letter," Gundar said.

"And I," said Svein.

"We will *all* see it," Rune said, and the group gathered round as Havtor held it up. This gave Havtor time to think.

By Bendik's account the man had given up usurping Rune's position, and Rune knew it; therefore Rune had no known motive to kill Bendik. Havtor breathed surprisingly easier, knowing that.

Yet Havtor was sure of De-Zhen's eyewitness account. One of the gothar had killed Bendik while the others were distracted in the fog. That left Svein or Gundar.

"Did you know he meant to retire?" Gundar demanded of Rune.

"I did," Rune said.

"I did not," Gundar said.

"Nor I," said Svein. "Why did you keep this from us?"

"It was not for me to tell," Rune said. "As head gothi, however, it was for me to know."

Havtor thought, *Svein, with his interest in human sacrifice, might have wanted to sacrifice Bendik, especially if he'd known about the retirement. He might have thought Bendik was past usefulness anyway. Gundar, known to be greedy, had little to gain by killing the retiring Bendik, but he might truly not have known that.*

At last Rune said, "This is valuable information. But you still should not have run away with that woman. Where is she?"

"We were nearly at her sky-ship when your nøkken intercepted me."

"Then she may have made it there," Rune stroked his beard. "We can't let this matter be. We need to settle if she herself had a hand in Bendik's death, by deliberately distracting him or attacking him from overhead in some way."

Svein said, "We all know how clumsy Bendik is. Was. There is all the answer you need."

"I am not satisfied with that," Gundar said. "I too would speak to this girl and see her sky-ship."

"We will go," Rune said, and the others agreed. "Lead us, Havtor."

The two of them walked a little ahead. Havtor wanted to speak of the murder but it wasn't easily possible with his suspects walking just behind. Thus Rune spoke first.

"Son," he said, "what made you think your actions would be acceptable?"

"I didn't think," Havtor answered immediately and honestly. "I acted."

Rune grunted. "So you did. And confirmed all my fears about you. Still, I am glad you survived the forest. Indeed, I am impressed. But your place is back at the temple. Safe."

"I want to accomplish real deeds, Father."

"Deeds are like scars, son. You can't get rid of them, and you're damn lucky if they make you look any better."

"How did you track us?"

"We kept searching at night, along the lake. I spotted a mushroom trail, glowing in the dark," said Rune. "I knew what it implied, and thought it just possible you were at the end of the trail. I begged the others to let me ashore at that point."

"You followed alone at first?"

"I am Rune the gothi. I had fears for my son, but not for myself. I lost your trail, but I had the good fortune to find a nøkken I could bind. With such a fast-moving servant I could both search for you and stay in touch with other searchers. In time I gathered this party."

"I know you did not kill Bendik, Father."

"Perhaps no one did." Rune sighed. "Bendik — or you — would not be the first man distracted by the sight of a striking woman."

"Her name is De-Zhen. And she needed me."

"That's what I told myself about your mother." Rune laughed. "She eventually agreed." To Havtor's scowl Rune added, "You know, your mother told me the secret of life is this: What you worry about today may not be what you worry about tomorrow. Because a worrier always finds something to worry about. Knowing that, why worry at all?"

"That's it?"

"That is what I said to her! She said it might not make sense until

I was an older man and had worried a lot more. Women are more practiced at worrying, she said. Sometimes I think I see what she was getting at. I am very glad you're alive, Havtor. You are still going to clean every inch of the temple. But I'm glad you're alive."

"Father, the things De-Zhen said ..."

Rune lowered his voice. "I know. I can't discount it. The waves at Herkeby — we've put it down to Bror the nøkken causing trouble. But I don't think so. Yet I can't decide which is the likely one."

"Keep your eyes open, Father."

"Always."

Manna and her little sister shone high and silver in the sky, and Havtor kept moving in what he thought was the right direction. Maintaining a course on the lake was much easier than doing it in the forest. Nevertheless he was fairly sure of his path until he heard the shouts and screams and clanging of metal. Then he was fully sure.

"They're under attack!" he cried to the others. "We have to help!"

And then he was off, his father bellowing, "Havtor, wait!" in his wake, and cursing.

By the sounds of battle Havtor easily found the sky-ship. It was perhaps sixty feet long, three-masted, and lit by lanterns. It hovered a few feet above the ground, quivering as combatants raged upon it. Havtor saw dark elves in melee with people garbed similarly to De-Zhen.

He ran up to the ship. "Let me help you!" he called out. "I'm a friend of De-Zhen —"

An arrow fired from one of the ship's men caught him in the shoulder.

It hurt more than anything he'd experienced in his life, even the soul-drinking attack of the draugr. Luckily — if you could call it that — the shot had been quick and not given full draw. The force of the arrow could have been much worse. Havtor stumbled against the keel of the vessel. Snapping the haft of the arrow, pain chewing at his innards as though a ferret had gotten inside him, Havtor yelled, "I'm a friend of De-Zhen, you bastard!"

In answer a rope ladder dropped beside him. Havtor climbed it with agonized alacrity. At the top the man who'd shot him looked at the arrow-wound sheepishly but unapologetically. Havtor wasn't sure if the man was more perplexed at hitting an ally or that his target still lived. Havtor would decide whether to forgive him later.

For now Havtor just pointed behind him to where his father's party was approaching through the trees. The archer from LongGuo seemed to decide any help was welcome. The archer ran toward the center mast to join the main fight but first pointed Havtor toward a stairway and a lower deck. "De-Zhen," he called back, before raising his bow.

Havtor descended to a lantern-lit realm of polished wood and bright red paint. "De-Zhen!" he called out.

"*Wǒ zài zhèlǐ*," came a weak voice. "I'm here."

Havtor entered a large cabin and found hammocks full of wounded. There were crew tending to the injured, but De-Zhen was left to herself. Havtor felt a flash of anger at that, but surely there were people worse off. He crouched beside her. For a moment he attracted stares from De-Zhen's crewmates, but they seemed too busy to worry much over a strange barbarian with an arrow haft sticking out of his shoulder, at least if De-Zhen accepted his presence.

"What happened to you?" he said, seeing bandaged cuts upon her but no injury explaining her being bedridden.

"Poison. What happened to you?"

"Arrow. Not poisoned. I think. Who poisoned you?"

"That Svartálfar who fell with me finally caught up with me. He's done for." She flashed a grin, but the effort weakened her. "As for me, we will see what we will see. My crewmates spotted me but it took time to bring me here. They have been fighting over the ship for hours."

"You'll make it," he said fiercely, willing it so.

"So will you. You got away from the nøkken?"

"No. It brought me to my father. He and the gothar and others are here."

Worry creased her face. "Havtor. Listen. I found this on the Svartálfar." She handed him a holy symbol. It was a metallic representation of two ravens facing opposite directions. The metalwork was fine, and the eyes were little rubies. "It's not a dark elf token, is it?"

"No."

"He said he was working with someone important."

"Oh no. I know who it must be." Havtor grabbed the holy symbol and steadied himself with one of the ropes of the hammock. "I have to stop him."

"I will help," De-Zhen said, and nearly fell out of the hammock in her attempts to rise. A crewman stitching another woman's bloody wound called out in alarm.

"No," Havtor said. "I see a way to stop him, and help your people. I just have to —"

He was dizzy himself; he wobbled as he staggered up the steps. He must be more wounded than he thought.

Good.

He reached the deck and thought that the battle at the twilight of the world couldn't be crazier.

The ship was slowly rising over the trees and in the moonslight Havtor could see it was aimed back toward the Mikillvatn and Herkeby. A female Svartálfar was at the wheel, and though the battle was far from done, members of Rune's party were now fighting on either side.

Rune and Gundar were guarding the dark elf at the wheel, aided by the two Wolf Warriors. Trygve the Trustworthy and Svein and the housecarls of Inga the Undaunted fought among the LongGuo crew, trying to regain control.

As Havtor lurched into view, Inga's raven fluttered off from Trygve's shoulder toward Herkeby. But the sky-ship gained speed and the raven was left squawking in the darkness behind, unable to warn Inga of what might come.

And what might be coming? Havtor had guesses, but that wasn't important right now. He focused on walking forward. The man who'd shot him was lying on the deck with a dagger in his eye. That almost made Havtor lose his balance with queasiness and vertigo. But he must not waver.

"Havtor!" Trygve called. "Fight with us!"

"Boy!" snapped Svein. "Stand with us. Your father's gone mad! He's always held us back. Even Bendik saw it. Let us sacrifice these fools to the gods."

Rune called out, "Son! Fight with us against the foreigners!"

"They were scouting an invasion!" Gundar yelled. "The dark elves will stand with us for the freedom of the north!"

"You all talk too much," Havtor gasped. He yanked out the arrow shaft.

And on the deck he drew in blood, with a shaking but determined hand, ᛗ.

It should not have worked, not by the rules he'd been taught. He needed to be near death before learning the deep rune-lore. He should not be able to learn it merely in the midst of collapsing from blood loss. But the Chooser of the Slain had said, *I come only to aid your victims, for they fought you valiantly.* The gods valued courage. They had to, or this would come to naught.

The Mannaz rune blazed for a moment like fire.

"Truth!" Havtor called out on his knees as all but the dark elf at the helm stared at him. "The Mannaz rune prevents lying! Truth, Gundar! How did Bendik die?"

"I ... I ... you must ... you ..."

"Truth, Svein! Did you sacrifice Bendik?"

"No!" called out Svein. "I meant to sacrifice a goat! I swear!"

"Truth, Father!" Havtor gasped. "Did you kill Bendik?"

"No," said Rune. "I did not see how he fell. At first I thought it must be his clumsiness."

"Answer me, Gundar the Greedy!" Havtor said. "He pulled out the holy symbol of the twin ravens. "How did a dark elf come by this holy symbol? The most expensive holy symbol of Aurvímnir I've ever seen. What are you up to? How did Bendik die?"

"I ..." said Gundar. "You ... must already know ... What could I add?"

But Rune understood now. He knew, having felt its power, that the Mannaz rune was alive with magic.

He grabbed Gundar from behind and held a sword to his neck. The Wolf Warriors watched carefully. The dark elves made to rush Rune but the Wolf Warriors growled them back.

"Speak!" said Rune. "Speak with breath or your throat will speak with blood! How did Bendik die?"

"I ... I pushed him. In the fog that I created you couldn't tell."

"The fog you *created*?" Svein bellowed.

"My allies had a small version of the magical device that lifts this ship like a cloud. It can also be used to create a cloud. With it I hoped to lift the treasure."

"What treasure?"

"The orichalcum chain around the middle of the temple."

"*What*?" Rune cried out.

"Why would you even plan to steal such a thing?" Trygve demanded.

"'Why?'" Svein exclaimed. "Leave alone 'why.' *How*? The thing's immense! And you'd have to destroy the temple to even get at it!"

Gundar laughed. He clearly did not care anymore about dissembling — things had gone too far. "I was about to burn it all down. Does that really shock you? I am a man of little power, always in Rune's shadow. But having sold that orichalcum to the Svartálfar I'd live like a high king! Bendik suspected my plan. He'd seen me stuffing alcohol-soused hay in the storage areas of the temple. I was going to light it later today."

One of the LongGuo crew, a gray-bearded man with ornate

armor, made a fist. He cursed in his own language before adding in Norrønian, "So that is what became of our secondary Fu Yun Qi!"

Gundar chuckled. "Yes. The Svartálfar stole the device from you when you took on supplies near Nilmgard. I was to prepare things for them."

Svein spat. "Yet you've confessed now. And your plan was foiled."

Gundar snarled at the Svartálfar woman at the wheel. "By the dark elves themselves! They couldn't resist chasing the sky-ship!"

The old LongGuo man, whom Havtor suspected was the captain, said, "It was not merely chance. We were magically tracking the stolen Fu Yun Qi."

The Svartálfar at the wheel smiled and said, "No matter. The plan can still succeed." She nodded once and one of her compatriots threw something that produced a smoke field. In the confusion Gundar broke free, laughing, as Rune was stabbed by a dark elf knife.

The fight renewed with fresh ferocity, though this time Gundar's only allies were the Svartálfar.

"Father —" Havtor gasped.

He didn't think he could rise, but he could press his luck another way. Though his vision swirled with purple around the edges he began drawing another rune with his blood. But he found himself falling over before he could finish ...

Someone caught him. De-Zhen knelt beside him. She saw the symbol he was trying to make, and how he was making it, and knew it for what it was.

She jabbed her palm with a dagger and began sketching the rest of it in sure strokes: ᛞ.

The Dagaz rune flared once with red, and then a glare like noontime blazed forth from beneath Havtor and De-Zhen. They toppled against each other as the Svartálfar screeched in sudden anguish. With his allies temporarily blinded, Gundar found himself overwhelmed by the other Norrønir. The Wolf Warriors had no mercy in their hearts. One hacked an axe into Gundar's ribcage and the other flung the shocked-looking gothi over the side of the sky-ship.

The LongGuo and Norrøngard folk quickly subdued the dark elves. Most were taken alive, and despite some grumbling from the Norrønir, the ship's captain had the survivors locked up.

But Havtor had no time for that. With De-Zhen's help he stumbled to his father. De-Zhen was calling to her crewmates for help.

Havtor slumped down beside Rune. "I don't want you to die," he said, compelled to speak truth.

"I don't want to die either," Rune said. And he added, "I want to know you better, son. I love you. I'm proud of you."

"I want you both to save your strength," said De-Zhen. "I find the Norrønir stupidly stubborn. It's very irritating that I find Havtor attractive. What would my mother say? I should stop talking now."

"I want you to talk as much as you like," Havtor said. "Both of you." But then it all went dark.

The next thing he knew it was daytime, real daytime, and the captain was bellowing in Norrønian, "All barbarians off my ship! Now! Then we can talk."

Dazedly Havtor found himself and De-Zhen walking arm and arm down a ramp onto the plateau of Fornuppsalir with the sky-ship settled beside the temple opposite the great tree. They followed the cot bearing the still-weak, but still-living Rune.

When all the inhabitants of these lands were escorted off the ship, and the Svartálfar were secured inside the temple, and men had moved the hay bales outside of it, and Jarl Inga had arrived from Herkeby, and all interested parties were assembled in the hall of the High Father as though for worship, Havtor and De-Zhen at last had a moment to talk while the important people argued and laughed and shouted.

"I have no idea how this is going," Havtor told De-Zhen.

"This?" she said, looking a bit startled. She gestured, shyly, at her and then at him.

He blushed. "This — I mean this meeting."

"Oh," she said, looking perhaps a bit disappointed.

Havtor thought he should probably say something, something that wasn't directly about how thrilling it was to be sitting next to the most wonderful woman on any continent, but perhaps something that should be *informed* by that sentiment; but despite the constant churn of thoughts in his brain absolutely no words formed. For once he thought he'd almost be better off writing.

"I wanted to ask you something," she said.

"Yes?"

"We have informants from many lands. And you are very knowledgeable. Perhaps ... you would like to come with us? For a time? We would get you home eventually."

He blurted, "What would your mother say?"

"My mother has nothing to do with it."

"Is that what you would say if we were in the power of the Mannaz rune?"

"Be careful what you say, Havtor Runeson. I saw the runes in my dreams. I think I may be able to call upon them too."

"That would not surprise me ..." He took her hand. She didn't squeeze it, but she didn't pull away. "Do you know how 'eventually' it would be? Before I could see home?"

"There is no way to say. But I think if you go with me — us — you will return a grown man."

He nodded.

When the meeting concluded, or rather drifted apart like a cloud, Havtor and De-Zhen understood that a truce was agreed upon, that the LongGuo folk would regain their cloud-maker, that the dark elves would be ransomed but not slain, and that in all other respects debts were cancelled, should any arise.

Rune was at last free to speak, though he remained too weak to rise from his bench. Havtor and De-Zhen sat down on either side of him and explained what was in their hearts.

Rune scowled. "I feel as though I just found you again, son. In more ways than one. The old Rune ... had to crumble a bit. The new Rune would like to be a better father to you."

"You already are," Havtor said.

"And adventure is just trouble!" rumbled Rune. "Remember the sagas! All that running around and feuding. Most of those tales are good fun until someone puts an eye out. Or an arm. Or a skull."

"But you sought adventure," Havtor said, "when you were my age. I think you needed to. It's what I need too."

Rune was silent.

Startling both men, De-Zhen got to her knees beside the bench. "Think of this, honored elder. The Emperor is outward-looking, sending our Treasure Fleet far and wide. But a successor may keep the Fleet home. Most of our rulers have preferred to keep LongGuo to LongGuo. Everyone else, they say, is a barbarian, not worth knowing. It could happen right away. You know how this is, even here in your land. Havtor said the current peace could fail if your high king falls —"

But it was Rune who fell to his own knees then, for all that it pained him. "Rise, girl," Rune said, offering her a hand. "Rise up with me." Havtor joined him there and helped him up. When they'd all at last risen, Rune said, "No one can tell the future."

"Of course," De-Zhen said. "That's just it. There could be plague killing any of us. Or war, demanding we stay home. And no matter what there is old age waiting for all of us. If we're lucky!"

"We don't consider old age lucky," grumbled Rune.

"That is a difference between us, yes. But the differences are so interesting to learn. And the things in common too." She grabbed Havtor's hand; Rune's eyebrows went up but he let her keep talking: "Those of us who want to reach out and see the world and taste of life — we only have so much time. We should take those chances while we have them. That's why Havtor should come with us."

Rune turned to Havtor with a fleeting smile almost hidden

beneath his beard. "I can see why it's hard to say no to this girl, my son. But I don't want you to be an old man regretting rash choices."

Havtor said, "Father, what if I become an old man regretting never being rash? I'd rather have strong memories than unfulfilled dreams. Think of it! I may never see Korjengard but I will see the unknown West. I may regret some of it. But are we not all fated for regrets?"

Rune grunted. "*I* have few." Then he scratched his beard, studying Havtor. "You remind me of your mother. I think she'd have wandered wild if she'd had a man who could have endured it. Or if she'd chosen to leave me. Instead, she gave up the road and took care of me — and you." He met De-Zhen's eyes. "This young woman here reminds me of her as well." Rune shook his head. "I don't regret what I did to myself. That's my path. But ... I sometimes regret what she gave up for me."

He grasped their linked hands. "If this is what you truly want ... Then yes — go. Go with my blessing. Go, son, be a Norrønur such as none have been before. But if you can, come back one day. I have few regrets, but losing you forever would be one indeed."

Havtor embraced him.

The temple, the plateau, the town, the lake — they were like places on one of the ship's maps or paintings. Not quite real-looking. But still home. Clouds crossed over his view until the world was a blank scroll, ready for his unsteady but eager hand.

De-Zhen nudged him with an elbow. "There is work to do, sky-sailor. Do not forget, I am an officer in the Emperor's aerial navy, and I outrank you."

He smiled. "I assure you that's hard to forget."

"Your behavior is my responsibility. You will learn our language, our table manners, and especially our hygiene."

"Yes, ma'am."

"And you will serve this ship with cleaning and Norrønian language lessons and knowledge of your homeland."

"So long as I don't betray any trusts, I am delighted to give it."

"And do not get any overly romantic ideas! Not until you meet my family."

"I will get romantic ideas to exactly the right amount."

"I beg your pardon, sky-sailor — I didn't quite catch that."

"I, of course, said nothing."

"Very good." She let a smile escape. "What we are to each other … That is a mystery we will have to explore, like an unknown continent."

He stole one last look over the edge. *How did I come to soar into the sky, Me?* he thought. *Whatever happens, I'm grateful. I'm ready to draw that map. Shaky hand and all.*

CHRIS WILLRICH's short fiction has appeared in *Asimov's*, *Beneath Ceaseless Skies*, *Clarkesworld*, *Fantasy & Science Fiction*, *Lightspeed*, *Tales from the Magician's Skull*, and elsewhere. Many of these stories are part of his "Gaunt and Bone" fantasy series, which also includes the novel *The Scroll of Years* (Pyr, 2013) and its sequels *The Silk Map* (Pyr, 2014) and *The Chart of Tomorrows* (Pyr, 2015). He's also the author of the Pathfinder Tales novel *The Dagger of Trust* (Paizo, 2014). In "Runefall" Chris was partly inspired by family history. The female lead is named after his wife's maternal grandmother, and the male lead is named after Chris' maternal grandfather. Chris' family is proud of their immigrant connections to China and Norway and they hope their ancestors would look kindly upon this story. Visit Chris on the web at chriswillrich.com for news about his worlds or his more casual blog at chriswillrich.blogspot.com/ for talk of books, games, cats and whatnot.

About the Editor

LOU ANDERS is the author of the novel *Once Upon a Unicorn*, the Thrones & Bones trilogy of fantasy adventure novels (*Frostborn*, *Nightborn*, and *Skyborn*), and the novel *Star Wars: Pirate's Price*. He is the recipient of a Hugo Award for editing and a Chesley Award for art direction. In the tabletop roleplaying game world, Anders is the creator and publisher of the *Thrones & Bones: Norrøngard* campaign setting. He has also done game design for Kobold Press, River Horse, and 3D Printed Tabletop. In 2016, he was named a Thurber House Writer-in-Residence and spent a month in Columbus, Ohio, teaching, writing, and living in a haunted house. When not writing, designing, and editing, he enjoys playing roleplaying games, 3D printing, weightlifting, and watching movies. He lives with his wife, children, and two golden doodles in Birmingham, Alabama. You can visit Anders online at louanders.com or on Facebook, Instagram, and other social networks.

ADVENTURE IN NORRØNGARD

The ***Thrones & Bones: Norrøngard*** 5e campaign setting draws upon world mythology and the novels of Lou Anders. Inside these pages you will find everything you need to play a campaign in Norrøngard, setting of the novel *Frostborn*, including new ancestries, new subclasses, new backgrounds, new feats, ten Norrønian towns, new spells and magic items, a brand new system of rune magic, a system for tracking honor, new creatures and monsters, two complete adventures, and pages and pages of lore.

Thrones & Bones: Sagas of Norrøngard features seven more adventures, for levels 3 to 8, in the land of the ice and snow from designers Lou Anders, Jeff Lee, Sarah Madsen, Ben McFarland, and Brian Suskind.

Thrones & Bones: Vengeance of the Valravn is a stand-alone adventure designed by Lou Anders and Kelly Pawlik intended for characters of 7th level set in the land of Norrøngard from the *Thrones & Bones* campaign setting. It can be played as part of that setting or dropped into any northern-themed campaign. The Jarl of Sindholm has a problem. People are being slain in the outlying farms and villages north of his city. By the savage bite and claw marks on the victims, the jarl suspects that wolves are to blame. He seeks adventurers to find the creatures responsible and put a stop to their savage attacks. But the jarl is wrong in his assumptions. The danger to Sindholm is far greater than wolves and far older than he suspects.

The **Player's Guide to Norrøngard** excerpts pertinent information from chapters 1 and 3 of the *Thrones & Bones: Norrøngard* campaign setting, presenting a short overview of the world and all the player-focused character mechanics in a spoiler-free package so that you can build a character that fits authentically into the land without ruining any surprises. As a bonus, it also includes the rules of the board game Thrones & Bones, a popular pastime that every self-respecting Norrønur learns how to play from an early age!

ALSO FROM LOU ANDERS

Frostborn

Nightborn

Skyborn

Once Upon a Unicorn

www.ingramcontent.com/pod-product-compliance
Lightning Source LLC
Chambersburg PA
CBHW030424310726
48979CB00009B/1602/J